M000222841

A SONG TO DROWN RIVERS

ALSO BY
ANN LIANG

If You Could See the Sun
This Time It's Real
I Hope This Doesn't Find You

A
SONG
TO
DROWN
RIVERS

ANN
LIANG

ST. MARTIN'S PRESS
NEW YORK

First published in the United States by St. Martin's Press, an imprint of St. Martin's Publishing Group

A SONG TO DROWN RIVERS. Copyright © 2024 by Ann Liang. All rights reserved. Printed in the United States of America. For information, address St. Martin's Publishing Group, 120 Broadway, New York, NY 10271.

Designed by Devan Norman

ISBN 978-1-250-28946-9

TO KATHLEEN RUSHALL,
FOR ALL YOUR FAITH AND GUIDANCE

A
SONG
TO
DROWN
RIVERS

CHAPTER ONE

THEY SAY THAT WHEN I WAS BORN, ALL THE WILD geese flew down from the sky, and the fish sank beneath the waves, having forgotten how to swim. Even the lotus flowers in our gardens quivered and turned their heads away, so ashamed they were of their own diminished allure in my presence. I have always found such stories to be laughably exaggerated, but they prove the same thing: that my beauty was something unnatural, transcending nature itself. And that beauty is not so different from destruction.

This was why my mother insisted I cover my face before leaving the house.

"Do not draw unwanted attention to yourself, Xishi," she cautioned, holding up the veil. It rippled and gleamed in the midday light, the edges glowing white. "It is dangerous, for a girl like you."

A girl like me.

There were a thousand meanings tucked in those words, and I tried not to dwell on them, even as the old memories boiled up in response. The clucking, red-cheeked village aunties, who once came over to visit and marveled at the sight of me. *She is so pretty,* one of them had murmured. *Someone of such exquisite loveliness— she has the power to topple kingdoms and overturn cities.* She had meant it as a compliment. Another had sought to introduce me to her son, who was thrice my age, worked as a woodcutter like my father, and had a face that reminded me of a bitter gourd.

"Come here," Mother said.

I stepped forward and let her wrap the veil around my head, feeling her thin, calloused fingers—worn from scrubbing raw silk in the day and scrubbing rusted woks in the evening—fiddle with the strings. The fabric fell gently over my nose, my lips, my chin, cool against the sticky summer heat. I supposed I ought to be thankful for her desire to shield me from outside eyes. Zhengdan's mother all but dragged her out onto the streets and paraded her good looks for everyone to see. And it worked. Already, seven of the men in our village had shown up on their doorstep, bearing lavish gifts and begging for her hand in marriage. It was Zhengdan who told me this late at night, her mouth puckered in disgust, her hand clenched into a fist beneath mine.

"I'll return before it's dark," I promised Mother, who I knew would start worrying long before that, even though the river was not far from our western corner of the village, and I had walked the same route countless times.

But girls like me sometimes went missing. Though *missing* was too soft a word for it. The truth was uglier: stolen, slaughtered, sold. Traded between men like rare porcelains. It was especially true these days, with the wounds of war still running fresh in our kingdom, the Wu breathing down our people's necks, and our remaining soldiers too jaded and thinly spread to be bothered by trivial matters like dead girls.

"Return as soon as you can," Mother urged, and pressed a

rough-woven bamboo basket into my arms, bolts of silk piled inside it.

I walked through the village alone, alert. The long veil tickled my cheek and soon clung to me, damp with sweat, but it helped subdue the less-pleasant smells of goatskin and dirt and uncooked fish. Around me, most of the houses still lay in ruins, with gaping holes in the walls like puncture wounds, or cracked stones strewn across the yard like skulls. There were black marks in the earth from when the Wu soldiers had come, fires blazing, swords swinging, our people's blood dripping from their hands. The scene was fresh as ever in my mind, less a memory than a haunting. Sometimes at night, I thought I could see ghosts hovering over the yellow dust paths. All the villagers who hadn't survived.

A door creaked to my right, yanking me back to the present. Voices spilled out through the cracks. A man hacked up thick phlegm. I moved faster, the basket drawn close to my chest.

As always, I heard the river before I saw it. The steady, songlike trickle of water, joined by the calling of geese from beyond the trees, its blue-sweet scent a relief. Then the elms parted, offering a clear, stunning view of the riverbank, with the grass rising and swaying in the breeze and the smooth pebbles strewn along the edges, patterned with white and gray specks like quail eggs. The place was empty, save for me—and I was glad of it. I had always enjoyed the sound of my solitude, the quiet of my own breathing. Often, when I was around other people and felt their gazes on me, I had the strange, encroaching sense that my face and body did not belong to me. As if I had been designed purely for the pleasure of their viewing.

Slowly, I unrolled the first bolt of silk from the basket and plunged it into the cool river water. Once, twice, again. Then I wrung it dry, the water running in rivulets down my wrists. The task looked simple but was harder than most people knew. Unwashed, the silk was rough against my skin, leaving pink blisters in its wake; washed, it was so heavy it weighed on my arms like sheepskin. I paused for short breaks between, to catch my breath and unclench my muscles. To massage the tender skin over my heart with one hand. The stranger stories claim that my mother had been washing silk on this very river when she was struck by a pearl, and soon after became pregnant with me. In these stories, I am reduced to someone barely even human, a creature of myth, but at least they would explain my ill health from when I was a child, the ache in my chest that occasionally subsided but never fully went away. At times, I imagined there was a fissure running through my heart, one I could not stitch up no matter what I tried.

Now the pain grew sharper. I winced, my brows knitting as I set the silk down with a splash. Tried to exhale. There was no fighting the pain when it came; all I could hope for was to let it pass. I was still clutching at my chest when I heard a distant yell.

It sounded like a child.

Susu was my first thought, but that was foolish.

I straightened and squinted, my heart pounding from both pain and fear. Two figures were drawing closer down the riverbank—a stick-thin, disheveled girl at the front, pursued by a much larger man. My blood ran cold at the sight of him. His black hair was cut short in the traditional Wu style.

Monster.

An enemy in the flesh. Right here in Zhuji, in our village. On our riverbank.

"Please, help," the girl cried, her wide eyes landing on me. She could not have been alive for more than one full zodiac cycle—around Susu's age, if Susu had been given the chance to grow up. When she lifted her scrawny arms, I saw the violet bruises marring her sunburned skin. They looked fresh.

The girl and her pursuer were only a few yards away now. Less.

Do something. The words pressed against my mind, but they felt detached, as if another person had thought of them. My hands were still wet from the river, the cold silt stuck beneath my nails. My teeth chattered. I scanned the area for something—someone—but there was only the yellow sunlight glancing off the water and the geese soaring over the horizon and the silk crumpled within the basket.

The girl stumbled. Fell forward, knees knocking against the pebbles. The sound jolted through my own bones, and I felt a secondary pain that wasn't mine. A cry escaped her lips, but in my ears, it morphed into another child's cry. A familiar one, shrill with panic and confusion. Someone who needed me more than anything.

Susu. No, don't go there, we must keep hiding.

Listen to me.

Come back.

For one moment, time seemed to divide, and I saw my baby sister, her round eyes, her soft face, made from everything good in the world. I saw the sword pierce her side. I saw her fall—

"Help!"

The girl was scrambling to rise again, but the man towered over her, as giant as Pangu from the early myths, his shadow spreading beneath the sun. He closed in, one boot stamping down hard on the corner of her threadbare tunic. She was pinned to the ground, a bird with an arrow pierced through its wing.

"Little thief," he spat, the Wu accent obvious in his words, in the way he crushed the syllables between his teeth. "Did you really think you could take the pear from right under my nose and get away with it?"

The girl's face was white and stark as bone, but her eyes, when she turned them to her attacker, seemed to burn from within. "It was just *one* pear."

"It's mine. Everything here," the man said, gesturing to our village and beyond, to the sloping blue mountains, the capital city, all of the Yue Kingdom, "belongs to us now. Don't forget."

The girl responded with a series of expletives so foul I could only wonder where she had learned them from—

"Enough," the man barked, and drew his sword.

The sharp, metallic hiss cut through all noise. I had heard the Wu were masters of metallurgy, just like we were; that their swords were so fine they could slice into rock and would remain sharp even after centuries. With great despair, I saw firsthand that it was true. The blade glinted in midair, the sun split open on its lethal tip. One swift strike, and it would sever bone.

I jerked free from my horrified daze. There came the thought again, louder: *Do something. Save her.*

Don't fail again.

My fingers groped the ground wildly and closed around a loose stone. No bigger than an egg, but solid in its weight, with a jagged edge. The man wasn't watching me; his gaze was only on the cowering girl. In the split second before the sword swung down, I threw the stone at him. What I hoped to achieve then, I do not know. I like to think that murder was not at the forefront of my mind, that I only wished to distract, rather than to hurt. But when the stone struck the man's nose with a loud *crunch*, and he staggered backward, yelling, hands flying to his face—

I will admit to feeling a small, sharp curl of satisfaction.

Yet fear rapidly surged up to take its place. The man had turned his full attention to me, and even if murder had not been *my* intention, I could tell it was his. His chin was smeared with thick blood, and as he stepped toward me, more blood trickled from his nose into his mouth. He turned and spat. Wiped at his face with his left sleeve. In his right hand, his sword gleamed, pointed directly at me.

"In the Wu Kingdom," he said, "we have a saying about people who can't mind their own business: They often die unpleasant deaths."

My throat tightened.

I knew then, with a certainty that sang through my very bones, that I was going to die right there on the riverbank, where the water met the sky, and where my mother waited less than a mile away for me to come home. The man's footsteps crunched over the pebbles, closer. In my panic, my mind skipped to absurd places, pulled up flimsy, half-formed protests. That I was too young, that surely I had done nothing so bad as to deserve this, even if I did not always finish my rice or fold my sheets; that I had yet to fall in love, to see the sea, to set foot on land beyond my village.

Yet all my protests went unheard by the vast universe. I flung another stone at the man, desperate, but he was prepared now. He dodged it easily, and the next one, his lips pulling back to reveal blackened teeth. Again, he raised his sword. I felt the coolness of the metal as if it had already collected my soul, kissed my flesh.

No, I thought nonsensically. *Not yet, not yet, not yet*—

A bright flash across my vision.

The clang of metal against metal. I blinked. An unnatural wind fanned my veil, and it took me a moment to understand what had happened. Another sword had shot out and knocked the man's weapon off its trajectory before it could reach me. But where had the other sword come from?

I twisted around, searching, and the answer soon revealed itself to me. A tall, lean figure strode forward across the banks with all the eerie grace of a lynx, the sun blazing behind him, his features blurred by light. I wondered faintly if this was someone sent by the heavens, a warrior from the legends—or if perhaps I were already dead, and had dreamed the scene up.

But no, this was real. Nothing had felt more real in my life. I could taste the rich salt of the river, mingling with the blood from where I'd bitten down too hard on my own tongue. Then the figure turned a few degrees, and the light changed, illuminating the planes of his face. I was surprised to find that it was the face of a young man, and a beautifully refined one at that. All the angles were clean, sharp, harmonious, the natural curve of his lips almost arrogant; together, they were too intimidating to study for long.

"Who are *you*?" the Wu man cried, though his question came out a rough gurgle, thickened with blood. "Where do you people keep coming from?"

"You have no right to speak to me," the stranger replied calmly. His voice was like his appearance: cold and quiet, but only in the way a blunt sheath conceals a deadly blade.

The Wu man's face twisted. He lunged for his sword where it had been knocked astray into the grass, then made a violent stabbing motion at the stranger.

"Look out!" I cried.

I need not have spoken. The stranger crossed his hands behind his back and swerved easily out of the sword's path. His expression didn't even change. He wore that same cold look, his eyes dark and intelligent, the corner of his mouth lifted contemptuously, as if this were all an annoying inconvenience.

The quick movement threw his attacker off-balance. The man's arms flailed wildly as his body weight teetered, following his empty swing. Panting, he steadied himself and tried again, this time aiming straight for the stranger's exposed neck. But no sooner than he'd shifted position, the stranger did too; a most subtle change, one you might miss if you blinked. And so it continued, back and forth. The Wu man striking, pouncing, charging like an enraged bull until he was bright red in the face, and the stranger gracefully sidestepping, dodging, ducking without so much as lifting a hand.

"Who are you?" the Wu man repeated, but there was a note of real fear in his tone.

The stranger did not reply. Instead, he lifted his leg a fraction just as the Wu man came charging once more. With a noisy crash, he went sprawling on all fours, his sword flying free from his grip. Before he could try to retrieve it, the stranger paced over, picked up the sword between two slender fingers, and tossed it ever so casually into the river's depths. The water rippled outward.

In the silence, only the defeated man's harsh, frustrated grunts could be heard.

"Leave," the stranger said coolly, turning away with a swish of his robes. "Or it will be your body that is thrown into the water next."

The man blanched, then—cursing under his breath the entire time, his crooked nose still dripping red—staggered to his feet and fled, disappearing behind the copse of elms without a glance back. Once his footsteps had faded into the distance, the stranger finally faced me. Up close, he was even more striking than I'd realized, his beauty so sharp as to be unsettling, his gaze of such a clear, black-eyed intensity I could not look away.

"Are you hurt?" he asked. His voice was gentler than it had been when he spoke to the Wu man, but no warmer.

I drew myself up to full height—though even then, my head only came up to his shoulders—and scanned my body for any signs of pain. There were none, other than the faint stinging in my palms from where I'd gripped the stone. Even the ache in my chest was gone, as if it had never been there at all.

"No," I replied slowly, smoothing out my veil. Then I remembered his sword. It had planted itself into the dirt, but much of the blade was still a shiny, polished silver, with a diamond pattern repeating down the front and back and little jade fragments embedded in the hilt. There were words engraved into the blade too.

I read them as I tugged the sword free: *The mind destroys; the heart devours.* They stirred something inside me, like the slow pluck of a guqin string, but I could not name why.

"Thank you for—everything," I said, passing the sword to him rather awkwardly on two outstretched hands. I did not know if this was the right way to do it. He was clearly from some sort of noble background, with robes that alone were worth more than a dozen of our best water buffalo.

He sheathed his sword in one silver, fluid motion. "It was nothing." He did not sound like he was being polite, but rather stating the truth.

"I should repay you," I insisted, standing straighter. "I owe you a life debt."

His lips quirked, as if wondering what I could possibly give that he did not already have. "That won't be necessary," he said. "It is satisfying enough to humble a man from Wu." He paused, tilting his head. "Were you the one who broke his nose?"

I briefly considered lying, to act the part of the wide-eyed, innocent maiden, as most people expected from me. But something compelled me to nod.

Now his lips curved higher into some semblance of a smile. "Impressive." Then his gaze slid over to the little girl, who was still lying where she'd fallen, her mouth hanging agape in shock. "Is she a relative?"

I felt an ache inside me. How I wished she was. How I wished I could still point to someone and call them *sibling.*

"I don't know who she is," I admitted, walking over to her, the stranger following behind me. "She just looked like she needed help."

"Yet you saved her," he said with a touch of surprise. Something told me he was rarely surprised, and a strange pride bloomed beneath my breastbone, knowing I had done the unexpected.

"You saved me," I pointed out. "And we don't know each other."

"Yes, but I was certain I would be in no danger. Protecting your interests could not have harmed mine." He glanced at me sidelong, though I pretended not to see it. "It is quite a different thing to help someone when it puts yourself at risk."

I opened my mouth to respond, but the little girl spoke up first.

"Is—is the bad man really gone?"

"He is. But don't get up just yet," I added hastily, seeing her struggle to rise onto her elbows. I crouched and inspected her wounds. The bruises were a terrible purple-blue shade, like an overripe plum, and she had grazed her skin open in multiple places when she'd stumbled. It was difficult to tell how many of the dark splotches in her tunic were blood or mud. Then I drew my attention down to her small hands and recoiled. All her nails had been torn clean off, leaving only little semicircles of raw, uneven flesh. These injuries were older. And they did not look like accidents. "What . . . happened to you?" I breathed, swallowing the bile in my mouth. "Where are your parents?"

"They're dead." She said it in a listless way, as if reciting a poem that had long lost its meaning.

"Dead?"

"Killed," she amended, staring out at the glittering river.

"By who?"

"Who else? The monsters of Wu. I managed to escape while they were distracted by my mother's screams. I didn't want to," she said, almost defensive, as if she thought we might judge her for surviving. "But I wasn't going to wait around for them to cut my throat too. It was what my mother would have wished for."

Good, I wanted to tell her, the ache deepening. *You should have fled. You should have done whatever you needed to get away from them. Because if your mother had lived and you died, she would spend the rest of her days in unimaginable pain, weeping until her voice went hoarse. She would drag herself around the house like someone had torn half her soul from her body. It is the cruelest fate for the gray-haired to bury the dark-haired.*

I would know.

"You did the right thing," the stranger spoke up. His features had tightened, and I thought I caught a flash of resentment beneath his icelike complexion. "What is your name?"

"Wuyuan," she whispered.

"Wuyuan. I see." He did not offer his name in return, nor lower himself to the ground as I did, but he retrieved a skin of water and a clean handkerchief from his robes, then turned to me. "Her injuries will likely grow infected if left unattended. Do you have any experience with cleaning wounds?"

"Some," I said, taking the supplies from him. The handkerchief had been embroidered with an image of two fish circling each other in a lotus pond, and the silk was of the finest quality, wonderfully soft to the touch. It felt wrong to stain it with blood, but he did not seem to care. "This might sting," I told Wuyuan as I smoothed out the handkerchief.

She just nodded, her gaze still on the river. It was not the reaction a normal child would have to pain. Then again, perhaps there could be no normal children raised in an age of war. As I dabbed at her bloodied palms, I felt a vicious stab of hatred toward the Wu. There had been no end to the turmoil in our kingdom ever since the Wu armies captured Kuaiji, and now there grew a generation of parentless children who were more familiar with pain than peace.

I expected the stranger to leave, but he merely stood to the side and watched me while I worked. It was a foreign feeling. Few ever paid much attention to me when my face was covered, and fewer still looked at me as if they could see me—not the smooth, pretty surface of things, but the thorns that grew underneath.

"You are not from around here, are you?" I asked without glancing up at him.

"How can you tell?" From his mild tone, it was difficult to judge whether or not he was genuinely asking.

To be safe, I responded anyway. "Your . . . air. Your mannerisms. It is not like the men around here."

"No? And what kind of air do I possess?"

Now I did glance at him, at the sword in its carved sheath and the rich-colored robes wrapped tight around his waist, the elegant topknot his raven-black hair was arranged in, the tassels and jade swinging from his belt. "A dignified one," I said at last. "The air of somebody important. Perhaps you are a nobleman. Or a traveling scholar. Or a leader in the military—you fight so well." I wanted him to correct me, to confirm my guesses, but he just smiled slightly and said nothing else.

When Wuyuan's wounds had been treated to the best of my abilities, he placed a pouch in her hands. I only needed to hear its faint jangle to know it was filled with coins.

Wuyuan stared, wide-eyed, her shock mirroring mine. "What—"

"Buy yourself some food and new clothes," he said. "But make sure you do not spend all of it. Leave half the coins to purchase unripe plums at the lowest price you can get—I suggest the market two miles south from here, right down the river. Store them in a safe place, away from the sun. You will find that the prices for plums will rise dramatically three days later. When that time comes, sell the plums again at triple the price. Do you understand?"

Wuyuan nodded, even though she was now openly gaping, as if unsure whether the young man before her was a mortal or god. I was no longer sure myself. "Yes."

"Good."

How do you know? I wanted to ask him. How could he possibly predict what the prices would be three days from now? And he sounded so certain of it. But he had smoothed his robes and started back down the riverbank, away from us.

Without thinking, I ran after him.

"Wait, before you go—" I scrambled to pick up the best bolt of silk I could find in my basket, the one I had finished washing, and passed it to him. "Please, take this."

He slowed, and cocked his head. "For what?"

I pointed downward at the hem of his robes. There was a tiny tear from where he must've caught it on some rock earlier in his fight with the Wu man. "To patch it up. Or make a new set of robes. And if not," I said louder, when he looked about to protest, "then take it as a token of my thanks. I know it is not the most equal of trades: a bolt of silk in exchange for a life. But perhaps you can better remember me this way."

"I do not need the silk to remember you," he said, so quiet I barely heard him, but accepted my offering with a small dip of his head. "If fate wills it, may we meet again."

I gazed after his retreating figure, the sun beating down on the knife-straight line of his shoulders, until his silhouette was but a smudge in the distant horizon. Yet as soon as he was out of sight, my chest seized, and I gasped, fingers grabbing uselessly at my robe collar. Just like that, the pain had returned.

I made no mention of my close brush with death, nor my strange encounter with the young man, when I returned home. I knew my parents would worry themselves to pieces over the first part, and even more so over the second. Besides, in the old, familiar light of my room, with its rammed-earth walls and low, thatched roof, everything that had transpired now took on a dreamlike air. Would they even believe me if I spoke of a beautiful, mysterious stranger who could win a duel against an armed man without moving a finger, who could predict the rise and fall of the market in the future, who stood and spoke like someone raised in a palace? I barely believed myself, and I had been there. I had seen him.

So I collected the washed silk, cleaned the tables, and prepared dinner. Our supply of beans was low, and our supply of rice lower; when I took the amount needed for one full pot of porridge, my ladle scraped the jar bottom. I ignored the pinch of worry in my belly. Tomorrow, I would clean twice the amount of silk I did today, so we could sell more at the market. That would be enough. It needed to be. And when that ran out—

I snipped the thought before it could grow. I had learned to think of time in days, the stretch between two meals, from sunup to sundown. Sometimes it felt like that was all my life was, all it ever could be: the repetition of tasks necessary for survival until I grew older and my time expired. Yet strange as it was—whenever I tried to imagine myself as an old woman, I couldn't. It was like trying to see the tail end of a river; the image only grew blurry and faded to black.

"Do you need help with that?"

My father's face in the doorway, beaten brown by the sun. He was not an old man, I didn't think, but his hair was already graying, and his frame was stooped from the weight of thick tree trunks and giant axes.

"No, Father," I said. He always offered to help, and he always said it sincerely enough, yet somehow, he never ended up helping. Perhaps because it would be worth more trouble teaching him than simply doing the task myself; I doubted he even knew how to boil water on his own. But he was still better than some of the other fathers, who beat their children for not cooking fast enough, or simply to release their own rage on someone who couldn't hit back.

"Very well, then." I listened to him shuffling across the room, the low heave and exhale as he settled into his chair, and not long after, his soft, rumbling snores. And then there was the boiling water, the green beans floating to the surface, their insides splitting open. I stirred as I had been taught by my mother, and her mother before her.

After dinner, I sat beside the window, knees hugged to my chest, and stared out. Although the huts themselves were not much to look at, little more than an ugly reminder of the violence that had touched our part of the kingdom, all the trees and wildflowers and mountains were painted in saturated shades of blue and green. Lush grass grew over the places corpses had been left to rot, back when there weren't enough villagers remaining to help bury the bodies. Butterflies fluttered from one branch to another, where blood had once stained the leaves.

Nature had healed faster than we had.

A warm breeze drifted in and sighed against my skin. At times like these, the dusky air held a breathless quality, as if it were waiting for darkness to descend. I was waiting too—but for what, I did not know yet.

CHAPTER TWO

EARLY THE NEXT MORNING, WHEN THE SKY WAS STILL a sleepy shade of pink, a knock came at the door.

This was highly unusual. Many of the villagers believed the most direct and efficient form of communication was to call out at the top of their lungs when passing by; some simply wandered straight inside without warning, armed with either a favor or snippet of gossip. My pulse picked up at the possibilities. Was it an official? Was there to be another war? Had something terrible happened?

My mother reached the door before I did, her robes wrapped hastily over her white inner garments like a cloak, still rubbing the sleep from her bleary eyes. When she opened it, I stifled a gasp.

There, standing before our crumbling, decades-old house, was the same young man from yesterday. My memory had not done his beauty justice, just as remembered pain was always duller than actual pain. He had changed his robes into something of a darker, more somber shade, and his hair was tied back tighter, accentuating the fine angles of his jaw and cheekbones. He looked . . . different.

Older. Though he had not been warm toward me upon our first meeting, his stance had still been reasonably relaxed, his manner laced with some private touch of amusement. Now, all that was scoured away. I could detect no emotion in those intelligent, pitch-black eyes, nothing to suggest at why he had come.

Yet the pang in my chest, which was always worse upon waking, eased.

"Good morning," he was saying to my mother, bowing low. "I hope I'm not intruding."

"I— No," Mother said, but I could sense her quiet alarm. "I'm sorry, but you are . . . ?"

"Fanli," he replied, and straightened. "Political and military advisor to King Goujian of Yue."

This time, I was unable to suppress my surprise. *Fanli*. But of course—I should have known. All the rumors sang of him: the advisor with a mind sharper than blades and beauty finer than jade, only twenty-two years of age yet more accomplished than men twice as old. He had managed to impress the king when he was but a mere adolescent and quickly climbed his way up the ranks to become one of King Goujian's most trusted ministers. There were already folktales about him, poems praising his name. He was, in the eyes of the Yue, incorruptible. The last pure thing under Heaven. He was said to have none of a commoner's wanton wants and lowly desires; he was of the few who truly put the state before the self.

"Oh!" After a delayed beat, my mother quickly dropped into some attempt at a curtsy. So rarely did nobles venture into our village that there were no customs to look toward for reference, nothing to prepare us for this. "We are honored . . . Most honored to have you here . . ."

Fanli's eyes moved past her shoulder to me, but there was no spark of recognition there. Only a calm, calculated curiosity. I remembered then that he could not possibly recognize me; he had only seen me by the river with my veil on. But then, his arrival made even less sense. What did he want?

"Is this the girl everyone calls Xishi?" he asked.

My mother paused, and then, with a new wariness, nodded. "Yes. My daughter."

He had not looked away from me, and it was now to me alone that he spoke. "They were right," he said evenly, studying me with a quiet, burning intensity. "You really are beautiful." It did not sound like a compliment, designed to flatter and charm, but rather a confirmation of something.

I stayed silent, not yet recovered from my shock. I could not think of a fitting response anyhow. People always prefer the beauty who is oblivious, unaware of her own power, who blushes easily and is taken aback by strangers' approval, who is soft and demure and lacking in just enough confidence so as to seek it out in the opinions of men. But these are such lies. All my life, the very same people had told me time and time again how gorgeous I was. How could I not know it? That was like growing up not knowing you were tall.

"Is there something you seek here?" Mother said, stepping in between us, a protective hand resting against the crook of my elbow. She squeezed once, lightly. It was our code, her way of letting me know everything would be all right.

"I'm afraid it is a rather long story," Fanli said, breaking eye contact at last. I felt it like the snap of a thread. "Could I come in?"

I saw my mother hesitate, but of course she could not refuse him entry. He worked for the king—*the king*. And the king's wish was law.

"Certainly. Xishi, lead him inside," she said, moving away. "I'll go boil some tea."

The truth was, there was very little room for me to lead him anywhere. Only a few steps in, we came to a stop at the table, where he smoothed the back of his robes out, adjusted his broad sleeves, and sat gracefully on one of our low chairs. I sat across from him. The stillness between us felt solid. It threw everything else into clarity. From the other room, I could hear my mother scraping the tea leaves into the pot—she would be using the expensive tea, what we had been saving up for the Lunar Festival—and hissing something low and unintelligible at my father. The two of them emerged together later, my mother carrying the steaming clay pot on a tray, my father with a slightly dazed look on his face, as if unsure whether he was really awake.

"Thank you," Fanli said as my mother filled his teacup, the rich, dark green fragrance of the leaves sweetening the air. The cup in fact belonged to me, but we had no spares. "And as for why I'm here—I was sent directly by King Goujian to seek out a potential bride of unmatched beauty."

My pulse hammered harder. *Bride.* A word I had grown up hearing, yet here, with the king's advisor sitting opposite me, the golden sun rising outside our window, it seemed to acquire a new meaning.

Mother and Father exchanged a look. "For—for you?" Mother asked, frowning. "Surely there are already plenty of women who wish to marry you, why must it—"

"No, you misunderstand me," Fanli said, setting his tea down. "The bride would be for King Fuchai of the Wu Kingdom, as a tribute from the Yue. And after much searching, I believe Xishi would make the perfect candidate."

I made a small, involuntary sound: of shock, or fury, or fear, I did not know. My gut churned at the mere mention of the name. Fuchai was infamous for his love of wine and women; he was said to have frequented every single brothel in the Wu capital, and took his personal pleasures more seriously than state affairs. Yet he had crushed our armies, defeated our king. He was the enemy of my people, the cause of our suffering.

He was why the soldiers had come.

Why Susu had been killed.

"What?" I burst out. "But he's horrible."

At the sound of my voice, Fanli looked at me with a new emotion. There it was, the recognition come too late. Something like sorrow, regret, even, flickered across his features before he collected himself. All this, in seconds. I doubted an onlooker would have even noticed the change, subtle as it was.

"It is certainly not a pleasant mission," he continued, as if nothing had happened. Only his voice came out more restrained. "But you would be a bride only in name. In practice, you would be a spy—our spy. You would distract him from his duties, and influence him to our liking, all while gathering key information from within the palace. You would, in short, be the integral piece of our plan to take revenge on the Wu and conquer them for good."

A stunned silence fell over the room.

Fanli's expression was somber, his hands clasped over the teacup, the white steam trailing through the air like ghosts. He looked entirely serious.

"That's—" A laugh tore out of me, the sheer absurdity of it sinking in. "Forgive me, but that's ridiculous. I cannot marry a king. I've never married anyone before. I've never even wandered farther than the borders of my village. I do not know how to curtsy properly, or eat whatever royals eat—"

"You would receive intensive training over the course of ten weeks," he said, as if he'd been expecting this response. "I will oversee it myself, to ensure everything goes as planned. With my guidance, you will be more than ready when I escort you to the Wu palace. Believe me."

A lump rose in my throat. The room suddenly felt too small, the tea's fragrance too strong, too heady. I couldn't think.

"She's only a commoner," my mother said, shaking her head. Her voice trembled when she spoke. She seldom refused anything, let alone the request of a king; to do so was dangerously close to treason. But she did not leave my side. "This marriage—this mission—is there really nobody better suited for it?"

"The plan is to send two tributes," Fanli replied. "A concubine, and a palace lady to accompany her. I have already found another candidate from your village who I believe will be fitting for the role of the latter. But to be frank . . . ever since I set out in search of this bride, I have visited countless places and seen plenty of beautiful women. Those with the elegance of swans and the voices of larks. Yet compared to Xishi, they wink out into obscurity, like the stars beside the moon. It was the villagers' gossip which led me here, but now I have seen it with my own eyes, and I know it to be irrefutably true: Xishi is a beauty for the legends. Our chances of success will only be high if she is the one to go."

"And if I do succeed?" I whispered.

His gaze met mine, and for a moment, all else ceased to be. The mournful cry of the geese, the rustling of trees. Everything seemed to shrink down to just the two of us. A shiver raced through my body, as if I already knew in my core, even then, the significance of what came next. "If you do succeed, Xishi," he said quietly, "you will be the savior of our kingdom. You will forever alter the course of history."

I ran out into the yard, gasping.

Though the air was warm, the sky lightening to blue, the chill in my bones only deepened. My head swam. My knees buckled beneath me. Alone outside, I tried to envision the future Fanli had drawn for me, one of gilded halls and vermilion robes and secrecy—but my imagination could not extend much further than that. All my life, I had known only the hushed song of the river and the lotus flowers abloom over the pond near my feet.

I squeezed my eyes shut, pressed my head against the unyielding wall of the house. My breathing grew shallow. Yet his words did not leave me. *Legend. Kingdom. History.* These were new words in my vocabulary. They carried weight, solidity. I turned them over on my tongue, and they tasted sharp, like metal and blood. They were so different from what I was used to hearing: *beautiful.* That old blessing, that tired curse. So flimsy and temporal, so easily faded, like the plum blossoms that withered in midwinter. And then, as I considered it, a small, quiet laugh of disbelief fell from my lips.

The village aunties had always said that my beauty would be what changed my fate. I doubted anybody had thought it would mean this.

Footsteps sounded behind me.

I tensed. They were too quiet to belong to my father and too slow to belong to my mother.

"I haven't made up my mind yet," I called out.

"I know," came Fanli's mild response. He stepped out in full, the light falling on the intricate blue threads of his robes, the sharp planes of his face. "I understand that it is a lot to absorb."

"It is my whole life," I couldn't help saying. Perhaps it was unwise to say these things aloud, especially to him. But I went on. "It would change everything."

"I know," he said again, coming to a stop two feet away from me, though I wasn't sure what kept him there. Propriety? Politeness? Consideration of my feelings? Or did he simply keep his distance from everybody?

"What about my parents? If I go, who will take care of them?" Without realizing, my nails had bitten red crescents into my palms. I made a conscious effort to unfurl them, hide them behind my back. "I'm their only child." The words bruised my throat. *Their only child left* was more accurate, but that would hurt too much. And I did not know if I could even still consider myself someone's sister. Such a term was a string, linking one to another, implying two parts of a whole. Without Susu, the string went slack; the term had no meaning.

"That, you need not worry about. I will ensure they receive a handsome compensation, with their clothes and food provided for as long as they live. They will never have to work a day again, unless they wish to."

"Truly?" I asked, hardly daring to believe it.

But his gaze was clear, free of deceit. "I give you my word."

"I'm afraid a man's word alone is not enough. I would prefer a written document, with the king's seal, stipulating all that you have promised."

Again, I had managed to surprise him. "If you would like," he said slowly. "That can all be arranged for you. So long as you go."

I could admit: It was tempting. It was so tempting, but—

"I am not going to assure you it is an easy mission. On the contrary, it will be most demanding, not to mention dangerous. You will have to leave your family behind. You will have to adapt quickly to the ways of the royals and nobles, who are all wolves wearing sheepskin. Life in a village like yours is simple; everything happens on the surface. In the palace, everything happens in the shadows. Someone could smile at you one moment and stab you the next. And of course—" His voice grew clipped, grave. "Of course, there is the matter of the king himself."

I exhaled heavily, my skin breaking out into goose bumps. *Yes*, I thought. *That one small matter.*

"You will be sharing his bed," he stated, his expression cool and collected, as if he were discussing state affairs. Which, I supposed in a way, was what this was. Politics and power, the opposite of romance. "You will need to charm him, win his trust, until he cares about nothing in the world except you. He is not the most moral of men, and he has never shown devotion to a single person before."

"And you really think I can do it?" I asked, turning my head an inch to meet his eyes. "I have never tried to charm a man before. Not deliberately."

"I doubt you would have needed to."

"I have never even been kissed," I confessed.

Now he paused. Cleared his throat. While he had spoken so openly of seduction without a trace of emotion, it was somehow this that drew a flush of shyness from him. For the first time, I saw how close he was in age to me. Only two years older.

I smiled a little, despite myself. With a sudden boldness, I said, "And you say that you will teach me how to bewitch the king. Could you truly help me?"

His left hand curled, a slight, unthinking movement, half-hidden by the sleeve of his robes. "You are mistaken."

"About what?"

"If you agree to the mission, I won't be the one helping you. You'll be the one helping me."

I stared at him, my humor vanishing, my pulse striking faster in my veins.

"I am the one who needs you." He said it like a grave confession. "I am the one who suggested the plan to His Majesty, who is responsible for organizing this mission. Without you, I will fail."

I chewed the inside of my cheek, unsure what to make of this. Of anything. Plenty of people had made it clear how much they wanted me: my face, my beauty, my company. But nobody had ever really *needed* me before.

From all around us, the village began to stir: the gurgles of young children, the splash of water from the well, the whisper of dried corn, the wet slap of straw sandals over mud. For the villagers, it was only another morning, one of thousands just like this. But for me, this morning might be my last here.

As if reading my thoughts, Fanli said, "I tell you all this not to sway you in either direction. Some may prefer the comfort of lies to the sting of truths, but I wish to be completely honest with you from the beginning, even if the picture I paint is not always pretty."

"What if I were to say no?"

"I would leave," he said at once, "and never disturb you again. There will be no repercussions for your choice."

No direct repercussions, I corrected in my head, tilting my chin up to the yellow wash of sunlight. Because if the plan did not work out, the king of Wu would go on undefeated, safe in the riches of his palace, while the people of Yue suffered and grew weaker day by day, living in constant fear of another war. I took in the view of the great green elms, the ripe mulberries glistening like little red jewels from the trees, the wooden toys strewn along the cobbled path, the hoofprints pressed into the dirt. All the signs of hard-won life. All that had survived through the first battle. But would it survive the next? Or the one after?

I thought of Wuyuan, her skin stretched painfully thin over bones, the raw, pink scabs where her nails had once been. I thought of my parents inside the house, who were getting older and frailer; already my mother's eyesight had started blurring, though she would never admit it, and my father had never recovered from his fall in the forest. I thought of their faces when they ran inside and saw Susu crumpled on the floor, the harsh sob that had left my mother's body, as if something inside her had shattered.

And I thought of Susu herself from *before*, her sweet smile, her pockets filled with berries, her eyes filled with light.

When it came down to it, the choice was this: a kingdom, or my happiness.

And how many people under Heaven were really fortunate enough to know happiness? Happiness was a side dish, like the sweet, sticky rice cakes Mother made during the festivals, or the glutinous balls stuffed with rich sesame paste. But *revenge*—that was the salt of life. Necessary. Essential.

"It is a difficult decision," Fanli said from beside me. "But it is yours to make."

"Let me think about it some more," I told him, though the answer had already come to me. The answer had always been there, as if scrawled across the scripts of history. I was only deluding myself now, pushing back against time. "I will give you an answer by midnight."

"Then I will be waiting for you at the eastern gates, where the river flows. The same place we met." It was the first time he had acknowledged aloud our encounter from yesterday, and it flickered between us like a secret, a silent flame. His gaze was heavy on mine, dark and appraising. Yet the instant he turned away, I felt the sudden absence of its weight. "Find me there."

All day and night I thought about it. It was impossible to think of anything else.

My mother said very little, yet the mournful look in her eyes, how she held me longer than she ever had before, her hands soft despite their calluses, told me that perhaps she already knew the answer too. What was it that people said about mothers having a sixth sense? Sometimes she seemed to see my heart even before I did.

"I wish I could keep you safe forever," she whispered, and I heard the unspoken part of her sentence, the fresh pain of it. *But I cannot.* "My daughter . . . I do not wish to lose a child again."

A sharp, sour feeling twisted inside my chest.

"And your health," she continued, her voice steady, even as her lips trembled. "You have always been so frail. What if . . ."

"I am not as frail as you think," I told her, and it was true. My whole life, ever since that inexplicable pain had flared up in my heart, I had been protected and treated like a precious vase, capable of cracking at the lightest touch. But even if I could not rid myself of the pain, I could live with it. One could live with almost anything, so long as they had something to live for.

My mother placed a warm palm on the back of my head, but said nothing. She just looked at me for a long time in the quiet, as though hoping to memorize my features. Then she returned to the chores.

Fanli had left the house already. The tea was all but cold now, the leaves sunk to the bottom, the water deepening to a murky, bitter green. All the cups were still full. A waste.

Perhaps I would have spent my remaining time wandering around the house like a ghost, at turns terrifying myself with visions of King Fuchai—someone with teeth like fangs and brutal hands and a greedy, blood-soaked smile—and attempting to console myself with visions of a fallen Wu Kingdom, their flag trampled beneath the feet of our soldiers as they marched in to an unobstructed victory. Yet not long after my parents had retired to bed, a familiar voice called from outside—

"Xishi-jiejie! Xishi-jie, did he find you too?"

Zhengdan barged through the door without pausing, her robes fluttering in her wake. In her rush to get here, her black hair had started coming loose from its elaborate bun; she yanked out the wooden hairpins with an impatient hiss until it tumbled freely down her back. Two severe spots of color had risen to her cheeks, and her voice was urgent. It took me a second to understand what she had asked.

"Who? You don't mean—the advisor?"

"I knew it," she said, shaking her head. The expression on her face was a peculiar one, tragic and triumphant at once. "If he came here in search of a great beauty, of course he could not leave without meeting you."

"Wait." I sat down on the closest stool; or rather, my knees sank on their own accord, my shock pressing down on me like a physical weight. She remained standing, her hands on her hips. "You were the other girl he spoke of? Did you . . . You've agreed to go? As a *palace lady?*"

"What better choice do I have?" She scoffed. "My mother was going to marry me off to that old man Lidan—you know, the one who is already balding, and smells like fish all the time. I would rather be a palace lady than his wife."

Not for the first time, I marveled at my friend's nature. Everyone spoke of her loveliness—particularly her brows, which were slender and arched like willow leaves, and expressed all the emotion she did not say out loud—but they overlooked the smaller, more significant things. They forgot that it was she who had scared away the group of bandits that had once tried to steal from our village, injuring one so badly with a blunt cleaver that he'd limped away whimpering; that it was also she, and she alone, who had trained the village horses, and fixed the main road, and hunted down the fox that had broken through the fences and eaten half our hens. The first time I had ever witnessed her cry was when she'd snapped the animal's neck.

"Have you already agreed to the advisor's request?" she asked, those famous, delicate brows arching.

"No. Not yet."

"Not yet," she repeated. Then, with a startling fierceness, she crouched low beside me and grabbed my hand. The pads of her fingers were thick with blisters old and new; not from cleaning and cooking, as one might have assumed, but from secretly training with a sword. "Think over it carefully, Xishi-jie. The mission is— It's dangerous—"

"Yet you're going anyway," I said. "Aren't you afraid?"

Her chin jutted forth. "Of course not."

But I knew she was lying. Just as I knew that she was too proud to admit otherwise.

It was awfully familiar to me, that dark, steely look in her eyes. One early morning, during the height of war, I had spotted her with her father outside their house. She was engulfed in his old armor, lugging his sword behind her, her teeth clenched from the effort. The scene was almost comical, the helmet so large it kept sliding down over her eyes. Her father had laughed aloud, then gently lifted the helmet from her head with both hands.

Don't go to the battlefield again, she'd begged, reaching up on her tiptoes and trying to grab it back from him. It was useless; she was only half his height. *Let me fight in your stead.*

This is my duty, he'd said. *The heavens have something else planned for you, Zhengdan. I can feel it.*

Her eyes had shone with ferocity, but in the end, she had watched him leave. Every morning after that, I'd find her standing outside, her spine rigid, her hopeful, anxious face turned to the horizon.

Two years later, in that very same spot, a grim-looking official had returned, holding only her father's blood-splattered helmet. *It was the highest honor a soldier could ask for*, I'd overheard the officer say. His last fight was against the general of the Wu Kingdom himself. General Ma.

Now, gazing over at her, it was as if the past had rushed back to us. Or perhaps the past had never left.

"I'm coming with you," I told her. The words rang clear in the cramped room, and I heard the conviction in my own voice. The air seemed to ripple against my skin, and the wind outside suddenly slammed against the window-paper, as if even the heavens knew of my decision. Was it the right one? I could not tell. Perhaps it did not matter. Either decision led to pain; I had merely chosen one kind over another.

Zhengdan had known me all her life. She made no further attempts to dissuade me. It would be futile, whatever she said. "If your mission is to seduce the king, then my mission will be to keep you safe." She reached for my hand once more as she spoke, her eyes blazing in the dark.

"We'll *both* be safe," I corrected. "We'll come out of the palace together, alive and well."

She gave me a faint smile but said nothing.

"Promise me," I urged her.

"All right, I promise," she said, laughing. It was like blowing cold air at a wound; it did not heal, but at least it soothed. I could have pretended then, with Zhengdan smiling next to me and the moonlight shining through the small holes in the window, that the world awaiting us was not so terrible. That it would only be a grand adventure, just like the ones we heard about in the stories.

But it was much harder once she had gone home, leaving me in the dim quiet.

I tiptoed into my parents' room, watching their familiar, sleeping figures, the blanket stretched just over their stomachs. My mother was hugging Susu's unwashed tunic, even though its scent had long faded, and the threads were starting to fray. She seemed to be having a nightmare. Every now and then, she would shiver and clutch at the air as if something were being taken away from her. I wanted to wake her from it, but also could not bear to. She slept too little as it was. And if she woke and saw my face, she would know right away what I was thinking.

A sharp spasm of pain tore through my chest again. I drew in a silent breath, tried to ignore it.

Now that my decision had been made, everything I had once taken for granted was repainted in shades of yellow nostalgia. Already I missed the warmth of my parents' presence, the faded straw fan laid out by their bed, the wooden comb my mother used to brush my hair back every morning, the lingering scent of smoke from the stove. Gently, I undid the jade pendant around my neck, then set it on a wooden chest. It was the single most valuable thing I owned, a gift from my parents on my first birthday. They would see it tomorrow, when I was already gone, and know what it meant.

Later, though, I would wish I had stayed longer. Woken them up, held them close. Given them the chance to say a proper goodbye. But such things only occur to you in hindsight, framed by the before and after of everything you've endured; when it is still happening, all you care about is what lies ahead.

CHAPTER THREE

JUST AS PROMISED, FANLI WAS WAITING ON THE RIVER-banks, illuminated by the pale, ghostly light of the full moon.

He was not alone. Behind him stood a line of horses: three beautiful mares, each of their dark coats gleaming, muscles rippling as they pawed the ground, their bridles polished until they shone even in the darkness. Zhengdan was already mounted atop one of them, her spine as straight as a soldier's, one hand stroking her horse's withers. These majestic creatures were to the dull-eyed, half-lame animals of our village what silk is to ramie. As my footsteps crunched over the twigs, one of them tossed her great head and whickered softly.

Fanli looked up too, and met me halfway.

"You came." The moonlight rendered his features lovelier than ever, tracing out the slope of his jawbone and nose. If my beauty was of the destructive kind, his was a beauty that pressed exquisitely close to sorrow; something as cold and untouchable as the stars scattered overhead.

"I would like the finest quality rice," I said in response.

He tilted his head; a question.

"For my parents," I clarified, before I could lose my nerve. If he truly needed me as much as he claimed, he ought to agree, no matter how bold my demands. "You said you would compensate them. They must be cared for as one would care for their own blood. They are to receive fresh fish from the rivers, duck meat, and lamb every day. Especially duck meat. That is my mother's favorite. My father—he has a bad leg. He will need a proper cane, and warm bedding in the winter to prevent it from acting up. The window-paper also needs to be repaired, and there are holes in the roof, which always leak when it rains."

"Very well." If I did not know better, I would say he looked almost amused. "Is that all?"

My heart had started pounding as it had not since I snuck out of the house. I fought to maintain a façade of calm. If I were leaving, I would do so with my hands steady by my sides and my chin held high. "For now. But I will let you know, should I think of anything later."

"So you are ready to depart?"

Of course I was not. "Yes."

To my shock, he bowed to me then, his head at such a low angle that it came down to my waist. "I do not take your choice tonight lightly," he said, his voice hushed. "All of Yue will remember you; I swear it." As he righted himself again, slowly, he gazed up at me from beneath the shadow of his lashes. There was a look in his eyes, one I did not have the vocabulary for yet. Then it vanished entirely, and in a brisk, businesslike manner, he guided me over to the mare in the middle.

She was the shortest of the steeds and had a white patch like a star on her noble forehead. Still, I could not quite reach the stirrups on my own. After Fanli helped me up with one arm, careful

not to brush any skin, then strode forward to his mount, I looked
out at the river and thought to myself: *How fitting that the one who
saved my life should now be the one to lead me away from it.*

We traveled in darkness, guided only by the song of the river.

It was halfway that I realized this was a strategic choice on Fanli's part. There would be nobody around to witness us at night,
to question this sight: a young man dressed in the finest robes,
accompanied by two girls of marrying age. Nobody to make their
own erroneous assumptions about what this meant.

My mare had been trained well. Even when we passed rock-
strewn roads and barbed bushes rustling with nocturnal prey, she
did not flinch, nor spook. The lightest touch of the stirrups against
her belly, the flick of the reins, was sufficient to prompt a response
from the creature. The sound of her steady gait was soothing, an
echo to my own heartbeat. I tried not to think about everything I
was leaving behind. Or about the dark waters I was wading into,
the murky, outflung stretch of black. We were already too far from
my village to turn back.

At dawn, with the air rising warm around us, we finally arrived.

I had not known what to expect—only that we were headed
to someplace private, where we would live and be trained in secret. But perhaps that was for the best, for my imagination would
have failed me anyway. The cottage was raised up on the slope of
a mountain, high enough to have an open view of the city below,
yet fringed by enough plum blossom trees and shrubbery to remain well concealed. Its green-painted roofs flared out like wings
on both sides, and its vermilion walls shone with dew. Just above
the front doors, the words RIVERSONG COTTAGE had been etched
into the wood from right to left. When I inhaled, there was a new,

foreign scent to my surroundings: something clear and sweet, like the first melting of ice in the spring.

A man was waiting at the entrance.

The sun had risen to cast his face in reddish hues. He was neither young nor old, yet he carried himself with the weary, hardened air of one who had already seen too much of the world. His features themselves were on the plainer side, broad-jawed and firm, albeit not fine enough to be handsome. The thing that caught my attention, though, was his gaze.

He watched us like a hawk as we dismounted and approached the gates on foot. A suspicion stirred under my skin. My throat tightened at the possibility. Could it really be that—

"You've found her?" he asked, speaking only to Fanli, even while his eyes remained on me.

"She is the best of the best, just as promised. A beauty like no other; you can see for yourself," Fanli returned. Then he clapped his hands together before him and lowered his head. "Your Majesty."

Your Majesty.

I exchanged a quick, startled look with Zhengdan before hastily lowering myself too, mimicking Fanli's position. From this angle, I could only see the bright emerald grass and the polish of King Goujian's boots. Above me, as if from a great distance, I heard him remark:

"Neither of them have an understanding of basic etiquette? Girls are meant to curtsy, not bow."

I flushed and straightened at once. Both King Goujian and Fanli were looking toward me; Goujian, with sharp appraisal; and Fanli, without any visible emotion at all.

"I discovered them in a remote village," Fanli said. "You cannot expect them to be as well versed in etiquette as those of the court. There's no need for concern though—such things can be taught."

Goujian's brows rose. "Oh, I forget: You were once like them too, weren't you, Fanli?"

Surprise flickered through me. What exactly did he mean by that? Fanli's expression remained impassive, yet his spine stiffened. Before he could reply, Goujian had already moved on—to me.

"Could they really be taught within ten weeks? You know we do not have much time left, and I have waited too long for this." The gleam in his eyes was almost crazed. "We'd promised the Wu the tributes would arrive before midwinter—if we fail to deliver, the little trust we've built up will go to waste. We cannot afford that."

"It is enough time, I guarantee it," Fanli said.

"Well, you are certainly right about her," Goujian said, examining me closely, as one would a well-forged sword. I resisted the urge to jerk away. This was the king, after all. And I would have to endure far more in the Wu Kingdom. "She *is* quite captivating. With proper training . . . Fuchai won't stand a chance." The soft vehemence with which he spoke Fuchai's name startled me.

Goujian saw, and smiled again. "What is your name?"

"Xishi," I said, even though it was not actually my real name, but the one everyone in my village had given me. Somehow, it felt most fitting. Then, remembering too late: "Your Majesty."

"Xishi," he repeated. "A pretty name. Tell me, Xishi, what is your opinion of the Wu?"

I might not yet have received any official training, but I saw the answer ablaze in those dark, hawklike eyes. Besides, I did not have to think up a lie; I needed only to remember the blood gurgling in my sister's throat, her tiny hands reaching for me as the soldier drove the sword deeper into her flesh. When Susu died, it'd felt as though the whole universe had been tipped off-balance. Here was the chance to restore it. "I hate them," I said quietly. "They are monsters, raised on violence and trickery. I wish only to bring the kingdom to its knees."

King Goujian nodded, satisfied, and said to Fanli, "She is perfect."

The cottage was empty, save for the quiet, shadowlike presence of a maidservant, who retreated into the kitchens upon our arrival, and the far noisier presence of a guard our age. He had told me his name, though I had forgotten it just as quickly, too distracted by everything else that was happening. If I was to become a spy, I would have to learn to pay better attention. The guard kept up a rapid stream of chatter as he led us to our rooms in the eastern wing.

"I take it you've met the king already?" he asked.

My straw sandals padded over the smooth floors after him, which were made of a wood so dark I could see my reflection blurred in it, like the surface of water. The halls here were much wider, and there was not a single crack or leak to be found in the walls.

"We have," I said.

He glanced back over his shoulder, a sly, conspiratorial look on his face. He reminded me a little of a fox, with his arched brows and crooked grin. "What do you think?"

I hesitated. I had watched the king leave moments earlier, yet I couldn't be sure where this guard's loyalties lay, how these relationships worked. He seemed to serve Fanli, who served Goujian; surely that meant he was working for King Goujian, too?

Yet while all this raced through my mind, along with all the vague replies I could give, Zhengdan had already responded.

"In complete honesty? Rather disappointing."

My next step faltered, but she went on:

"I expected him to be more . . . well, kingly."

To both my shock and relief, the guard did not immediately execute her on the spot. Instead, he laughed, the sound muffled by his hand, as if he were sharing a secret with the both of us. "Interesting. What would you define as *kingly*? A carriage of gold? A crown on his head? A line of servants waiting at his disposal?"

Zhengdan shrugged. As much as I admired her brazen courage, sometimes it was also a great source of my concern. "To me, he does not look so different from a common man."

"But haven't you heard?" The guard's smile tugged higher on one side, and he made a dramatic show of looking around us—though we were the only people in these halls—before continuing in a whisper, "He insists on living like a common man too. It's said that he sleeps on brushwood, and hangs a piece of gallbladder in his room, from which he drinks every night. He also refuses to indulge in any form of luxury, even when they are offered to him on opened hands. All this, so he will not forget Kuaiji."

"*Gallbladder?*" Zhengdan repeated, her eyebrows drawing together.

"Kuaiji?" I said with shallow recognition. It was the fallen city where Goujian had been forced to surrender to the Wu soldiers. Still, the way the guard spoke of it suggested at another story there, something even more shameful than a military defeat.

The guard merely winked. "If you two would prefer not to lose your head to a very sharp and expensive sword, I'd advise that you don't mention Kuaiji in Goujian's presence, should you see him again."

"But what happened there?" I asked.

"Oh, that's not for me to say." The guard paused outside a wide doorway, seeming to enjoy the suspense, or just the attention. "Perhaps Fanli will be so generous as to tell you the details, when he is in an agreeable mood."

"And when will that be?"

"Most likely never," the guard said, laughing. "I've known him since I was fifteen, and the advisor is many things: noble, strategic, judicious, too intelligent for his own good. But agreeable is unfortunately not one of them."

We entered a vast chamber that smelled faintly of rosewood and something else, something new. Its furnishings were simple yet elegant, with two canopy beds and a cabinet so large I doubted all my possessions could fill even a single drawer. There were mirrors, too, laid out on the table, their golden-bronze sheen like the light of small suns. The entire room was brightly lit. Across from where we stood was a window; through its lattice frame, I could glimpse the lotus pond in the courtyard and the old greens of a camphor tree.

This, I realized, was where we would be staying for the next ten weeks.

A sudden wave of homesickness crashed over me. I tightened my grip on my satchel, which contained within it only a few roughspun tunics and a hairpin Father had carved for me himself from wood. I had not known what else to bring. The skin above my sternum felt empty without the familiar weight of my jade pendant.

Would my parents have woken by now? Did they know I was gone?

Someone touched my wrist. I looked up, blinked the ache from my eyes. It was Zhengdan. There was a knowing in her expression; even though she did not appear so sad to have left the village behind, she understood.

"You can just set your things down here," the guard told us. "Fanli is expecting you in the dining hall."

I quickly collected myself and tucked the satchel away. I would not think about my parents anymore. I would grow into a different person here, with a new room and new clothes and new wants.

Someone who could cast spells on the most powerful of men and deceive without any softening of the heart.

The dining hall was not difficult to find. The scent of roasted meat wafted out to greet us yards before we had even stepped into the room. My stomach grumbled, a sharp pang of hollowness striking me with full force. On the ride here, I had not even entertained the thought of food. But now, it was all I could think about. Not the coarse millet buns from our village, the mung bean porridge that was too often diluted down to mildly flavored water, but real *meat*.

My footsteps quickened.

Inside, a feast was already laid out on a low table. Fanli sat alone on one side, his bowl of rice untouched, his chopsticks set down, hardly even interested in what had been spread out right under his nose: plates of crisp bamboo shoots; a whole fish slathered in a golden-brown sauce, the white meat so tender it sprung apart on its own; slices of chicken cooked with fresh chestnuts and chilies. I could imagine the taste just from the scent—the give of the bamboo between my teeth, the notes of sweetness mixed with the richer tang of dark soy sauce and oil—

"Hungry?" Fanli asked, catching my eye. "Sit down. This is for the two of you."

We needed no further invitation. I grabbed the pair of chopsticks to my left and pushed as much food into my bowl as it could physically contain. It was so hot still that I could see the steam rising from the fish.

Fanli waited until we had both eaten a few bites of everything before speaking. "In the palace, that is not how you take your meals."

I paused, my chopsticks hovering in midair. "What do you mean?"

Zhengdan did not even stop chewing. Through a mouthful of food, she said, "Don't tell me we are meant to learn etiquette for *eating* too."

"You must." Fanli rose from the table, his eyes cold. "First, you are supposed to wait outside the door until you are called in. You must then curtsy—with your hands like this." He clasped his own hands together, then shifted them to one side while bending the knee ever so slightly. "Do not make eye contact with him. Do not tilt your head. Wait for him to excuse you before approaching the table from the side." He gestured to our left. "When you sit, your feet must remain like so."

Zhengdan stared at him. "We must do all of that? Every time?"

"Not only that." He lowered himself back down in his seat. "Nobody is allowed to touch their chopsticks—much less eat—until the king has eaten first. If he raises a goblet of wine in toast, then you must ensure your goblet is placed lower than his. And when you do lift your chopsticks, you must take care to arrange your robes." He made a series of elaborate movements with his broad sleeves, fanning them out almost like a dance before slowly lifting them up to cover his mouth.

Catching my eye, Zhengdan muttered to me, "By the time we finish, all the dishes will have gone cold."

I bit back a smile. It *did* seem somewhat absurd, all these unnecessary flourishes of movement, all the subtle rules and expectations. And what was their purpose, exactly? To make the king feel more important? In our village, there was barely enough time to eat as it was. Nobody would waste it on such hollow gestures as these. I couldn't even count the number of times I had seen a villager crouching in one corner, shoving chunks of millet bun into their mouth as though in fear somebody would snatch it away.

"You may find it laughable now," Fanli said evenly. "But only the other lunar month, a court official was beheaded for lifting his wine higher than the king's. They found it a blatant sign of disrespect."

All my mirth withered, and my stomach clenched. The images that flashed through my mind were enough to dissolve my appetite: the young official who had forgotten himself for only a second, who raised his goblet with perhaps too much enthusiasm, so eager was he to please—and the wine dropped from his trembling hands, the dark red spill of it like blood against the smooth palace floors. A sick feeling frothed inside me. I paid closer attention when Fanli showed us the eating rituals once more, and managed to emulate him on the fifth try. Zhengdan succeeded on the eighth.

"Now you understand the basics," Fanli said, "it is important to perform them in such a way that is pleasing to the eye. Remember, you will be watched the whole time."

And so our lessons began.

CHAPTER FOUR

DO YOU KNOW WHAT YOUR PROBLEM IS?"
These were the first words Fanli spoke to me the next day when he found me sitting alone by the lotus pond, my fingers skimming the water. The coolness of it felt divine, like silk against skin. It was a strange thing to realize that I might never have to wash silk again in my life.

I jerked my head up, then hastily wiped my wet hands on my robes. I had not been expecting Fanli so soon. The evening before, he had said he planned to see each of us alone, to better assess what our strengths and weaknesses were and tailor our training accordingly. I'd thought he was still with Zhengdan, who'd been away so long by the time I woke that her sheets had already turned cold.

"My problem?" I echoed, somewhat affronted. "What?"

He sat beside me, taking his time to smooth the layered fabrics of his robes before replying, "You wear everything you feel on your face."

I blinked. "I don't—"

"You do," he countered calmly. "For instance, right now you are wondering how I even came to such a conclusion."

"That's not—"

"And now, you are wondering how I read you so easily."

I felt a prickling of annoyance. Worse, he was right. "Those are just guesses."

"Is that so?" He cocked his head just so, a small smile flickering over his lips. "You are now contemplating how it is that I'm right. And you would not mind if I were to fall into the water."

"I'm not," I lied, biting the inside of my cheek. How did he *know*? I was suddenly self-conscious of every shift in my facial muscles, every minor movement in my body. Was I giving something of myself away, even now?

"Don't be self-conscious," he said, smiling still. He reached over and placed his palm above the surface of the pond, in the very same place I had touched the water moments earlier. I watched the silvery light ripple over his skin. His hands were surprisingly slender for a swordsman, each bone as long and delicate as the shaft of an arrow. "You see how easily the water changes upon the slightest breeze, the faintest stir of the lotus petals, the lightest touch?" As he spoke, he skimmed his fingers over the water, and the pond rippled, our reflections distorting within it. "It is the same with your expressions. I do not have to look hard to tell if you are overjoyed; if you are homesick; if you are resentful. Only yesterday, I could see when the sight of a flock of geese soaring through the skies delighted you, or when the sound of the flowing creek reminded you of something tragic."

It was an unwelcome shock to know your most vulnerable thoughts were all but public to those who cared enough to read them.

"Then tell me," I said, angling my chin higher, willing my features to flatten, to prove him wrong, "what am I thinking at present?"

Perhaps it was a mistake to challenge him. To invite his full attention. As he searched my face, I could focus on nothing but the unnatural darkness of his eyes, the curious sensation of the air thinning between us. When his gaze drifted lower, down to my nose and lips, there came a fierce rushing in my chest, like the howl of wind over a sheer cliff.

In the same instance, something beneath his calm mask flinched. He drew back, just an inch, yet enough for the change to feel significant. "You are thinking," he said slowly, looking out at the courtyard instead, "of something you know you should not."

Warmth rose up the nape of my neck. "So what is your point?"

"My point is that it is a dangerous thing for a spy to wear their emotions so openly. If the king detects something off, the entire mission falls apart. But," he added, perhaps sensing my despair, "this can be controlled over time. As with anything, it is a matter of willpower and technique."

"How?"

"Look here," he said, gesturing to the pond. The water had stilled, and the surface served as a mirror. I gazed down at my own features. It is always difficult for one to see themselves with any objectivity, but I had come to understand that the slender column of my neck was pleasing, the natural cherry-red tint of my lips harmonious with my thick-lashed eyes and small nose. Yet when I looked closer, I saw for the first time how my lips were puckered at the edges, as if I had tasted something sour, and my brows were knitted together, as though in confusion. "Try to smile."

I tried. My mouth curved, but my eyes remained dark and heavy.

"If you smiled at me like that," Fanli said, a wry note to his voice, "I would think you were plotting to murder me."

I watched my reflection twist instantly into a scowl. A scowl which only deepened when I realized just how obvious the changes in my expression were.

Fanli laughed aloud.

The shock of the sound wiped my face free of any irritation. It was the first time I had heard him laugh; I'd been starting to wonder if he even knew how.

But he composed himself just as quickly. "Try again," he suggested. "This time, think of the mind and body as two separate entities. There is no connection between them. Your body is merely a tool, a canvas, a weapon. It is entirely subject to your control."

Again, I smiled at nothing, feeling more and more like a fool by the minute. The planes of my face remained stiff as ever. I could deceive nobody, not even myself. Had Zhengdan also been subjected to this? For some reason I doubted it; though she was blunter than I in many ways, she also did not experience such intense emotions.

"Perhaps we will find another approach," Fanli decided. "But I'd suggest you practice as often as you can with a mirror. Study your expressions. See how they change, what causes those changes. That is one place to begin, at least."

The fake smile slipped from my face. I sighed and massaged my cheeks. This was not quite the type of training I'd had in mind.

"Patience. There will be other things to come," Fanli said. "But I want you to practice this for the time being."

I was not as well trained in reading expressions as he, but even I could see the dismissal written over his features. I rose to my feet and began to leave—

"Are you not going to curtsy?"

I froze mid-step, then forced myself to turn back slowly, to lower my head and bend my knees. The position felt so unnatural that I feared I would topple over at any second. I was like a foal, just learning to stand. My legs shook beneath me.

"Yes," Fanli murmured, half to himself, "I see we will have to work on that as well."

"How was your meeting with Fanli?" Zhengdan asked from the doorway.

I was sitting before a bronze mirror in our chambers, assessing my expressions as critically as possible. I did not know how much control I could exert over my muscles, but I was growing rather tired of my own face.

"Lovely," I told her. "He believes I cannot hide anything."

"He believes I cannot charm anyone," Zhengdan said. She walked across the room and sat beside me, her head coming to rest on my shoulder. "I suppose that is further reason why you are the concubine, and not me."

I had to laugh. "So what does he propose for your training?"

Zhengdan's reflection glowed in the mirror, her eyes bright, her skin suffused with healthy color. We had only been away from our village a day, but already she looked more alive than I'd ever seen her. "He asked me to show him my hands instead."

"Your hands?"

She nodded. "It was quite astounding, really. He took only one glimpse of them and said that he knew I trained with a sword in secret. He even seemed to know how long I had been training for, and the general extent of my abilities."

I thought about the sharp, calculating look in his eyes, like he could see everything.

"I was worried he would give me the usual lecture," Zhengdan said, "about how it is unfitting for a young woman to fight, or how it would only scare men away. But guess what he said."

I shook my head, mystified. There was a smile sneaking its way up the corners of her lips.

"He's going to instruct me in swordsmanship. Proper swordsmanship." Her words tumbled out in a rapid, excited stream. "For one, it will allow me to better protect you. But he also wants me to focus on the Wu military. While you distract the king from his duties, I'm to observe the movements of their soldiers and watch their training. As a palace lady, it will be easier for me to slip in and out without people noticing."

I tried to smile at her. I *was* happy for her; I knew she was most herself when she had a sword in her hands. But at the same time, I was reminded again that the burden of bewitching the king fell on me and me alone. If I failed, everything would be rendered futile. All these people, all those lives, the weight of kingdoms balanced on my shoulders, and here I sat, unable to even school my features into an expression of false delight.

It did not help that Zhengdan peered at me then, and observed, "You look worried."

"I will fix that," I said, focusing on the mirror again. My brows were pinched, my mouth pressed into a tight, anxious line. "I just need to practice."

At night, I tucked myself into a foreign bed, miles and miles away from home—but still the old nightmare found me.

It was always the same. The same place, the same time. The same beginning.

Susu and I were alone in the house when they came; our parents had left for the forest to gather fresh wood for the coming winter. Already the air was so cold I could see Susu's breaths clinging to the air when she laughed. I was telling her a story about Nüwa, and how she had made the first mortals.

"She took great care, handcrafting them and shaping them from yellow clay," I said, smiling as Susu slumped against my legs, her small mouth open in mid-yawn. "These became the nobles and royals."

"And the rest?" She had only learned to speak the year prior, and her words came out in a mumble. Sometimes she grew frustrated when she could not express herself as clearly as we could. But that was fine, we reassured her, she had plenty of time to learn.

"And the rest were created when she was tired. She dipped a long rope into mud and she swung it, and the droplets that landed became commoners. Like us."

Susu frowned. "You're not made of mud."

"No?"

"You are made of flowers," she said decisively, crawling onto my lap. She was getting too heavy to do so, but I sat back without protest and let her anyway, stroking her soft hair, inhaling the sweet milk scent of her skin. I would protect her with my life, I thought to myself. "And rainwater. And silk. And lanterns. You are made of good things."

And that was when the shrieks started.

In my nightmares I felt my panic more sharply than I had even in memory, a feeling so intense it tore through my whole body. Because I knew how this ended. I knew there was no escaping it, even as I pulled Susu into the cramped closet with me, even as I buried us in old coats and tried to hold on to her squirming body.

"We must hide," I whispered into her ear. My heart was pounding so loud I could hear it in the dark space, its every strained, heaving movement, the rush of blood like wind. "Please—Susu, listen to me—you have to keep quiet—"

But she had started crying. "Mama," she choked out. "Mama, I *want Mama*—"

The crash of the door. The pounding of footsteps. Something cracking.

The soldiers were here.

"Mama," Susu sobbed, pulling back from my arms, her short legs thrashing. She was strong for her age; each kick was hard enough to bruise, but I didn't let go. "I'm *scared*. Mama, take me to find Mama—"

"She'll be back," I whispered, desperation squeezing my throat hoarse. I was trembling. Through the crack in the closet doors, I could see the soldiers storming into the room. Two men, their dark hair cropped, their swords stained with blood. "Just stay here, and we'll be safe, I promise. Don't go out."

Susu shook her head furiously and twisted her torso away from me, wrenching her arms free. The sleeves of my robes were damp with her tears. Her tiny fists pushed against the closet door—

"*Susu—*"

I tried to grab for her. I tried to reach for the doors. But my fingers curled around nothing, and in the instant she stumbled out from the closet, a terrible physical pain seized my heart.

No.

Not now.

The illness that had plagued me since childhood. The curse I could not cure. My body failed me; it felt as though someone had thrust a spear into my chest, the blade sliding between my ribs. I doubled over, gasping, useless, as Susu walked straight into the soldiers.

Please.

Don't hurt her. My mouth moved silently over the words, the pain burning through my blood. *She is only a child. I promised to teach her how to ride a horse, and braid her own hair, and tomorrow our mother is making her favorite lotus root soup, which she has been looking forward to for weeks. This war—your territory—the difference between kingdoms—it means nothing to her. It means nothing at all. Just let her live.*

When the sword rose, I searched the soldier's face. I did not know what I wanted to find—perhaps the faintest trace of hesitation, of remorse, of self-loathing. But it was like staring into a tiger's eyes as it mauled its prey. There was only darkness. The gleam of violence.

The sword streaked through the air.

Blood splattered the floor. Her blood. The blood we shared.

And I was screaming, screaming until my throat split open, until I could taste the copper on my tongue, until I couldn't see her anymore—

My eyes snapped open. I lay on the bed, my hand clutching my chest, remembering how to breathe. There was an ache in me, like a decayed tooth.

Susu.

Across the room, under a sliver of filtered moonlight, Zhengdan turned onto her side, snoring softly. Outside, the branches rustled, a cicada chirped, the river water flowed onward. All was peaceful. But something about it felt unreal, like *this* was the dream. Perhaps I had not been awake since Susu was taken from me.

For the rest of the night, I stayed staring up at the ceiling, my fingers itching with the promise of revenge.

CHAPTER FIVE

IN THOSE EARLY DAYS, FANLI WOULD ALWAYS SEEK ME out by the lotus pond. Sometimes he wore robes of inkstone black, his sash belt embroidered with the finest gold threads, creating repeating patterns of open magnolias, layered clouds, cranes in flight. Sometimes he was dressed in silver, his broad sleeves floating in the breeze and flowing like water, soft and ethereal, and he would wave a white fan to match. I could not decide which appearance suited him more: god of war, or muse of poets. To me, he was both.

"We are learning something new," he told me one morning. He was in pure black, the smooth planes of his face made colder by contrast. "I believe you are ready."

"For what?"

In response, Fanli merely called: "Luyi. Bring it here."

The guard ambled out from behind the covered corridor, carrying a long wooden instrument in his hands. I recognized it from its distinctive features, rather than my own experience: the silk-thin strings stretched horizontally across it, the warm gleam of the wood under the sun. One end was curved and slightly wider than the other, and it was so large that if it were stood up next to me, it would be taller than my shoulders.

"Hurry up," Fanli told Luyi, but without any real impatience. "Don't tell me that instrument is too heavy for you."

Luyi made an exaggerated pout and walked no faster. "After searching every spot in the mountains the other day? Consider it a miracle I can even hold my body upright. My leg muscles are still sore."

"Do you truly care so little about your reputation as a guard?" Fanli said dryly. "Nobody will hire a guard who whines just because he was made to climb a few miles."

"A *few*?" Luyi repeated, indignant, setting the zither down before us with a loud *thud*. "I doubt even the Kunlun Mountains are so high. And better yet, if nobody else wishes to hire me"—he grinned—"you'll be stuck with me all your life."

"Incredible."

Luyi's grin broadened. "I am, aren't I? About time you took notice."

"No," Fanli said, voice flat. "I meant it is incredible how your impertinence grows by the day."

I looked between the two of them.

"Why . . . were you searching the mountains?" I asked.

"Oh, security measures," Luyi said, waving a dismissive hand. "Seeing as both the great military advisor of Yue and future tributes to the Wu king are all gathered here in one place, Fanli wanted to ensure there were no assassins of sorts lurking around these mountains. Because, as you can imagine, that would be rather inconvenient."

Assassins. My blood beat faster within me. The word conjured up visions of blood and blades, men masked in black, the stuff of folklore. They barely seemed real. "Did you find anything?"

Luyi shook his head and offered me a wide smile that was perhaps meant to reassure. "Good news: Nobody wishes to kill you."

"How wonderful," I murmured.

"Yet," Fanli added, his eyes sharp as knifepoints on me. "It's no reason to let your guard down. Have you not heard that the loveliest flowers are usually the first to be plucked? Your beauty is dangerous—to others, but also to yourself."

"You're scaring her," Luyi said, jabbing a thumb at my face. I flushed, remembering again what Fanli had told me about my expressions showing. Were they truly *that* obvious? "Look."

"Yes, I can see quite plainly. It is another problem we must contend with." Fanli turned back to Luyi. "You may go now."

He pouted. "But I was hoping to watch—"

"If you truly have nothing better to do, then you can search the mountains again."

"Just joking," Luyi said hastily, backing away with impressive speed. The next moment, he was gone.

Fanli rolled his eyes at the wall around which Luyi had disappeared, then adjusted his position behind the instrument and gestured to it. "Do you know what this is?"

The word rose clumsily to my lips. I had only ever heard it spoken by others. "A guqin."

"Correct. And do you know how to play it?"

I lifted a tentative hand to the strings. Though I'd thought them to resemble silk, they were in fact so sharp to the touch I wondered how anyone could strum them without splitting open skin. Slowly, I shook my head. Such instruments were the pastimes of fancy noblewomen, girls born into royal blood.

"Let me show you." He leaned forward, swept his sleeves back in a great swishing motion, pressed down the string on one end, and plucked it on the other. A low, melancholic note reverberated through the air. It was so beautiful, so pure, I felt a stirring in my blood. The breath swelled in my lungs. Then he strummed the instrument in earnest, his fingers moving too fast for me to make out. Without pausing, he looked up and asked, "What does this remind you of?"

I closed my eyes. A breeze kissed my skin, and the music rose around me, like heat. "It reminds me of . . . a river running south. Water on rocks." I had no idea if this was anywhere close to the right answer, if there could even be a right answer to whatever test this was.

Fanli was quiet for a long moment.

"And now?" The melody changed, slowed down. There was a dark tone to it, something sad and terrible and slightly ominous.

"A fallen city. The aftermath of a war. Two lovers separated over two shores."

"Now?"

"Wisps of clouds moving over a full moon. The silence of solitude. An empty room, dust motes floating in a slant of pale sunlight. Regret for something you cannot take back. Happiness for somebody you cannot have."

The music stopped completely, and when my eyes fluttered open, Fanli was looking at me in a new way. Almost perplexed. As though a calculation he'd been certain of had suddenly rearranged itself, and he wasn't sure what to make of it.

"Yes," he said at last, that look falling away.

"Yes . . . what?"

But he did not elaborate. He just motioned for me to sit down before him. I did so, and was quickly made aware of his presence. We were so close I could feel the soft exhale of his breath against the back of my bare neck. Though we were barely even touching, his arms encircled my body, and his hands hovered over mine, guiding them to the strings. I was glad, then, that he could not see my face from his angle, for my expression surely would've betrayed everything I was thinking.

"Try to play it," he told me, demonstrating a few times and explaining all the different playing techniques and pitch positions until my head swam with unfamiliar terms.

I plucked the string just as he had, but the sound it made was dull, grating to the ears. Disappointment curled in my belly alongside a pinch of panic. What if I proved awful at everything Fanli attempted to show me? What if I was like all the villagers said: beautiful to look at, but little more than that? The entire mission suddenly seemed overwhelming, absurd. Impossible. I would never be ready, let alone within the mere eight weeks we had remaining.

"That is to be expected, for your first time," he said. "It would be a wonder if you could play it well right away."

For a moment I wondered if he'd sensed my tension, and sought to comfort me. But his voice was too matter-of-fact for that. I gave myself a small shake. I needed to stop scrabbling for sentimentality where there was none to be found.

"Adjust your finger positions here." He moved my wrist forward, his fingers cool through the thin fabric of my sleeves. "And do not pluck it with such blunt force. These strings are sensitive. A slight change in pressure can change the sound also. Listen."

All morning we stayed out by the pond, practicing with the instrument. I played again and again until my skin had been rubbed raw, but uttered no sound of complaint. It was Fanli who saw the fresh blood smeared over the hair-thin strings, and came to an abrupt stop.

"Why didn't you say anything?" he asked, frowning. "We could have taken a break."

"No." I didn't lift my fingers off the guqin. "I think I'm starting to get it. Let me try a little longer."

"You will ruin your hands this way."

I ignored him. I had always hated leaving things unfinished. But it was more than that: I needed to prove to someone, if only myself, that I *could* do this. That I was equipped not just with the pretty features I had been born into. That I would be just as good, if not better, than the sheltered girls who were instructed in dance and song and classical instruments from childhood.

When both my hands were slick with my own blood, I found that I was able to play a simple tune on the guqin from beginning to end. The heady rush of satisfaction instantly swept all the pain aside. I turned around, grinning, to Fanli. *See?* I wished to gloat. *I can do it after all.*

"Good" was all he said.

But he was staring at my hands.

We quickly settled into a routine. The mornings were dedicated to learning the guqin, among other instruments, singing, and all styles of dance. Some of them I had never even heard of before— they involved the swishing of brightly colored fans that flared out at the edges, while others required spinning around in rapid circles on the same spot. The first few times I attempted this, I ended up falling on all fours, the world swaying before me so violently I thought I would be sick.

"Watch the movement of the swans," Fanli would tell Zheng- dan and me, pointing at the creatures' slender necks, the way they glided over the waters. "Dancing is an expression of beauty, and what is beautiful is always derived from nature itself."

"He only says such things to avoid demonstrating the dance for us himself," Zhengdan muttered into my ear one session. I had to fight so hard to control my laughter that I almost lost my balance on the second spin.

Lunchtimes were just as rigorous. There seemed no end to the number of rules that came with a single meal. Eating was no longer just a means of nourishing the body, of appeasing the empty stomach and ensuring one had the energy to work another day, but a highly complex ritual. It was considered a great offense to have the head of a fish dish turned toward the king; an offense to make audible noises while chewing in the king's presence. It seemed to me that the problem lay more with the king; who else would have the energy to be offended by nearly everything? Of course, I kept these thoughts to myself. I had not forgotten what Fanli told us the first day about the beheaded official.

But despite all this, what I looked forward to most were the afternoons. Here the focus shifted to classics, poetry, politics, and history. The stories Fanli told us—and to me, they felt exactly like stories, these romantic, dramatic, and tragic tales that did not happen to ordinary people—were wildly fascinating, made even more engaging by the fact that he himself was acquainted with many of the characters.

"What do you know about Wu Zixu?" Fanli asked, stepping around his desk.

We were sitting in his study, a closed-off room on the other end of the courtyard from our bedchambers. The late orange sunlight moved in filtered patches over Fanli's desk. A map of the fractured empire lay across it, marking the borders between the Wu and the Yue, and places beyond our two kingdoms, places so far away they felt to me like they belonged to another world entirely: the Chu to the west, the steppes to the higher north, the Yellow Sea stretched along the coast. From afar, the fragments of land looked like shattered porcelain.

Beside the map was a dense diagram of various figures, their relationships drawn out in a series of dotted ink lines and Fanli's tiny annotations.

"Wu Zixu . . ." The name was familiar, but I could not quite place where I'd heard it. Then I remembered the common saying, passed from villager to villager. Out loud, I recalled, "Wu Zixu is to King Fuchai what Fanli is to King Goujian."

Fanli's brows rose a fraction. "You are correct, in some sense. Though I'd argue he was more valued as an advisor by Fuchai's father, King Helü. Wu Zixu was the one who helped Helü assassinate his cousin and ascend the throne. From the inside reports I've received, Fuchai does not trust Wu Zixu quite as much as his father did. Which is good for us. Why do you think?"

I rummaged through what little I knew for an answer. The Wu's and the Yue's interests were forever at odds. What was good for us had to be terrible for them. "Because . . . Wu Zixu's advice could make the Wu stronger before we have a chance to attack. Because a king who doesn't trust his own advisor is easier to deceive. Or because . . . Wu Zixu is most likely to suspect King Goujian's plan for revenge?"

Zhengdan nodded beside me. "That makes sense. It takes like to know like, and Wu Zixu has always wanted revenge himself, hasn't he?"

I turned to her. Zhengdan spent more time in the village center than I did, and gossip sometimes proved a surprisingly reliable source of information. "Revenge for what?"

"For his father," Fanli explained, returning to his position behind the desk. He pointed an ink brush at another name on the cluttered diagram and traced it back to Wu Zixu. "Wu Zixu originally came from the State of Chu; his father was grand tutor to their crown prince. But this official"—he drew his brush farther down to a name written in red—"spread the rumor that his father and the prince were plotting a rebellion. While awaiting his execution, the grand tutor was forced to write a letter to his sons, asking that they come to the capital. Wu Zixu recognized it was a trap, and fled to the Wu Kingdom instead."

My stomach turned cold.

Treason. Traps. Treachery. The more I learned about these men and their methods of obtaining power, the more I dreaded entering the court myself. I was just one person. Could I really stand to outwit them all, to seduce their king right under their noses? How did any of them even manage to fall asleep at night, knowing that one wrong move could rip everything away from them?

As if I had spoken my thoughts aloud, Fanli fixed his gaze on me. "Zhengdan is right. Wu Zixu is a naturally suspicious man, who cannot tolerate the slightest speck of sand in his eye. Watch out for him. If my predictions are correct, he will be the first to suspect you, and will do everything he can to make your life in the palace difficult." His eyes darkened with urgency. "You must find a way to remove him from King Fuchai's side as soon as possible."

"Or else?" I could barely breathe, dreading the answer.

"Or else he will remove you."

When all the training was over for the day, I lay in bed, my mind swimming with fresh information and new threats and my body aching quietly. I could not remember ever being so exhausted in my life, even when washing giant baskets of raw silk on my own.

Then I felt a weight lower itself beside me. The tickle of long hair.

"Xishi-jie." Zhengdan's voice. She was whispering, even though it was just the two of us here. "Are you asleep?"

Without opening my eyes, I murmured, "Yes."

She snorted and shuffled closer until her pointy chin dug into my shoulder. "Talk to me. I'm bored."

"You're *bored?*" My eyes snapped open in my incredulity. I blinked thrice in the blue darkness, before her face came into focus. "How are you not exhausted? I don't believe it's physically possible for our daily schedule to be busier than it already is." My hands stung even as I said it. The places where I'd rubbed my fingers over the guqin strings had already started to harden and form calluses.

"Yes, but there are so few people around here."

"What's wrong with that?" Privately, this was perhaps one of the things I most enjoyed about the cottage. There were fewer prying eyes, fewer bitter tongues, fewer people to worry over. "It's peaceful."

"For you, maybe," she grumbled, flipping over onto her belly. She was silent for so long I wondered if she had drifted off to sleep already. Then she asked, "What do you think about Fanli?"

Irrationally, I felt myself tense. "Why?"

"What do you mean, *why?* I just want to know. It's not as if there is anyone else around here to gossip about."

I made a noncommittal sound. In truth, I did not want to discuss anything about Fanli or entertain any thoughts of him while lying in the dark of my bedchambers; it was enough that I had to be around him every hour of the day.

Just as I was debating how to change the topic, Zhengdan went on. "I wonder if he has a lover of his own."

"Wait—what?"

"I doubt it," she said. "If he spends all his time around *us*, and his heart remains still as water, and his face as cold as ice, then he must not be tempted by anything whatsoever. It's no wonder the king trusts only him with this mission. Perhaps he is not even interested in love. He will be one of those people who devote themselves to their kingdom, and pass through their whole lives alone."

A strange taste crept into my mouth, like day-old tea. I drew the sheets higher to my chin. "Is it really any of our business?"

"Come on, Xishi-jiejie." She nudged me. "Don't tell me you have no opinions of him."

For a moment I considered telling her about the riverbank, the little girl with bruises trailing down her limbs, and Fanli approaching with the sun blazing behind him, like a warrior from the stories made real. Yet something stopped my tongue. It was like telling someone that you'd dreamed of them; even if there was little meaning to it, it still felt too intimate.

"He doesn't reveal much of himself," I settled on in the end, gazing up at the high windows. A delicate latticework of branches could be seen through the thin rice paper, their flowers faintly visible as splotches of color. "All I know is that he would do anything for his kingdom."

"That alone reveals plenty," Zhengdan said. "Think: a man who has severed all worldly desires in order to save the world, who has sworn total loyalty to the state and so is loyal to nobody. Someone like him would put a sword through his own heart for the greater good. It's probably for the better," she added as an afterthought, "that he takes no lovers. He is too virtuous to have a good ending with any woman. In a world where everyone will demand something from you, it requires a certain degree of selfishness to be happy, you know."

Zhengdan, the great beauty and philosopher. There were times when she reminded me of a young, wide-eyed girl, a little sister to be protected and doted on, and others when she seemed possessed by a century-old sage who has already seen through the red dust of the world.

I reached over and flicked her forehead lightly, glad for the concealing properties of the dark. "Enough, now."

But even after she went quiet, it took me forever to fall asleep. I could not stop turning and prodding at what she'd said about Fanli passing his life alone. The thought sent a pang through my chest, though of course I wasn't able to fathom why. What did any of it have to do with me? Yet even then, there was another voice inside me that answered differently.

CHAPTER SIX

IN THE COTTAGE, THE DAYS FLEW AWAY FROM US LIKE AUtumn leaves snatched by a violent wind. I learned how to pluck the sweetest melodies from the guqin; how to win and lose deliberately at a game of chess; how to drink my wine in silent, delicate sips, with my face hidden behind my sleeve. I memorized the names of the Five Hegemons, and could recite in my sleep the series of conflicts between the Yue and the Wu, the attempts of King Helü to invade our kingdom, only to lose the Battle of Suli and eventually die from his battle wounds. I trained my facial features into obedience and learned to turn my mind to beautiful fantasies when I wished to fake smiles and laughter. When I tired of the training, I picked a deep-ripened plum from the tree and relished it alone, the cool juice dribbling down my wrist.

At times, I would stray to the courtyard, where Fanli and Zhengdan were practicing. It seemed a privilege to simply stand there and watch Fanli fight. In his hands the sword became fluid, moving silver. His blade would pierce the air, his hand following in a silent line, and the plum blossom petals would shower down on him like spring rain. But when he stopped, and looked up, his breathing just slightly uneven from exertion, I was always quick to avert my eyes.

Throughout those final weeks, I could feel myself changing; in the mirror, or the reflection of the still pond, the face that stared back was lovelier yet more cunning, with a new sharpness to the gaze. Sometimes, if I pretended that time could slow and the rest of my days would pass just like this, I could even be happy.

But I was always reminded yet again that there was a point to what I learned, and *that* was my life, my destiny, not this calm interlude among the plum blossoms and windfall fruit.

And my destiny was rapidly approaching.

"In a week, you will be meeting King Fuchai," Fanli told us. The weather had started to cool, and we were indoors, a controlled fire blazing close by. I held my fingers closer to the flames, watching the red-orange light flicker over my skin. "From your very first encounter, you must make him desire you. But what is desire?"

"Greed," Zhengdan replied at once, with a curl of contempt in her voice. I wondered if she was thinking of the village men throwing themselves at her door, how their eyes lingered on her figure, how they called after her whenever she walked the streets. "Possession."

"Absence," I said, after some thought.

Fanli looked at me and made a silent gesture for me to continue.

"We are most tempted by what we cannot have. Men will dream of the mountains they have yet to scale, the rivers they have yet to set sail upon, the plains they have yet to conquer. They are told from birth everything belongs to them, and so when something does not, they view it as a personal challenge." I thought about it longer. "But also, from a distance, everything looks more beautiful; we are better able to conjure our own fantasies about them. Sometimes the fragrance of a feast is better than the taste itself."

"Absence," Fanli repeated, and nodded. He stood, began to walk in slow circles. "That is true enough. And that is what you must keep in the back of your mind when you are with King Fuchai. More than any man, he believes he owns the world. Do not fall straight into his arms. It is too easy; he will grow bored within days. He is more likely to be intrigued if you keep him reaching for you. And every time he believes he is close, close enough to touch"—he held his hand out toward me, and for one foolish moment, I wondered if he would do something like brush my hair from my cheeks—"you pull away. Again and again." His voice was low. For the first time, I noticed there was a faintly hoarse quality to it. "Until he is consumed by thoughts of you." He withdrew his hand, a snap of the sleeve, and resumed walking.

I swallowed. My skin was hot from the flames, yet there was another, more potent heat rising behind my ribs. Absence. The forbidden object, the thing you cannot have. Why had I said it, and said it so easily? Where had the answer even come from?

Zhengdan nudged me. I startled, a strange, guilty flush spreading through my skin, though I had not done or thought anything wrong.

"What's wrong?" she whispered while Fanli's back was to us. "You have an odd look on your face."

"Nothing," I whispered back.

She squinted, then pointed at me. "You're turning red—"

"I'm *not*—"

"What's the issue?" Fanli asked, whirling around.

I quickly shook my head, remembering everything he had ever taught me about controlling my emotions. I imagined my face as a frozen lake, hard stone, blank and impenetrable. Perhaps it worked, for he asked nothing more.

I was returning from the dining hall that evening when I saw the candlelight flicker in Fanli's room. A shadow moved.

I did not know what slowed my steps. The sky had already darkened to a heavy purple, the air sweet and cold the way it is when it approaches nightfall, and I was eager to stretch across the comfort of my own bed, to sleep my exhaustion away. But instead, I crept closer. The sliding lattice door had been left ajar just a sliver, and through the gap, I saw Fanli just as he lowered himself to the floor.

My heart skipped.

It was only him inside, his ink-black hair glistening wet from the bath and running freely over his shoulder. I had never seen him with his hair out of its usual high knot before. He was facing the other direction, and as I watched, hardly breathing, he shrugged himself free of the thin white robes he'd been wearing. A sound rose in my throat, though I quickly squashed it down. He could not know that I was here, what I had seen. The entirety of his upper back was exposed, from the shoulder to the column of his spine to the narrow curve of his waist, but that was not what made me freeze.

His back had been split into a brutal map of scars. They looked obscene against his skin, which was otherwise smooth and delicate as first snow. Each was the rough width of a whip, and all were old enough to have faded into a darker, purplish shade. There was no order to them, where they started and ended, nothing but evidence of blunt violence, pain inflicted for the sake of pain.

Then he dipped his fingers into a jar of ointment, the motion rehearsed, routine, and began the labor of rubbing it slowly into his ruined flesh. The strong scent of herbs wafted toward me where I stood, like flower fragrance but more bitter, with a biting edge. My nose stung from it, and my throat prickled. Yet for all Fanli's efforts, he could not quite reach the scars running through the center of his spine. After a few attempts, stretching his body this way and that, he gave up completely with a just-audible sigh.

I considered stepping inside and offering to help. But then I would have to explain why I had stopped here in the first place, and I would surely wound his pride.

While I weighed out my options, he suddenly stiffened, then whipped around. I tried to duck out of view, but he was too fast.

"I know you're there," he called. "Come in."

I entered, feeling like a thief who had been caught by the very master of the house they intended to rob. It felt more difficult than ever to maintain control over my facial muscles, even after so many lessons. My guilt and shock must've burned like a flame in my gaze.

"Sorry," I stammered out, unsure where to look. In the time it took me to step forward, he had already finished dressing, a black outer cloak thrown on over his robes, a broad sash tied tight around his waist. But the sight of the scars was seared into my mind. "I didn't mean to—"

"Spy on me?" He said it without accusation.

I said nothing. My mind was racing with questions: What had happened to him? Who had done it to him? Who *dared* to? Did the scars still hurt? Did anybody else know about them? Was I the first? A wild, dangerous impulse seized me. I imagined myself tracing those jagged lines with my fingertips, pressing my lips to the wounds. Would he flinch away from me? Or would he break his own rules and let me stay? Then I gave myself a shake; it was like being doused in cold water. These were not things I should be wondering. What was wrong with me today?

"I can hardly blame you for the spying," Fanli continued. "It's what you've been trained to do. My main complaint is that your presence was too obvious. I should not have discovered you at all."

"Next time, I will be sure to . . ." I paused. *Spy on you more silently?* That hardly seemed like the right response.

His mouth twitched. But despite his calm demeanor, I noticed that he held himself with more care than he usually did, as if he were guarding a secret. At the same moment, I noticed that we were alone. Alone, and in his room, which I had never visited before. The awareness of this struck me like flint.

"Let's both forget about it and get to the point. Was there something you came here for?" he asked, studying my face.

There wasn't, but I felt the need to say something, anything, to distract both him and myself from the forbidden sensation in my chest. I searched the room desperately for inspiration. It was messier than I had expected from someone as disciplined as he, scrolls laid about everywhere, badges of honor scattered over his desk, maps weighed under little figurines that represented navies and armies, his bed covered by so many books I wondered if he even had room to sleep, or if he slept at all. At last my eyes fell on his sword, which had been set down just beside him. He always kept it close.

"What does it mean?" I blurted.

He looked taken aback. "What?"

"The inscription on your sword. I've been wanting to ask for a while now. Is there a special meaning to it?"

What a foolish question, I chided myself. *Do you really expect him to answer?*

But to my surprise, he picked up his sword and drew it out, the blade whispering from the sheath. In the warm candlelight, the metal gleamed as if freshly forged from flame. And there were those words again: *The mind destroys; the heart devours.* "I had it engraved to remind myself," he said mildly.

"Of?"

He hesitated. "The heart is a fickle thing; it takes and takes. It is easily swayed, and tempted, and made weak. Too many have fallen victims to their own irrational desires. But the mind—the mind is dependable, accurate, deadly. It destroys the enemy, not the self, and ensures that we do what we need to, not what we want."

My pulse beat faster in my veins. Somehow, it felt like a warning.

My final test took place inside a teahouse.

When the doors swung open, light and noise instantly rose to greet us, so overwhelming I did not know where to look first: the customers squeezed into the square stools, their money pouches rattling; the servers scuttling up and down the steep steps with boiling pots of tea; or the performers gathered on the first level, plucking an upbeat melody that reminded me of wild horses galloping on an open plain. The teahouse itself was vast, with bright wooden beams crisscrossing over the high ceiling. In the air hung the rich, green scent of wet earth and moss from the drizzle earlier, and beneath that, a cloying fragrance.

I hurried in after Fanli, who strode forward in the same manner he did anywhere: with grace and with purpose. Ever since he'd informed me that there would be an assessment to mark the end of our training, my stomach had been a tight coil of nerves. I could not even enjoy my surroundings—unlike Luyi, who was clearly in good spirits.

"Finally, I can stretch my limbs out," he said, grinning as he surveyed the area and raised both arms above his head with an open-mouthed yawn. A server had to duck around him last minute to avoid being punched. "And meet real people. Do you know what a waste it is, for someone with *my* looks and charm to be cooped up in a cottage all day? Not that I personally mind it, but it's a shame for the others: Can you imagine living your whole life without the chance to witness one of Heaven's greatest masterpieces?" He gestured to his own face.

Fanli had not stopped walking up ahead, but he turned his head a fraction. "Luyi," he said.

Luyi snapped to attention at once. "Yes?"

"I see you are making good use of your tongue."

Confusion flickered over one of Heaven's greatest masterpieces before he smiled slyly like a cat. "Well, yes, I suppose. Though if I'm being honest, if we were able to travel around more, I could always make *better* use of it—"

"Careful that I don't cut it off."

Luyi clapped a hand to his mouth, as if Fanli had already unsheathed his sword, and obediently fell into step behind me. I shared a half-amused look with Zhengdan. We were both used to their exchanges now and had witnessed Fanli threaten Luyi enough times to know he would not follow through with it. Though I wasn't so sure that'd be the case if it were someone else.

On the second level, we settled in at one of the corner tables, with Fanli and me sitting directly across each other and Luyi and Zhengdan seated beside us. Immediately, a server hurried over with menus and a stack of teacups.

"Esteemed guest," he said, speaking only to Fanli. Perhaps it was obvious who would be paying for our visit. "Is there anything you would like—"

"Just green tea is fine," Fanli said.

Luyi opened his mouth as if to add something, then closed it again in a pout.

Fanli saw, and sighed. "And red bean rice balls for the gentleman over there."

Luyi perked up at once. "How did you know?"

"One need not be a fortune teller to guess," Fanli said, tone dry. "You always choose the sweetest possible item, do you not?"

"So you *do* care," Luyi said, lifting a dramatic hand to his breastbone. "And here I was thinking that all your attention went only to state affairs—"

Fanli spoke over him, cutting the server a look. "That is all. And be quick, please."

The server nodded and left. Outside, rain had started to fall again in a steady rhythm, tapping against the roof and the delicate window-paper. The lantern lights of the teahouse seemed to flare brighter in contrast, and the natural flow of conversation picked up to be heard over the background noise. I examined the other customers more carefully. There were not many women here at all, and the few I could see were stuck performing down below, playing the flute or dancing as they sang. Before, I would've easily been impressed by their movements, the sweetness of their voices, the nimbleness of their steps. But now I saw the mistakes, too, signs that their training had been less than perfect. In the palace, mistakes would not be tolerated.

"You've both made observable progress in your training," Fanli said, sitting up straight in his seat. "But for you, Xishi, the real test comes here."

"What do you want me to do?" I asked.

"The task is simple. Find the most difficult-to-please man here, and preoccupy him for the amount of time it takes for his tea to go completely cold."

I contemplated this for a moment. "Just that?"

The faint ghost of a smile. "You are so confident?"

Admittedly, I had my own doubts. All this time we'd been training in the cottage, I had yet to try to charm a real flesh-and-blood man, to observe their reaction. But Fanli could not know this. "All the customers here look fairly easy to distract," I said, shrugging.

"What about that man over there?" Zhengdan nodded subtly to the customer sitting alone two tables away. Aside from Fanli, he was easily the most attractive man here; so young his face was smooth, with a pleasant-shaped nose and full lips. He had not glanced up once the entire time we observed him.

But Fanli shook his head. "I said difficult to please, not handsome. The two are not always the same."

We were interrupted when the server came back with our orders, then disappeared again just as fast. The tea leaves were pressed smooth and flat, a beautiful jade-green color, with a warm, mellow aroma. I watched them sink slowly inside my teacup, my hands braced around the porcelain. Beyond the windows, the rain poured harder, intensified into a loud beating.

"Who do you propose, then?" I asked Fanli.

He tipped his head toward another man. This customer sat closest to the railings, with the best view of the performers below. Everything about him was plain, nondescript. If Fanli had not pointed him out, I never would've even noticed him.

"*Him?*" Zhengdan said with a frown, not hiding her incredulity. "I've seen plenty of men just like him in my village."

"Don't be fooled by appearances. Notice how the servers did not even ask him for his order before bringing him his meal? It means that he must come here often enough to be a regular, and that he sticks to the same order every time. So he enjoys his routine. Not only that, but the tea here is horribly overpriced; so he must not be lacking in fortune. And the rich are always picky, with higher standards for everything." Fanli's voice remained calm, muted, yet here he was, dissecting a complete stranger from head to toe. "Notice also that he has been pretending to read the same scroll for the length of an incense now. His eyes have not so much as moved. It means he cares for appearances, but lacks the patience or culture to actually study. And finally—see what's hanging from his belt?"

I squinted. There was a pink pouch attached to his belt with an image of two mandarin ducks sewn into it. The embroidery was clumsy, done by an untrained hand.

"A gift from another woman. Perhaps a lover. He is not afraid to display it in clear view, even if it means potentially turning off those who might take an interest to him. There is already someone else who has his heart," Fanli concluded. "It will not be easy to hold his attention."

"Well, let me try," I said, rising.

My pulse began thrumming as I approached the man. I could feel keenly the eyes trained on the back of my head, imagine the assessing look on Fanli's face even without turning. My steps quickened, my spine righting itself. I wanted to prove to him—what? That I had learned even more than he'd thought? That others desired me? That I was no longer the girl he first found by the riverbank, so new and tender to the world, so defenseless I could not even use the weapon I'd been born with?

I slowed deliberately beside the man's table.

He glanced up. He really was plain, so plain as to be forgettable. My eyes kept slipping past his face, that broad jaw and bulbous nose, but I forced myself to gaze straight at him, calm and level.

"Is . . . there something you want, miss?" he asked after a beat, frowning. He spoke with a polished accent, his vowels smooth.

I feigned a blush. "Sorry. I don't mean to intrude—I was just . . ." My words felt incredibly clumsy and too sweet, like my lips were swollen with pollen. He was barely looking at me. "The music," I tried. "It's lovely, don't you agree?"

Now he did look at me, but it was with an irritable expression. "I don't know. I can't hear it very well, what with you talking."

My face stung. It did not help that I knew Fanli was observing me. "Sorry," I said again. "I—I only—"

"What is your point here, miss?" he cut in. Even the word *miss* was tacked on with great insincerity, his tone increasingly impatient. "Are you trying to sell me something?"

"No. Nothing." The heat in my cheeks rose. "You just seemed so captivated by the performance—"

"Which you are still interrupting. If there's really nothing else, then please stop bothering me. I'm busy." With that, he snapped his head back to the show below, denying me even his side profile. The dismissal could not have been more clear.

I backed up a step, humiliation burning down my throat. Out of the corner of my eye, I spotted Fanli and the others. Zhengdan looked concerned, and Luyi greatly amused. Only Fanli's expression revealed little outward emotion, his eyes pitch-black in the dim light. Yet, after so many sessions together, I could almost hear him: *Have you learned nothing? Are you going to give up after a single attempt? Think about what he wants, Xishi. Appeal to his ego, not his heart.*

Steeling myself, I studied the man more closely, taking in every detail. So he did not wish to talk about the music, and he would not be charmed by another's attention alone. What else? My eyes trailed finally to the scroll in his hands. This whole time, he had not let it go.

"Why are you back?" the man asked.

Because the king's famous military advisor sent me over here with a task, and he is even more difficult to please than you. "I was just . . . curious about what you were reading."

"This?" He held up the scroll, his brows raised. At least he was not shooing me away.

"That's the real reason I came here earlier," I said, a half lie. Hopefully it would help heal his first impression of me. "It looks very important, like—like something only the scholars or noblemen would read. May I see what it is?"

His expression cleared, all the impatience in his features melting away. "Aiya, you should've said so earlier." He held the scroll out to me. "Can you read?"

I leaned closer, pretending to study the scroll, when really I was offering him a better view of my face. I recognized the moment he was made truly aware of me, my physical presence. His breath drew in, a soft quickening, and in my peripheral vision, I could sense how his eyes lingered on the arch of my brows, the slope of my nose. *Good.* This was a beginning, at least.

"These are poems," I mused, lowering my voice to offer the illusion of intimacy. Admittedly such tactics made me embarrassed, so basic and shameless they were, but perhaps it worked. The man's gaze drew closer. "I've always loved poetry, though I don't know many myself." A lie. I had now memorized every poem there was worth knowing. I could have spent a day speaking in nothing but couplets, and I was certain that I knew more about poetry than the man sitting before me. "Do you . . . have a favorite among these?"

"I see you are quite well-read," he said admiringly, though of course the emphasis was on *quite.* Well-read enough to make him feel smart and cultured, but not so well-read as to challenge his views on anything. "Well, sit down, sit down. Let me show you this ode—isn't it beautiful, the imagery of the trilling geese?"

I sat, taking care to smooth my skirt, to tuck my ankles, my movements slowed so he could take in the full length of my figure. He was pretending not to watch, but when I looked over at him, our gazes collided. I shaped my lips into a small, demure smile, then averted my eyes again. "The imagery is beautiful indeed," I said softly. "What does it all mean?"

"Oh, yes, well. It is perhaps too depressing for a young lady like you," he said, his tone changing. It was deeper, deliberate, affecting the airs of a wise scholar. "See the repetition of the sinking sun, and the—the rising river? Everything is thrown into a state of despair. One can only watch, powerless to change anything. A tragedy through and through."

I raised my sleeve to my lips with a muted gasp. "How terrible. And you can tell all that just from so few lines?"

He smiled, his chest puffing out. One of his front teeth was crooked. I tried not to stare at it. "It is nothing for someone like me. When you've read as many poems as I, you start to sense a pattern in the imagery, and all the motifs."

The urge to roll my eyes was overwhelming. I knew this poem already, and to read it as a tragedy was to misunderstand the poet's intention entirely. The very heart of it lay in finding power in small and beautiful things. But of course I did not correct him. When men say they want a lover, what they often mean is they want a mirror; they wish to see themselves reflected back at them in the best light. "Why, I could *never* imagine being able to do that," I marveled. "Still. Don't you think there is something inherently romantic about tragedy?"

He blinked. "Romantic?"

I slid closer to him so my forearm was brushing against his. Out of the corner of my eye, I watched his cup of tea. He had not tried to refill it yet, and the steam had stopped rising. Only a little longer now. "Yes, romantic," I said, rolling the word on my tongue like honey. His breathing was unsteady. "All those lost opportunities; everything gone and wilted and buried. Divided loves and shattered hearts. Devastating, but beautiful. Memorable. How deeply it stirs the soul."

He did not say anything for a long while; he was too busy staring at me. A feeling expanded in my chest then, like an eagle spreading its wings for the first time. *Power.* I knew in that moment, with a cool, solid certainty, that if I were to rise, his eyes would follow. If I were to go home, he would trail after me. If I were to touch his neck, he would let me. I had him enraptured, the way a snake has its tail coiled around its prey. And yet a strange thought slithered into my mind: *Would any of this work on Fanli?* I remembered him from last night, standing with his back bared to me. If I ever used these tricks on him, would some part of him weaken too? Or would he remain as stony-faced as ever, remote and utterly unmoved?

Stop. I willed myself to pay attention to the person who actually mattered in this instance.

"Beautiful," the man repeated in a murmur.

I smiled, still that faint, guarded smile, without revealing any teeth, and turned to face him fully. I saw my own reflection swimming in his widened eyes, his dark, dilated pupils. It was true: I *was* beautiful, but it was less how I looked, and more what I felt.

"Would you mind me asking—what is your name, miss?" the man said. "And where are you from? I don't believe I've ever seen you around before. Trust me, I would remember."

"Guess," I said coyly, gazing up at him from under my lashes.

He laughed, the sound too eager, too strained. "Are you trying to make me curious? Because I must say you've already succeeded."

No, I am simply trying to delay the time. I checked the tea again, touching the cup with the back of my hand in a quick movement. It was ice cold. A heady rush of triumph and relief swept through me. I had succeeded. Passed the test. Yet as soon as the thought crossed my mind, another realization settled into my skin like frostbite. This was it, then—the end of everything. My training was complete. From here, what awaited me was the Wu palace.

"Excuse me," I said, with a shallow dip of my head. "There's somewhere else I must be."

"No, don't go yet." The words spilled from his lips. He pressed them together, as if to stop himself, then blurted out: "Is this because I was rude to you before? I apologize—I'm not usually very accepting of strangers; one must have standards, after all. But I can't remember the last time I connected to someone so quickly . . ."

Perhaps because nobody has ever been so quick to flatter your mediocre literacy. "Consider it forgiven. Still, I really do have to go."

I pushed my chair back, but he held up a hand. "Surely it's nothing important. Not as important as me. What urgent matters do women really have anyway, other than the cooking and washing? Stay," he said, with emphasis. "I insist."

I let the smile melt off my face. Thank the heavens; my muscles were starting to ache. "I would really rather not," I told him, no longer bothering to sweeten my tone. I rose just as abruptly, and saw the bewilderment flashing over his features. He looked as if someone had jolted him out of a pleasant dream.

"Wait—" The chair squeaked. He scrambled out of his seat. "You— You're just leaving?"

"There are people waiting for me," I said. "Thank you for your time."

"No, wait." He caught me by the arm. His hand was giant and callous, his grip hard. And tightening. I felt a frisson of panic through my pride. "What was that just now? A joke? You were—you're interested in me, are you not?"

My heart pounded. Still, I tried to remain calm, to keep my voice down. "I don't know what you're talking about. Now, please, excuse me—"

He didn't loosen his grip. "You *are* interested," he insisted, splotchy color rising in his face. He leaned closer, uncomfortably close. "You must be. I saw the way you were looking at me earlier. Don't pretend otherwise."

How strange that seconds ago I felt so powerful, a serpent with flashing eyes and cutting fangs, and now I felt like a rabbit caught in a trap. I struggled to pull myself free, my panic rising to my throat. "Let go," I said.

"I don't see anyone else around here," the man insisted. His eyes glinted like black beetle shells. "You're alone, aren't you? Come with me instead—"

"*No.*"

The man was still leering down at me like I was a meal. "Behave, now—"

"I told you to *let go*." In my peripheral vision, I saw Fanli rise, but I was faster. My heart beating wildly, I did the only thing I could think of: I bit his wrist as hard as I could.

My teeth sank into flesh. I tasted blood.

With a yelp, the man dropped his hand. "You—"

But I wasn't done yet. I grabbed the tea from the table and splashed it in his face. He stood frozen to the spot, his eyes squeezed shut, mouth half-open in horror or protest. The liquid ran in rivulets down his nose and neck, soaking through the collar of his robes.

"Next time you refuse to listen," I said, letting all my contempt seep into my voice, "I will make sure the tea is hot enough to burn."

As the man wiped his face with his sleeve, Fanli appeared beside me. He did not make any move to strike, but there was a cold violence to his gaze, like the silent swish of a blade right before it drew blood. Yet instead of terror, I felt only warmth, safety, an anchoring. My whole body relaxed in his presence. By instinct, I leaned toward him, and was surprised when his hand came to rest against the small of my back, even as he kept his eyes ahead. We had passed many full moons together, and it was the first time he'd ever touched me willingly.

And what a difference it makes, I wondered dimly. Where the man had grabbed my wrist earlier, it had felt as though my skin were crawling with centipedes. But with Fanli, I did not mind the coolness of his palm, the long, elegant shape of his fingers, their protective curve against my spine, his touch just light enough to let me know he was there.

I did not mind it at all.

"Are you hurt?" he asked me, his voice low. There was something in it that foretold of bloodshed, so long as the answer was *yes*.

I managed to shake my head.

"Let us go, then."

I expected him to simply lead me back to our table, but we passed right by Luyi and Zhengdan, who were both watching with open concern, and descended the steps. We did not stop until we were outside the teahouse, standing in the cool gray air, sheltered by the roof's overhanging eaves. The rain was pouring harder than ever. I watched the water slap the wet tiles behind Fanli, turning every color darker. I could feel the cool spray of it against my cheeks.

"Are you sure you're unharmed?" Fanli asked again. Something about the rain changed him too. Lent an ethereal quality to his features, his dark hair shining with all the luster of a pearl. Involuntarily, I remembered afresh how it had trailed over his strong shoulders after his bath, the water dripping from the ends.

I stared up at him, confused. "You've already asked me that."

"Yes, but—" He stopped himself. I had never seen him quite so unsettled, so agitated. "I'm sorry, Xishi."

My confusion grew. "Sorry for what? You did nothing to me."

"I can do nothing for you," he said. He seemed to be talking more to himself now than to me; all his emotions were turned inward to some unreachable place, his expression bleak, his eyes dark as a gathering storm. "In the future . . . When you are gone—I cannot. I will not be there. Even if he—" He drew in a sharp breath. His hands stretched out before me, empty, the tendons straining in his flute-thin fingers. "I won't be able to make it stop. No matter how . . . And I—I am sending you straight into the thick of it."

I could hardly make sense of what he was saying. I only wished to clear the furrow between his brows, to still his hands.

"You must hate me," he said abruptly, looking me in the eye.

"What?"

"You should," he said in a strange, cold tone, tempered with self-loathing, but this time it sounded almost like a question. Like he wanted me to tell him. Like he was offering me the whip, and turning his scarred back to me.

"I . . ." *I don't hate you at all.* The scent of the rain filled my nose. "You are only doing your job," I said in the end. "And I am doing mine. This is how the story goes; these are the roles we have chosen for ourselves."

He did not look satisfied, but he nodded once. Drew back.

"In any case," I said, hoping to ease this knot between us, whatever it was, "did I pass?"

"Pass?"

"The test." I tried for a smile. "Proof that I can make any man want me."

There was a pause. The pounding of the rain quickened like a heartbeat.

"Yes, Xishi," he said at last, his voice pained, looking anywhere but at me. "You passed it perfectly."

CHAPTER SEVEN

THE RAIN HAD STOPPED BY THE TIME ZHENGDAN AND Luyi moved down to join us. They were not the only ones. Now that the sky was an immaculate blue, the dark shine of water on stone and wet lick of the breeze the sole remnants of the storm, the civilians had come out with the sun. Around us, the alleys and paved roads were filling rapidly with carts, horses, merchants. It was as if the day had just begun.

"Are you all right?" Zhengdan asked, grabbing my hand.

I nodded and smiled at her. "Of course."

She gave my hand a gentle squeeze, though her voice was fierce. "That cursed turtle egg. I would have killed him if he held on a second longer."

"I'm sure Fanli would have gotten the job done before you," Luyi muttered.

We all turned to him. Fanli, especially, with a tightness in his expression, like a warning.

"What is that supposed to mean?" Zhengdan asked.

"Nothing," Luyi said hastily, catching Fanli's eye. Some silent exchange passed between the two. Whatever it was, Luyi was the first to retreat. "Don't take anything I say to heart; I only ever spew out nonsense."

"It's good that you're self-aware," Fanli said.

Luyi beamed at him. "Yes, you're right. You're always right, my most honorable minister. I'm just glad we're all here and nobody has been charged with murder."

"I'm glad we're here too," Zhengdan said, nudging me with emphasis. I recognized the look on her face. It was the look she wore when she used to sneak into my house after dark to exchange stories; when she plucked the fresh plums from Old Wang's backyard; when she fashioned poles out of branches and went fishing barefoot in the creeks, the murky waters up to her knees; when she dragged me out into the forest to show off a new sword technique she had taught herself. The look she wore when she was about to do something she knew she shouldn't, but wanted to anyway. "Now that the weather is better, can't we stay out a little longer? We haven't had a break from training since we first arrived, and we'll be gone in just three days. I barely even know what the town looks like."

"You can see it from here," Fanli said, waving a sleeve at the stalls on both sides of the street. A long line had started to form in front of a cart that sold fat slices of watermelon and waxberries and cherries, their firm, red-purple skin glowing in the light. Two children trotted past us, laughing, watermelon juice running down their chins, coins jingling in their purses. They must have been from noble families; only the wealthy could show such joyous carelessness in an age of war and instability. They assumed their money protected them from everything. The ultimate injustice was that sometimes it did.

"It's not the same thing," Zhengdan protested.

Fanli retrieved a fan from his inner robes and flipped it open with a clean snapping sound. He waved it slowly with one hand as he spoke. "We still have three texts to go through this afternoon."

Zhengdan turned to me, sulking like a child, and mouthed: *You try.*

I had always considered myself more principled than Zhengdan. But I was also the one who had held out the basket for her to throw in her stolen plums, who had opened the door at night to let her inside; I never knew how to refuse her. And so I gazed up at Fanli. "Just this once," I said, not expecting anything to come of it. "Please."

He hesitated. The fan in his hand went still.

"We can head back before it's dark," I pressed. "And when was the last time you did anything for leisure? You deserve a break too."

Something rippled over his features, and the frost in his eyes receded as he met my gaze. I stifled my next breath. All this time I had thought his eyes to be pure black, but now I could see the warm flecks of brown, the ring of molten gold around his iris, like preserved amber, the reflection of a gleaming crown. "All right," he said.

Luyi made a spluttering sound. I could not quite believe it myself. "All right?" he repeated, then promptly snapped his mouth shut as Fanli's face turned to ice again. "I merely meant—I had not thought it possible to sway you on any matter."

Fanli's voice was dry. "Do you wish for me to change my mind?"

"No," Luyi said in a hurry, and, as if afraid Fanli really would regret his decision, twisted on his heel to join the crowds swarming the streets. Zhengdan followed close after him, leaving me with Fanli.

A beat of silence passed between us. It felt new. It *was* new—to have such freedom, or at least some semblance of it, the paths ahead of us open and scattered with fallen pink petals, the scent of firecracker smoke and osmanthus honey hanging in the air.

"What would you like to see?" he asked, tilting his head. There was a rare touch of uncertainty to his demeanor too. "I will follow you."

"Really? Anywhere?"

"Anywhere," he said.

He spoke the truth. As I pushed my way through the wagons and ran from stall to stall, he followed quietly after me, without complaint. Every time I turned around, he was there, one hand behind his arrow-straight back, the other waving his white fan so it covered the lower half of his face. And though I was surrounded by stunning sights I had never even dreamed of—rolls of glimmering fabric so soft they looked to have been spun with magic, glittering hairpins carved into the shape of butterflies and cranes with jewels for eyes, zodiac animals shaped from melted gold sugar, pastries pressed into intricate flower molds—I found myself distracted again and again by his beauty. How he walked down the street like everything else was insubstantial.

But it was not just me who had noticed. A group of young women giggled from the shade, their eyes sweeping hungrily over Fanli.

"He must be a scholar," one said in a whisper designed to be heard. "He has such pretty hands, and the air of a poet."

"Or perhaps he is a warrior. He looks like he knows how to hold a sword."

"Hush, now, he is watching."

"Shall we invite him over?"

I skidded to a stop beside the closest stall and motioned for Fanli to come over. There was a sour taste in my mouth, like I had bitten into an unripe grapefruit.

"Yes?" he said, moving to my side in an instant. "Would you like to buy something?"

The idea was far from my mind, certainly further than the

image of those women inviting Fanli to do anything, but the vendor leaned in with great eagerness, his gray beard trembling as he spoke. "How about these?" he asked, gesturing to the rows of crimson bracelets laid out over the cloth. They were all made of simple string and tied together with a small silver bead. "The string of fate," he said. "It ensures that you are bound for eternity, that your souls will find their way back to each other in every life. Perfect for a pair of young lovers."

It took a moment for the assumption to sink in, and once it did, fierce heat rushed up my neck. I waited for Fanli to clarify, but he only swallowed, like he was pushing an emotion down.

"Do you want it?" he asked me.

I had the sense, then, that we were standing on the brink of something; one step in the wrong direction, and we would both fall in. "It is pretty," I said, in the same neutral voice he'd used.

He turned to the vendor. "How much?"

The vendor started to reply, but I reached for my purse, and shook out a light handful of coins.

"This is all we have," I told him.

The vendor's mouth puckered. "That's hardly enough," he said. "A single bracelet is worth twice that."

I smiled sweetly at him. "Unless your bracelets are woven from gold, I doubt it. If you are unwilling to sell for such a reasonable price, then we will find something elsewhere." I spun around and had taken but two steps when the vendor heaved a sigh.

"How did you know to do that?" Fanli asked as I set my coins down on the cloth. He spoke with genuine wonder, and watched me with sharp attention, like a boy who had just witnessed a magic trick.

"Have you never bartered before?"

He shook his head.

"But surely you must negotiate often in court?"

"Those tricks would not work here," he said, his tone thoughtful. "I would have needed a day in advance to gather intelligence and root out my opponent's weaknesses, their greatest fears, their attachments, and search through their past records for any crimes I could hold against them."

I laughed, then realized he was not joking.

"Here you go," the vendor said, holding out the two bracelets. "Have a good day."

I took one and extended the other to Fanli, my heart beating oddly in my chest. When he didn't move, just gazed at me with that unreadable expression of his, I faltered. Perhaps I had already stepped too far, pushed too hard against the invisible constraints. "You don't have to wear it," I said, feigning indifference. "Do with it whatever you like. You can even throw it away, if you wish, or give it to someone else."

"No," he said, taking the red string, his fingers brushing briefly against mine. His skin was soft, warm. I fought hard not to react, to recognize the feelings stirring inside me. "I'll keep it."

But as he slipped it inside his inner robes, a commotion sounded down the street. The violent drum of a horse's hooves, yellow dust blowing into the air, clouding the antique displays and fresh fruit stands. There came a succession of loud crashes, broken by screams. A whip hissing.

"*Make way for General Ma,*" someone roared. "*Make way or die.*"

At once Fanli tensed, his mannerisms shifting, his fan exchanged in one movement for the hilt of his sword.

I was alert too.

They came like the monsters from my memory: ten men in bronze armor, rising tall on their powerful steeds, the Wu flag racing in the wind behind them. They rode on without care, without discipline, leaving utter chaos in their wake. Their long whips fell again and again on the horses' flanks, but were swung with such recklessness that they cut close to anyone within their vicinity, lashing open sleeves and overturning cartons of berries. Howling children were yanked to the side seconds before they were trampled by those merciless hooves. Porcelains tipped over and shattered on the tiles.

My stomach lurched.

Then I spotted one of the women from earlier. She stood frozen in the middle of the street, her eyes wide with horror. The soldiers showed no signs of slowing.

Without thinking, I rushed forward and seized her wrist, pulling her back with all the strength I possessed. Just in time. The horses charged so close I could feel the heat of their breath prickling my bare neck, smell the oil and leather. The air trembled with their raw strength. Even the ground seemed to shake beneath my feet.

"A shame we didn't run you over," one of the soldiers called behind him. The others cackled with mad laughter.

My heart was still pounding as I drew back from the woman, though I no longer knew if it was from fear, or rage. Now the immediate danger was gone, I saw that the woman was really just a girl, her skin pressed with thick powder, her lips dabbed crimson to appear more mature. She was the one who had remarked on Fanli's hands, though that already felt like it had happened a long time ago. It all seemed so trivial by comparison, so frivolous.

"Th-thank you," she whispered, rearranging her robes with trembling fingers. "The soldiers have never come to this side of town before . . . I didn't know—I wasn't expecting it . . ."

"It's all right," I said. "Be more careful next time. The Wu are all monsters."

She flushed, the redness of her cheeks visible even beneath that heavy powder. "I am from the Wu Kingdom myself," she told me.

I stared at her. Something in my mind seemed to fracture, and briefly, for only an instant, the state borders faded away. The enemy lines shifted, separating girls like us from men like them, commoners from soldiers, the powerless from the powerful.

But then I remembered the look of wide-eyed terror on Susu's face, the way she had struggled against the blade—

My teeth clenched. No, the enemy was and had always been the Wu.

I stepped back from the girl, letting her friends come forth and flock around her in a hurricane of silks and perfumes. At the same time, Fanli approached, with Zhengdan and Luyi trailing after him.

"That was very brave," he said, his eyes dark, the line of his jaw hard, "and very foolish."

"I will choose to believe you're complimenting me," I told him, straightening. "In which case, I am flattered."

Zhengdan was gazing into the horizon, tracking the silhouettes of the soldiers as they rode farther and farther away. Her fist was clenched by her side. "I can't believe I missed him," she hissed. "He was *right there*, and I couldn't do anything."

"Who?" I asked, taken aback by the venom in her tone.

"General Ma."

It was only then that the name truly clicked. *General Ma.* In my mind, I saw the dented helmet in the official's outstretched hands, the bronze smeared with blood. Zhengdan hadn't shed a tear when she received the news. Instead she had grabbed her father's sword and raced off into the forest. She had come back later that night with weeping calluses, shaking limbs, scratches slicing through her skin. I had found her and pressed a jar of homemade ointment into her hands and said nothing. I still didn't have the words to hold my own grief. But she understood me.

"You couldn't have done anything anyway," I told her gently. "Not without exposing your identity."

"One day, then," she said, the lines of her face set with furious resolve. "One day, I will raise a sword to his neck, even if it is the last thing I ever do. I swear it."

CHAPTER EIGHT

THE FOLLOWING MORNING, KING GOUJIAN CAME TO VISIT. He was dressed like last time, without any of his royal finery, and rode alone on a chestnut steed. But I recognized his face instantly. It was as if his thirst for vengeance had been permanently carved into his features—his black, hungry gaze and sunken cheeks.

I hurried out to the cottage gates to greet him, with Zhengdan following close behind me, our bright skirts billowing around us like clouds. He stopped to watch us, and I imagined what he saw. Faces lovely as shimmering jewels. Dark hair shining down our backs like silk. Broad ribbons fluttering past our slender arms. How we treaded the tiles as if they were all water, how we moved like swans prepared for flight. Or perhaps we only appeared as weapons to him, daggers to be thrust into the heart of the enemy. However we glinted and shone in his eyes, it was because of our sharp edges, our potential to cut.

"Your Majesty," I said, dipping into a low curtsy. At the same time, Zhengdan curtsied behind me, as a palace lady ought to.

"*Well.*" Goujian sounded quite pleased. He was looking at some place above our shoulder, and I knew, just from the subtle change in the air, the shadow falling over me, that Fanli had come out as well. "You have definitely been training them."

"When have I ever failed a task assigned to me?" Fanli returned calmly.

I understood what he meant by it, that this was the proper way to speak to a king, yet I felt a twinge in my gut. This was all that I meant to him: a task. An assignment. Fanli and his unshakable sense of duty. Of course—what else could I expect from him?

"Ah, I've missed seeing you often in court," Goujian said, moving past us to clap Fanli on the shoulder. Still, I did not fully lift my head, did not sway in my curtsy, even as the muscles in my neck began to cramp. "Though I see I was right to leave you here. If it had been any other man, I fear they would've already run away with one of the girls. But you—you can resist any temptation, can't you?"

Though I had been taught otherwise, I wanted nothing more than to stand up, to see Fanli's expression. Then again, knowing Fanli, his face would look as it always did, cool and controlled, giving none of his feelings away.

"If this plan of yours succeeds," Goujian continued, "and my revenge is secured, I will make sure that you are handsomely rewarded for your efforts."

"No need, Your Majesty." His voice was even. "It is my duty to serve the kingdom."

"Don't be like that, now. You must want *something*. Gold, perhaps? Wine? Land? A marriage with a daughter from one of the noble families? There are many girls who have already expressed interest, you know, and I dare say they'd make excellent concubines, good enough to satisfy even somebody like you. It would be no trouble."

My stomach sank. *Many* girls. What number was that? Six? A dozen? Perhaps Zhengdan had been wrong, and he would not live his life alone. Perhaps he would get married the second I stepped into the Wu palace. A sour taste crept into my mouth at the thought, as if I'd just swallowed vinegar.

"I thank you, Your Majesty, but such things would be wasted on me."

Goujian scoffed, a sound of equal parts admiration and bemusement. "Of all the men who have served me, only you are so insistent on denying yourself the basic pleasures of life. It's almost masochistic—"

"Let us go in, shall we?" Fanli cut in. "I believe there was something you wished to show us before our departure?"

"Oh yes, yes," Goujian said hastily. To us, he commanded, "You may rise."

My neck ached, stiff from being held in one place so long and hot from where the sun had beaten down on it. When Fanli had first shown us the right positions for a curtsy, I'd wondered aloud if discomfort was the primary purpose of it. What better way to show that you took another person's power seriously than to suffer for their sake?

It was a relief to be back indoors, in the cool air of the study.

"Look here," Goujian said, unrolling a map over the low mahogany table. To my surprise, I saw that he was gesturing to us. I crept closer, close enough to see the sprawling territories, the drawings of the mountain peaks and rivers and valleys, the meticulously labeled cities, but not so close to the king as to forget propriety.

"That is Lake Tai," I said in slow recognition, looking to the place he had jabbed a finger.

"Precisely." He nodded. "This will be our opening."

It took me a moment to understand. "Into the Kingdom of Wu, you mean?"

"I have familiarized myself well enough with the territory. The quickest and easiest way inside is not by horse, but by boat."

"But . . . there are no waterways," Zhengdan said.

Goujian shrugged. "So build one."

The way he said it, he might have been suggesting that we build a small mound of dirt, not a highly sophisticated structure that required the physical labor of thousands.

"Or, to be more accurate, convince Fuchai to build one," Goujian continued, tapping the map sharply. "I do not care what excuse you use. Tell him you like the scenery there, or that you wish to spend more alone time with him on the canal, or that you believe you may uncover some mythical creature in the waters. If you have bewitched him sufficiently, won him over body and soul, he should be willing to do whatever to meet your requests, no matter how irrational they may seem."

My throat constricted. Suddenly the air in the room felt too stuffy, too solid. I had tried desperately to ward off thoughts of the Wu king, to stop myself from dreading the journey ahead. Yet it was only now, with the king of my own homeland addressing me, this map of two kingdoms unfurled before me, that it felt *real*. Everyone was looking at me. I would have to do this. It would have to be me, and I would have to succeed, or else—

"Now that the carriages and boats have all been arranged, you'll be leaving as planned in two days. Fanli will escort you there, of course, and Luyi will come as well. I had hoped to send you off even sooner, but Fanli insisted that I give you the full ten weeks to train until you were perfect . . ."

Two days. I had braced myself for it, had known this was coming, yet still I felt as though I had been thrown into a dark room and was watching the door swing shut right in front of me. A foolish impulse gripped me then—to beg the king for more time. More time to taste the sweet plums in the yard, to admire the lantern lights of the village at night, to fall asleep with Zhengdan's quiet snores in my ear. More time with—

In that exact instant, Fanli's gaze touched mine, and something in the air tightened, as if there ran a thread between us, and it had suddenly been plucked. It had to be my imagination. Wishful thinking. A manifestation of my own black, churning despair. But his eyes appeared darker, and I thought I caught a flicker of sorrow in them, like a bird's shadow flitting over a still pond.

"Is there a problem, Xishi?" Goujian asked. The weight of the question hung like a mallet, poised to crush my neck. I had once heard that kings never asked anything, no matter how it was phrased; they merely made requests.

"No, Your Majesty," I murmured, bowing my head, the lie scalding my tongue. "I am ready."

On my last day, I sat perched atop the ledge of the highest cottage wall, my legs dangling over the side. It was my favorite place to go, with its clear view of the village below: the serene sky of dawn casting its soft light over everything, the dense clusters of houses connected by crooked paths and dusty roads, the little boats floating over the waterways, and farther beyond that, the winding river that flashed silver like the body of an eel. Sometimes I thought I could see where the very edges of the kingdom lay, the simmering lines that marked out Wu from Yue soil, where the colors turned deeper and darker and even the clouds formed different shapes.

Behind me, footsteps sounded.

I knew, without even having to turn, who had come. Only Fanli walked with the grace of a dancer and the quiet precision of a killer. Yet something in my blood skipped as his presence drew near.

Stop, I told myself firmly, keeping my eyes on the horizon. *There is nothing to anticipate from him.*

"It's beautiful, is it not?" he asked as he lifted himself onto the ledge beside me. A few feet of space remained between us. The safe distance, always there, in everything he did. Always so careful not to cross some invisible line that separated duty from—whatever else there could be.

"It is," I murmured.

I expected him to turn the topic to some difficult chess technique, or perhaps the journey up ahead, but he remained sitting like that for a while, quiet. Unable to help myself, I snuck a glance at him. His profile was sharp against the early light, and there was a faraway look in his eyes, as though he could see something I could not.

"Often, before a battle," he said, "I would climb somewhere high with a view such as this."

I stifled a breath of surprise, afraid the slightest sound would discourage him from continuing. He had never spoken of his own experiences in battle before.

"That way, it was easy to remember how small my existence really was. It did not matter if I was afraid, or in pain, or if I was to die on the battlefield. What mattered was what lay ahead of me." He gestured to the mountains, the river, the slowly filling streets. "All that lies under Heaven. All the lives I must protect. My pledge of loyalty to the Kingdom of Yue."

I drew my legs up and held them to my chest, resting my chin atop them. He had never admitted to being afraid before. He did so well in maintaining his façade of ice and stone, cool intellect through and through, that sometimes I wondered if he was even mortal, if he felt anything like I did. "Can you tell me what happened?" I asked after a beat. My blood pounded harder in my ears, my nerves tingling. *Perhaps Fanli will be so generous as to tell you the details, when he is in an agreeable mood,* Luyi had once said. Well, I could not be entirely sure whether Fanli's current state was *agreeable*, but I was certain this was the closest he would ever come to it. And there would be no other opportunities after today.

He looked at me so sharply that I almost withdrew the question. "What happened where?"

"In—" The word was thick in my throat. "In Kuaiji."

Something in his features tightened. "You'd really like to know?"

I nodded.

He breathed out, his shoulders tensed, as if bracing for someone to remove an arrow shaft from a deep wound. "After the Wu soldiers surrounded us, we were essentially given two options: to die, or to serve King Fuchai. Goujian, being as proud as he is, was of course ready to give up his life before bowing to the enemy. But I convinced him otherwise." He lifted his chin. "I have always believed that knowing when to yield is even more important than winning. If we were to bow our heads and humble ourselves before the king, and earn his trust over time, then we could hope to one day return, and devise a plan for revenge." He looked to me in acknowledgment, and I felt a strange roaring in my blood, a kind of drifting away from my own body, until I was not blood and flesh but the things that mountain soil and river water and starlight are made of. Something ancient, eternal. *I* was that plan. I was part of the kingdom's history. "I told him death was the coward's way out. That death was final; it eradicated all possibility. If he were to fall to the sword then, his legacy would only be his failures, his defeats. How would he be able to face his ancestors in the Yellow Springs of the underworld?

"It took a great deal of persuasion, but eventually, Goujian agreed. Part of him, I'm sure, resents me for it even to this day. But we went and submitted ourselves to King Fuchai, and were assigned to sweeping the stables. We were treated as servants, worse even. It was bearable when Fuchai neglected our existence entirely, and left us to the chores; but sometimes he would grow bored, and remember. Then he'd summon Goujian to see him in private . . ." A pause. "You must understand: It is not quite so uncomfortable to claw your way up through the ranks when you have been born into a lowly position. If you were raised in robes of rough ramie, you'd find yourself adjusting quickly to the feeling of silk. But when you have known nothing but power and riches all your life, and your skin is a delicate thing, used to the softest material—anything less causes instant pain."

No wonder Goujian hates the Wu king so, I realized, leaning back on the ledge. I remembered the dark, poisonous look in Goujian's eyes, how he'd spat out Fuchai's name. *It is not just political—it is personal. He has been wounded in every way.*

Then something else occurred to me.

"Was Goujian really the only one Fuchai humiliated for entertainment?"

His tone was wary. "What do you mean?"

"The . . . the scars on your back." To acknowledge it out loud felt illicit. "Were those also from the Wu? When you were made to serve them?"

"They do not hurt," he said after a beat, which meant *yes.* "I am already used to them."

He could have been telling the truth. The planes of his face were cold and unmoved as the moon overhead. Yet I felt a vivid rush of rage, a reckless impulse for violence. I would remember this. I would torment the ones who had done this to him, who had carved their hatred into his flesh. I would gladly bring down their entire kingdom for this one wrong. My nails dug into the stone.

"It's not worth being upset over," Fanli said softly. Then, in a clear attempt to change the subject: "Now you see why Goujian is so bent on revenge."

"And you?" I asked, my lingering anger loosening my tongue.

"What about me?"

"You always speak of kingdoms and grand plans, of history and duty, of Heaven and those under it . . ." I could not resist looking at him, at the moonlight lining his lips. And once I did, I could not look away. "Do you have no desires of your own? Have you never wanted anything just for yourself?"

His gaze cut to mine. A cold shock pierced through me, and I made a careful, active effort to school my expression into neutrality, so he could not tell what answer I wished to hear.

A long silence.

Something shifted in the trees: a bird's weight, lifting, or a breeze.

Then he turned, pushing himself off the wall and landing as quietly as a cat on the ground. I swallowed my heart. So that was it. He would not offer any information he didn't want me to know. Perhaps it was for the better this way. There were certain things that, once said, could not be taken back. And we would be leaving soon; I'd likely never see him again after that. Fanli began to walk toward the cottage. I watched him go, his shadow stretching out behind him—

Until he stopped. His head moved fractionally, so I could just make out the sharp angles of his face over his shoulder. His lips were pressed tight, his brows furrowed, everything in his expression warring with itself.

Quietly, so quietly I would wonder later if I had dreamed it, he said, "I have."

A set of wedding robes had been laid out on my bed that night.

They were the deepest red—the red of spilled blood, of spoiled wine, of kissed lips—and embroidered with gold thread. All along the sides and down the wide sleeves and sash, there were images of soaring birds and phoenix tails and floating clouds, chrysanthemums and lilies in full bloom, stars crowded around a blazing sun. It was the most beautiful and terrible thing I had ever seen. It made my heart halt its next beat. Sitting atop the robes was a note, written in Fanli's neat, slanted calligraphy: *See if it fits.*

The fabric was as soft as it looked, made of the kind of silk I had only ever washed but never worn. The long skirt flowed down past my ankles like water and puddled crimson at my feet. It fit perfectly, the measurements exact, as if it had been made just for me.

I fastened all the ribbons myself with shaking hands, smoothed out the waist, and tied my hair back, pinning it into coils atop my head with a slender jade hairpin. Beads of amber dangled from its end, rattling as I walked.

I had no idea what I meant to do until I reached Fanli's room. I swallowed the hard lump in my throat, my hand hovering over the door in a half-formed fist, hesitating. *Knock. Go inside. It is your last chance to do so.* Before my courage could abandon me, I pushed the door open. It creaked loudly, and there Fanli sat with his back to me, outlined against the candlelight.

His robes were undone, left to fall around his narrow waist. He had stiffened at the sound of the door, but he did not turn around.

"Xishi?" It was a question, in more ways than one.

My eyes went to the ointment in his hand, and I stepped forward with a boldness that did not feel like my own. "Let me," I said, quiet, lowering myself to the ground behind him and plucking the ointment from his closed fingers. "Let me help you."

I heard him swallow. "This is not for you to do."

"I know." The words rang out; like coins tossed down a waterfall, I could not tell when they landed, where. But he did not stop me; he simply held himself with even more stiffness than usual, his eyes ahead. I dipped one finger into the jar. The ointment was cool, smooth with oil, and almost sweet, the fragrance of a winter flower I thought I recognized.

The seconds expanded. We both seemed to be waiting.

Very carefully, I pressed one finger to the scar snaking down the center of his spine, where he could not reach. His skin burned to the touch. And something burned inside me, too, a flame behind my ribs. We had never been so close; he had never been so exposed. I could feel the resistance of hard, tensed muscle, the unnatural rise of his scars as I traced my fingertip down the jagged line.

He shuddered.

"Am I hurting you?" I asked, pausing.

A silence, before the reply came: "You could never hurt me."

But when I shifted closer and touched the ruined space between his shoulder blades, his whole body was trembling, the muscles under his skin pulled as taut as if he were in battle. The scent of the crushed flower soon suffused the tight space between us. I felt almost dizzy from it, though my attention did not waver. Every time I moved to apply the ointment, he flinched, then tried to twist his head to look back at me.

"Stay still," I told him.

"It is difficult," he said, "to not see you."

"I'm almost done now." I hoped he could not detect the hitch in my breathing. When I had smeared the last of the ointment into his skin, I stood and stepped back, letting him dress, my gaze following the subtle movement of his shoulders.

"Thank you," he said, hoarse. "Nobody has . . . before."

Then he turned around fully, and his lips parted at the sight of me. He looked almost . . . afraid. A primordial emotion, something that crept up through his ice mask.

"I came to show you this. Do you think it fits?" I asked, spinning a slow circle before him, feeling how the air moved against my skirt and the gems swung in my hair. *Reckless*, a voice in the back of my mind chided. *Foolish.* I had already toed over the invisible line too many times tonight, crossed into forbidden territory. But there was another voice, a memory of Fanli, the expression on his face: *I have.*

"Yes," he replied. His hands flexed, then curled at his sides, so tight that his knuckles strained white. "I believe so."

"Really?" A gale blew against the window panels, scattering petals through the gaps into the room. The door slammed shut behind me. My blood pounded in my ears as I lifted my chin at a calculated angle. "Look closer."

"Xishi." There was a strain in his voice, a note of caution. He did not move.

"What?"

"Stop it."

I raised my brows at him. "Stop what?"

"You know what you're doing." He released a soft huff of air, like a laugh, but there was an edge to it. The collar of his normally immaculate robes was creased, the sash around his waist tied in a hasty, uneven knot. "This is not—meant for me. It is for their king."

"Am I beautiful enough for him, do you think?" I kneeled beside him, my skirts spilling around me like blood from a mortal wound. My fingers tingled, even though they held nothing. Would it be like this with the Wu king? Like standing on a great precipice, one move away from tumbling through the air, from losing or gaining everything? I doubted it. "Am I all that you hoped I could be?"

"You are . . . ," Fanli began, then trailed off. Swallowed. He angled his head away from me, toward the wall, so I could see the strain in his jaw. His breathing was uneven. It grew less steady the closer I drew. I do not know what gave me the nerve, but I grabbed his chin. Gently. Forced him to look back up at me. His skin was even smoother than I'd expected. Faultless. Delicate.

"What am I to you, Fanli?" I whispered. It felt illicit, saying his name without the title, without any kind of address. As intimate and impulsive as if I were to reach out and stroke his hair.

His eyes flashed, then flicked down to my robes. My wedding robes. What I would wear when I greeted his greatest enemy—the same man who had humiliated him and degraded him and overseen his torment, the one responsible for the scars on his back—as my own lover. Fanli seemed to be holding his breath. His fists were clenched so tight I could see the bones of his fingers. "Why—" he managed, his voice shedding some of its usual neutrality. "Why are you doing this?"

"I want to know," I said. My fingers trembled against his face. The polish was starting to rub off from my performance. I cared too deeply to affect nonchalance. To act as if my heart were not straining against my ribs, as if it did not hurt to be this close, *this close*, and know that I could not go any farther. "I have to know. Before we leave. Everything will be different and—" I stopped talking before my voice could waver. I had been trained better than that. "You will never get to look at me like this again."

"Xishi," he said, voice low. "I cannot—"

"Speak to me normally," I demanded.

"What do you want me to say?"

"Tell me . . ." I dropped my hand, keeping my gaze level with his. "Tell me what I am to you. Please," I added when he began to protest, to maneuver his way free from the conversation. "Am I your greatest weapon? Or something else?"

He inhaled. Seemed to steel himself. Then he made that sound again, that half laugh, with its undertone of incredulity and self-mockery. "So this is how it feels," he murmured, almost under his breath, "to be cut by your own blade."

The candles flickered. Everything felt pressed close, warm, like air cupped inside a palm. I could see our shadows splashed across the magnolia-patterned folding screen; the trick of the light made it so they looked closer than we actually were, our faces touching. Even now, after all that has passed, I can visualize the scene in fresh, intimate detail: the guqin set beside his desk, the way the gold and crimson threads of my robes gleamed, the jar of ointment lying open on the floor, the silhouette of the plum blossom trees just outside the window. In the days to come, when I was alone, I would wonder what might've happened if I had been a little braver, a little more selfish, a little more reckless. If I had pulled his shadow to mine until our hearts collided, if I had just spoken outside our silent glances, acknowledged what blazed between us in those brief, quiet moments together. Perhaps then, all would be different. But these things tend to make sense only in fantasies, in memory. In reality we were just two mortals, bound by our respective roles in history, and whatever flickered between us felt so terribly fragile compared to the immovable weight of mountains, of kingdoms, of war.

He shifted forward, lifted a hand to my hair. Stopped. Up close, his pupils were blown wide, black as bottomless pools in the deepest winter. Very slowly, as if afraid I would disappear right before him, he touched one fingertip to the jade hairpin. The pressure was no more than a butterfly landing on a petal, but I felt it travel down to my bones. My heart thudded harder, my mouth dry with everything I could not say.

Then his gaze hardened, and he withdrew his hand. A flash of fabric. Just like that. The shock of it was like bursting through water after a long, long swim. The empty air stung my skin.

"You should get some rest," he said, twisting away, denying me his face. His voice was cold again, curt, removed to a place I could not reach. "It will be a long journey."

CHAPTER NINE

OUR DEPARTURE WAS A QUIET AFFAIR.

A carriage had been prepared outside the cottage gates, with a scarlet veil draped over the windows on both sides and the raised roof decorated with intricate blue-and-green carvings. Luyi was already at the front, dressed in leather armor and adjusting the horses' bridles.

"Do you have everything?" Fanli asked as I climbed into the carriage after Zhengdan. He did not look at me as he spoke, but rather seemed fixated on a small scratch in the door. His lips were pale, and when I snuck a glance at his face, I saw the dark gray shadows under his eyes. Perhaps he had not slept well.

"Yes," I said, my voice as stiff as his. I patted the satchel hanging across my shoulders. It was far heavier than it'd been when we first arrived at Riversong Cottage, now stuffed full of different robes and powders and pretty ornamental things.

He nodded, still without facing me. "Good."

The door snapped shut.

I sighed and leaned back in the cushioned seats, only to find Zhengdan staring at me.

"What?" I asked.

"Did something happen between you two?"

"What do you mean?" It came out sharper than I intended, and a treacherous flush rose to my cheeks. *I wish something had happened*, I thought to myself. But it was a forbidden thought, not meant to be shared with any soul, no matter how I trusted Zhengdan like my own sister.

"He's been rather . . ." She paused, then lifted the veil an inch to watch Fanli through the round window. He was saying something to Luyi too quiet for us to hear, but Luyi's back snapped straight, and his free hand flew to the sword at his belt. ". . . on edge this morning," she finished, brows arching. "Wouldn't you agree?"

"It must be the trip," I said, dodging the question as best I could. "It's a lot of pressure, after all. If anything happens to us, he will have to take full responsibility."

Zhengdan let the veil fall back down and snorted quietly. It was one of the many things Fanli had warned her against when we reached the palace; it was not considered ladylike. *Why does it seem to me that the court's idea of a lady is a beautiful, dull shell who has no personality and makes no sound*, Zhengdan had complained to me afterward. *They would be better off marrying a statue.* "Typical of you."

"Hm?"

"If anything happens to us, I would be concerned first and foremost with getting kidnapped or killed, not the consequences someone else must bear."

The carriage lurched into motion. Soon the steady *clip-clop* of hooves and occasional swish of the whip reached our ears, and the song of the river grew fainter and fainter. It was an uncomfortable ride, stretching on and on for what seemed like forever. Even with the cushions padding the seats, I felt every stone and twig crushed under the wheels, every jolt of the carriage when we turned a corner. I could not tell what was worse: the sheer boredom, or the undercurrent of dread that ran beneath it. It was like being forced to lie paralyzed on the ground while your enemy approached you slowly with a blade raised. The only times we left the carriage were when night fell and we needed to find an inn to rest; then, in the morning, the journey continued again. More than once, I considered shoving the carriage door open, running far away, and never coming back. Such a quick, simple movement. But my fingers remained clasped and clammy in my lap.

When the sky started to darken beyond the carriage curtains, Zhengdan rested her head on my shoulder and dozed off, her breathing deepening into snores. I was amazed she could fall asleep so quickly, or at all. My muscles were so tense that the idea of sleep seemed absurd. As my thoughts ran ahead to the looming palace in its faraway land and the king I loathed but would have to pretend to love, I could not imagine myself ever sleeping again.

A strange hissing sound outside jerked me from my reverie.

At first I wondered if it was just the wind. But then the hissing sound came again, even closer, and through the veil I saw the black flashing shadow of something thin and sharp. My body seemed to understand what it was before my mind did. My heart slammed against my ribs. I straightened in my seat, one hand braced against the door.

We were under attack.

"Zhengdan," I whispered, shaking her awake. "*Zhengdan.*"

She opened one bleary eye, rubbing at her face. "What?" Her voice was still groggy. "Are we almost there? That was faster than I—"

Up ahead, the horses let out a whinny that was almost a shriek, stamping their hooves madly. The entire carriage shook with the motion. My stomach flipped. I stifled a gasp, grabbing blindly for the sides of the seat to steady myself.

Zhengdan's eyes widened, fully awake now. "What's going on?"

I shook my head, unable to speak. More arrows swished through the air, raining down like lightning. There had to be dozens. This was no random attack; it was coordinated. I couldn't help it. My throat tight, I brushed the veil aside an inch and squinted into the falling purple darkness. We were in the middle of some kind of forest path, surrounded by patches of overgrown trees. Fanli had already leaped to the ground, sword at the ready. Both he and Luyi were cutting down the arrows as they fell, severing them in midflight. I had no idea how they were doing it; the arrows moved so fast you could barely track them with the human eye, their lethal points glinting in the moonlight. I strained to find the attackers, but they were hiding somewhere behind the trees—

The carriage door flew open.

I felt the rush of cold night air against my back, and something else. Something that made all the hairs on my neck stand up.

Zhengdan screamed.

Gloved hands gripped my arm, yanked me out backward as if I weighed no more than a doll. I thrashed, but it was useless. Another pair of rough hands grabbed my hair and pulled; my eyes stung with the sudden, tearing pain. Zhengdan moved to unsheathe her sword, but there were too many of them, at least six attackers, all dressed in black. I could not see any faces, only the darkness, and the silver storm of arrows shooting through the air. *Distractions*, I realized too late. They were designed to keep Fanli and Luyi preoccupied, while they took us and—

My bleak imagination ran wild with the possibilities, my heart thudding so hard it hurt my chest. I kicked out again, gasping. In response the hands around me tightened into burning bands around my wrists. Though I had eaten nothing all day, my stomach heaved. I was remembering the horror stories I had heard, what happened to pretty girls, young girls, girls who dared walk alone in the dark. Was this what I would become? Just another story, a warning mothers whispered to their daughters at night, for fear they would venture too far from home?

Then I looked ahead, and all the air left my lungs.

An archer stood between the trees. Their bow was raised, their knee slightly bent, the string pulled taut. The arrow aimed directly at Fanli's back.

No.

There was no way he could anticipate it. He was already fending off countless arrows at once, his sword slashing through the air in a frenzied blur. I could not move against these strangers' iron grips, could not even run forward to warn him. So I did the only thing I could: I cried out.

Just as the archer released the arrow.

He had flinched at the very last second, startled by the sudden sound. Instead of flying forward, in a perfect curve, the arrow flew askew. And shot straight toward me.

I did not have time to react. One second I was watching the arrow being expelled into the air, and the next I felt an explosion of pain in my left shoulder, white-hot and instant. Brutal. I jerked backward, agony tearing through my body. I could *feel* it, the place where cold metal sank into flesh, the unnatural object piercing through skin. And then—and then—everything happened in a blur. There was Fanli, racing toward me, fast as a shadow, like a figure from the fables. My sight had started to fade already, black spots swimming before me, and so perhaps I only thought I saw the wild, raw emotion ablaze on his face, a wretched look I'd never witnessed before, like the world was crumbling around him. There was the slice of his sword, its cold light streaking through my vision. A horrible gurgling sound came from the man closest to me. Warm blood sprayed my cheeks, the sickening, coppery taste filling my tongue. His hands slackened, and he fell limp to the ground, alongside an odd *thud*. Something rolled off to the side. At first I assumed it was a stone, but a cloud moved over the moon, and a slant of light illuminated the tangled hair, the glazed-over eyes, the severed neck, blood still gushing freely from it. My heart slammed so hard against my chest I was afraid I would throw up. It was a head.

Amid the chaos, there came a moment of pure, eerie silence. Nothingness. Like the earth had frozen over.

Then somebody yelled out, and everyone jolted into action once more. Fanli swung his sword to the side, one great, vicious slash, more fat droplets of blood splashing across the leaves. And he was holding me, lifting me into his arms, even as he held on to his weapon, cut through anyone who stood in our way. My lashes fluttered. The searing pain had started to dull into a persistent throbbing, and I could no longer tell if the blood soaking through my robes was my own, or someone else's. All I knew was that I was tired, so tired. My body felt heavy as stone. It was a wonder Fanli could carry my weight at all and move as fast as he was.

"Xishi." His voice, hoarse and rough in my ear. A whisper. "Xishi, hold on. We're almost there."

Almost where? I had lost control over my senses. My head spun. Dimly, in Fanli's arms, I could see the clouds floating up above, their edges lined with pearlescent light, and the black branches of the trees rushing past us on both sides. Were we leaving the forest? Going deeper in? More arrows sailed overhead, their metal ends whispering through the leaves, yet miraculously, none of them touched me.

"Be careful," I panted. It cost me to speak; my chest rattled and heaved, and the arrow in my shoulder seemed to drive deeper, splitting through flesh. I bit back a scream. "It's—dangerous."

"You're safe with me."

Funny how that felt like the truth, even when everything about our current situation suggested otherwise. The soft, steady fall of his steps, the slight sway of his arms as he carried me, the warmth of his robes against my cheek, pressed so close I could hear his strong, thudding heartbeat—I could have curled up like this forever. I could have fallen asleep. It would be so easy; my eyelids were already heavy. I needed only close them, and then maybe the terrible pain would stop, maybe I could rest—

"Don't close your eyes." The sharpness of Fanli's tone split through my thoughts. His steps sounded faster; his arms tightened around me. "Focus on me, Xishi."

I didn't want to listen to him. Sleep was much more tempting. But there was a part of me, a shameful, burning, inextinguishable part, that always wanted to please him. So I made myself look up. My eyes tracked the knife-sharp cut of his jaw, the gentle curve of his lips. A small cut ran down his cheekbone, still wet with his blood. My heart seized. I wanted to lift my fingers to touch him, make it all better, but my arms were dead wood, falling uselessly at my sides.

"You—You're injured," I whispered, the words grazing my throat like sand.

He stared down at me, his face strained, eyes black as the night around us. "Ironic that you should mention it."

"What?"

"You're bleeding out in my arms as we speak, Xishi." His voice caught on the end of the sentence. He cleared it, smoothed it out. More evenly, he added, "It would be wiser to worry about yourself first."

"Why? I don't look pretty this way?" I managed to smile as I said it, teasing.

He cast me a dark look. "Are you trying to make a joke?"

"No. That's why I'm important to you. Because I'm beautiful."

He said nothing for a long time. Almost imperceptibly, his hold on my body seemed to tighten. At last, he muttered, "Well, at least your confidence has not been injured."

I huffed a soft laugh, then winced; the faint movement drove a black spike of pain through me. Still, I croaked, "Could you not be sweeter to me? Even just a little?"

Something flashed across his face. But I could not identify it. My vision was growing duller, white bleeding into the edges. Everything—the trees blurring past us, the dark sky looming overhead, the salt scent of blood and dirt and old bark—felt farther and farther away as he ran on, drifting beyond reach. We had crossed into some kind of new terrain. The shrubbery thinned out, and the low rush and hiss of waves traveled to my ears. The air felt crisper, damper, cold on my skin. We were on a riverbank.

"Fanli," I murmured, or at least I tried to speak. My voice was so faint it was little more than air, dissolving in the breeze. "I can't . . . keep my eyes open much longer."

"You have to." His footsteps slapped over rocks and mud. Something splashed in the water before us; there was the groan of wood, a loud clattering. "Listen to me. *Listen*. If you die, my . . ."

But I couldn't hear the rest of it. The roar of blood in my ears was too loud, drowning everything out. I could only guess at what he'd meant to say. *If you die, my great plan will be ruined, my most valuable weapon lost forever. If you die, my reputation will suffer, and His Majesty will never forgive me. If you die, my kingdom will have no savior.* More voices rustled past my head. Unfamiliar, but urgent. An incomprehensible mumbling, no more meaningful than the rustle of wind through grass. All I knew was the solidity of Fanli's presence, the way a red-crowned crane knows the sweetness of the pine trees, or how a cormorant knows the melodies of the river water. He had not let me go. The last thing I saw before my eyes fell shut was his face, its cold, ineluctable beauty pinched tight with concern and hovering over me.

I woke to the world swaying.

My mouth was dry, as if it had been stuffed with a rough cloth, and tasted bitter, like old blood. My whole body felt cavernous. At first glance, I was in a small room of sorts, with a single bed and wooden planks covering the walls. When I tried to sit, a sharp pain speared through my shoulder, and I gasped. Looked down. A white bandage had been wrapped snugly around my wound, a small patch of crimson blossoming from the center. The violence of the night suddenly pressed close against my memory: the arrow that had missed Fanli and caught me instead, the men leaping from the trees like monsters, the sound of Fanli's breathing hot and harsh in my ears as he ran—

"Xishi-jie! Oh, thank the heavens, you're finally awake."

Zhengdan rushed over to my bedside, her bright skirts brushing against the wood. Her face looked more wan than usual, and there was a slight tremor to her hand that had not been there before, but otherwise she looked safe. Unharmed.

I felt a dizzying rush of relief.

"What happened?" I asked. My lips cracked, and my voice came out a rasp.

"Drink this first. Fanli said you would need it." She handed me a cup of water, still warm. I took a long swig, then another. It was as if I had never tasted water before; it was so sweet, so filling, so soothing down my throat. "Slow down," Zhengdan chided, her expression torn between concern and amusement. "You're going to choke."

I shook my head, not even willing to lift my mouth from the

cup to reply. When I had finished every last drop, I set it down again. "Tell me now," I urged. "Where are we? How long has it been since they attacked? *Why* did they attack? Is Fanli all right? Is Luyi?"

"One thing at a time," she said, scooting closer, a placating hand resting on my hair. It was a gesture that reminded me sharply of my mother, and I felt a deep tug of homesickness in my gut. "We're on the boat King Goujian had prepared for us. Fanli thinks the attackers had timed it so they could intercept us right before we boarded, to stop us from reaching the Wu Kingdom at all. We set sail a little over a week ago from Xiaoshan."

"*A week?*" I shot up, then instantly regretted it. Pain blazed through my stiff muscles like a flame.

"Careful—your wound's only just closed." Zhengdan grabbed my arm and helped me shift into a less torturous position. "And yes, you're lucky Fanli had thought ahead to request a physician to come along with us. Whatever medicine he brewed for you put you to sleep right away. Though for a while . . ." Her voice wobbled, and she averted her gaze to the bucket below my bed. The water inside was tainted dark red. A blood-soaked cloth hung over the edge. *My* blood, I realized with a sickening jolt. "For a while, you were so still . . . I was afraid you had left us already. Fanli must've feared it too, because he . . . You should've seen him, Xishi-jie. I've never seen him so—" She shook her head, seemingly unable to find the words. "It was terrifying. He refused to let the physician tend to his injuries, and forced him to focus only on treating you. He has not moved from the place outside your door. Nobody has dared approach him these past couple days, not even Luyi."

I stared at my hands, my heart quickening, remembering the way he had lifted me as if I weighed no more than a feather and hugged me tight to his chest, even as arrows rained down on either side of us. "Well, of course he was afraid. He has invested so much time and effort into training me." I tried to smile, to play it off as a jest. "If I had died, it would all have gone to waste."

"It's not just that—"

The curtain to the room flipped open. Fanli stood in the doorway, the dark moss-green of the river glittering behind him. His eyes widened marginally as he took me in, before he crossed the room in three quick strides. Stopped a foot away from the bed. His fingers flexed in my direction, as if to reach out to me, but he curled them again into a tight fist at his side.

It was to Zhengdan that he spoke. "You could have told me she'd woken." There was a hard edge to his voice, a faint creep of irritation. If I had not heard it, I would've thought Zhengdan had been exaggerating. *Nobody has dared approach him.*

"Don't blame her," I said quickly. "I only just woke."

His eyes flickered to me, lingering on the bandage covering my shoulder. "How do you feel?"

"Well," I said.

He cast me a look of disbelief.

"Well enough," I amended. "Thank you for . . . for saving me." *Again,* I wanted to add, the unspoken word clawing at my throat. What a bittersweet fate we shared, balanced so precariously on the fine line between life and death, union and separation, joy and despair.

"You saved me first," he said, shaking his head. "You should have just let the archer shoot."

Even the thought—the possibility—sent a blistering ache through me. "I don't regret it."

Silence unspooled between us, save for the faint splash of oars against the waves, the faraway call of herons. I remembered the last words he had said to me, right before darkness fell. *If you die, my . . .* What? The question burned within me, but there were certain things that could only be admitted under certain circumstances. It was too different now, with the danger behind us and the warm yellow daylight filtering through the windows and Zhengdan waiting next to us, watching. The moment had expired.

I cleared my throat and sat up straighter. "The attackers. Who were they? Did you see?"

"I didn't, but I can guess." His tone mirrored mine, serious now, carefully stripped of feeling. "As you must know by now—and as you will soon see yourself—the court of the Wu Kingdom is . . . complicated. They've long been divided among themselves, split into factions. You have those who have allied themselves in the favor of Fuchai—they are usually younger, of weaker disposition, more likely to be tempted by the promise of pretty porcelains and concubines for their harem. And you have those who secretly scorn the king for being too frivolous and self-indulgent, and remain loyal to the one they've served longest: his father, King Helü. They have never forgotten Helü's death from battle, nor his last words, which were to remain vigilant against the Yue at all costs."

"So they do not want me there," I said slowly, my head clearing. "Right? If they know that tributes from the Yue king are coming, they must see it as an offering of goodwill, an extension of peace. Either they believe it to be an insult to King Helü's memory or—"

"Or they suspect it may be a trap," Zhengdan offered, her expression grave. "They know that Fuchai won't listen to them, and so they took matters into their own hands. Fuchai would never know they were the ones behind it."

"Not only that," I said, a chill crawling down my spine, "but it would look like a careless mistake on His Majesty's part, perhaps even some kind of dark joke, to promise a tribute of beautiful women only to announce that they had died on the journey. Fuchai would've taken it as a personal offense, and the conflict between our kingdoms would only escalate to new heights."

Fanli nodded.

I was trying not to panic. We had been warned countless times that our mission was dangerous, that we would have to be cautious, watch our every move, trust nobody, lest someone stab us when we were looking the other way. But it was another thing to have felt the cold, ruthless force of the arrowhead splitting my own flesh; to have been seized by rough, gloved hands and yanked out of a carriage; to have tasted blood and death on my tongue as we fled through the night.

"Has this delayed our journey?" I asked Fanli. I did not know what I wanted the answer to be. Part of me wished the boat would turn back, wished to hold off my arrival in Wu as long as possible.

"No," he said. "But about the attack, and your wound . . ." His eyes flashed black as he said it.

"I understand," I assured him, knowing what he meant. When I arrived at the palace, I could not breathe a word of what I had survived, of my suspicions. Whoever had ordered the failed attack would only have more reason to dispose of me, and quickly. Instead, I would have to spin a convincing lie, feign ignorance, put those in court at ease.

He looked like he wished to say something more, something else. But then he glanced over at Zhengdan, who sat beside me still, letting me lean against her for support. After a beat, he merely nodded. "We are almost there. I'll tell you when it's time."

CHAPTER
TEN

THE KINGDOM SPRAWLED BEFORE ME WAS NOT THE kingdom of my nightmares.

I had imagined a barren land, with a perpetually overcast sky and dirt pressed thick with the blood of my people. I had imagined empty, crooked streets squeezing in together like dungeons, and houses with jutting roofs like teeth, swords and skeletons lining the yards. Perhaps there would be bats flying low in the horizon, and snakes slithering through yellowed grass, and lions waiting to spring from the shadows. There would be no sweets, no silk, no clear water, no flowers.

Yet, with something almost like disappointment, I saw that the place we sailed into now could almost be mistaken for Yue. A series of wide green canals glittered in the late afternoon light, the clouds fat and heavy and brushed gold-pink at the edges. On each side of the banks stood neat clusters of houses, their smooth walls faded white from the steady erosion of wind and water, their roofs curved with slate-gray tiles, strings of round lanterns hung from their balconies, fringed with delicate silk tassels. We floated under little arched bridges, their reflections swimming over the canal surface so that from afar, they formed the perfect shape of a full moon. It was not a land of corpses and smoke as I'd thought, but one of ponds and gardens, water and earth, fishing boats and floating lights.

But even its beauty left my bones cold. I drew my cloak tighter around my body, steadied myself on the deck of the boat. The physician had advised that I come out here to breathe in fresh air, let my wound heal faster in the sunlight, but I wasn't sure if I felt better, or worse.

"Odd, isn't it?" Luyi asked from beside me. He was gazing out at the canal, too, his dark hair blown back in the breeze, his expression uncharacteristically serious, devoid of its usual mischief.

"What?"

"How . . . normal everything looks," he said, nodding at the civilians on the raised stone platforms around us: silver-haired old women carrying baskets of dried dates and herbs, giddy children racing one another across a bridge. "There goes this saying, that for somebody from Chu, they would not be able to tell a Wu and Yue man apart. You would think that after all our fighting—well, you'd think there would be some marker at the least. A good reason."

I cast him a curious look. He seldom spoke of such topics. "You never told me how you came to be in Fanli's service."

He shifted slightly, keeping his eyes ahead. "It's quite the boring story. My father died on the battlefield, and my mother was taken by a Wu soldier. I begged on the streets for a while before Fanli found me when I was fifteen and asked how good I was with a sword. He likes to say he saw potential in me as a fighter, but *I* believe he keeps me around for my charm." His gaze flickered back to me, and he smiled with what seemed like great effort. "Like I said, boring."

I swallowed. "I'm sorry."

"Don't be. While Fanli may subject me to the most rigorous training any man in this world has ever endured, and could stand to laugh at my jokes every once in a while—I *know* they're funny—I'm lucky he took me in. He's . . . good, you know? Deep in the core of him." He breathed out, turned to me fully, his eyes dark with an understanding I didn't want to see. An echo. A likeness. My pulse skipped. It was as if he had sensed every forbidden feeling I'd tucked away, every desire I'd smothered like a candle flame. "If heroes are born from tumultuous times, then he must be one of them. Perhaps very little from our kingdom will survive through the tides of history, but Fanli—I believe he will. Even hundreds or thousands of years from now, I believe they will remember him a hero."

"But heroes always have tragic endings," I said softly, a lump in my throat.

"Yes, well. One cannot save the world and live in peace. That's not how these things work."

Something about his words reminded me of my own thoughts from when I was standing outside my house, scared, my decision weighing on my chest: *a kingdom, or my happiness.* We had both made our choices. Was it too late now to regret them?

"What will you do?" I asked. "When we are gone?"

He was quiet. The oars creaked and splashed the water in a rhythmic motion, and a gentle mist rose around us like white steam.

"I cannot be sure. But I will stay by his side." The planes of his face were smooth, certain, his shoulders squared. "Wherever he goes, I will follow, for as long as he lets me."

Perhaps a flicker of envy or longing showed in my eyes, because he took one look at me, then threw his head back and laughed, the sound half-bitter. "Trust me, it's not so much better a position, compared to you," he said. "I know he will be thinking of someone else."

Before I could reply, the boat lurched, the planks wobbling beneath my feet, and came to a stop on one side of the canal. Fanli emerged from behind the curtains, his sword gripped in one hand.

"Are we there already?" I asked, confused. I couldn't see the palace, only the emerald water flowing on and on ahead of us, and the crimson glow of the lanterns.

Fanli shook his head. "We're not, but I'm getting off here."

It was as though someone had flipped the boat over, yanked the world out from under me. I couldn't breathe. A sharp pain tore through my throat, even fiercer than where the arrowhead had pierced me. "You're—not coming with me?"

"No." His expression was impossible to read, his eyes unfathomably dark. "I've given it some thought, and there is no need for a dramatic farewell. You should arrive at the palace alone, without any attachments to the Yue Kingdom; Luyi will be there to ensure your safety. It is best."

It is best. Such simple words, so cold in their practicality, so unfeeling. I wanted to hit him then, to shake him, seize his wrist and squeeze. Would he not miss me at all? Did he not understand that this was his last chance to see me, our last moments together? Could he not be so rational, just for once?

He stepped forward and held out his sword to me on two opened hands. The same way I had given the sword to him, back on the riverbank.

"What is . . ."

"Take it," he said. "It is yours now, for protection."

I stared at him. "But—you always carry this—"

"You need it more than I do. Keep it. Please." There was something else behind his words, but he said no more, just extended the sword farther to me, concealed in its familiar sheath. I swallowed, taking it from him. As I did, our knuckles brushed; just the barest second, skin against skin, yet my whole body shivered from the awareness, my throat tightening.

The sword was heavier than I recalled. I pulled it out a fraction, enough to see the inscription in the polished metal: *The mind destroys, the heart devours.*

"Remember," he said quietly.

When I looked up, he was already stepping onto the stone-paved platform, his chin lifted, his hands clasped behind his back. Removed, detached. Only his fingers trembled. Without turning to me, he motioned for the boat to continue on. The oars picked up again, water misting the air. He remained standing. The distance between us spread, inch by irreconcilable inch.

"Wait!" I cried out, desperation rising inside me. I scrambled forward, as close to the edge of the boat as it would allow without my weight tipping everything over. Tears pressed against my eyes, burned in the back of my throat. My hands grabbed on to nothing. Civilians had started to stare from the overhead bridge, the other side of the canal, but I didn't care. "Wait—stop—I don't—" I whipped around to Luyi. His expression was bleak, his lips pressed into a tight, resigned line. "Help me," I said, half pleading. "Turn the boat back. Only for a few more seconds. I just want to tell him—I never got to tell him . . ."

But Luyi gave a small shake of his head and rested a hand on my good shoulder. It was meant to comfort, I knew, but in that moment I only wanted the familiarity of Fanli's touch, his presence, his scent. I only wanted him. "Can't you make this a little easier for him?" Luyi said, his tone laced with pity. Not for me, I realized, but for Fanli.

"*Him?*" My mind spun. The boat was drifting farther and farther away from the platform. "What—what do you mean?"

He sighed. Gave me a look that was almost exasperated. "Why do you think he's getting off early, Xishi? When he so rarely leaves anything before its completion?"

Because he's heartless, I wished to say out of spite, though I understood even then it wasn't true. *Because he does not care as much as I do. Because he wishes to be rid of me sooner. Because he will always choose the kingdom before me.*

"Can you not imagine," Luyi continued, "that it might be difficult for him to deliver you straight into the jaws of the enemy palace, and watch you marry another man? He is disciplined, Xishi," he said as his words buzzed in my head like a wild swarm of hornets, "but he is not made of stone. He suffers too. Privately."

I clutched at my throat, made a choked, anguished sound I'd never made before. I could not bear it. The realization was overpowering. There would be no more dinners with him by the warm, gentle candlelight of the hall. No more strolls in the hazy purple evening, no more coming across him by the pond, his reflection swimming under the lotuses. There would be no more stolen glances in the corridors, footsteps slowing in his shadow. No more suppressed smiles and almost-touches, slender fingers skimming over silk. No more finding him in his room, his silhouette outlined against the fire, opening the door a crack just to see him more clearly. No more spring flowers and autumn rain. No more sneaking onto the highest ledge, watching the mortal smoke and fire of the distant city with him beside me. No more words of advice or words of caution, no more stories coaxed from him when he was in a lighter mood. No more morning greetings. No more watching him secretly, with his head bowed, an ink brush in his hands. No more tenderness. No more solace. No more possibility.

Now there was just me, standing on the prow of the boat, gazing at his lone figure on the opposite bank. He was already too far away for me to make out the lovely details of his face, only the lines of his shoulders, his knife-straight spine. The water rippled and glimmered between us, expanding, the tides pushing the boat onward, away from all I knew and toward the terrible palace. My fingers curled tight around the cool hilt of his sword, as if I could feel the ghost of his grip, the impressions his hands had made in the wood. I had been prepared for this, had taken everything with me except what I really wanted. I wished to weep, but my own tears felt insubstantial, a broken gesture. The feeling swelling within me like churning waves was greater, heavier, absolute.

I tore my gaze away from Fanli's fading silhouette, unable to look anymore, to see what I would miss. Yet as soon as I did, a fresh pain tore through my chest, a pain I had not felt since the day I first met him, as if my heart had been wrenched apart.

I arrived at the Wu palace a ghost.

I was dressed in crimson, the bright, joyous color of a bride, my lips pressed with carmine powder and my cheeks brushed with rouge. The jewels in my hair rattled and whispered softly as I made my way through the giant, bronze-studded gates, led by a line of maids, their faces blank as stones smoothed by waves. They were well trained. More goodbyes had been made: I bid farewell to Luyi, who squeezed my hand and promised to look after Fanli. If tradition had allowed it, I would have pulled him into a crushing hug, buried my head in his robes; but propriety reigned as it always did, and we merely nodded at each other, his face lined with understanding. I touched the worn wood of the boat, the cold of the water, until my fingers smelled faintly like river brine. Each of these small goodbyes was a hollowing; a hole had been punctured through my ribs, and there was my spirit, my essence, seeping out through it. But that did not matter. The worst goodbye was already behind me. My heart had already died.

And so I stepped into my new life.

My face was a mask. I hid behind a feigned look of admiration while I tracked my new surroundings. The palace buildings gleamed red, with sloping gold and emerald roofs and statues of one-legged cranes and tigers standing on top of them. Dusk had turned the sky pink, its light glittering off the diamond-lattice windows and gold-framed doors. I made note of where one gate opened to another as opportunities for invasion; where brilliant gardens bloomed behind fences, offering protection from sharp eyes; where crimson-lacquered pillars and marble balustrades might deflect incoming arrows; where guards had been positioned at five-foot intervals, silent as shadows. The lanes here were wide and swept spotless, the distance from one to another like that between the heavens and the earth, and all pointed toward a palace that rose above the magnificence on steep steps.

This, I realized, was where King Fuchai awaited.

My heart hammered in my chest. I glanced over at Zhengdan, who walked behind me, eyes cast down like any obedient palace lady. Only I could have noticed how tightly her hands were clasped and known the depth of her fear.

At last the maids left us, and we entered the palace alone. The air was darker inside, colder. Our steps echoed over the vast polished floors. The tapestry-covered walls were so high that I felt like an ant inside them, something primordial and insignificant, scuttling for shelter. I fought to keep my expression pleasant, to stop myself from shaking. An elaborate throne stood on a dais before us, gleaming like dark jade. And sprawled across it, in a posture so lazy he might have been about to fall asleep, was the enemy king.

He was young. That was the first thing I noticed, foolish and simple as it was. I had been picturing a graying man, with a wisp of a beard and skin so rough and withered it looked like bark, a chin that melted into the loose folds of his neck. But Fuchai appeared to be at the age more fitting for a prince than a king: a mere couple of years past twenty. He was also surprisingly, disturbingly handsome, with clear black brows and the sharp, assertive features of a wolf. And like the other men of Wu, he wore his hair cropped short, the dark, wavy strands ending just above his eyes and the nape of his neck. I wanted to recoil from the unnatural sight. It was a practice that defied the heavens. Our hair, our skin, our body; these were all gifts from our parents. They were not to be damaged.

Loathing bubbled inside me, black and rapid. This was the man who had ripped me away from my old life, from my family, from Fanli. This was the man who had tormented my people, who lounged on his throne while his soldiers picked our civilians off like vultures after hares. I should have unsheathed Fanli's sword and run it through his heart until he bled out on the cold stone floors. I wanted so badly to. My fingers itched with the impulse.

Instead, a few feet away from him, I dropped into a low curtsy as I had been instructed, my face held at the perfect angle to catch his eye.

"Come forward, come forward," he said. While Fanli's syllables were crisp and cool, his were smooth, almost a purr, flowing off the tongue like wine. "Let me see you properly."

I acquiesced, my steps nimble, silent on the palace floors. Women were not supposed to make a sound unless it was to sing. I bit the inside of my cheeks to keep from screaming.

Fuchai's voice traveled over my head to one of the ministers waiting on the sides. "She is the concubine Goujian promised?" *Goujian.* Not even a title placed before the name. It was how you spoke of a servant, or an old friend.

"Yes, Your Majesty," came the minister's low reply. I snuck a glance at him out of the corner of my eye. He was a tall, strongly built man, also younger than I'd imagined, somewhere in his late twenties, with a sharp jaw and dark set of brows which were currently furrowed in my direction.

"He has not underdelivered; she is lovely to look at. She has a slightly different . . . quality than our women, doesn't she?" I stiffened, but he went on, "A good thing, to have some variety around here. What is her name?"

This was my cue. I lifted my head a fraction. Four scantily clad girls lingered around his throne, silk sashes flowing from their sparrow-boned shoulders to their slender waists. Their perfume thickened the air, a cloying scent like wilted flowers and cinnabar powder. When Fuchai waved an impatient hand, they immediately curtsied and retreated into the background.

"I am Xishi," I greeted him, holding his gaze for three heartbeats. It was a bold move; most were afraid to look the king directly in the eye. But he gazed back down at me with increased fascination.

He descended the dais and stopped before me, so close I could count the glint of every jade button sewn into his robes. There was a black, wolfish gleam in his eyes; his lips were sculpted into a smile that looked more like a smirk. Without warning, he grabbed my face, his thumb and forefinger pressed to my cheeks, and lifted it up higher. His touch was not rough—in fact, I do not think he could have been any gentler. Yet my skin burned from it. *Enemy.* The dark word pulsed through me like another heart.

"Xishi," he murmured; I wanted to rip my name from his tongue, to stop him from corrupting it, from replacing the sound of how Fanli called me. I could not bear to forget anything. "Do you know how beautiful you are?"

Did he know how numb I was to hearing such lines? But of course I reacted with necessary humility. "I'm only a peasant girl from a faraway village, Your Majesty," I said with sickly sweetness. "It is an honor to be here." In my head, I corrected bitterly: *It is a torment. There are a million places I would rather be, including a pigsty.*

"Don't be so polite. You're one of us now." He brandished his sleeve toward the high-ceilinged palace, the gilded chambers, the golden hangings, the dozens of ministers and concubines and servants waiting to do his bidding. "Welcome to the Wu Kingdom, Xishi. Welcome home."

I smiled so I would not cry.

"You must dine with me," he said abruptly, snapping his fingers with an almost childlike excitement. "Are you hungry? What is your favorite dish? I will see that it is prepared at once."

"I . . ." Fanli's lessons flashed through my mind. I steeled myself, remembering the other concubines who had surrounded his throne. Fuchai must have once treated them with such enthusiasm too, but now he did not even spare them a second look. Men like him liked challenges, and novelty, the thrill of the hunt. I had to pull away, to keep him intrigued. "I would love to, Your Majesty, truly . . . but I'm afraid I'm rather tired from the journey here. Perhaps another time?"

He looked, for a moment, stunned. He had not been prepared for a rejection; he had so little experience with it. I felt a sudden, spine-tingling rush of fear. What if I had played my cards too soon? What if instead of reeling him in, I had done the opposite, and insulted him so greatly he would never wish to see me again? My stomach churned.

After a long, terrible silence, he nodded. A trace of disbelief clung to his countenance. "Of course. You should go rest; there will be plenty of opportunities for us to spend time together in the future."

"Thank you, Your Majesty." I hoped he could not detect the relief in my voice.

He was already returning to his throne, throwing himself carelessly across it without even bothering to smooth out his robes. The gold crown on his head had slid askew, only further accentuating his wild, dark features, his unruly black waves. He flicked his wrist at the same minister from earlier, eyes heavy-lidded, almost falling shut. "Zixu, you have finished assigning their rooms, haven't you?"

Zixu. Wu Zixu. My pulse skipped. So this was the man Fanli had warned me about.

The minister stepped forward and dipped his head. Fuchai's eyes were nearly closed now, so he could not see what I did: the tension that ran through Zixu's frame, the charged look in his gaze. "All has been arranged."

"Good, good. Make sure they know where to go."

I heard the dismissal in his words, and was glad. I did not know how much longer my mask would hold. I could feel the wound in my shoulder starting to bleed again, my bandages sticking to my skin, drenched in warm liquid. They would have to be changed soon. Yet as I exited the palace and turned around slowly, my neck prickled with the dangerous, telltale sensation of being watched by multiple pairs of eyes.

CHAPTER ELEVEN

OUR CHAMBERS WERE LOCATED IN THE FARTHEST corner of the palace.

I did not realize this until the third day, when it became clear something was amiss. No maids came to change our bedding or bring fresh water; no concubines came holding gifts or even to give their greetings. And the sound I had been waiting for—the sway of the king's carriage as he traveled down the lanes, looking for a partner to spend the night with—was absent. It was as if we did not exist, as if we had never entered the palace at all. A panicked part of me wondered if I had already failed, if the king had always meant it to be this way, to accept Goujian's gifts on the surface while really leaving us abandoned in some shadowy, remote corner, never to be seen or heard. But I had seen the way Fuchai looked at me. Even if he was not *fond* of me just yet, he ought to at least be interested.

"This is Zixu's doing," I complained to Zhengdan as I paced the length of my bedchambers. As my palace lady, her room was next to mine; it was much smaller, without any ponds or gardens or elaborate furnishings. "You heard him; he was the one who arranged our rooms."

She folded her arms across her chest, leaning back on the cushioned seat. "He doesn't trust us."

"No," I agreed. "And this is the easiest solution for him. I bet the king has hundreds of concubines to choose from. So long as he does not pass my chambers, and nobody else in court brings my name up, he'll soon forget my existence entirely."

"What a pain." Zhengdan huffed. "What do we do, then? Perhaps I can sneak out to find the other palace ladies? Ask them where the king is?"

I shook my head. "I'll bet Zixu already has guards planted around the palace to watch us, just in case. If we venture too far from our chambers, somebody will come to escort us back. We cannot seek out the king on our own. Besides, it will look too deliberate. Plenty of women go forgotten until their chambers are cold."

She caught my eye and raised a slender brow. The expression was endearingly familiar, reminiscent of our days in the village; she might have been asking me to hide out in the trees with her to escape her mother's fussing, or leave pebbles in the shoes of an auntie who'd insulted her. "So you think we should lure him to you?"

"Precisely."

She considered it. "But what event will be so significant the king must come himself?"

"It does have to be significant. Life-threatening, even," I said, my eyes going to the wound in my shoulder. The skin had just started to close, but it was still raw and tender, delicate.

Zhengdan followed my gaze, then blanched. "You don't mean . . . No, surely, you can't—"

"Can you think of anything more effective?"

She opened her mouth, then snapped it shut, a resigned look on her face.

"We only have one chance," I said, already rifling through the drawers for something sharp. A mirror I could break into shards, perhaps, or a jar. "If we do not successfully draw the king's attention, we'll only alert Wu Zixu and the other ministers that we are planning something. They may look for an opportunity to imprison us, or worse, kill us. It is so simple, to make things appear as an accident when there are few others around as witness." At last I came across Fanli's sword. I had hidden it carefully at the very bottom of the drawer, concealed in crimson fabric so nobody could find it. Now I brushed the fabric aside and lifted the weapon. The blade rasped against the sheath as I pulled it out slowly, imagining Fanli's hands curled around the same bejeweled hilt, memories rising like ghosts before me. How many times had I seen him holding his sword at his side, ready to protect or to strike; training with it in the cottage gardens, plum blossom petals falling around him; slicing it through the air, blood spilling from the whetted tip. A pang filled my chest, as if someone were squeezing my heart inside their fist.

Stop. Focus.

The sword was heavy in my grip, yet I derived some strange solace from it. It was the closest thing I had to Fanli's presence, the sword a stand-in for the self.

"Xishi-jie." Zhengdan rose, then stopped. Her lips were set in a grim line, her eyes worried. "You shouldn't— It's too big a sacrifice. What if you just feigned illness? Said your stomach hurt, or you had come down with a fever?"

"Do you really think I could fool the royal physician? He will know I'm lying, and tell Wu Zixu."

Her chin jutted out, every bit as stubborn as I was. "There must be another option—"

I shook my head. "This is the best we can do. Don't worry, I'm already injured. The skin's ruined either way." My voice came out impressively steady. Only I could feel how fast my heart was beating. It was so childish, to be afraid of pain. But perhaps it was also biological, inbuilt, the body's natural means of self-defense. Even once my mind had been made, my fingers trembled over the sword. Another doubt snagged at my heart; I had scorned the Wu for cutting their hair, but now here I was ready to cut open skin. Surprisingly, it was Fanli's voice that drifted to me, as clear as if he were standing right there in the room: *What is the bigger cause?* To him, almost anything could be done, so long as the end result was more beneficial. And I knew exactly what he would do in my position.

It was quick; at least there was that.

My skin parted easily under the blade, my wound reopening. Fat droplets of blood oozed out and trickled down my sides, dampening my robes. The blaze of pain came soon after, so acute I found myself stamping my feet, trying anything to distract myself from the agony in my shoulder. The sword clattered to the marble-veined tiles. *I will be so angry,* I thought half-hysterically, gasping, *if the king does not end up coming, and I am left to just bleed all over the floor on my own.*

I was still bleeding when Zhengdan ran to the doors, threw them open, and yelled out, with real distress: "Help! Someone help—please! Call the physician!"

King Fuchai swept through the room first, his robes swishing over the floors, his crown catching the light. An old physician trotted in after him, carrying a black lacquered box with countless little knobs and compartments.

"What happened?" Fuchai asked, eyes scanning the area. Then

they fell on me, and he came over, two clean, wide strides, his boots clapping against the tiles.

I gritted my teeth against a cry. I was lying in bed, my hands gripping the blood-soaked fabric around my shoulder. Zhengdan had already cleaned the sword and hidden it back in its drawer, and a vase lay shattered on the floor. Despite the physician's uttered warnings, Fuchai skirted around the fragments with surprising ease and stopped beside me. His hair hung dark and tousled past his face, and two hectic spots of color had risen to his high cheekbones.

"Your Majesty," I croaked out, making my voice tremble with pain. The pain was real; everything else was not. "I did not mean to alarm you—"

He waved a hand, and the physician immediately scurried forward, his already-stooped back bent so low I thought it might break in two. "Tell me what happened." Fuchai's eyes flashed like lightning across a storm-black sky. "Nothing of mine should be injured within these palace walls."

Nothing of his. No wonder he was so worried. He took it as a personal insult to see a possession damaged, just as he would distress over the wounding of one of his best steeds, or his favorite coat.

"No, it's really nothing," I gasped. The physician bent closer, examining the cut in my flesh, careful not to touch me without the king's permission. "It's my own fault . . ."

I like to think that Zhengdan and I had developed a mutual understanding, a shared sensitivity by this point, for she picked this moment to speak over me. "It's *my* fault, Your Majesty. I was trying to dust the upper shelves, and she—she insisted on helping—and the vase slipped from the top and shattered. She didn't want to call you away from state affairs, but the cut was so deep . . . I was afraid . . ."

Fuchai's brows creased. "Why would *you* be dusting the upper shelves? That's work for servants, not palace ladies, and certainly not concubines."

We both went silent, letting him figure it out for himself. I supposed I was lucky then, that the king of Wu was not so dull-witted as our kingdom's rumors said, or else we might have remained like that forever, my shoulder bleeding and the physician crouched before me and him just standing there, waiting for an answer.

"Have no servants come to aid you?" He stared around the chambers, as if truly seeing it for the first time. The cobwebs sticking to the high beams and closets, the fine layer of yellow dust that covered the window ledge, the barrels left empty, the sheets unchanged. His eyes narrowed. "Have no servants been here *at all?*"

The physician, who had started applying some herbal paste to my wound using a long swab, trembled violently at the change in his tone, as though he were the one who'd drawn the king's ire. Even I felt a prickling of fear. There was an alchemy to such things; even if I did not recognize Fuchai as *my* king, and even if I were plotting to bring an end to his kingdom, I was keenly attuned to what the crown on his head could do, the power it carried. Perhaps this was another survival instinct.

"Ridiculous," he muttered under his breath, still looking around him. "And what chambers have you been assigned to? It is so far away from everything. No," he said decisively, "this kind of gross negligence will not do. I must speak to the maids."

Suddenly an image of ten young girls felled like stalks of grass sprang to my mind, their blood flowing to form a river over the golden halls. If the palace was a place of tigers and wolves, then the servants were rats, easy prey. My stomach clenched.

"I do not believe the maids were aware of where we stayed, Your Majesty," I said as softly as I could. The paste had started to sting, its bitter herbal smell burning my nostrils. "Perhaps—perhaps there was a miscommunication."

His expression softened. He lowered himself on the side of the bed, shaking his head. "You are so considerate of them. Know that if the positions were reversed, they would not hesitate to throw your life away, so long as it diverted the blame from their own necks."

I knew. Of course I knew.

"It's all right," I insisted. "The wound looks worse than it is. I'm embarrassed you even had to come in person for such a matter."

Fuchai made an impatient, batting motion at the physician. "Leave the medicine with me," he ordered, taking over the herbal paste. "I'll handle it."

"B-but—but Your Majesty." The physician's voice quavered, his body shaking like a leaf. "Your Majesty, I thought you had a court session scheduled for this afternoon . . ."

Fuchai hesitated.

Sensing an opportunity, I let out a pitiful gasp, and pretended to double over, clutching at my shoulder. The medicine was surprisingly effective; in truth, the pain had already began to numb. But he could not know that.

"No," Fuchai said firmly, waving his sleeve again, his gaze on me. "Tell them I have other matters to attend to."

The physician didn't dare say anything else. To speak up the first time could be interpreted as offering a kind reminder; to speak up again would be to defy the king's orders. He quickly bowed and left the building. Zhengdan excused herself shortly afterward too, but not before turning slightly at the front doors and catching my eye with the subtlest nod. A look that said *be careful*, and *good luck*. Then it was just me and the king. I felt as if I had been left alone with a wolf.

"Now that everyone's gone," Fuchai said, a small smile playing at his lips, "we can speak to each other casually. It's so tedious, isn't it? *Court speech.*" He rolled his eyes, as if he were speaking of some dull play. "All those ministers as stiff as wood."

It could have been a trap. But it could also be a chance to draw him closer, to do what few other concubines dared, leave a mark on his mind. Before I made him love me, I needed to make him remember me. "Then . . . may I call you by your name?" I ventured. "Or do you prefer *Your Majesty?*"

He did not reply at first, he was so focused on applying the medicine. His hands were surprisingly gentle, and after each light dab of the swab, he leaned forward and blew on the wound. And every now and then, when I flinched sharply for dramatic effect, he would apologize and slow his movements. I'll admit: I would never have expected such tenderness from a wolf.

But still, some part of me kept waiting for him to bare his fangs. Who knew when he might change his mind, whether he would grow bored of playing the healer and seek out a more pleasurable activity? We were already sitting on my bed, the doors shut, the windows locked. And this was the king who had a reputation for his visits to the brothels, his love of pretty women.

"You can," he said, jolting me from my thoughts.

It took me a moment to remember what he was referring to. "All right," I said slowly, testing the waters. "Fuchai."

His mouth split into a wide grin, and he gazed at me with sudden charm. "I like how it sounds. Say it again."

"Fuchai."

He leaned back a moment, eyes closed, content, like a cat lapping up the sun. "God, it's been so long since anybody has called me that."

In my kingdom, even the king did not refer to himself by his real name. But I acted surprised. "Nobody?"

"They seem under the impression that I'm tricking them," he

said dryly, eyes fluttering open to look at me sidelong, his grin settling back into its usual smirk. "That they'll speak my name once and"—he made an abrupt slashing motion with his free hand—"they'll lose their heads. Of course, they're not totally without reason. It may be because I killed that soldier once for doing just that, but in my defense, he was being *very* annoying."

Little darts of fear pulsed through me. How casually he spoke of a man's death. But beneath my fear boiled an old, familiar rage. It did not matter how gently he treated and wrapped up my wounds now; he had inflicted far greater injuries upon my family, my people, my land. My love.

All of this, I swept clean from my face.

"Zixu is always saying that I cannot kill people just because I find them especially irritating. His issue, of course, is less with the killing itself than how I go about it. *Imagine if your wise, perfect, never-wrong father were here,*" Fuchai mimicked in a voice so like the minister's stern rasp I half expected him to appear in my room. "*He would know which strings to pull to achieve the same results without appearing like a drunken tyrant.* But why should I have to figure out a complicated series of thirty-something steps just to dispose of one man? What fun is it, being king, if I cannot do even this? Of course," he added, with a conspiratorial look, "don't go repeating my words to Zixu. God knows the lengthy speeches I must endure, and all supposedly for my own good."

"Zixu," I repeated, schooling my features into mild wonderment. "The name is familiar . . . Is that the minister who assigned us our rooms?"

He frowned. I could almost see the threads connecting in his mind; sometimes a little nudge was all it took to steer someone in the direction you wanted. "And so it is. I'll have to ask him why he had to choose the least convenient of places for you to live. Really, he always claims to have his reasons, but sometimes . . ." He trailed off with an irritable sigh, then laid a hand over mine. His skin was unbearably warm, unbearably foreign, smooth and devoid of calluses. I forced myself to stay still. "Don't worry, I'll make sure a new accommodation is prepared for you. What kind of place do you prefer? Somewhere with a nice view of the ponds, or perhaps more room for dancing—"

"Whatever place is close to yours," I said sweetly, resisting the urge to gag, "so you may come visit me when you please." *And so it is easier for me to track the movements of your generals and ministers.*

His face brightened like a young boy's. "Consider it done," he said.

The king's word really was law.

We were moved into another set of chambers that very night, one where the windows were vast and open and allowed rhombus patches of light to filter in, and where great rockeries and pink-flowering trees sat in the yard outside, lanterns strung across the branches like stars. Now we were so close to the heart of the palace that the sounds of footsteps often reached our ears, along with a wavering call and chime that I soon learned signaled the arrival of the king.

Yet even though we were closer, I still did not have the chance to see him—and it was not for lack of trying.

In the first week, I sought to use my injuries to my advantage, calling out for frequent visits from the physician, complaining of a sudden stabbing pain or of bleeding through my robes. But the physician who appeared was different, and Fuchai did not accompany him.

"Where is the one who treated me before?" I asked him.

He sniffed, then poured alcohol directly onto my wound without any care or gentleness. It burned like liquid flames. I had to bite back a yelp, dig my nails into my skin. "That is the royal physician, the highest ranked in the palace. He should serve only His Majesty."

"Then who do you serve?" I asked, shaking from the pain. He did not reply, but I could guess. Wu Zixu. He must have sent the physician before anyone else could.

In the second week, when my shoulder was mostly healed, I fashioned a kite out of old fabric and twigs and thread. Zhengdan and I made these often in our village, but I understood it to be a novelty for those raised in the lavish confines of the palace. When the chimes sounded, and Fuchai drew near, I ran down the lanes with the kite soaring high above my head, willing him to come. Yet, I had flown the kite for only a few seconds when a mysterious black dart pierced through it, and it tumbled back down to the ground like an injured sparrow. I clenched the dart in my fist while the tinkling of chimes faded away.

In the third week, I wrapped little golden bells around my ankles and wrists and ventured out to the palace gardens. When he passed by on his high carriage, I began to dance, the bells jingling sweetly with my movements, the music rising through the air. Just when I heard his carriage slow, and felt the hope lift in my chest, it was Wu Zixu's dreaded voice that drifted toward me over the trees. "We mustn't delay our next meeting, Your Majesty," he said. "It is of the utmost importance."

In the fourth week, after Zhengdan had found out that Fuchai was to arrive soon, I drew a warm bath for myself and sank into the jasmine-infused waters, the steam swirling hot and thick around me. I had shooed away all the maids, and left the door just slightly ajar, designed for him to walk straight in and see me. But when footsteps finally drew near, they were the wrong ones, too light and nimble.

Water splashed to the floor as I twisted around.

One of the maids had returned. "Minister Wu Zixu has called His Majesty away for the afternoon to approve his birthday preparations. The minister asked that I inform you, so you are not kept waiting for nothing."

"I understand," I said tightly, and I did. I saw what Zixu was doing. It did not matter how charming I was, how well I'd been trained, if he would not even allow me the opportunity to see the king.

But he had unwittingly reminded me of something else. The king's birthday, just one moon away. Everyone would be expected to attend, from the most esteemed ministers to the lowliest servants. And even Wu Zixu could not prevent me from being there.

CHAPTER
TWELVE

THE KING'S BIRTHDAY WAS A TRULY JOYOUS OCCASION to him alone. To everyone else in the palace, it was a source of great anxiety.

In the weeks leading up to the event, the servants could be seen scrambling up and down the interlinked halls with a frenetic energy, putting up banners and scrubbing every lacquered surface until they were clean enough to be licked. The cooks sent for men to climb the remote mountains in search of rare herbs, and brewed clay pots of chicken soup for seven nights and seven days. And within the sprawling estates and embroidered screen doors, the concubines wrote letters to calligraphy masters and jewelry suppliers, arranging the most elaborate gifts.

I had no wealth or connections in this kingdom, so I could rely only on my two hands. For weeks, I'd stayed up by the flickering flame of the candles, threading a rich embroidery of dragons and phoenixes. Each glossy scale and feather contained a myriad of colors, a collection of a hundred tiny, careful stitches.

When the day came, I folded the embroidery into a rosewood

box for the maids to carry, then joined the others outside in the grand pavilion.

There, amid the overhanging lilac blossoms and wisteria, sheltered from the sun, the king sat on a raised throne of white stone. He wore layers of brocade robes so fine it was difficult to believe they had been spun from mortal fabric. The hems were lined with soft fur, the sleeves decorated with silver flames. He looked terribly beautiful, the way wolves might look beautiful in blood-splattered snow.

I would have him today, I decided. I would sink my nails into his heart and force him to remember me.

For a moment, he seemed to glance my way, though it was hard to be certain. I had joined a line of twenty concubines, each dressed in their very best, their palace ladies positioned beside them. The air was thick with the unnatural fragrance of a dozen different perfumes. It made my nose itch, but I kept my expression pleasant.

One by one, the concubines stepped up and gave their blessings. The content was painfully derivative, some variation of *May His Majesty live ten thousand years* or *May His Majesty be blessed with peace, good health, and prosperity.*

"You may now present your gift," Fuchai said in a bored tone, waving them forward as though they were doing him a favor.

Precious boxes and scrolls were passed down and opened. A goose egg made from pure gold. A ship carved from ivory. A nightingale that had been trained to recite a poem praising the king—which was rather impressive the first time around, but quickly grew maddening.

"Put it somewhere far from my chambers," Fuchai said, handing the bamboo cage to one of the servants. The bird had started its tenth recitation of the poem. "Who's next?"

Lady Yu went. She had brought a mahogany statue of a leaping lion. The knife work was immaculate, the details so finely rendered it looked almost alive.

"Pretty," Fuchai said absently. That was all.

By now my palms were sweating, my throat tight with pressure. The world's greatest riches were on display before him, and he would barely give them a second glance. As Lady Yu curtsied and moved to the side, I motioned for the maid to bring my gift.

"I hope you will surprise me," Fuchai said, tilting his head to the side.

Though we were outdoors, the space felt too small, too suffocating, the pillars of the pavilion looming tall. Everyone was silent, watching me. Yet I knew even before I opened the box that something was amiss. The lock was loose. I glanced up, and I saw Wu Zixu standing in the shadows beside the king, his expression carefully blank, save for the slight curl of his lip.

Dread sliced through me.

"What is the matter?" a concubine asked aloud. "Don't take too long now."

Fuchai leaned forward too.

"Nothing," I said, keeping my tone airy. On my left, Zhengdan had stiffened, worry flashing through her eyes. She must have also sensed something was wrong. "It *is* a surprise, after all. Some suspense is necessary." I lifted the lid slowly, fearing the worst, and still my stomach plummeted. The embroidery had been torn into unrecognizable pieces, the threads mangled as if run through by a hasty knife. To present this to the king was not an option. But then I would be without a gift, and even if I was not punished by the whip for disrespecting the throne, I could be sure I would never win his affections.

I stood, frozen, holding that cursed box, my mind working so fast I felt dizzy. What to do? It was an impossible task, like being asked to part the seas or conjure the moon. I wanted to scream with frustration, to march up to Wu Zixu and tackle him to the ground. He was always there, always ruining everything. This was meant to be my one opportunity.

Do not react. Think, I willed myself, my blood pulsing. *Find a way out of this.*

"Lady Xishi?" a servant prompted, not hiding his impatience. "We do not have time to wait about—"

"Look!" Zhengdan's voice rang out from beside me.

I snapped my head up. Everyone turned to stare in the direction Zhengdan was pointing, but there was only the clear azure sky, the distant impression of the mountains.

"What?" someone asked.

"A bird," Zhengdan said, with such conviction nobody could guess that she was trying to buy me time. Gratitude swelled in my chest. "It was a giant bird with iridescent feathers and a red beak—I've read about it. It only appears in the presence of a divine being . . ."

Never one to miss out on an opening for flattery, a servant cried, "The divine being must be His Majesty! What an auspicious sign."

As the others murmured among themselves and craned their necks in search of a nonexistent bird, I stared around me. I had but a few seconds. My eyes fell on the pebbles near my feet, and a most ridiculous idea hit me. Ridiculous—yet I was desperate. In one quick motion, I bent down and seized a smooth pebble, wiping it clean with my sleeves before dropping it into the box.

When everyone had lost interest in the bird sighting, I was already standing upright and smiling, as though nothing had happened.

"Here is my gift," I said, my mouth dry, and held out the single pebble.

There was a long, significant pause.

My heart thudded like a startled hare. The expression on Fuchai's face was inscrutable, his dark brows just slightly raised, his eyes on me.

"This?" he said. "It's a pebble."

Even with their training, the servants standing on both sides of him dissolved into snickers. Others looked on in horror, as if they could already foresee the whip cutting open my skin. As if I were already dead.

But retreat was no longer an option. Steeling myself, I pushed ahead, my voice steady as I wove out my lie. "There are plenty who will wish for your glory and success, but such things tend to come at the expense of your personal happiness and sanity. For your birthday, Your Majesty, and every day after, I hope only that you have more time to yourself. That you may indulge in life's quiet pleasures, like skipping pebbles over water, or hand-picking a ripe fruit from a tree, or strolling through the gardens at dusk—"

"How presumptuous," a servant cut in, glaring at me. "How could someone like *His Majesty* lower himself to do such—such common activities?"

From the uneasy glances shared between the other attendants, they all seemed to think the same thing.

A fresh wave of fear crashed against my ribs. Would the king take offense? Would he assume I was mocking him? Would he see straight through me?

Then Fuchai smiled. He had not done so all morning, and the entire atmosphere shifted in response, the air lightening at once.

"Bring it here, Xishi," he said.

My knees were so weak from both fear and relief that I had to focus on walking in a straight line, the small pebble gripped tight in my fingers. When I reached his throne, he held out his palm, and waited, still smiling. His gaze was disarmingly gentle, like the breeze that had risen around us.

I placed the pebble into his hand, and he stared down at the coarse, rudimentary thing as if it were a treasured prize, better than all the gold and jade and porcelain the others had showered him with, unlike anything he had ever seen.

"Thank you," he said quietly. "I will remember you."

CHAPTER THIRTEEN

THE BIRTHDAY DECORATIONS HAD BARELY BEEN TAKEN down before the king's servant appeared outside my chambers.

"His Majesty has asked for you to accompany him tonight," he called.

My heart pounded. *Finally.* It seemed my gift had made an impression after all; he really had remembered me. But I did not move to bathe in rose water and change into a set of fresh robes, as was expected of me. I could not relinquish an opportunity so easily. If I went to him tonight, like a beautiful, obedient bride, there would be no anticipation left, no intrigue.

So instead I turned my back to the lattice sliding doors and replied with forced calm, "Tell him I am too tired. Perhaps another time."

A beat of drawn silence.

I could feel my heartbeat quickening, my blood rushing fiercely through my veins. There was a risk, I was aware. A chance his goodwill from the gift would shatter. A chance his impatience would triumph over his curiosity, and he would order my banishment from the palace, or perhaps my immediate execution. I squeezed my eyes shut against the image of a falling blade, my blood seeping through cold stone.

"One should be most honored by such an invitation," came the servant's eventual reply. I could hear the incredulity in his voice, and beneath it, the unspoken accusation: *Who do you think you are to deny the king what he wants?* "Many would kill for it."

"That does not change the fact that I'm tired," I said firmly, and walked deeper into my chambers, my long robes sweeping the floors. I spent the rest of the night wide awake, restless, listening for the sound of footsteps, half convinced the servant would return with my sentence. But only the osmanthus branches tapped my window, and the flames of lanterns burned low.

Another invitation came the next evening.

"His Majesty hopes you are well rested now," the servant said. Even with the door between us, his sneer was obvious. "He would like to see you tonight."

I chewed my lip. I ought to already be grateful I had been kept alive. But how long could I stretch this out for? How far until the king's tolerance snapped? "I'm afraid I cannot. My heart has been acting up again," I said, and it was not a lie. Ever since I had parted with Fanli on the canal, the pain had burrowed deep into my chest like a scrabbling creature. In everything I did, I felt its terrible ache, my body's betrayal.

"No wonder they say the girls of Yue are raised without man- ners," the servant muttered, his footsteps turning away.

But he was back by the next evening, and again, the one af- ter that. Each time I turned him away with bated breath, aware that my excuses were wearing thinner and thinner, that at this rate the king would either grow obsessed with me, or grow to hate me. I wish I could say it was all strategy, but there was also fear. I did not know how he would act once we really were alone together.

"Are you sure this will work?" Zhengdan asked one afternoon, when the servant left.

"Of course," I said, with far more certainty than I felt. It had been ten days already. Perhaps the king would give up. Perhaps he would find someone more willing, more eager to please. There were so many women in the palace, each as lovely as a water lily. "It must work."

When I heard the footsteps outside my chambers, I was already prepared.

"Tell His Majesty I am about to sleep," I said, running a comb through my glossy hair. "Perhaps another day."

But I was not met with the servant's bitter complaints, as I was accustomed to. Instead, the doors creaked open, and King Fuchai himself stood in the entrance, a black brocade cloak draped around his shoulders, the sky darkening to violet behind him. His eyes glinted, the corner of his mouth twisting upward. Too sharp to be a smile, too sincere to be a sneer.

The air froze in my lungs. "Your Majesty." I set the comb down and dropped into a low curtsy, keeping my eyes on his face.

"What game are you playing?" he asked softly, closing the door behind him. At once the space inside seemed to shrink, the distance between us narrowing. I wished to retreat, but that would be a sign of weakness.

Instead I tipped my chin up. "I am not playing any games," I said.

"Then why do you not wish to see me?" he pressed, stepping

forward. His voice gave me pause. There was something surprising in it; he sounded almost hurt.

"I am seeing you now, aren't I?" I said, all innocence and poise. He could not know how fast my heart was beating.

He took another step. Lifted a hand to a stray strand of my hair, then brushed his knuckles gently over the side of my cheek. His hands did not feel like a killer's hands. They were smooth, unscarred. Warm. "I have been thinking about you," he told me, agitated, in the tones of a drunken confession. Or perhaps he really had been drinking. I could smell the faint notes of yellow wine clinging to his robes. "I cannot stop thinking about you."

I smiled. "Then don't."

His features blazed with wanting. It made him look younger, less cruel. He leaned in, and I shifted back, just slightly, just out of reach. His hands curled as he tried again. This time I let his lips brush mine before I moved, angling my face away from his.

What is desire?

Absence.

He stared at me in the stillness, his eyes burning.

Fear knotted my throat. If he really wanted to, he could overpower me now, kiss me without asking. Kings never needed permission. But though his breathing was uneven, his hands still clenched, he withdrew. "We don't have to," he said at last. "There is no point, if you aren't willing."

I did my best to conceal my surprise. This was not what the rumors had warned me of.

"May I stay here tonight?" he asked, then, following the direction of my gaze, clarified, "Only to sleep beside you."

My attention drifted to the shadows waiting outside the windows. Guards. If Fuchai left now, word would flow through the corridors that the king was uninterested, that I had failed to gain his favor. But if he stayed, it did not matter what we did or didn't do. The assumption alone would be enough.

"If you wish," I said, careful not to sound too eager, nor too dismissive. It was like walking along a cliff's edge.

As Fuchai unfastened his cloak, I picked up the comb again, praying he couldn't see the tremor in my fingers.

I fell asleep long after he did. And when I dreamed, I dreamed of blood.

Susu's blood, trickling from her mouth, pooling over the floor. The terrible gurgling sound in her throat. Her small, tiny fingers clutching feebly at the air. Her skin, so soft and tender only in the way of children who had not lived long enough to be marked by the world. Until now. How easily the sword tore through it. I remembered my mother fussing over her when she had scraped her thumb on the corner of a wooden toy; the thinnest red line, barely more than a scratch, but even that had been too much. We gathered around her, my mother squeezing her wrist, my father gathering fresh water to clean it, wiping her tears away, humming to make her laugh. She was the sun in our family, the source of all our light.

I shouted for her, even though it was useless. *Susu. My sister, my life.* The blood was spreading, smearing over the wood. I could undo it, I kept telling myself. It was only a few seconds' difference. One single movement. How could that be enough to take her away from me?

But I couldn't move. I could only watch.

The same nightmare, the same ghosts, the same terrible, unforgivable ending.

The soldier tightened his grip on the sword hilt. His face was blank, shrouded in darkness. Then I blinked, and his features morphed into Fuchai's.

No.

My eyes flew open. I was drenched with cold sweat, my chest heaving as though I had run the distance here. *Here:* tangled in silk sheets in a luxurious canopy bed, in the enemy's palace, next to their king.

He was still sleeping.

I gazed across the dark stretch of pillow between us, at the moonlight gliding over his skin. His lashes cast shadows over his cheekbones. His brows were smooth, his lips slightly parted, his breathing slow. He looked so peaceful I almost could not fathom it. I found myself staring at the hollow of his throat. *One single movement.* All that had been needed to rip Susu away from me. All that I needed now, to jam my hairpin into his vein, to end him for good.

The temptation was so strong it formed a jagged stone in my belly. I knew, with a cool certainty, that if he were gone, everything would be made right again. But I couldn't, just yet. That was not part of the plan.

Be patient, I reminded myself, holding my breath. Outside, an owl hooted into the night, and the clouds moved silver across the sky, and the palace grounds lay in utter stillness, while inside, the king went on sleeping soundly beside me.

He visited my chambers every day after that. Some nights I would rise and smile to greet him, teasing him lightly about the extravagant robes he'd chosen, or the countless servants who followed him everywhere. Other nights I would pretend to be absorbed in a scroll, or an ink painting, and make him wait. To him this must have been the greatest novelty, for nobody ever denied him anything. And it was this that compelled him to come back, time and time again. At the end of the evening, he would blow out the candles and lie down to rest next to me, and whisper, "Goodnight, Xishi."

There was always a trace of anticipation in those words. I would lean in, close enough to watch his eyes widen, but no farther. "Goodnight."

While I filled the king's mind with thoughts of me, Zhengdan filled her schedule with the other palace ladies. She accompanied them to watch the soldiers train every morning, pretending to admire their strength and power while really noting their sword techniques. Often, she would gather critical information just from the ladies' gossip, about which general was due for a promotion, or which skilled soldier had suffered a bad injury. They sometimes spoke about Fuchai too—his likes and preferences—and whatever she learned, she would report back to me.

"They say he's particularly fond of the scent of jasmine," Zheng-dan said one morning. We sat together in the dining room, cush-ioned by furs and silks.

"Is that so?" I mused. "Perhaps I'll dab some jasmine perfume on my wrists tonight . . . Or my neck."

"You're going to make that poor king lose his mind over you," Zhengdan said without sympathy, clicking her tongue.

"Good. The sooner he loses his mind, the sooner his kingdom—"

Suddenly, the doors swung open. A maid entered, holding my meal.

My heart thudded in my chest as I tried to look natural. Had she overheard our conversation? Could she guess at what we were planning? The maid did not say anything, but she was staring at us oddly when she came forward and presented the tray. Up close, I saw that she had a flat, round face, with thin brows and eyes set wide apart. She was not the one who usually delivered my meals.

"We have a new drink from the kitchen today," she murmured, her eyes cast down. There was an unpolished, regional accent to her words. Her hands were coarse too, peasant's hands, and they trembled as she lifted the lid from a pretty cloisonné cup. A rich fragrance wafted toward us, sweet like honeyed osmanthus and dates. Inside was a dark green liquid that resembled tea. "It's good for digestion. Do try it."

I searched her face for any lingering signs of suspicion as I lifted the cup to my lips—

"Don't drink that," Zhengdan said sharply, swiping at my arm.

The cup slipped from my hand and shattered with a loud tinkling sound, the murky liquid pooling over the ground. The silence that followed was deafening. I could hear my own furious breathing, my pounding heartbeat.

Zhengdan's eyes were bright with fear. "Don't," she said again. "It's poison."

CHAPTER FOURTEEN

THE MAID STUMBLED BACK, HER FACE STARK WHITE.
Her widened gaze darted from the liquid spilled before our
feet, up to my face, then down again.

"It's not," she stammered, shaking her head so hard her braided
knot threatened to unravel. She could barely get the words out
through chattering teeth. "I—I swear it—I don't know anything—
please, miss—"

"I recognize you," Zhengdan was saying, and I saw the immediate effect of her words. The maid stiffened and recoiled as
though Zhengdan had raised a hand to slap her. "You were with
the palace ladies the other day. You're one of Lady Yu's maids,
aren't you?"

The maid didn't reply, just uttered a low whimpering sound.

Somehow, her panic worked like an antidote, counteracting
mine. I felt a curious sense of calm descend over me, my head
clearing. A path opened up before me, as natural and obvious as if
it were predetermined by the heavens itself. I needed only follow it.

"Lady Yu's maid," I repeated slowly. Now, I saw that what I'd taken for suspicion had in fact been guilt. "She's the one who set you up with the poison?"

The maid shook her head again. "N-no. No, it's not like that. It isn't poison—"

"Really?" I took a step forward. I felt the power of my own presence, my dark eyes bearing down on her. "Then drink it."

She flinched. "W-what?"

I pointed at the puddle of liquid. "There's still some left. Just drink it, and I'll believe you."

The maid seemed completely frozen for a moment, her face contorted in despair. She looked very young, perhaps fourteen or fifteen at most. Perhaps she had been sent into the palace by her parents, in hopes of advancing their social standing—the typical commoner's fantasy of working in the palace, only to one day be noticed and adored by the king and eventually picked as his concubine. Or perhaps her family was already dead, and she had nowhere else to go. I felt a prickling of guilt, but my stance did not soften. Then there was a loud *thud*. With a choked sob, she threw herself down on all fours and kowtowed, all but banging her head against the hard wood, her voice trembling as much as her small body. "P-please, forgive me, miss. I'm sorry. I'm so sorry. I really didn't mean to—"

"You clearly did mean to," I said with a dry huff of laughter. "You knew what you were doing. If my palace lady hadn't intervened, I would be dead right now."

"I'm sorry," she babbled. "I just—I don't want to die. I'll do anything, whatever you ask. Please. Please, miss, spare me."

Over the young maid's shivering, curled-up form, Zhengdan gave me a hard look. A nod of confirmation. I knew that if the one almost poisoned had been her, she would be happy to turn the page, to let the maid go with only a warning. But because it was me, she had no room for mercy.

"Look at me," I instructed.

The maid hesitated, then lifted her head slowly. Her cheeks were streaked with tears, her skin splotched pink and red.

"What is your name?" I asked.

Clearly, she thought it was a trap; perhaps I would take her name and immediately run off with it to the king. She clamped her mouth shut.

Zhengdan crouched down beside the maid and placed a hand on her shoulder. The maid tensed under her touch as if it were a killing blow. "If you don't want to die, then I suggest you answer whatever Lady Xishi asks of you."

A beat. The maid swallowed thickly, then replied, "Xiaomin."

"Xiaomin." I regarded her without any outward feeling. This was a rare opportunity to come by, and I would not waste it. "I'm going to give you two choices. I can invite King Fuchai over now, and tell him you attempted to poison me. He will most definitely sentence you to death; *how* is the key question here. Perhaps it will be death by a thousand cuts. Perhaps it will be a public beheading. Perhaps it will be by attaching your head and four limbs to different chariots, so you are torn apart. Perhaps it will be by cutting off your nose, and letting you bleed to death on your own."

Another piteous whine rose from Xiaomin's lips. She clutched her nose as if it had already been severed.

"Or," I said, louder, over her sobs, "I can pardon you for your crimes. I will not speak a word of what transpired today to another soul. We can settle this matter personally, so long as you pledge your unwavering loyalty to me from now on."

Xiaomin stilled mid-sob, her warm brown eyes glassy with tears. "You—you mean it?"

"If you agree." I stared down at her and raised a finger before she could speak. "But if you ever give me reason to question your trust again . . ." I let the threat hang in the cold, dark air.

"I promise," she gasped, scrambling to stand. "I will prove that I'm trustworthy."

I nodded, satisfied at last. In my head, I had already started to compile a list of information she could retrieve for me, errands she could run without anyone else knowing. A thrill shot through my blood. The thing about maids was that they'd been trained to stick to the shadows, so nobody ever noticed them, but really, they were the eyes and ears of the palace, always listening, always watching. "Good. You can begin by telling me where Lady Yu is. I would like to speak to her."

I found Lady Yu alone in her private gardens. Her back was turned to me, her lovely head bowed as she pruned a bright bloom of peonies. She could have blended in with those flowers herself, dressed in carefully arranged layers of pink gauze, intricate floral patterns threaded down her spine. A white fountain ran beside her, its quicksilver waters tinkling like little chimes. The air was thick and redolent with the fragrance of chrysanthemums and pale azaleas and countless other plants I could not name, a kind of secluded heaven on earth.

My footsteps crunched over the fallen petals, and she whipped around, her face brightening for a moment—perhaps assuming it was the king—before she saw me. Immediately, her features soured, as if she'd just bitten into a rotten plum.

"You," she said stiffly, not bothering with pleasantries. At least this would be quick. "What are you doing here?"

"Surprised to see me alive?"

Her expression did not change. She was a good actress, I could credit her with that. Only her hand gave her away; the slightest tremble, the flowers quivering under her fingers. A petal fluttered to the ground. "I have no idea what you mean," she said.

I affected an indulgent air, my tone amiable. "Would you like me to explain it to you in detail, then?"

She pressed her lips together. I studied her face while I waited. She was undoubtedly beautiful, less in the way her physical features were arranged and more in the way she wore them. We'd never spoken more than a few words before, but I'd heard the palace gossip about how her kisses were worth dying for, how her skin was soft as silk, her waist slim and sleek as an eel's, and I'd seen for myself how many of the ministers and guards secretly lusted after her, though they would never dare act upon it. It was said that the king used to visit her at least seven nights for every full moon, charming her with honeyed words and promises and generous gifts: this garden was one of them. But in recent weeks, I did not think the king had set foot into her chambers even once.

"To save both of us time, your maid has already confessed," I said, keeping my tone pleasant. We might have been discussing the flowers, or admiring the butterflies dancing over the blossoms. "Perhaps you should have just done it yourself. It would have been less obvious, at least. You may even have succeeded."

She tensed, covering her face with her sleeve. "I still don't know what you're talking about."

"How about this, as a reminder?" I unearthed the vial from my inner robes; the poison swirled within it. Her pupils narrowed, turning thin and black as a cat's. In another fluid motion, I pocketed the vial again. "If I were to bring it to the royal physician now, what do you think he will say?"

"You wouldn't," she said, but she sounded uncertain.

"You're right. I have a better idea: I will summon His Majesty to my chambers—"

Her complexion paled; it was like watching fresh snow harden to ice. "The king is not to be—to be *summoned* by a lowly concubine—it should be the other way around—"

"With me, he can be," I said, smiling. I knew I was being callous, that if the positions were reversed, I would've wished to slap myself; as it was, I felt more sorry than anything for the girl before me. Still I continued. "I need only say the word, and he will come running, everything else forgotten." A pause. Another smile. "Why, is he not like that with you?"

She was silent.

"But what was I saying? Oh yes, I shall ask him to come, along with the physician, and his food taster, and my palace lady, Zhengdan, and of course your *ever-loyal* maid, Xiaomin—it will be like a party, with all of us there. We can go through the day's events and decide on your punishment together." When she made no response, I spun around on my heel, turning my back to her. "Don't believe me? I will go there right now. *I* certainly have nothing to lose." I walked as I spoke, counting every step I took away from her.

One.

Two.

Three.

Four—

"Wait." Her voice cut through the air. "Are you . . . really going to tell His Majesty?" she asked at last, her façade falling.

"That depends." I shrugged, pretending to admire one of the begonias dangling from a clay pot. The wide petals were tinged a deep blood-red at the edges, and slowly lightened toward the center. "I may not mention it to Fuchai if I'm pleased enough with our conversation."

A stem snapped between her fingers. "You dare call him directly by name?"

I had used it deliberately to provoke her, to assess her reaction. "I do," I said, calm. "He asked me to."

The sour look was back. "How sweet."

"Tell me something: Do you truly love him?"

She blinked. I had surprised her. "Love," she repeated slowly, in a tone veering toward contempt. "Girls like me are not made for love; we are made to be wanted." Then she cast me a careful, side-long look from under her heavy lids, and amended: "Girls like us."

The familiar words stung my throat. Briefly, against my will, I remembered Fanli's fading figure, the blue-white mist rising up around him, the canal waters lapping against the boat as it floated farther and farther away. *Stop*, I instructed myself, before my heart could fracture again. *Do what's useful.*

"Of course, there are things I love," she went on, "if power counts as one of them. And pretty things. Maybe that makes me vain, but isn't it natural to be drawn toward what's beautiful?" She stroked one of the budding flowers, then touched the gold brace-lets jangling around her delicate wrists, the inlaid gems luminous under the sun's light. Finally, she glanced back up at me. "Is that response satisfactory enough?"

I drifted forward through all that lush greenery and stopped by the fountain, lowering myself to the ledge. The stone was cold against my skin. I patted the empty spot next to me. "Tell me more."

"What is there to tell?"

I waited until she was seated—with all the reluctance of one coming to sit beside a leopard—before continuing. "I'm just trying to understand you. Poison is a rather dire tactic, don't you think? Messy, as well. You must have been desperate."

Confusion flickered over her features. Dryly, she said, "You don't sound too angry about it, for someone who could have died."

"Oh, I am angry," I reassured her. "Furious, in fact." A beat. "But at more than just you." These were the rules that shaped our lives from when we were born: *Be beautiful, be charming, be the most coveted girl in the room, or else you will be nothing.* For men, it was so easy; the path to power was so direct. But we had to manipulate and maneuver and claw our way to gain half of what they did.

Lady Yu's brows furrowed, the only crease to be seen in her smooth, petal-like face. When she spoke again, her voice was lower, softly bitter. "You wouldn't understand. My father commands a portion of the royal guard. Whenever my position in the palace slips, his falls as well. All the servants have been talking about it; how His Majesty used to frequent my chambers as if it hurt to be separated from me for more than a day . . . and how he doesn't even seem to remember me now."

My heart leaped. *The royal guard.* I had come here in search of an ally, but I had found something even better. "How about we make a deal?"

She eyed me warily. "A deal?"

"I can ask Fuchai to visit you more often, and remind him of everything that's good about you, and kindly omit your personal defects, such as your occasional impulse to poison the people around you. It will be enough to stop the servants from whispering, and anyone with eyes shall be convinced of your worth to him. Your father's rank will be secured, and your family's power will only grow from here on."

"What, you don't mind sharing?" Her tone was still dry, barbed with mockery, but I could see the fresh glow of interest spreading over her face, the apt attention in her gaze. She was right, after all. Neither of us were in this for something so trivial as love.

I shook my head.

"And what's the catch?"

I could not disclose my plans with her, not yet. So I only said, "Remember this favor. What I've done for you, and what I've forgiven. When I need you and your father, I'll provide you with more details."

She scoffed, but it was a sound without much malice. "You are different from how I imagined, you know."

I smiled slightly. "Aren't we all?"

There was a silence. A strong, abrupt wind blew through the azaleas, a torrent of flushed petals picking up and swirling around us, some landing in the fountain waters, so light they barely made a ripple. My robes fluttered out like bird wings, my hair tickling my cheeks, wisps flying loose from their elaborate knots. Yet I remained motionless, my breath held tight, while Lady Yu rearranged the gauze covering her shoulders. Her eyes were contemplative.

"So? Do we have a deal?" I prompted, holding out a hand.

She stared down at it for the longest time, then nodded, curling her thin fingers around mine. Her bracelets sang softly as we shook, gleaming in the light.

CHAPTER FIFTEEN

WINTER CREPT IN SLOWLY.

The flowers in the gardens wilted and withered, their rose blushes fading into dry browns. Sheets of ice hardened over the palace's curving artificial creeks. Flimsy gauze dresses were swapped for thick, luxurious coats made of silver-white fox fur and wolfskin. The maids busied themselves filling and refilling buckets of boiling water and wheeling in carts of fresh firewood. Whenever I went outside, my breath trembled in the cold, pale air, and my fingertips quickly lost all feeling. My shoulder healed, but the pain in my chest sharpened, though I could not tell if it was from the bone-deep chill or my old illness or something else. Throughout everything, I could feel time trickling away from me. Back in the Yue Kingdom, they would already be preparing for the next step of the plan, training their soldiers, forging new swords, mapping out the lines of battle with what information they had . . . and waiting for me to do my part too.

It was snowing when I arrived outside the king's court. The white shone starkly against the dark emerald roofs and crimson ledges,

the frost glistening like fine crystals. The palace looked more remote than ever in the falling snow, a place made for ghosts instead
of mortals, its cold stillness like the silence between breaths. All
the marble steps had been swept clean by maids at hourly intervals, with salt spread over them to melt the ice and prevent anyone
from slipping. From both sides, a silent row of guards waited, their
halberds raised to head height, their eyes staring straight ahead. I
tightened my grip on the tray of wine and made my way carefully
up, my cheeks pink from the cold.

The court was empty, with only Fuchai spread out on his throne,
head dipped back, one leg dangling over the gilded armrest. Locks
of crow-black hair tumbled past his brows, and the black fox fur
draped around his neck made him resemble a deity of devastation
and destruction.

Then he saw me, and he snapped instantly into a sitting position, a smile blooming at the corners of his lips. There were times
when he gazed at me with such pure sincerity, such boyish eagerness, that I almost forgot how much I loathed him.

But I always remembered again.

"I brought wine," I said, crossing the distance between us.

He surveyed the tray in my hands, his eyes bright with a rapid
quickening of interest. Then he glanced up at the windows, where
fat squares of daylight streamed in. "At this hour?" he asked. "I'm
meeting with a few ministers soon—it's important, according to
them anyway."

I know, I thought to myself as I smiled at him with utmost
indulgence. That was why I'd come. Yesterday, Xiaomin had overheard Wu Zixu preparing for the meeting. "It's only a few sips," I
said, pouring the yellow wine out into a deep goblet. "It'll help you
relax. And besides, I've already warmed it for you."

"It seems quite unwise," he said, but he was already reaching
for the goblet, as though his mouth and body were divorced. He

swished the liquid around a few times, took a careful sip, then a long swig. I quickly refilled it again and held it up for him. "You are my weakness, you know that?" he murmured, but drank obediently, eyes fluttering closed.

I watched the rolling movement in his throat and felt a flicker of anticipation. He was always more pliant when he was drunk, easier to manipulate, eager to agree to anything. But all those years of drinking meant he'd built up a considerable tolerance for alcohol; it would take more than a few cups to achieve the intended effect.

"I was wondering," I began slowly, filling the goblet until the wine was close to overbrimming, "whether I might join you in your meeting today. Just to watch."

He turned to me, his brows raised in surprise, though there was no trace of suspicion in his expression. "Why? It's terribly boring; I have trouble staying awake half the time, and the ministers are always busy yapping among themselves like dogs over the most ridiculous things. Most of their requests could be answered in a few simple words: *Yes,* or *Absolutely not, you utter buffoon,* or *Call the executioner.*" He made an exasperated sound, as if it pained him just thinking of it, and downed the goblet in two gulps. "I wouldn't want to subject you to that kind of torture."

Spoken like a truly great king, I mused dryly to myself. But I met his gaze and lifted my lips into a coy smile. "I know very well how boring it is for you—that is why I'm here. To keep you entertained."

He tilted his head up, studying me over the polished edge of his cup.

"After all," I went on, "it would be cruel to leave you to such tedious affairs by yourself."

He wrapped an arm around my waist, drawing me close to him in one swift movement, the action so abrupt his wine threatened to spill over. He barely seemed to notice. "Entertained, you say," he repeated. "How so?"

I chewed the inside of my cheek. Steeled myself. If I wanted to sit in on this meeting, I would need more than just wine to soften his mind. "Like this." Then I pressed one hand slowly to the flat planes of his chest, lifted my head, and kissed him.

He made a small, surprised sound with the back of his throat; perhaps he had not expected me to be so forward. But soon he was kissing me back without restraint, his hand curving against the nape of my neck, fingers tangled in my hair. He smelled like sweet wine and cold smoke; he tasted like treachery. I could feel his heart drumming under my palm, hard and fast as a sparrow's wings. His every sharply exhaled breath echoed in that vast, empty, ancient hall.

I closed my eyes and pretended it was someone else. Someone with skin as cold as ice, hair as dark as a river at midnight. His lips would be soft, his touch light. He would be controlled and careful and precise, no matter how hard his heart hammered, and I would do everything in my power to test if I could make his heart beat even faster.

When enough time had lapsed and I broke free, Fuchai's eyes were shining, his crooked smile barely suppressed, his crown tilting precariously on his head. Bright streaks of color painted his cheeks and neck. He looked already drunk. Perhaps he was. "So this is what they meant, in all the poems," he murmured under his breath, half to himself, then laughed. "And I'd thought they were just over-sentimental fools, exaggerating. Now I understand. It has never been this way, before."

With difficulty, I pushed all thoughts of Fanli from my mind, and stared up at the king of Wu. I had not withdrawn my hand yet; my fingers curled around the front of his robes. "Don't you agree that things are more fun when I'm around?"

He took another swig of his wine and dabbed absently at his lips. "Yes. Yes, indeed."

When the ministers filed into the hall, in all their stiff court finery and somber silence, they found me curled up next to Fuchai, sharing the seat of his throne. I was serving him another drink; he had drank more goblets than I could count by now, and the flushed color in his face had spread to the tips of his ears. When he spoke, his speech was slurred. "Don't just mill about; take your places."

The ministers were well trained enough to control their expressions, but I'd been trained better to read the most subtle flicker of emotions. In their eyes I saw the unspoken passages of shock, exasperation, resentment, contempt. There were ten of them in total, and I recognized the men standing at the front: Wu Zixu, with his cold eyes and lifted chin; Bo Pi, with his beefy neck and stout frame, who'd long ago started accepting bribes from Fanli and had provided us with valuable intelligence. And General Ma. I felt a sharp lurch of resentment on Zhengdan's behalf. Now that his face was no longer obscured by a heavy helmet, and he was not charging down the streets on his steed, I saw that he was good-looking, but hardly good-looking enough to carry himself with the smugness he did.

"Your Majesty." Zixu stepped forward, then hesitated. "Are you . . . drunk?" There was the faintest, upward curl of distaste to his words, the question more like an accusation, but Fuchai did not seem to notice it.

"No, not at all," he slurred, the redness in his cheeks rising. "Just having some refreshments. Surely I am allowed to keep such simple pleasures for myself? Or must every court meeting be so dull as to leave me with a headache?"

A muscle twitched in Zixu's jaw, but he dipped his head low. "Of course, of course, Your Majesty. And as for Lady Xishi . . ."

"Is there a problem? I wish for her to be here," Fuchai said with a dark, steely look that threatened death to anyone who disobeyed. Yet his hands were still gentle around my waist.

General Ma shifted forward too. Even though the meeting was indoors, he was still dressed in armor, the bronze plates on his chest and shoulders creaking and clanking together when he moved. It was not for necessity, I observed, but a mark of honor, to remind others of his position. "Your Majesty. Forgive me for being presumptuous, but . . . do you really believe it's appropriate to have Lady Xishi listen in on this meeting? For one, she is a woman—"

"Yes, believe it or not, I'm very well aware of the fact," Fuchai said dryly, his goblet dangling between his thumb and forefinger, the wine swirling within it.

General Ma looked wildly uncomfortable, but pressed on. "Still, the topics are—highly sensitive, not for just anyone to be involved in, and should any information fall upon a foreigner's ears . . ." He had said too much. He seemed to realize this even before Fuchai glowered down at him from the raised throne, the air around them deadly still with the king's power.

"Xishi is no foreigner," Fuchai snapped. "And she's certainly not just *anyone*."

I remained strategically silent, my face blank as I resumed pouring out wine.

The ministers exchanged a few uneasy looks, but after a silence, Bo Pi cleared his throat and spoke up. "Your Majesty is right. Any concubine of the king's is a valued and trusted member of the Wu Kingdom. Let us proceed with today's agenda, regarding our current military stance toward the Yue Kingdom . . ."

As he ran through a few introductory points, I studied the minister with quiet approval. So Fanli had not bribed him for nothing.

"We should launch another attack," Zixu spoke up first, his expression hard. "Strike while they're still weak. Their economy has yet to recover from the last war, and their soldiers are either injured or dead; last I heard, there were only a few thousand left in their command. It's the perfect opportunity to eradicate one of the biggest threats to our borders."

My heart struck my throat. *Another attack.* Faces and places flashed through my mind: my mother's, my father's, the frustrating but defenseless aunties down the road from our house, the morning market and riverbanks, all burned to rubble. The Yue Kingdom would not be able to withstand it.

Fuchai sipped his wine in silence, then jerked his goblet in General Ma's direction. "You," he said. "What do you think of this strategy?"

General Ma bowed. "I believe it wise, Your Majesty. The Yue may not have bothered us much in recent times, but they are like cockroaches, draining resources and scuttling about everywhere." He wrinkled his nose. "We should crush them under the heel of our boot when we can, lest they duplicate and infest our kingdom."

Remain calm, I willed myself, fighting against my rising rage. *Don't give them reason to suspect you have the Yue's interests at heart.* So instead of breaking General Ma's face with my fist, I ran my fingers down Fuchai's arm and angled my chin up at him. I felt him shiver under my touch.

"That . . . seems slightly exaggerated, don't you think?" Fuchai said, his eyes on me. "And Goujian promised he would not harm our kingdom."

The ministers exchanged another dark look among themselves.

"Can we really trust him to keep his promise?" Zixu asked. "He could be speaking with their war committee right now, readying their forces for invasion."

Before Fuchai could reply, I leaned forward. "War committee?" I repeated, frowning like a puzzled student in class. "But I thought the Yue's war committee had been disbanded after they lost, and most of the ministers were either killed or dismissed. Is there a new one I don't know about?"

Wu Zixu glowered at me. "Your Majesty, again, I must ask whether it's appropriate for Lady Xishi to be present—"

"She's only curious," Fuchai said, while I made a show of looking chastened, my gaze turned down. "And didn't you hear her? The Yue have already gotten rid of their war committee. How can they be preparing for war?"

Wu Zixu did not falter. "You don't think it possible that Goujian holds a grudge?"

"I'm so sorry to ask," I said, blinking with feigned confusion, "but . . . I don't understand. Why would he hold a grudge? Everyone knows how much Goujian looks up to His Majesty. They're friends, aren't they?"

"Yes, yes indeed," Bo Pi put in. "And he's sent many offerings of friendship: the one hundred thousand bolts of hemp cloth, the nine wooden containers of honey, the ten boats and fox pelts . . ."

Fuchai nodded, drunk and content. "He has been good to me, hasn't he? He's a humble man. Harmless."

I'd barely breathed a sigh of relief when, below us, I saw a shadow move over Wu Zixu's face. "Even if Goujian is harmless," he said, in a tone that suggested he highly doubted it, "one cannot underestimate his military advisor, Fanli."

The sound of Fanli's name—spoken out loud, in these cold halls—sent a piercing pain through my chest. I almost gasped, a tangle of emotions surfacing inside me. Nostalgia and loss and a kind of . . . possessiveness. It felt wrong, to have the enemy discuss him so casually right in front of me.

"Ah, yes, Fanli," Fuchai said. "He was the one who insisted on accompanying Goujian to our kingdom, wasn't he? That statue of ice and jade? I do remember him clearly; even in rags, he had a fine face. Lovelier than a woman's, they say."

Wu Zixu clenched his jaw. Likely, he had not expected his king's first key impression of the military advisor to be how pretty he looked. "I'm afraid you are forgetting the complete saying, Your Majesty: a face lovelier than a woman's, with *a mind deadlier than a snake's*. If he retaliates—"

"But wouldn't he have retaliated already?" Bo Pi cut in quickly. "After all the humiliation he endured at our hands?"

My heart spasmed.

"That's right," Fuchai said, as if reminiscing a distant but fond memory. I felt a frisson of panic. Whatever came next, I did not want to hear it. I could not bear to. "I remember it too. He had some pride. Even when I made him kneel on all fours, he refused to bend his spine. Not when we used the bamboos, nor when I used my boot. So much blood spilled—yet he wouldn't even beg for mercy."

I was suddenly sick. My imagination ran free with those terrible words, and I saw a vivid image of Fanli, the esteemed military and political advisor of Yue, the young prodigy, forced onto his knees before a jeering crowd of Wu noblemen and soldiers. His head would still be raised at that cool, arrogant angle, his eyes intensely black, even as the bamboo sticks whipped his back open into bloodied cuts. Soon his pristine white robes were stained red, his breaths coming out short and fast. And Fuchai loomed over him. Cruel, haughty, careless Fuchai, his leather boot coming to rest first under Fanli's chin, forcing him to meet his gloating smirk. The crowd roared in anticipation, their faces dripping with glee . . .

Wave after wave of nausea rolled through my stomach. The place where my skin still grazed against Fuchai's robes prickled.

Yet he drank on, completely oblivious. It was the easy arrogance of one who had emerged the victor of a long battle, who had seen the best men from another kingdom brought down before him. *This is why I must succeed.* My resolve curled around that one crucial line like a tightening fist.

"I still don't understand," I said timidly, my eyes wide. "Why are we spending so much time debating whether or not to defeat a kingdom that's already been defeated?"

"You make a good point," Fuchai murmured, leaning into the palm of my hand.

"*Your Majesty.*" Wu Zixu stalked forward until he was standing right under the throne, then spoke with barely controlled fierceness. "Your Majesty, please. Don't lower your guard against the Yue. Have you already forgotten your father's dying wish?"

At this, Fuchai's eyes, which were close to falling shut, opened again. "Of course I haven't," he said brusquely. "I am reminded of it every day." He squinted around the court. "Reminder! Where are you?"

Immediately, a scrawny servant ran into the hall and fell to his knees with a loud *thump*. "Your Majesty, you must remember your grudge against the Yue king for causing the death of your father!" Then, as soon as he'd finished this dramatic little declaration, he got up and exited the room.

"See?" Fuchai said to the speechless court, swishing his sleeve in an irritable gesture as he sat back. "It's rather hard to forget."

"But—" Wu Zixu tried again, his fingers quivering.

"This meeting is over," Fuchai decided, speaking over him. "I've made up my mind: We will not attack the Yue Kingdom, and focus instead on strengthening our kingdom from within. Goujian is not my enemy, nor a threat."

There was no opening left for protests. As my heart lightened, all the ministers in the room sank into a deep bow and spoke in unison: "Yes, Your Majesty."

But when Wu Zixu rose again, his glittering black eyes snapped to me, and the odd look in them made a chill snake down my spine.

"Do you know what they're all saying about you?"

I raised my eyebrows at Zhengdan and shook my head silently. We were sitting together by the palace lake, warmed by fox furs and boiled ginger tea. Above us, the bare tree branches spread themselves out silently, dusted with white snow.

Zhengdan shot me a conspiratorial smile over her teacup. "They say you're a nine-tailed fox spirit."

I laughed. "A *fox spirit?* Really?"

"Well, that's the most popular explanation. Everyone's convinced you've cast some sort of spell on the king. Or else why would he keep returning to your chambers again and again?"

"What else do they say?" I asked, curious.

Zhengdan turned to Xiaomin, who was standing behind us. Ever since the incident with the poison, she'd proved just as loyal as she'd promised, coming early every morning to greet me with both fresh gossip and an ever-changing assortment of sweets from the kitchens. *Don't tell me you've poisoned these too,* I'd said the first time she brought them. She had immediately fallen to her knees, babbling madly and swearing her innocence, until she realized I was joking.

"Xiaomin, come sit with us," Zhengdan said, beckoning the young girl over.

She startled, as if unsure whether we were really talking to her. In the palace, maids were only summoned and spoken to when there was something that needed to be done. Then she approached us with small, hesitant steps, and lowered herself slowly onto the stone bench next to us.

"What have you heard from the maids?" Zhengdan asked.

She cleared her throat. "I— Well . . . Please don't take offense, but—"

"Don't worry, Lady Xishi is very hard to offend," Zhengdan said, grinning at me. I rolled my eyes. "Just tell the truth."

Xiaomin checked the area to make sure nobody was around, then lowered her voice. "In that case . . . the ministers—not all of them, but many . . . they're concerned that Lady Xishi is too—*involved*—"

"Please don't bother phrasing it delicately," I told her, propping my chin up on my hands. "And don't sacrifice accuracy for niceties. Not when you're with me, at least."

"All right . . . They think you're meddling in affairs you shouldn't be, and you'll bring the whole kingdom to ruin," Xiaomin blurted. "And—and that all the foolish decisions the king has made can be traced back to you." As soon as the words left her lips, she flushed and looked at me with wide, terrified eyes, as if afraid I would suddenly spring down from the bench and strike her.

But I wasn't angry at all. In fact, I wasn't even surprised. How many women throughout history were blamed for the weaknesses of men? We made such convenient scapegoats. We were raised to be small, to be silent, to take whatever we were given and no more.

"Is this because of the palace?" Zhengdan asked. She absently picked up a pebble from the yellowed grass and threw it. It bounced once, twice, thrice before disappearing into the lake's icy depths with a faint splash. She frowned, unsatisfied, and tried again, her face tight with concentration. This time, it bounced seven times.

I bit back a snort. Only Zhengdan could be competitive about something like skipping pebbles when there wasn't even anybody around to compete with.

"Partly because of the palace," Xiaomin agreed. She looked sidelong at me, chewing her lower lip. The longer we spent together, the more conscious I became of just how young she was. Sometimes I was tempted to call her *xiaohai*, for little kid, but we weren't supposed to use such familiar language with the servants. And for all I joked with her, I would be lying if I said I trusted her completely.

"Whatever it is, just say it," I told her, amused.

"Is it true?" she asked. "That you asked the king to build a palace just—just for you?"

"It's true enough," I said, watching Zhengdan as she flicked another flat pebble out. It skimmed the lake thirteen times, barely glancing the water surface. "Though it'd perhaps be more accurate to say that I won a palace."

A week ago, I had brought Fuchai to this very spot and pressed a pebble into his hand, much like the one I'd given him for his birthday. "How about a competition?" I had challenged, grinning. "To make things more interesting."

"What will the winner get?" Fuchai asked.

"A wish," I said, prepared. "Any wish."

His eyes glittered. "All right. You go first."

I found another pebble half buried in the damp soil and flung it out wide at the waters, watching it hop only once, then sink somewhere far from the shore. I whirled around to find Fuchai laughing at me, clutching his side as if he'd just witnessed the world's most amusing play.

When it was his turn, his pebble skipped twice—barely more than mine, yet he cheered like a child. "Did you see that?" he asked, gloating.

"I did. And I win," I informed him.

He paused. "What?"

"I never specified the rules of the competition," I said slyly, dusting my hands. "The goal was to see who threw their pebble the farthest."

"You tricked me," he said, but without any anger. Compared to winning, he would prefer novelty; compared to a wish, he would prefer the unexpected. Still, the truth buzzed like a wasp in my stomach: this was the least of my tricks. "So," he said, arms folded, his gaze warm on me, "what do you wish for?"

"How about . . . somewhere to dance in private for you?" I replied, like it was an idea I had thought of just then. "Somewhere beautiful. Our own palace, up in the hills." Of course, I did not truly care for such a place. But I needed to drain the national treasury, divert all the funds for the military elsewhere, and a palace was the most expensive option I could think of. It was better than prized jewels, better than rare paintings, for the scale of construction involved would require extensive labor too, and resources. And once the coffers slowly bled out, every time the maids and guards and ministers walked past that new, gleaming palace, they would be reminded of their king's indulgence, his reckless, excessive spending. Even those who originally sided with him would run out of excuses to defend him, until all he had left was the illusion of me.

"I heard from the other maids that construction is already underway," Xiaomin said, snatching my thoughts away from the memory. "And he's calling it the Palace of Beautiful Women. After you."

I made myself smile. "It's sweet of him."

Xiaomin took my words with utmost sincerity. "Oh, it *is* sweet. It's so romantic. Like something from the old ballads. So many girls would be jealous—imagine having the *king* build a palace just for you." Then she caught herself and added hastily, "Not—not that *I'm* jealous—I'm not saying—I just think it's nice, is what I mean. This lowly maid would never dare develop any affections for the king . . ."

Luckily, Zhengdan turned away from the lake and spoke up before the poor girl could give herself a heart attack. "Is there anybody you *do* have affections for?" Her tone was playful, teasing. It was how you spoke to a friend.

Xiaomin lowered her head, but I could see the color creeping up her cheeks.

"There is," I said. "Clearly."

"It's nobody," she mumbled, but the color deepened, and her lips twitched into a shy smile, as if she couldn't help herself. "Just—just one of the guards—"

"Oh, so he works in the palace?" Zhengdan asked with interest.

I was suddenly interested, too, though for different reasons. Already I was imagining all the ways this relationship could play out to our advantage. If there was a guard we could distract, one we could lure to our side, then it would be so much easier to slip in and out. And guards were the key to communicating with the world outside the palace. For the longest time, this had been my dilemma: I'd gathered plenty of information but had no way of sending it to Fanli. Until now.

"He does," she said, blushing more furiously. "The first time we met—I walked by while he was training, and he was just . . . beautiful, you know? I've never seen anybody move like him."

"Does he like you back?" I wanted to know.

She didn't reply, but touched her neck. A small painted bead dangled from her necklace. It was answer enough.

"You should introduce him to us sometime," I said, keeping my voice casual. Beside me, Zhengdan flung another pebble, the motion of her wrist quick as a whip. Seventeen times. A new record. "Point him out the next time we're walking through the palace grounds."

"He's being sent off to guard the borders soon," Xiaomin told me. "But . . . he'll be returning next year, if you'd still like to meet him. He said . . . He said he'll ask for my hand in marriage once he returns." There was a distant look in her eyes as she spoke, and though her lips were chapped and her skin roughened by working through the severe winter winds, the smile on her face was serene. Joyous. The winter sun spilled light over her. It was the look of someone wholly, utterly in love. *Be careful*, I wanted to warn her, a pang in my chest, that old affliction of the heart. *Love is a knife; it cuts both ways.*

But I remained quiet.

The following winter, the construction for the Palace of Beautiful Women was complete at last. In that time, I had nearly finished my own construction of a grand map, filled with all I'd taken note of while I was here, between countless feasts and trips to Fuchai's private study and chess matches in the pavilions. It contained the entire interior of the palace, every entry and exit, every garden and chamber labeled, every pond and lake, every hidden passageway known only to the palace ladies, even the path to Fuchai's summer retreat in Mount Guxu.

I had just tucked the map away when Fuchai rushed in to invite me to visit the new palace with him. He was excited, as if the gift were made for him instead of me. I looked at the boyish flush in his neck, the thrill of anticipation written all over his face, and almost took pity.

Either way we arrived together, my arm laced through his. We must have made for quite the scene: the king with his crown hanging crooked over his midnight hair, his black eyes bright, and the lovely, wicked beauty of the legends beside him, glittering in fresh jewels and casting her silent enchantments. None of the servants lined up at the entrance dared look at me directly, but I could feel their gazes trailing after me as I walked. Perhaps they were searching for my fox tail. By the next day, I was certain the rumors would reach my ears, one more exaggerated than the other. *Let them spread*, I thought, my chin lifted. So many rumors about me had surfaced in the past year that I'd come to find them amusing;

sometimes I asked Xiaomin to recount them as bedside stories while I drifted off to sleep.

The palace rose up on the slope of Yanshi Hill. We'd timed our arrival perfectly. The sun's slanting light touched the walls in its descent over the mountainous horizon. Everything burned white and gold. And even though I had not really wanted the palace for myself, my breath still caught in my throat. It really was beautiful. It could have been a home to the gods, their divinity illuminating those tiles until they gleamed like abalone shells, skilled fingers carving out intricate designs of clouds and constellations in the pillars. Streams and ponds flowed around it, glowing blue, and the gardens were dotted with rockeries and pavilions and thickets of osmanthus trees.

"Do you like it?" Fuchai asked. He wasn't even looking at the palace, but watching me intently.

"Of course," I said.

"Truly?"

"It's even better than what I'd imagined. It's a place of dreams."

A wide smile flashed over his lips, and he led me forward by the hand. Everywhere I turned was some new wonder, some great marvel: marbled chambers and precious stones and mother-of-pearl columns and the most ornate bronze wares forged from new flame, flocks of white swans and peacocks drifting over the neatly cut lawns. Their feathers fell like snow.

"Since you like it, can you do me a favor?" Fuchai said. The chambers were so vast that his voice echoed.

I played coy, as usual. "Depends on what it is."

"Will you dance for me right now?" He made the request almost shyly.

"But there is no music," I said, laughing.

"There is. I had it prepared." He gestured to a corner I had not paid attention to yet, and indeed there were already instrumentalists setting up, guqins gleaming in the light, flutes and drums all ready.

And so I danced. My slender arms moved in graceful circles, like the swans taking flight around me, my feet soundless and nimble over the stone. I was in perfect control of my body, every limb and muscle, and as the music swelled, I felt—not happy, never quite that. But accomplished. The sun shone down on my face and Fuchai gazed on, as if everything in the world had dissolved and he would gladly relinquish anything, except me.

CHAPTER SIXTEEN

THE TRAINING GROUNDS LAY FLAT AND SERENE IN THE winter chill. The dirt was bright red, the sky behind it a deep blue; together, it looked as if the horizon had been sliced in two. The palace's best soldiers were lined up from one end of the open arena to another, their faces pink from the cold, hands gripping their swords. All stared straight ahead. They must have been freezing, yet they did not shiver, did not even waver from their positions.

But up high in the raised wooden stands, next to the king and the other concubines and palace ladies, I was warm. We were provided refreshments at five-minute intervals, and we were all dressed in the thickest coats. A hearty fire blazed below, its heat rising up to us in waves.

"This is always the most entertaining event of the year," Fuchai was explaining as he absently stroked the back of my hand. We sat at the very front, with the best view of the soldiers. Even our seats were well cushioned. "There are prizes on the line: gold, promotions, better equipment. But of course, the real thing everyone is fighting for is honor. Watch."

A gong sounded.

The soldiers broke formation and moved into a wide circle as two men stepped forward into the center. The air seemed to change, to tighten, crackling with tension. The contestants were both young, their chins still smooth, and the way they moved reminded me of the yearlings raised in the palace stables, all that raw energy and rippling muscle.

I barely managed to catch the moment when the first soldier drew his sword. It was just the rushing of silver, a blade of light. The sword clashed with the other in midair. There was a violent scraping sound before both stepped back, panting.

Yet mere seconds later, the soldier attacked again, charging forward this time with his sword raised. Dust flew from his heels, picking up in billowing red clouds. His body was a blur; light flashed off his armor. With a grunt, he swung all his weight into his next strike, his sword streaking through the air. Metal clanged. The second soldier caught the blow in his shoulder. He staggered, his sword arm shaking.

Cheers rose from the crowd.

"Is . . . that all?" I asked. "Has he won?"

Fuchai just smiled. "Keep watching."

The injured soldier seemed to sense the king's attention on him. His face burned crimson. Then he gritted his teeth and ran—tackling the other man to the ground. The *thud* of their bodies was so loud I could feel it in my own bones, but neither slowed. Their swords lay discarded in the dust. Now they were simply exchanging brutal punches, fists slamming repeatedly into flesh. One of them turned and spat out something thick and red with a white fragment mixed inside it. It looked like a tooth.

"Ah, see?" Fuchai tilted his head. "It's only just begun."

The cheers grew louder, but there was a cold churning in my belly, a sickness crawling up the back of my throat. It was difficult to forget that these were likely the very same soldiers who had invaded our lands, killed our men. The fight was so—violent. Ruthless. The first soldier was straddling the other, driving his fist again and again into the man's jaw while he squirmed, fighting for release. Seconds later, I heard the distinct crack of bone.

The concubines and palace ladies gasped in unison, but no matter where I looked, everyone was watching with glee. Everyone except Zhengdan, who was seated just behind us. Her face was tense, her brows pinched together.

She was not staring at the fight, but at General Ma in the corner.

A hoarse cry pulled my attention back to the soldiers. The current victor was grinding the heel of his boot into the other man's stomach, his expression one of cold satisfaction. For a moment, in the shifting light and shadow, he looked exactly like the man who had stormed into our house. Who had cut Susu open, left her to bleed out on the floor—

Fuchai's touch on my hand suddenly felt like ice. But I couldn't pull away on my own, not without reason. I turned around and spotted Lady Yu sitting in the back, sheltered under a painted umbrella. Despite the dust swirling around the training grounds, she was wearing a set of pristine peach-pink robes, her makeup as impeccable as ever, highlighting the fullness of her lips and the round goose-egg curve of her face.

We were trained to sense other people's attention. At once, she returned my gaze, her expression more curious than venomous. It posed a question: *Do you remember our agreement?*

Of course I did. Lady Yu's family was a crucial part of my plan.

"Fuchai," I murmured, dropping my voice close to his ear. Below us, the soldiers' cries and grunts continued, like that of animals in pain. "Fuchai, doesn't Lady Yu look beautiful today?"

"Hm?" Fuchai said distractedly, staring ahead at the training ground.

"Is that a new hairstyle?" I persisted. "It really frames her face and her figure, don't you agree?"

At last, Fuchai yanked his attention away from the bloody fight and glanced back too. Lady Yu was cooperative; she chose that exact instance to rearrange her coat, opening it up at the front so all that milky, supple skin below her collarbones was on display. Her hair was luminous, her eyes lit up like the sun on the great Lake Tai. You certainly had to give her some credit; all those years before I came, she had not enjoyed the king's affections for nothing.

By now I knew of my worth to Fuchai, but I was not arrogant enough to assume I had changed him completely from that wine-loving, women-seeking, debauched king in the stories. His eyes clung to her. "Hm," he said again, in a considering way. "I suppose you're right."

"I hear there are countless soldiers who secretly pine after her," I told him. It was a dramatic statement, but not a lie. "You see the ones who are fighting?"

Fuchai frowned. By now one of the soldiers had his arm twisted at a grotesque angle, his face white with pain as he scrabbled and writhed against the dust like a fish on land. "Yes?"

"It may be honor that they're fighting for. But . . . don't you think they might also be trying to impress?" I said no more, letting him figure it out for himself.

Soon, a dark cloud moved over Fuchai's face. There was nothing more tempting than someone others wanted, nothing more thrilling than the possibility of competition. It was like my mother used to say: The food in another's bowl is always more appealing than the food in your own.

I expected him to go to Lady Yu's side right away, but he hesitated, squeezing my hand. "Will you be lonely, if I leave?"

I will be nothing but thankful. "A little," I lied. "But I've been selfish, keeping you all to myself. And as long as you are satisfied, I'm satisfied also."

He gave my hand another light squeeze and left, moving up through the stands. There was a loud commotion. Immediately all the concubines and ladies stood and bowed low, their necks bared to him. The show was still going on in the arena, but the real show was up here now. As Fuchai took his seat next to Lady Yu, I watched how all the spectators took this detail in, their eyes flickering and mouths moving quietly. Lady Yu straightened and smiled. She was gloating.

The gong clanged again, a rich, reverberating sound. The victor staggered from the circle to wild cheers. The other soldier was dragged out. Those who had been watching from the sidelines regrouped, and new competitors entered to take their place. And so it began again: the slash of swords, singing metal, weeping wounds. One step forward, one step back. Again and again, the dirt beneath the soldiers darkened, running a deeper red with their blood, while the concubines sank comfortably into their seats, ensconced by shiny furs, and the servants came to us bearing fresh grapes on platters.

I picked at the fruits but ate very little. The sick feeling inside me grew as the rust scent of violence wafted toward us from the arena.

The sun rose higher in the cold blue sky. The circle had dwindled as more and more soldiers stepped up, only to be beaten down again. Losers were immediately eliminated. Winners then warred against winners until the strongest remained. To nobody's surprise, the only person left in the victor's circle—the one with the longest winning streak—was General Ma. A curious incident happened in every single duel he was involved in: The opponents who initially seemed both faster and stronger than he and were making notable progress would all tire dramatically near the end of the match. After all, power mattered more than competence. Those who *could* defeat General Ma didn't for fear of repercussion, of embarrassing someone of higher rank than them. The whole performance reeked of fragile egos and flattery.

One soldier had even tripped over his own feet and thrown himself flat to the ground before the general, begging for mercy.

A thin rivulet of blood trickled from General Ma's cut lip. He let it drip, then stared around him, a challenge in his eyes. "Is there anyone left to fight me?" he boomed. "Anyone at all?"

A silence. Everyone seemed quite determined to avoid his gaze.

The general smirked. "Really? Nobody dares to try their hand?"

"I will."

There was a confused pause, a rustling of fabric and metal as heads turned this way and that, trying to find the source. The voice had not come from one of the soldiers in the arena, but from the stands.

My heart seized.

Zhengdan stood up, her chin held high. She was already rolling back her sleeves, as if this moment in time was predetermined, as if she had been training for years just for this opportunity. Perhaps she had. There was a terrible sense of inevitability to it all, the cold sky and heavy silence. Years had passed since the official had appeared with her father's helmet, but she was still the same girl who had stood outside every winter morning, waiting for him to come home.

"Well?" she said. Her tone was light, almost in jest, but a dangerous note slid beneath it, like a snake through grass, prepared to strike.

It took a moment before General Ma recovered. "You?" He frowned.

"Yes, me. Is there a problem?"

General Ma spun to face the king, passing the question along silently: Is *there a problem?*

I couldn't imagine there being any specific rules that prevented palace ladies from participating in a mock duel, but I also couldn't imagine that there had been many, if any, predecessors.

Fuchai looked between the general and Zhengdan, his expression ambivalent. Everyone seemed to be holding their breath. I observed that the servants had already bent their knees, ready to throw themselves to the ground in a moment's notice if the king lost his temper. But after a beat, a smile flashed over his face like lightning. He leaned forward. "Well, this is even more entertaining than I'd anticipated," he purred. "Why not?"

Zhengdan's gaze sharpened into knives. "Thank you, Your Majesty," she said, curtsying even lower than normal.

"Are you sure you can handle him?" Fuchai asked, eyeing Zhengdan's frame. She was even smaller than I was, with arms so slender that even if you were to wrap your entire hand around her wrist, there would still be extra space left. "He will not go easy on you."

"I know," Zhengdan said, tossing her hair back. "I won't go easy on him either."

Fuchai's smile widened. "How . . . interesting. In that case, why don't you go and prepare? I'm sure we can find some spare armor for you, though it may be a bit loose."

Some of the soldiers below had started to jeer, barely suppressed snickers and side-eyed remarks fluttering among them. The concubines whispered too, though some looked genuinely impressed, while others were gazing at Zhengdan with worry, as if certain this was the last time they'd see her in one piece.

I felt a dark spike of dread. As Zhengdan made her way past me, her spine straight as any trained soldier's, I tried to summon her attention. *Stop,* I willed inside my head, clutching the edge of my seat and praying she could somehow hear me. *You're not thinking this through.*

When our eyes met, she only winked and mouthed: *Don't worry. I can win this.*

But that was exactly what I feared.

Zhengdan entered the ring transformed. Gone were the pretty butterfly hairpins, the pearls clutching her delicate throat. Her raven hair had been tucked neatly inside a bronze helmet just like the one her father had worn, her shoulders bolstered by thick padding, her body covered with shining plates that glowed like dragon scales beneath the sun. Even the lines of her face looked sharper as she took her place opposite General Ma, shifting into a fighting stance. She held a heavy sword in one hand, while her other hand was raised up, two fingers pointing to the general in a perfect straight line.

And in response, General Ma changed also. This whole time he had worn the somewhat bemused expression of one forced to fight a match that was barely worth winning. But now he must have recognized the certainty in Zhengdan's movements, the familiar way she readied her weapon.

My palms were clammy in my lap. I could scarcely breathe.

No sooner than the gong sounded, Zhengdan charged. Her sword speared through the air, shooting toward the general's throat. He swerved just in time, but it seemed more from muscle memory than strategy. His feet stumbled slightly, his heels digging into the dirt. There was a bewildered look on his face, a kind of stunned disbelief. That same look unfolded over many of the spectators sitting around me. The whispers died down; the only sound that could be heard throughout the whole training ground was the sharp hiss of Zhengdan's blade.

In action, she was so elegant. Beautiful. Her movements were fluid, like how water flows over rocks or how wind shifts through the trees. One strike bled into another, with no pauses or fumbles in between. I could have pictured her calling down red lightning with a flick of her wrist, leading a battalion of thousands into a war at the end of the world. This was her in her most natural state, doing what she truly wanted. Her footwork was unerringly certain, adjusting to the general's blunt, broad swings with ease.

One blow. Another. She advanced across the dirt, pushing him farther and farther back, her sword a blur.

All eyes were on her. Even the heavens seemed to be watching.

The girl against the general. The Yue against the Wu.

"Who trained you?" General Ma called out, barely dodging her next swing.

"Nobody," Zhengdan said. "I taught myself."

Despite my apprehension, some part of me felt a great swell of pride. If she had never left our village, if she had listened to her mother and married one of those old, lifeless, drooping-eyed men, she would have been trapped there forever, a bird caught in a cage. Everything within her would have wilted until only her beauty remained.

But here, she was radiant. She glowed with every thrust of the sword, every twist of her torso. And she was merciless.

At the next opening, she lunged, her blade stopping a bare inch from the general's throat. He froze. His sword clattered to the dust.

It was a reversal of the popular stories passed among the villagers. The beautiful girl with blood under her nails, who did not need saving from danger but was instead the danger itself.

She pressed the sword closer, close enough to slice skin if she wanted. And I knew how badly she wanted to. In my mind, I heard her voice like an echo: *One day, I will raise a sword to his neck* . . . I saw that violent impulse ride over her features now.

Before her, the general stood completely still, the tendons in his throat strained from the effort of resistance. His fear was palpable in the space between them.

"I won," Zhengdan said loudly, firmly, and let her sword arm drop.

In the aftermath, nobody moved. General Ma stared down at his own fallen weapon, his empty hands, as if unsure what had happened. He was panting, blood flowing freely from the gash in his lips, his forehead drenched in sweat. At first his cheeks splotched red. Then, as the moment stretched on, some black, ugly emotion twisted through his features. It was quick—quick enough to go unnoticed. But my fingertips tingled with foreboding.

Slow claps cut through the quiet.

They came from Fuchai. He had stood up, the silky black furs of his coat billowing around him, his mouth stretched into a wolf's grin. "That was quite the riveting performance," he said. "Truly. I've never seen anything like it."

Following his lead, the other spectators burst into applause. It sounded like the furious beat of war drums after a battle, trembling through the rust-red dirt, signaling one side's downfall. And Zhengdan stood in the victor's position, her eyes turned to the heavens, as if hoping that somebody else was watching. The sun shone bright as a god's eye; light showered over her.

Still, I could not stop myself from breaking out into a cold shudder.

I was warming my hands by the fire that night when Fuchai came into my chambers, a string of maids following close behind him. Each of them carried a lacquered box.

"What is this?" I asked, rising slowly, the silk of my robes trailing over my skin. I had freshened my powder earlier and slathered rose water over my neck, knowing he would come.

Fuchai just smiled and clapped his hands. Immediately, all the boxes were set on the ground and opened. For a moment, I was almost blinded. The brightest gems spilled out of them, forest-green jades and bronze mirrors and pearls overflowing, patterned porcelains and ivory sculptures carved in the shape of phoenixes.

"Yours, of course," Fuchai said, picking up one of the studded necklaces and walking slowly up to me. He made another small gesture, and all the maids curtsied, retreating. They had been trained well, shutting the doors behind them when they left to offer us privacy. "What do you think?"

I offered the back of my neck to him. "Is it some special occasion? Are they handing out free jewelry at the morning market?"

Behind me, I could feel him smiling. His fingers were surprisingly nimble, locking the clasp in one try. "Consider it . . . compensation. For making you sit through the rest of the duels alone." There was a sheepish note to his voice, like a child apologizing after playing when they shouldn't have, and I realized with a start that he felt guilty. This was very . . . unusual. Throughout all of recorded history, it was taken for granted that a king should have countless concubines. If he paid them the slightest attention, they ought to weep with gratitude. And if he neglected their existence, left them for dead—well, that was a natural part of the deal too. Had I managed to soften him so completely?

"That was an interesting match," I said, sidestepping the topic. Of course I wasn't really angry; I'd *wanted* him to go to Lady Yu. But it couldn't hurt to have him feel indebted to me.

"Oh, yes, wasn't it? I don't believe I've ever seen the general's face quite so red, even after seven jugs of wine. It should be a humbling experience for him."

I spun around to find him laughing.

"You're not upset?" I wondered aloud, turning back again.

"Why would I be?" His hands lingered in the place he'd clasped the necklace, the heat of his fingers brushing against my skin. "It was a competition between my palace lady and my general. Both are mine. No matter the outcome, I still win."

Sometimes he surprised me with the way his mind worked. "I doubt the general thinks of it that way," I said, feigning lightness.

"Probably not." He shrugged. "Zixu believes I should appeal to his ego a little, help him recover his pride."

Wu Zixu again. "And how does he propose you do that?"

But he was already bored of the topic. "Doesn't matter. Let's stop talking about it now," he murmured, his hand sliding down to the small of my waist. I could smell the day's blood on him, mixed with some kind of cold fragrance. "Hm?"

"It seems rather important," I tried.

He said nothing, just pressed his lips to my shoulder.

"Fuchai," I said. A mistake. I'd wanted to get his attention, but it seemed to have the opposite effect.

"I don't think I will ever tire of hearing you call me by my name." He wrapped his arm tighter around me. Pressed another kiss to my neck, his mouth grazing over the cool beads of the necklace. "Sometimes I swear—I only feel like a person when I'm around you. Does that make sense?"

"I—I think so—"

"Good."

"But Fuchai . . ."

He made a small, soft sound with the back of his throat, almost like a sigh, and in a flash, he stepped around to face me, his hand cupping my cheek. His eyes were black and dilated, his lashes so long they cast shadows in the lantern light. "You know, I used to believe," he began, his lips skimming my throat in a long, languorous line, "the heavens were especially cruel to me. They forced me onto the throne when I never wished to be king. They took my father away from me." Between every couple of words, he kissed me again, desperate and hungry and eager, like he'd been poisoned and I was the only thing that could save him. It was not unpleasant. That was the terrible thing. Physically speaking, it was . . . far from unpleasant. Even though deep in my heart of hearts I despised him, wanted him dead—my body could not help responding. "They took my friends away the instant this wretched crown was placed on my head. All those people I grew up with, studied beside; it was as if I had become a stranger to them. I had nobody to speak to, nobody to trust." He tugged at his crown as he spoke, and it slid free, his hair mussed and curling loosely in ink-black locks over his forehead. Another tug, and the crown fell onto the bed beside us, the polished gold glinting over the white sheets.

This has to violate some sort of law, I thought dimly as he kissed the edge of my jaw, the corner of my mouth, his breathing unsteady.

"I know what the ministers think of me," he continued, his voice rough. "They think I'm a disappointment, a shadow of my father. They all wish my father were the one ruling—" He huffed a bitter laugh, his nails curling against my robes. "Well, so do I. Then I would not be restricted by all this—*all this*. But the heavens must have mercy, still, because they led you to me. My beautiful Xishi." He pulled me impossibly closer, as if every inch of distance between us hurt. "You will be the death of me."

I let him run his fingers through my hair, let him push me slowly away from the blazing fire. Even as the heat spread through my body, I fought to keep my mind sober, clear as ice. It was like a game of chess. I couldn't just succumb to the experience, couldn't forget what I was here for.

"Kiss me," he said hoarsely, earnest and foolish. "Kiss me until I forget everything."

I obliged, wrapping my arms around his neck and standing on my tiptoes. His lips were terribly soft, yet they crushed mine, deepening the kiss. I could taste something sweet like peach blossom wine on his tongue. My thoughts raced ahead of my movements, jumping erratically from place to place, some less helpful than others. The rumors about him visiting every brothel in the city must have been true. His hands were skilled, clearly well practiced.

"What are you thinking about?" he asked. "Right now. I want to know."

"N-nothing."

He kissed me harder, until my mind turned to water. "Tell me."

"Nothing. Nobody, just—" *You* was what I meant to say. What had been poised on the tip of my tongue. But what came out was, "Fanli."

I did not even realize what I'd said until he jerked back as if he'd been slapped. He was still breathing hard, his lips swollen, but his eyes were wide, disbelieving. "What did you just say?"

"I—I didn't—" Hysteria surged inside me. *Explain.* I needed to explain, to make this all right again, but my head had gone completely blank. I could only hear a low buzzing sound in my ears. My heart crashed against my chest. "I—"

"You said the name Fanli," he said. There was still a raw note to his tone, like he wanted me to correct him. "Fanli. That's the military advisor of Yue."

If I didn't feel like fainting, I might have laughed. Sometimes Fuchai was so careless that he called his own ministers by the wrong name, and often addressed people directly as "you" instead of a proper title—yet *this* particular name, he recalled now without any difficulty.

"It was a slip of the tongue," I said, forcing my voice to remain level. I willed any trace of guilt away from my face. "I didn't mean it. It's just because . . ." I scrambled for some excuse. Anything. "It's only because we were talking about Wu Zixu earlier. And I—I was wondering who holds a similar position in the Yue court."

His expression was indecipherable. Even with the fire roaring, the room felt colder than ever. "While you were kissing me?"

For all my training, I could not help flushing slightly. "I . . . My mind wandered only for a second. That's all. It means nothing."

But his face was turned to the fire, his gaze distant, hands clasped behind his back, his whole body held rigid. It was a stupid thing to think at this time, especially when he had been so vulnerable only moments ago, his mouth grazing my throat like any excited, lovestruck boy, but he looked—like a king. Someone with the power to execute hundreds with a single command. Fear shot through me. "Perhaps Zixu was right after all," he murmured to himself.

It was as if someone had swung a heavy mallet to my lungs. My breathing stopped. Everything stopped. I was afraid I would shatter to the floor in pieces. This couldn't be happening. I couldn't have made such a terrible blunder, after all my planning and preparing. Yes, Zhengdan had been impulsive on the training grounds today, but I was meant to be the careful one. "Right . . . about what?"

He said nothing. His face was cold, unreachable. With a swish of his sleeves, he strode out the door. I heard the startled greetings of the maids planted outside, saw the flicker of lanterns as he passed, and felt a different kind of dread: By tomorrow, the gossip would spread about how the king had left my chambers before anything could have happened. They would all speculate over what

I'd done to enrage him, but I doubted anybody would come close to the truth. That my heart had betrayed my tongue. That for just a moment, I had been greedy and imagined somebody else's lips on my own.

Trembling, I sank to my knees, alone in that hollow room of shimmering jewels.

CHAPTER SEVENTEEN

I SPENT THE FOLLOWING WEEKS WAITING FOR SOME punishment to fall upon me. I almost wished the king had gone ahead and punished me that very night, instead of leaving my imagination to torment me. It was like holding your neck out for an execution, not knowing exactly when the axe head would fall, only that it would. Yet all was eerily calm. He made no mention of the event again, and still came to visit my chambers whenever he could. He was not cruel or cold or even petty. He admired me when I danced, listened when I sang. He smiled and teased just as easily as before, and made sure I lived in extravagant comfort. Every now and then when we were together, I would catch some shadow flickering over his face, but it was always so subtle I didn't know if it was conjured by my own paranoia, a ghost of my own guilt.

Five days passed, and all was quiet.

Another five days passed, and still all was quiet.

Just when I was starting to hope he had really forgotten about the incident, the axe swung down.

I had been summoned to the court.

There was no explanation, no information for me to glean. I could only obey. When I entered through the bronze-arched doors, everyone inside was silent, their heads bowed. A cold feeling prickled down my spine like ice water. Something was amiss. Fuchai sat high on his throne, his eyes finding mine at once. "You're here. Good."

My throat tightened. Whatever came next, I doubted it could be good.

He smiled at me, though there was an oddness to it, a stiffness. Only his skin moved, while the flesh and muscle beneath it was still as stone. His long fingers trembled slightly on the armrests. If I didn't know any better, I would say he was . . . nervous. But why? "There's someone I'd like you to meet."

"Who is it, Your Majesty?" I asked. My voice sounded so small in those grand halls, swallowed by all that dark space. I had not felt this uncertain, this powerless, since the very first day I entered the Wu palace.

Fuchai merely patted the spot next to his throne, summoning me forth. As soon as I'd taken my position beside him, he flicked his sleeve. "Bring him in," he called.

I turned, and everything inside me froze.

He entered from the far side of the hall, the sunlight flooding in from behind him, so all I could see was shadow at first, an outline. But I recognized him immediately. Even in dreams, in mist, in darkness, across the Yellow Springs, he would be as familiar to me as my own memories. His smooth stride, his straight shoulders, the proud tilt of his chin. His footsteps were silent over the well-trodden stone, his movements controlled and sleek as a predator in its own territory. My heart pounded in my throat. He drew closer, close enough for me to see his face. In all the time since we were last together, his ink-black hair had grown longer, and the marble planes of his face seemed to have been chiseled by a ruthless knife, hollowing out what little softness there'd once been. His eyes were the pitch-black of the dead, utterly unfeeling. Yet for the briefest moment, as if against his will, they swung to me, and my breath caught.

Fanli.

Flesh of my heart, light of my sun. He was here, in the enemy kingdom.

A wild storm of emotions brewed in my stomach, one nearly indecipherable from the other. If you asked me if I was happy, seeing him, I would have said yes. I felt a joy so radiant it could have transformed even those cold palace halls into a heaven, and me into a god. But in the very same instant I felt a pain worse than anything I'd endured before, sharper and hotter than when the arrowhead had impaled my shoulder, blistering and wrenching and merciless. And of course there was the dread, that cold shiver crawling down the back of my neck, all the way to my toes.

It was then that I became aware of someone watching me. No, more than one person. As Fanli moved forward, both Fuchai and Wu Zixu were studying my expression, as if determining something . . .

To determine whether you feel anything for him. Whether your heart is true. The answer came like a thunderclap. I pressed my horror down, forced my expression to remain pleasant, neutral. To look down at Fanli as if he were only an old acquaintance, nothing more.

My suspicions were confirmed when Fuchai made another lazy, halfhearted motion with his sleeve, and all the maids and ministers who'd been lining the sides of the court left, closing the wide doors behind them. All except Wu Zixu, who remained at the foot of the throne like a hound sniffing for blood.

"Do you recognize him?" Fuchai asked. He was still peering over at me, his black eyes narrowed.

I made myself look completely away from Fanli; it was like stepping over a cliff edge, like swinging an axe down on your own hand. Curving my lips into a smile of mild recognition, I replied, "I think so. He is the military advisor of the Yue Kingdom." *Yue Kingdom*, I said in that detached tone, as if it were not my home, the place that had birthed me, the place that would one day hold my bones. Sometimes it seemed Fuchai forgot I had any roots to begin with, that I was also a fully fleshed person with my own family and worldly attachments. I had often resented him for it, but today, I prayed to every deity in the sky, every god of the clouds and spirit of the earth, that he would continue forgetting.

The crease between Fuchai's brows cleared ever so slightly, though his jaw remained tensed. Then he stood, a king raised to his full height and glory, his crown perched atop his head, and opened his arms out to Fanli in what could almost have passed for a brotherly gesture if one did not know the dark history that ran between the two. "Fanli, how good to see you again. It's been too long."

Fanli stopped three feet away, his cold eyes focused only on the Wu king. My heart strained toward him. "Likewise," he said, his voice light, emotionless. He did not even acknowledge my presence.

All this time, I had missed him, missed him so potently my chest ached. But somehow I missed him more now that he stood here in the flesh, as if those few feet of distance burning between us stretched into miles. I could have bolted from the king's side, run to him, thrown my arms around him, damn all the consequences. I could have kissed him as if history did not exist, as if war was only myth. I could have grazed my fingertips over the line of his cheekbones, taken his slender hand in my own. *Could, could, could.* All those possibilities opening up again, blooming in his presence. But instead we remained in our respective positions, like two perfect strangers.

"Have you met my newest concubine?" Fuchai gestured toward me, as one would a grand prize. I dipped my head, hoping this would be the end of it. But he beckoned me closer, sliding me onto his lap, his arm draping over my bare shoulder. Just that morning, he'd asked me to wear the robes he'd had tailored for me, a set made of pink silk as thin and delicate as cobwebs, with lustrous pearls that glinted when I moved, the fabric all but falling down at the top and rising too high at the legs, revealing moon-bright skin and flesh. It was an impractical piece, made for the pleasure of the viewer rather than the wearer. Now I saw that this was by design too.

Quiet rage simmered in my veins, joined by some raw, bitter feeling like betrayal. How long had he been planning this? Since Fanli's name slipped my tongue, or perhaps even before that? How many nights had I lain beside him, all while he devised ways to test my feelings toward another man? I felt sick thinking about it.

But I was giving the king too much credit. Fuchai was my greatest enemy, but he was not a naturally suspicious person; it would have been Wu Zixu who'd conceived of the plan to begin with.

I would not allow him the satisfaction of succeeding.

"Isn't she beautiful?" Fuchai gloated, lifting my chin up on two sharp fingertips, another hand reaching over to stroke the side of my cheek. I made myself lean in, gaze up from under my lashes as though my eyes held only him.

Yet in my peripheral vision, I sensed Fanli's keen attention on the two of us. All his thoughts and emotions were wiped clean from his face. Only his left hand curled inward, forming a fist by his side.

His voice was impressively steady when he replied, "Of course she is, Your Majesty. We chose the best from our kingdom to pay tribute to you."

"Oh, I almost forgot." Fuchai laughed, the sound rolling through the vast chambers. "You played a role in picking her for me, didn't you? What excellent taste. I must admit I'd underestimated you, Fanli—from everything I'd heard about your reputation, I thought you had no opinions of women. Do you remember when you served me here in the Wu? All those pretty girls I sent your way—yet you refused to see a single one of them."

I stiffened. Though the king's voice was casual, there were little knives concealed behind those words, ready to cut upon the first glimpse of flesh.

"It is hardly a matter of taste, but objectivity," Fanli returned, as unflinching as ever. "I daresay anyone who sees her would be unable to deny her beauty."

"You're right, indeed." Fuchai drew me closer to him, so all I could breathe in was his scent, those dark, sweet notes of ink and sword polish and earth at midnight. When I had first entered the palace, I could always smell the fragrance of other girls' perfumes lingering on his clothes. But now his scent was entirely his, and whatever perfume marked him was mine. It ought to please me, to serve as proof of my power, my influence, but it was difficult to rejoice with Fanli standing before the throne, gazing up at the two of us. "Now that I think of it, I should thank you," Fuchai added, one corner of his lips lifting into a crooked, wolfish smile. "Truly. I don't believe I've slept so well ever since she came to my palace."

Fanli's expression remained inscrutable, carved from the purest jade, but I saw a faint muscle jump in his jaw. The color in his eyes deepened.

Stop talking, I willed Fuchai silently. *Please. Just let him go.*

He did stop talking—but it was only to lift his mouth to the shell of my ear. His warm breath tingled over my skin, as if nobody else was in the room. His pulse beat thick and hot next to mine, and I fantasized—a million terrible things. Most of all to run a blade through his neck, so his blood would flow and he would crumple on his own throne.

Before us Fanli stood still as a statue, his lips pale and set into an unyielding line. I saw the way Fuchai raised a brow at him, their gazes meeting as the king's arm tightened around my waist, everything in his eyes storm-dark and goading. If the two of them had been placed in battle, it would take the space of a breath for Fanli to triumph over Fuchai. But a battlefield was a battlefield, and a court was a court. They were separate spheres, and here, Fuchai held all the power.

A long moment passed. Silence. Only I could hear the violent rushing of blood in my ears, like the sound of ten thousand rivers flowing at once.

At last Fuchai reclined in his throne, his embrace loosening. Fanli had scarcely reacted, and I had forced my features to remain blank the entire time. Surely, by now we had passed whatever perverse test he and Wu Zixu had come up with? Fuchai nodded, a small, almost imperceptible motion, and relief shuddered through me. It was over. It had to be—

A flash of silver.

Then red.

I choked on a silent scream. Zixu had darted forth and drawn his sword, moving too quick for the eye to track. Now his blade had pierced Fanli's chest. Already blood was blooming from the wound, darkening his pale blue robes, slicking Zixu's outstretched hand. Fanli's features were strained with pain, a tendon standing in his neck, but he made no sound. No movement.

This can't be real. This can't be. I felt sick, delirious, like the world was spinning away from me. My skin flashed cold. I wanted to scream until my throat bled, to wrench the sword from Zixu's grip, to kill him. I wanted to kill everyone in this room except Fanli.

Fanli, who couldn't die. Fanli, who was bleeding.

Pain pulsed through me, as acute as if the blade were caught in my own chest, pushing past my ribs. It hurt to breathe.

"What—" There was a horrible gurgling sound when Fanli spoke, yet his tone was that of someone asking an innocuous, unrelated question, one they were only half-interested in. "What exactly—is the point of this?"

"Sorry," Fuchai said with a small, sheepish smile. I was still stuck on his lap, forced to watch from a distance. Zixu's grip on the sword hilt didn't waver. How close was it to Fanli's heart? "I was speaking with someone the other day, and I recalled that you'd killed a good deal of my men in war. Obviously not enough for you to *win*, but, well, a loss is still a loss. And I know, I know," he continued without any haste, his voice almost a purr, as if Fanli were not close to death, "these are old grudges. But wouldn't you rather me take whatever resentment I have out on you now, and call it even, then for me to remember at some later point, when I'm in a much fouler mood, and decide to raze all your villages? You are a person of intellect. You must agree with me."

Fanli did not answer. His face was draining of color by the second, his eyes two black stones. His blood dripped steadily, pooling beneath his feet.

I couldn't bear it any longer. I opened my mouth to yell, to demand that someone save him, but his eyes suddenly cut to me, a warning burning in them. Though the palace chambers were all but quiet, save for his ragged breathing, I heard his voice as clearly as if he'd spoken out loud: *It's a trap. Don't fall for it, Xishi. You're smarter than that.*

I clenched my jaw. Beneath the buzz of my panic, the thunderous beat of my heart, I understood that this was the ultimate test.

If I proved overly concerned for him, if I gave Wu Zixu and Fuchai any reason to suspect our relationship was anything beyond what was normal, then all our plans would be ruined. All that time I'd spent training with him, all my days wasted away from home, all my nights curled up alone in the cold, empty chambers, dreaming of him. All our scheming and strategizing, all our kingdom's hopes and dreams.

"What do you think, Xishi?" Fuchai asked, turning to me, his movements slow and leisurely, another hand coming up to tuck a strand of hair behind my ears. Before, I had thought that I couldn't possibly hate him more than I already did; I was horribly mistaken. "This man has wronged me in the past. How should I punish him?"

My throat ached as I made myself laugh, a bright, tinkling sound, as if the person suffering meant nothing to me, instead of everything. I had to convince the king. That was the only way he would release Fanli alive. "However you like, Your Majesty," I said, smiling slyly. I trailed a finger down his robe sleeves, over the place where a tiger was embroidered in silver thread. "Whatever makes you satisfied."

And there was that dog of a man, Wu Zixu, staring up at me. He twisted the sword in deeper, and a harsh breath escaped Fanli's clenched teeth, the first noise of pain. He swayed for a moment, his feet unsteady.

My head was on fire, my heart disintegrating. I wanted only to sob, but I just watched. I could not be the one to call for this to end. It had to be Fuchai, or Zixu.

"It hurts, doesn't it?" Fuchai drawled, casting him a smile that revealed two pointed teeth. "Does it hurt as much as those scars on your back?"

Fanli merely looked back at the Wu king, his gaze steady and sharp as sword points, his back held deliberately straight. I had learned this about him long ago: he would never give anyone the pleasure of seeing him struggle. He hid all his pain, his doubts, his fears, and was so successful at it that the rumors had immortalized him as someone who felt nothing, who had no weaknesses, no soft spots from which to draw blood. But I knew him. I'd felt the stuttering beat of his heart, listened to the hitch in his breath. At the end of the day he was only a boy, too stubborn and disciplined for his own good.

I clenched my fingers inside my sleeves so tight I thought my knuckles might crack. *Enough*, I willed. *Please. Enough. Stop this. I will do anything, so long as you stop this.*

Another hiss. Another cold inch of the blade, pressing into flesh. I bit down on my tongue to stop from sobbing. One more move, and—

"This is getting rather tedious," Fuchai said, rolling his eyes. He leaned back in his throne. "What is the point of tormenting someone if they won't even react? He really is made of stone. Zixu, you can stop now."

The minister looked unsatisfied, but nodded and tore his sword free with a terrible ripping noise. Blood splashed onto the palace floor. Fanli reeled back, his hand clutching at his wound, and steadied himself against the nearest pillar. I watched the sharp, staggered rise and fall of his shoulders. A dark strand of hair had slipped free from his neat topknot, hanging past his jaw. Sweat beaded above his brows. After a strained moment, he asked, his voice low and forcibly controlled, "Was there anything else you wanted, Your Majesty?"

Fuchai considered it for a beat. "No, nothing I can think of. Oh—do pass along my warm greetings to Goujian, won't you? You've been *so* wonderfully generous to me."

"Of course."

Fanli began to turn with the stiff, wooden movements of one

in silent agony. But as he did, he caught my eye. Just for a second, shorter than an exhaled breath. His complexion was pale and drenched in sweat, his mouth stained with his own blood. Yet I could've sworn his lips tugged up, the look on his face something like pride.

CHAPTER EIGHTEEN

FANLI LEFT A TRAIL OF BLOOD BEHIND HIM.

I waited until Fuchai was called away to another meeting before following. I kept my face neutral, my movements unhurried as I searched for the signs of where Fanli had gone. The dark red smeared over the flat white tiles, caught on the overhanging twigs. Like that of an animal injured during a hunt, dragging its weak body away from the hounds to lick its wounds in silence. Blood, blood, blood, in the shape of his footprints.

I imagined him collapsing somewhere in the vast palace all on his own, his body turning cold. I imagined him stumbling through the darkness, hands reaching for support where there was none to be found. Nothing to hold on to. Nobody to help him.

My heart felt as if it were shedding flesh.

Around the corner of an empty corridor, the blood seemed to thicken and spread. It dripped from the leaves of a bamboo stalk, violently bright against the subdued greens. The trail stopped here.

I looked around, my breathing faint, my panic swelling fast

beneath the surface. Nobody ever came to this part of the palace; the closest chambers belonged to Lady Gu. Zhengdan had heard from the other ladies that she possessed a strange aroma, one that caused the grass to wither and the water to grow stale. Lies, of course, likely spread by a scheming minister or another jealous concubine to discourage Fuchai from giving her his attention. The only thing I could smell in the air now was the fragrance of bamboos and the rust of blood.

He had to be here. He *had to*. But where—

Suddenly, a hand clamped down over my mouth.

My scream died in my throat when I saw his face. Fanli, his eyes dark and urgent as he dragged me behind the closest wall with him, so we were both hidden by the shadows.

For a moment there was only perfect, shocked silence between us. He was standing—or trying to. He dropped his hand from my lips and leaned a shoulder against the brick, his posture strained, his features stiff with pain. My gut lurched when I saw how far the blood had already spread. The front of his robes looked as if it had been dyed red.

"You shouldn't have followed me here," he whispered. Each word sounded like it cost him something.

I swallowed. Blinked back the burning sensation in my eyes. "I know," I said. "I know, I'll leave quickly. I just need to see—I need to keep you alive."

Somehow, he managed to smile. A thin trickle of light touched his face, patterned by the gaps between leaves. "I'm fine."

I could have hit him then, if he were not injured. "You're *not* fine. You have to get out of the palace. You were—You're bleeding, Fanli, and he used his sword—He cut you with . . . There's so much blood—" I was choking on some invisible blade in my throat, all the emotions I'd swallowed down in his absence. Everything was a haze, the background a distortion of shapes and colors. Nothing felt real. "God, how is there— How is there so much blood? What did he *do* to you? How could he—"

"Xishi." His voice was so tender. So familiar. "It's really not that terrible. I won't die from this; the wound should be a safe enough distance from my heart—"

"Don't move," I commanded, speaking over him. *Bandages.* I needed bandages, something to stem the blood, but my hands were empty. After a split second's hesitation, I grabbed his sleeve and tore a long, uneven strip of fabric from the hem.

"Has their king harmed you?" Fanli asked. His voice came from above me as I bent to wrap the fabric around his chest. I could see its staggered rise and fall, the effort of a single breath.

He has harmed me more by injuring you.

"No," I said. "He hasn't."

"Then has something . . . happened between you two?"

"It's my fault." I was glad not to be looking at him. Shame and guilt tore through me from heart to stomach. "It's all my fault. I wasn't thinking properly. I didn't . . . I made a mistake."

"What?"

It was hardly the time for embarrassment, yet I felt heat suffuse my cheeks when I replied, "I said your name. When he kissed me, I . . . I said your name."

A beat.

He was so quiet that I couldn't resist gazing up at his face, terrified of what I would see. I did it slowly, taking in the sharp tilt of his chin, the cold line of his lips—and at last his eyes, which were scorching on mine. My heart throbbed.

"I'm really sorry," I went on, scrambling to fill the silence. "I really . . . I shouldn't have said it. I should have prevented it, somehow, and . . . protected you from this. From all of this." I finished arranging the fabric over his wound, then stretched it out as hard as I could.

A hiss escaped his teeth.

"Sorry," I whispered again. My hands shook as I fastened the final knot. The makeshift bandage was messy, clearly wrapped in a haste. It would stop him from bleeding out for now, but what if he didn't make it out of the palace in time? What if the wound got infected on his way back to Yue? There was another trembling sensation deeper inside me, as if a fanged creature were burrowed under my skin and was desperate to escape.

As if I were one breath, one break away from shattering completely.

"What if I left with you?" I blurted. The very sight of his blood wounded me, made something in the back of my mind unravel.

Fanli's attention sharpened on me. I saw him waver, felt his heart falter—if only for a fleeting second. The possibilities seemed to flash across his eyes, like stars streaking across the sky. Then he steeled himself. Shook his head. "You can't."

"Who's to say? Who's there to stop us?" I knew that I was being irrational, that to even speak the fantasy out loud was dangerous, but I was so achingly tired of pretending. Of being selfless. "What if we snuck out of the palace together, right now? I'll bring you to a physician and take care of you while your wound heals. And afterward, you could resign as minister, and I could create a new identity— *Why do you keep shaking your head?*"

"I vowed to His Majesty that I would help him get his revenge," Fanli said softly. "You're right. He could not do anything to me if I really resigned. I've kept too many secrets of his; I have too many valuable connections. He cannot afford to hurt me without hurting himself also. But until your mission is complete, we have to honor our promises to the kingdom."

"But—"

"I know," he said. Closed his eyes. "I know."

My next breath deflated. We had made a choice. From the

moment we met by the river, we had been making choices—but this time, it felt fatal. Final. The forked road we'd been walking on ended here, and from now, no matter what happened next, there would be only one single path leading down into the darkness.

And as though the universe wished to hasten our descent, footsteps sounded over the stone in the distance. Guards. They would be patrolling the lanes at this hour. If they saw me emerge from behind Lady Gu's chambers, they would know something was wrong.

"You have to go," Fanli said. He pressed one hand to his chest, as if to physically force back the pain. "I'll be all right. Believe in me."

Liar, I wanted to scream, but we didn't have any time left. The footsteps were drawing closer. Still, I remained frozen to the spot, my gaze clinging to his face, his fragile complexion, his drawn posture. I wanted to stare at him just a little longer. I wanted the world to freeze.

"Xishi. Go."

How ironic it was, that when we were apart, all I wished for was to be with him. Yet as soon as we were reunited, all we did was tell each other to leave.

"Go," he said again. Pleaded. "Before you get caught. Run."

I ran without looking, without thinking. Tears stung my eyes, burned in the back of my throat, but I could not let them spill. Always those servants in the shadows, silently observing everything. I ran faster, my feet pelting the stone. My robes flowed loose behind me, tearing against the wind. Never before had I considered myself a violent person, but I wanted desperately to rip the world apart. To set fire to something, just for the perverse pleasure of watching it burn. The vermilion palace walls bled past my vision, every corridor and hall and footpath blurring together. It was all just a maze, I thought hysterically. A gilded prison. I would be doomed to wander this place forever and ever and ever, until my heart rotted in its depths. Still I ran onward, as if giving chase. I could see my future moving away from me, as distant as a star, my life caught in the tides of something so much greater than I was.

Powerless, powerless, powerless.

The word echoed in my head like a taunt. And no matter where I looked, it seemed to stare back at me, that age-old curse. The maids sweating as they hurried from chamber to chamber, carrying old sheets and fresh water. The seamstresses walking in a single uniform line, their hands rubbed raw from holding needle and thread.

I did not realize where I was headed, who I wanted to see, until I threw open the doors to Zhengdan's bedchambers.

"Zhengdan," I cried out. My voice echoed, then fell into the still air, like a stone in an empty well. An odd scent reached my nostrils. I should have sensed it then, but I was too distraught, my breath choked out in sobs. All I could see in my head was the sword piercing Fanli's chest, again and again. "Zhengdan. Zhengdan, are you—"

Then my eyes caught on her robes.

That was all I noticed, all I absorbed. I thought her robes must have fallen to the floor beneath her bed. She'd always been a little messy when it came to such matters, choosing to pile her dirty clothes together until she ran out of things to wear. But then I looked again, and my heart dropped. It wasn't just her clothes, but *her*. She was lying sprawled on the ground, her eyes half-open. Her skin was a terrible color, paler than death.

An empty vial rolled next to her limp form.

"Zhengdan." I crouched beside her, my fingers trembling. I couldn't see any injuries. "What—I don't understand—"

She was still conscious. She turned her head slightly, wincing, and frowned up at me. Fresh blood shone on her lips. "Have you been crying?" she asked, her voice a croak. "Did somebody hurt you? Tell me . . . who."

I shook my head fiercely. My mind had gone white, devoid of any thoughts except: "I'm—I'm going to get the physician. They'll know— They'll be able to help you— Just wait—"

"They won't come."

"What?" I couldn't make sense of it. I was panicking, my heart caught in my throat. "What do you mean? It's their job— They have to—"

Her lips worked into a weak smile. "I mean they're not allowed. I've already . . . been deemed guilty. Nobody can escape . . . punishment."

"By who? Who wouldn't—" I cut myself off. I knew, then. The bitter smell in the air seemed to sharpen, and I noticed for the first time the bejeweled dagger lying just out of reach of her fingers. It was an ornamental dagger, meant only to be admired, not used. I stared at the vial again. There was a special kind of poisonous ball made from herbs that dissolved the organs from within: It was the official punishment used for theft. "General Ma," I said with a creeping sense of disembodiment. My voice didn't seem to belong to me. "He framed you."

"I should have . . . expected it," she said, grimacing. Her breathing sounded fainter and fainter the more she spoke, like she barely had the energy left to do even that. "I—humiliated him—"

No, I should have expected it. Black bile filled my mouth. I had feared he would get his revenge one way or another, and this sort of cowardly trick—framing someone for stealing an expensive dagger—seemed exactly like something he'd do. I should've been on guard. I should've struck first, convinced Fuchai to have the general removed. Better yet, killed.

But just like with Fanli, I knew there was someone else behind the scenes, pulling all the strings. Someone who'd always suspected Zhengdan and me.

"I don't regret it though," Zhengdan said softly. "It was . . . the best moment of my life. Seeing the . . . look on his face. Do you think . . . my father was watching?"

It was the first time she had mentioned her father in years.

"Yes," I whispered. "Of—of course."

"Good. Good. If only I could have . . . fought them all." And she laughed, a huff of sound that quickly disintegrated into a horrible, hacking cough. She covered her mouth with a white napkin. When she lowered it again, it was speckled with blood.

My vision flashed red.

I was going to die.

I was going to kill someone.

"You still haven't . . . told me, Xishi-jiejie," Zhengdan whispered. "Who upset you? Perhaps—when I turn into a ghost . . . I can haunt them on your behalf—"

"*Don't say that*," I said sharply. I could feel the cracks forming under my skin, everything threatening to break apart. What would remain, even? I had nothing left. "Please," I said, quieter, desperate. "I can't bear it . . ."

"I'm not scared . . . of dying," Zhengdan said. "I just wish . . . I could accompany you for longer . . ."

"I'll murder him," I whispered vehemently, my nails digging into my palm. The images joined together in my mind: Zhengdan's pallid face, her crumpled form; Fanli's expression of silent pain, his limping figure. All that I held dear torn away from me, their suffering dangled right before my very eyes while I could only watch and pretend my heart wasn't eating itself whole. *Powerless, powerless, powerless.* "I'll cut him to pieces with his own sword."

"Don't, Xishi. I don't want you . . . staining your hands . . . for me." A violent tremor passed through her body. She winced and curled up against herself, like an infant in a mother's womb. Her eyelids drooped. "Why is it so . . . so cold in here . . ."

"It's because the maids haven't changed the firewood today," I babbled, drawing her body onto my lap and covering her with my coat. She was so light she barely weighed anything at all. "I'll start the fire later. Soon. And then—and then you'll feel better."

"Yes. That must be why," she murmured, closing her eyes. I had to lower my head just to hear her. "I feel . . . better already."

I wrapped my coat tighter around her, feeling the warmth of her skin fade. Her pulse ran as shallow as a mountain creek in the dry winter, and it was growing duller by the second. Zhengdan. My brave, beautiful, reckless friend. My family away from home. The girl who should have lived a hundred summers, burning as bright as a comet in the sky. Now I watched her light die.

"It hurts," she croaked.

"What does?"

"Everything." Then, as if she regretted saying it aloud, amended: "Only . . . a little, though. I can . . . handle it."

I cradled her neck and felt my heart collapse.

"Jiejie . . ." She looked like she was about to tell me something, but when she opened her mouth again, no sound came out, just a dark trickle of blood. *Jiejie.* A sound rose inside me, part sob and part scream. All this time, I had grieved the death of one sister—I could not bear to grieve another. It was too much.

Her head lolled back in my lap. She had gone completely still, her pulse silent as a grave, but I held on to her. Rubbed her limp, frozen hands to warm them. I would light the fire. I would heat up this whole room. And when that didn't work—I would burn this kingdom down to ashes, turn all its men into smoke. I would, I would.

I did not weep.

My tears had run dry, my heart a dark chasm. Any lingering sentiment, any softness—it had been scrubbed completely clean, like the sand from inside a dosinia shell. All that remained was a white, cold fury. And I knew exactly what I had to do.

I set Zhengdan's body back down on the ground. Wiped her blood from my fingers. Straightened my cloak. As I turned, I caught my reflection in the bronze mirror on her bedside table; my face looked hollow, my eyes so black they seemed to absorb all light. For the first time, I caught a shadow of the enchantress they all said I was, the legend I would become. I could barely even recognize myself.

Then I walked back to my chambers all alone, my back straight and my footsteps firm as though nothing had happened, and awaited the news.

Just as expected, Fuchai came later that afternoon, his mouth set into a grim line. "There's something I must tell you," he said. His voice was soft, and he looked genuinely regretful. Perhaps he already felt guilty about the meeting with Fanli, now that he'd come to the conclusion Fanli was no threat. "I'd suggest you sit down first."

I sat obediently on my bed with a look of perfect confusion. "What is it? What's wrong?"

"It's the palace lady, Zhengdan," he told me. *Of course it is.* He reached for my hands, the same hands that had cradled Zhengdan's cheeks while she withered, her insides eaten away by poison. I could still smell the stench of herbs and blood in her room. I could still feel the unnatural coolness of her skin. Bile bubbled in my throat; I swallowed it, forced myself to keep still. "She was caught stealing, and as a result . . ." He hesitated. "She has been punished. They've already buried her body."

It was then that I delivered one of the greatest performances of my life. My body swayed, as if I might faint. I let the shock show on my face, then anguish, my eyes wide and my lips trembling. A shame that nobody else was around to appreciate my acting. Zhengdan would have found it impressive. "What?" I said.

"I understand this can be quite overwhelming," he continued, rubbing a consoling hand over my back. "Especially since she has served you for a while now. But General Ma spotted her taking a highly valuable dagger with his own eyes. That same dagger was found later in her bedchambers. We are not sure what she intended to do with it but . . . The evidence is irrefutable."

I stared at him and wondered how big a role he'd played in helping plant that evidence there. Had he lent the dagger to General Ma himself? Or had he simply turned a blind eye as his ever-helpful minister, Wu Zixu, plotted the scheme under his nose? "That's terrible," I made myself say, dabbing at my eyes with my sleeve. "But—well, in that case . . . I'm glad you're safe. I hate to think what might've happened otherwise."

His pupils narrowed into two small, dark points. I felt his fingers tremble. "Truly?"

"Truly, what?"

"You care so much about my safety?" He gazed down at me fiercely, the look in his eyes wild and hopeful and terrible. His grip tightened over me, but for all his firmness, his kingly authority, I could sense the uncertainty quivering beneath it, like a young boy clutching desperately to a kite string, afraid it would fly away at any moment.

"Of course," I lied. It was all I ever did these days. "You are what matters most to me. There is nobody else but you."

He released a sigh through his teeth. Lay back on the bed beside me. "Sometimes," he murmured, "I admit . . . I find it hard to believe that you could ever reciprocate what I feel. You must know what you do to my heart." He tugged my hand down as he spoke, bringing it to his chest. I felt the rapid *thud-thud-thud* of his heart. How easy it would be, I wondered, my eyes fluttering shut briefly, to rip it out.

Patience, I willed myself. One step at a time.

"Are you convinced now, my king?" I asked, lying down next to him until our shoulders were close to touching. With my other hand, I turned and stroked his cheek with all the false tenderness I could muster. "Or do you need more convincing still?"

"I . . . No." He swallowed. "After today, you have more than persuaded me." Then he looked at me again, his eyes fringed by those long lashes. "Are you really all right? I always thought you were quite fond of her."

A dagger jumped to my throat. I savored the pain silently, let it harden me. "It's you I'm worried about, Fuchai," I said.

"Me?"

"Think: In one day, the Yue's military advisor has been greatly injured, and their hand-chosen tribute has been killed. If word of any of this reaches King Goujian, I'm afraid it would greatly sour the relationship between the two kingdoms. Wars have been waged for less, have they not?"

He frowned, but didn't speak.

I treaded on carefully, as though over ice. "I can help you smooth things over," I said. "I was born in Yue, after all, and am more familiar with their customs. And King Goujian is a reasonable man. We'd need only explain that Zhengdan had committed a grievous crime first. This need not devolve into something terrible. I am only afraid, well . . ."

"Afraid of what?"

"It sounds awful, I know, but . . ." Again I hesitated on purpose, pursed my lips. "Whoever advised this course of action seems not to have the interests of the Wu in mind. It is almost as if . . . they *wish* to spark a war." There was no need to specify who. It could only be Wu Zixu.

His gaze sharpened. He sat upright in an instant, his black hair lightly mussed and falling over his eyes. He raked an irritable hand through it. "What are you saying?"

"I have already said too much."

"No, I want you to tell me the truth." More quietly, he added, "There is nobody around me I can trust."

If this were any other day, I would have felt a dull stab of guilt. But Zhengdan's blood still lingered on my fingers. Fanli's silhouette still burned in my mind. As it was, I did not even flinch. "I was passing by the Hall of Celestial Harmony yesterday night when I heard this male voice . . ." I conveniently omitted the fact that I had passed by on purpose, having received notice from Xiaomin that Wu Zixu was there. "I could not quite place who the voice belonged to, only what they were saying. But the State of Chu came up."

Alarm rippled over Fuchai's face. "The State of Chu?"

"Something about it being the right opportunity, if everything went to plan . . . I did not pay it too much attention at the time, and perhaps I am wrong to think anything of it now—perhaps they were referring to some kind of trade. Yet I cannot help wondering . . . If the Wu and the Yue were to be reengaged in battle, who would stand to gain the greatest advantage?" I had finished weaving my embroidery. Now I could only hold my breath and pray he recognized the picture within it.

"That is . . . interesting indeed." His features were cast in shadow, so it was difficult to decipher his expression. But then he stood, brushing his robes, and muttered under his breath: "And here I thought Zixu had cut all ties with the Chu. He had sworn it."

I feigned surprise. "Zi-Zixu? As in . . . your advisor, Zixu?"

"The very one."

"Surely not," I said, clapping a hand to my heart. How naive I must have appeared, how wonderfully guileless. "Even though he's always been very adamant on conquering the Yue, surely he wouldn't go *so far*—and he is respected by many for his wise counsel to your father . . ."

The corner of Fuchai's lips twisted. His father had always been a sore subject, a constant wound in his pride. Sometimes you had to know precisely where to rub the salt. "My father may have trusted him. That doesn't mean I should."

I could almost see the poisonous seeds I'd planted sprouting before me, their darkness blooming in his mind. Trust was such a fragile thing; it took decades to consolidate, seconds to shatter, and a lifetime to repair again. I hid a smile. If the ministers called me a fox spirit, a witch—then a witch I would be. Whatever it took. "Come," I said, pulling him back to me and drawing down the veil of the canopy bed, so all our world was covered in red silk and thread. "Do not fret over it now, my king. We can always discuss again when the morning comes."

He sighed, massaging his temples. "It's all so exhausting."

"I know," I said. It was time for the next step of my plan. "What do you say we take a pleasure trip somewhere? Just the two of us? I've heard so much about the beautiful canals of the capital, yet I'm afraid I haven't had many chances to admire them."

"A pleasure trip," he repeated.

I waited, my heart thrumming like an eagle desperate for flight.

"Yes, that sounds wonderful," he said. "I will ask them to prepare a boat."

"Perfect." With that, I pressed my lips gently to his, sealing the poison within him.

When morning came, the boat had already been readied and docked outside the palace gates. It was made of a bright red wood so polished that it shone, and the side was carved into the shape of a dragon's undulating body, every individual scale etched into that glossy surface, its tail flaring out like flames. In motion, I imagined it looked like a real dragon diving in and out of the waters, its head reaching up from the emerald waves.

The trip was meant to be a private one, but as always, the king and I were not really alone. Among the crew on the boat were three maids, three servants, two chefs, a seamstress, a fisherman, and two experienced helmsmen who took turns with the oars. I was equally worried the boat would not be able to hold all our weight and curious as to how the seamstress would even serve her purpose.

"Where to?" Fuchai asked as the boat rocked back from the docks.

Home, I wanted to say, but I knew it was the one place I could not return to. Not yet.

"Anywhere," I said, breathing in. The air smelled like brine, like unshed rain. "Take me somewhere beautiful."

And so we went. The hour was early enough that a fine mist still hung over everything like a spell, softening the edges of the stone banks and arched bridges. Ancient buildings rose up around us, their walls a faded gray-white and covered with thick, crawling ivy. The sky shaded to a rose blush, then to a pale cornflower blue.

I sat by the very edge, as far as I could go without danger of falling overboard, letting the breeze whip my face. White foam frothed from the splashing oars, and the slow lull of the boat was almost a comfort. It was all fresh air, wide open space, the canals running to the end of the world. I could pretend the palace was gone, could act like there were no kingdom gates to hold me, only—

"What are you thinking about?" Fuchai's voice broke through the peace.

Only it was all an illusion. I had come here for a purpose, not pleasure. "Just . . . remembering," I said. Villagers filled the paths around the canals, noblewomen and vendors and scholars fanning themselves as they walked. Customers wove in and out of the stalls, buying slices of honeydew and jade trinkets and grasshoppers in little bamboo cages. Black smoke billowed from woks. *Smoke and salt*: It was how the poets always described the mortal realm. I could smell it, taste it on my tongue. The boat drifted on. We passed by a little girl carrying bolts of silk in her scrawny arms; the fabric was piled so high it nearly blocked her whole face from view. Yet her steps over the damp tiles were sure and steady.

"She seems quite young to already be working," Fuchai said.

I glanced at his face. He was being serious.

"You do not know what it's like out there," I told him. "In any village, girls half her age would be working harder jobs."

"Really?" His eyes widened.

Him and his sheltered naivete. "Of course."

"But why?"

Did he really not know? No, his expression was pure innocence, a boy who had spent his life behind golden walls. Even when blood flowed before him, it was onto marble tiles, and under his command. "They have to," I said, my tone light as our boat floated down the canals like a creature in the mist, "in order to survive."

I remembered the first time my mother had taught me how to wash raw silk. I was four years old then, only just big enough to walk without stumbling. She had been kind with me, and patient, treating it like a game. *See this?* she'd asked, holding the dry silk up to the light. *Watch how it changes.* Then she'd dipped it into the water, scrubbing hard with her rough and blistered fingers, and held it up again. I'd clapped in delight, and she'd passed the next roll of silk to me. *Now you try.*

This, I remembered too: The silk had been tougher than I expected. It hurt my fingers when I held on to it for long, and it was so heavy that when it was soaked through in water, I'd almost tumbled headfirst into the river with it. My mother had reached out at the last second, grabbing my shoulders to steady me.

Is it too difficult for you? she'd asked.

The skin on my hands burned. But I'd shaken my head firmly, not wanting to disappoint her.

Suddenly the boat gave a lurch, startling me back to the present. There was a flash of color in my vision, and time seemed to warp around me. I saw the entire scene unfurling in startling detail: the servant who'd been walking past us with a pot of boiling water—presumably to make tea—losing balance, the fear in his eyes as the lid fell and the water spilled out toward me.

"Careful!"

A warm arm encircled me, yanking me back. My eyes squeezed shut. But the burning pain I anticipated never came. There was only the servant's babbled words over the rushing water, his voice high and choked with panic.

"I'm so sorry— I'm so sorry, Your Majesty— Let me help you get something . . . I'm sorry, this clumsy servant deserves to die—"

Your Majesty? Slowly, heart pounding furiously, I opened my eyes again, and my breath stuck in my throat. Fuchai had wrapped his arms around me, shielding me with his own body. A patch of bright pink skin shone on his wrist, raw and ruined, his rolled-back sleeves soaked through. The water was so hot it was still steaming, little white wisps rising to the sky.

He had protected me.

There had been no room for hesitation. To have acted in time—it could only have been natural instinct, his very first reaction. A kind of inexpressible pain filled my chest, as if some part of my heart had been burned.

"Are you hurt?" he asked me, his voice rough. I shook my head, but still he stepped back and scanned me closely from head to toe, stopping only when he made sure that I was unscathed. "Good," he said, sounding genuinely relieved. "That's good."

Beside us, the servant seemed close to tears. He was disciplined enough that he prostrated himself on the deck of the boat without even being asked, his shoulders trembling like a leaf. "I'm sorry," he repeated. "I'm sorry, Your Majesty, please forgive me . . ."

"Stop your yapping," Fuchai said irritably. "Do you want to give me a headache as well as a burn mark?"

The servant made an audible gulp and said no more. Of course, it was possible he had gone into shock.

"How bad is it?" I asked Fuchai, inspecting his wrist. The skin had started to pucker. It was painful just to look at.

"Terrible," Fuchai said with a pronounced grimace. "It hurts so much I can't even think straight."

"Really?" My heart pinched, the concern showing on my face only half-pretend. I should not have felt anything at all, but—perhaps I was not as cold as I wanted to be. And I could not deny the truth either: that he had been injured because of me. None of this was how I'd planned the trip to go. "You," I called to the servant, who was still in that lowly, trembling position. "Go and fetch some soy sauce. And bandages, if you have any. If not—then clean cloth will do."

"Y-yes, Lady Xishi." He raised his head slowly. "I—I will go right now—right this very instant—"

"Hurry."

He scampered away, stumbling twice when the boat rocked against the waves, and disappeared behind the cabin.

Fuchai uttered a low sound of pain, dragging my attention back to him.

"It still hurts," he said.

"I know," I told him, my tone gentle. "I'll help you."

He blinked up at me, then furrowed his dark brows. "Just now . . . Was I hearing correctly? Did you ask the servant to bring soy sauce?"

The confusion in his expression was such that I could have laughed. "It's not for food. It is an old folk remedy; it should help with the pain, and prevent scarring." My mother was always getting burned in the kitchen, handling firewood and the stove and boiling water. It happened so often that she never even made a sound, just calmly reached for the soy sauce on the upper shelf and dabbed it onto her skin herself. How odd, to think of these things now. It was almost as if the memories belonged to somebody else. "I promise it works," I said.

"And here I thought you were concerned with seasoning your meals while I suffered."

My lips carved out a smile. "I would not be so heartless."

"You're right," he said, without any doubt whatsoever. That strange ache inside my chest again. I ignored it, or tried to. Then Fuchai hissed sharply between his teeth, holding his wrist higher for me to see. "It's awful, isn't it? Am I dying? Is this the end?"

"You're not dying."

"It feels like I am," he said, wincing again. "I cannot move without my skin stinging."

"Then maybe stop moving."

But instead of staying still, he shifted closer to me and laid his head on my lap like a petulant child. His hair was warm, his crow-black locks curling slightly from the damp, his eyes the color of sacred amber in the light. "I feel better like this," he said, snuggling tighter against me.

"I don't see why. It makes no difference to your arm."

"Could you not coax me a little, Xishi?" His full lower lip jutted out into a pout.

"Are you not afraid others will see you?" I asked, adopting the teasing voice I often used around him when we were alone. "The king in broad daylight, complaining of his wound and resting on his concubine's lap?"

"Let them see," he said carelessly, with the ease and arrogance of a young prince. "They will only envy me."

Loud footsteps drummed over the deck. The servant returned, carrying a small vial of soy sauce and strips of white cloth. He flushed at the sight of us together, but didn't look away. "Will— will this be okay?" he squeaked.

"Yes," I said, taking both from him. "Thank you."

He was still staring at Fuchai, perhaps hoping for the king to pardon him, or waiting to be sentenced to death. *Are you really so self-sacrificing?* I wanted to chide the boy. *Go, while he is distracted, and you may still live.*

"Is there anything else I can get for you, Your Majesty?" he asked.

I bit down an exasperated sigh.

Fuchai, who had been relaxing—a little *too* relaxed, I would even say—on my legs, frowned anew at the servant's voice, a muscle twitching in his jaw. Sensing danger, I spoke for him. "Let me take care of the king. You can go now."

Before Fuchai could call the poor boy back and whip him, as I was very sure he wished to, I tipped a few drops of soy sauce onto his wound and rubbed it in, then bandaged it up carefully. Yet still he flinched every few seconds, and whimpered with such persistence I half wondered if he had been burned not by plain water, but some kind of corrosive poison.

"It should feel better now," I said, frowning down at his wrist.

His pout deepened. "Perhaps it would if you blew on it."

Now I was certain that he was acting. But I humored him, bending my head and blowing cool air over the wrapped cloth. "Does it still hurt?"

"Yes." He gazed up at me from under his long, curving lashes. If not for the lashes and the fullness of his lips, he would have looked like a true tyrant, a cruel king. But those features added just the right touch of vulnerability to the sharp structure of his face. "Comfort me, Xishi. I'm in excruciating pain."

Shameless, I thought to myself, but of course I could not say so. Smiling with all the indulgent airs of someone caring for their one beloved, I raised my hand and threaded my fingers through his hair, patting the top of his head. He sighed then, like a cat being stroked behind its ears, leaning into my palm.

All the while, I could feel his black-eyed gaze on me. I busied myself pretending to check his bandages for a few moments, but his attention seemed to pierce through my skin, through my lungs.

"Would it be foolish if I said I'm happy to have been burned?" he murmured.

"It would," I said.

He didn't seem to mind. "Then let me be a fool. I am happier than I've ever been." He moved his head slowly against my hand, eyes half-closed. "You haven't looked at me so closely in a while."

I tensed, but forced myself to stay silent, even as my thoughts raced ahead. Had he noticed? Could he sense my resentment? Did he suspect my plans? No, he couldn't have. Or else he wouldn't be speaking to me with such sweetness.

"Don't be mad at me anymore, all right?" he said quietly. "I can't stand it."

I felt myself go very still. He spoke to me not as a king, but as a boy, pleading forgiveness. When he was with me he held nothing back, just laid it all out there, his heart and his thoughts bared to the bone. Yet with him I held back everything. He did not even know why I'd insisted on taking a trip down these canals.

"Everything is forgotten already," I reassured him, stroking his hair.

But in my head I saw Fanli, struggling to stand before the throne, his lips bled pale, the sword pressed into his flesh. I saw Zhengdan, curled up on the floor in my coat, still fighting to smile at me as her breathing slowed. I could never forget; I would not let myself forget.

Jiejie.

Xishi-jie . . .

If only I could have fought them all . . .

Whatever flicker of warmth I felt inside me died out. We had sailed far from the inner capital now, the painted houses giving way to lush green wilderness. I looked over the boat edge. The water was so clear here that I could see the weeds floating beneath the pale blue surface, the schools of silver fish darting sharply from left to right, avoiding the splashing oars. A large bird soared low over our heads, carrying what seemed to be every possible color on earth in its glossy feathers, like a phoenix reincarnated.

The boat slowed. "We cannot go any farther than this," a different servant told us, his head bowed.

I already knew, but I frowned at him. "Why not?"

"The canal ends here, Lady Xishi," he explained. "Farther up ahead is Lake Tai, but it cannot be reached by boat."

"But I was hoping to visit Lake Tai," I said, stealing a glance at Fuchai.

"Another time," he promised. "Just say the word."

"Y-yet I'm afraid that's not quite p-possible, Your Majesty," the servant stammered out. "Physically s-speaking. This canal does not reach the lake . . ."

I pursed my lips and lifted my fingers from Fuchai's hair. He made a small noise of protest, but I ignored him on purpose. "I wish there were an easier way to take pleasure trips around the area, don't you? I hear Lake Tai is so beautiful, especially in the spring. Imagine: Any time we wish to be alone together, to escape from the palace, all we'd have to do is set sail . . ." I turned back to the servant. "Are there really no other routes?"

"N-no, Lady Xishi. I'm afraid not . . ."

"I see." I let the disappointment fill my voice.

"Don't be absurd," Fuchai spoke up. "If there is no canal now, then surely we can build one. How hard can it be?"

My heart skipped. I had to fight to suppress any signs of excitement.

"That— It would be a significant endeavor, Your Majesty," the servant said. "I am no expert, but to build something of such a scale . . ."

I folded my arms over my chest with a loud, weary sigh. I could feel Fuchai's eyes on me.

"Can it be done or not?" Fuchai snapped at the servant.

"It can—it can," he said hurriedly. "So long as you decree it, Your Majesty."

"I want a complete plan on my desk by midday tomorrow."

"Yes, Your Majesty."

But Fuchai was already focused on me once more, nudging my hand with his, his intentions impossible to mistake. This time I acquiesced, lifting my fingers and running them through his soft hair. "You really would do anything for me, wouldn't you?" I murmured, staring down at him. The king who had just given his enemy the keys to his kingdom and didn't realize it at all, his lips lifted in a contented smile, his features smooth. When the historians wrote about the fate of the Wu years from now, would they be able to capture this very moment? Would they know how the idea had bloomed? Would they blame him, or me?

"Of course I would," he said, his smile widening. He looked at me how one would look upon a god. "Anything for you, my Xishi."

CHAPTER NINETEEN

*T*HIS WAS HOW EVERYTHING STARTED.
This was how everything came to an end.

The words beat against my skull like a mallet as I followed Xiaomin down the clean-swept lanes. Gripped tight in my hands was the finalized map, now including a detailed diagram of the canal connecting to Lake Tai. It was what King Goujian was waiting for. The information he needed before he launched his attack on the Wu. Then, perhaps, I would be free—to return home, to reunite with my parents, to see Fanli . . .

As we cut across an empty, shadowy corner, I folded the map carefully into a flower and arranged it in my hair, tucking it just behind my ears. When we moved into the pale sunlight again, both my hands were empty.

"I never had the chance to ask you," Xiaomin was saying, turning back to look at me. "Are you all right? After what happened with . . ."

Zhengdan. The name hovered in the air between us, unspoken.

I swallowed the lump in my throat. It violated the rule I'd made for myself, which was never to think of her, not unless it was to also think of revenge, of still bodies and spilled blood.

But Xiaomin continued, "I had someone like her too. Once." Her voice caught, just briefly. "We were born in the same village, on the same day. I still remember their yard: They grew everything, including their own apricots. They were the sweetest apricots I'd ever tasted, so soft and always fresh. Every summer, she would invite me and my little sister over to pick the fruits together; she was taller than me by a head, and so she'd pluck the ones I couldn't reach . . ."

We were almost at the southern gates now, the city looming beyond those crimson walls. Despite myself, I couldn't help asking, "What happened?"

"War," she said bitterly, and I found I wasn't surprised, as if I'd known it all along. It was the same narrative that coursed through the veins of our kingdom, only the characters were changed, the enemy reversed. "The monsters from Yue slaughtered their way through our village—few survived. I was one of them; I took my sister and fled. But she . . . was not."

My breathing suddenly felt very shallow. "You call the Yue monsters?"

"Of course. It's what we all call them." She looked at me in confusion, then seemed to remember something, her eyes widening. "So sorry, miss—I forgot you . . . Well, I don't consider you Yue anymore. You are as Wu as I am, and no monster at all."

I managed a small smile, but my gut roiled. I hastened my steps, eager to move past this next part, to outpace my own guilt. If Xiaomin knew what she was helping me accomplish, she would not consider me Wu in the slightest.

She came to an abrupt stop. "That's him." Her voice had changed, gone all soft and shy, and her cheeks were pink. Under different circumstances, I might have laughed at her. But strangely,

I felt a faint stab of jealousy. How easy it would be, how great a luxury, to simply look across the lane at the one you love and say, *That's him. There he is.*

The guard positioned outside the gates looked up, perhaps sensing our attention. He was young, seventeen or eighteen at most, with a naturally sunny, boyish face and crescent-shaped eyes. They crinkled at the edges when he caught sight of Xiaomin, though he did not forget to bow to me first. Etiquette reigned, after all.

"Lady Xishi," he greeted.

I was surprised. "You know who I am?"

"Yes," he said. He spoke a little quickly, and didn't dare lift his eyes to meet mine. "I—I doubt there is anyone in the palace who doesn't know of you."

"You may be at ease," I told him. "I am only passing by."

If anything, he tensed up further. Now I really did laugh.

"It was Xiaomin who wanted to pay you a visit," I added. "She speaks about you often."

His gaze flickered up to the blushing maid, and he looked for a moment like he'd just eaten the sun, the euphoria shining through his features. I did not wait around to witness their small gestures of affection, their bashful expressions, all the displays of innocent young love. I stepped past him, toward the gate—

"W-wait, Lady Xishi," the guard called, tearing his eyes away from Xiaomin with difficulty. Cold sweat broke out over my palms. "I'm afraid nobody is allowed to go through without written permission . . ."

"I only want to step out for a moment," I said, plastering a casual smile to my face. "I'll be quick."

He hesitated. "But . . . we were instructed that—"

"It shouldn't be a big problem, right?" Xiaomin spoke up, gazing at him expectantly.

"I . . ." I watched him waver, my heart flipping in my chest. But then he gazed back toward Xiaomin, her sweet, charming expression, and pursed his lips. "I suppose not."

I wasted no time. With a firm push, the gate doors creaked open. I slipped out through them like a ghost, the flower arranged in my hair. The difference between the world inside and outside the palace walls was like that between two realms. The harsh wind struck my cheeks, and yellow dust billowed in the air. Whereas everything in the palace was spacious and vast, giving the impression that you could wander the lanes forever and never reach the end, all the old houses and stores here were crammed close together. I squinted at the dozens of passing faces, young and old, and finally found the one I was looking for. He was manning a cart that sold jars of candied fruit, the contents glistening red-gold. A distinct scar ran down the side of his face and twisted into the corner of his mouth. This was the man Fanli had asked me to find if I ever needed to deliver information to him, a trusted servant of Goujian's.

I forced myself to walk over to him at a relaxed pace, my expression nonchalant. Pretending to inspect the jars, which all looked the same, I murmured, "Does the sparrow sing in the night?"

He stilled. With his head down, he replied, "Only when the river rises."

They were the correct code words. I released a silent sigh of relief, then plucked the flower from my hair, pressing it into his palm. It was made of only ink and fabric, yet it seemed to weigh like stone. "Hurry."

His fingers curled around it. He nodded once, understanding in his eyes.

When I returned through the gates, Xiaomin was laughing at something the guard had said. Her face was radiant, brighter than all the stars and the moon, her head tossed back, her giggles escaping through the spaces between her fingers. And he was there, watching her with such comfortable intimacy I wanted to turn away. The two were blinding in their shared joy.

"Tomorrow," she was saying to him, shy and eager. "The usual spot?"

His face split into a grin so wide she might have just promised him the whole world. "Always."

It felt as though someone had reached into my chest and yanked at my heart, made my old illness new again. I clutched at the front of my robes, waited for the worst of the pain to pass before walking up to Xiaomin, my face serene as that of a raised lotus flower. She immediately came to my side, but I could tell she did not want to leave him.

I'd never wanted to leave either.

I knew Wu Zixu would rise to the bait—it was only a matter of when.

I was in the king's bedchambers that night, lounging on his desk while he pretended to work. He pressed the royal seal down on document after document, the ink bleeding red, barely looking before moving from one thing to another, his movements impatient. The only sounds that could be heard were the thin rustling of paper and an owl hooting outside. To his credit, Fuchai had been focused when I first came in—his head down, his expression stern, the slightest crease between his dark brows, the bright lamplight clarifying his sharp profile. For a moment, I couldn't help hiding behind one of the carved rosewood pillars, just to study him in silence. It was rare to see him like that: proper, working hard. There was no malice or mockery to his features as he ground the ink and dipped his brush into the shallow pot.

Then I had stepped out, with my just-brushed hair and perfumed skin, and all that was forgotten.

"Am I distracting you, Your Majesty?" I asked now, adjusting my legs so they dangled just off the corner of his desk, my chin propped up on one hand. With my other hand, I combed my fingers slowly through his dark hair.

He stamped the seal down twice in the same spot, missed the next document completely, and said, "No, not at all."

I smiled. "Are you sure? I'd hate to keep you from something important . . ."

"Stay," he insisted. "I'm almost done here."

I sighed and continued stroking his hair, my motions lazy, all while I secretly read his documents with utmost care. There were military reports, with statistics on everything from the weapons supply to the number of soldiers and steeds available. I memorized the numbers, repeating them to myself inside my head. When Fuchai lifted his gaze, I shifted my attention to him. "Your hair is so soft," I said, tugging gently at a black, wavy lock. I knew it was what he liked.

Just as I expected, his breathing hitched, his eyes turned dark and almost drunk.

"What do you suppose people would say, seeing me treat the king this way?" I teased. "They must think me terribly impudent."

"Well, there's nobody around."

"You raise a good point," I said slyly. From outside, I sensed movement. Footsteps. The unmistakable silhouette of Wu Zixu was outlined against the thin windows, drawing closer and closer toward us. But Fuchai hadn't noticed yet. "We're all alone."

He faltered briefly, then understood. He swept the papers aside, the royal seal and brushes all clattering to the floor, and turned me around so I was gazing down at him from his desk. He stood, leaning in to kiss me—

I turned away on purpose. *Just a little longer now.* The footsteps were getting louder.

"Wait. Let me look at you first," I said, cupping his face. Every single time, it struck me anew how handsome he was. It seemed wrong; he ought to have the face of a beast, some malevolent creature, with blood-red eyes and deadly fangs. But instead his skin was smooth and clean-shaven and burning under my touch, his lips soft and parted. I wrestled down the uncomfortable emotion that reared its head inside me. No, I refused to be guilty. I had come too far already, lost too much.

And Zixu was here.

"My king," I murmured, bringing my lips to his. There were just bare inches between us when the doors burst open with a loud *thud*.

Zixu stalked inside, his hands balled into fists. "Your Majesty—"

I let out a faint squeal and pulled away at once, putting up the perfect performance of surprise, but Fuchai was slower to untangle himself from me, his hand remaining on the small of my waist. His expression had changed from open anticipation to impatience. He looked ready to kill.

"If you aren't here to tell me you've discovered the elixir of immortality, then I don't want to hear it," he said, his voice deadly soft, his eyes narrowed into knives. "Leave us."

Zixu averted his gaze hastily, but didn't retreat. "I'm sorry, Your Majesty. Please excuse this minister's brazen behavior, but this is a matter of great importance—"

"Funny, that is how you lead every conversation," Fuchai said dryly, straightening his robes and sitting back down behind his desk. I slid off too, stepping to the side with my head bent at a subservient angle. "The annual banquet, the *seating* for the annual banquet, the granaries, the construction of the new palace—even the purchase of new spoons for the royal kitchens. All supposedly deemed important."

For a split second, Zixu's eyes caught on me, deep distrust written all over his features. Then he bowed low to the king. Urgency bled through his tone. "This is different—this could determine the fate of the whole kingdom—"

"You should learn to relax more, Zixu," Fuchai continued in a slow drawl, leaning back in his seat. From appearances only, he seemed to be playing the role of king well enough, but he wore the look he always did when he wanted desperately to kiss me, the lines of his body tense and hungry. The minister prostrated before him might as well have been a wall, any inconvenient obstacle. "Spend time with your concubines, so I can spend time with mine. They would thank you for it, I'm sure."

Zixu made a choked sound and said with barely held composure, "I implore you, Your Majesty, if you would just let me speak—"

"Aren't you already speaking?" Fuchai said, annoyed.

Zixu flinched, but continued on. "There have been . . . strange movements along the Yue borders." My heart thundered in my chest. I listened harder, mouth dry, latching on to his every word. "We have no proof of what they're planning, but I'm certain they're planning *something*. It will not do to just lie here, waiting for the enemy to spring upon us. We have the advantage right now—we must use it and take swift action, conquer them before they can attack us—"

"The Yue again?" Fuchai interrupted. He sounded unimpressed, unconcerned. Still, I held my breath. "Zixu, this is getting dull. We've been through this conversation before, and I've made my decision perfectly clear. We are not to attack the Yue, and they will not attack us. The days of war are over."

A dark green vein twitched in Zixu's temple. He bowed impossibly lower, his face almost pressed to the floor. "I wish that were the case too, Your Majesty. Believe me. Who doesn't dream of peace? But Goujian is far more complex a character than you give him credit for—"

"You just said yourself you have no proof they will attack."

"No proof *yet*." Again his eyes snapped to me. "But I am confident that I will be able to find it, sooner or later."

Fear sawed at my stomach. I could not give him time to collect proof, to build up a stronger case for conquest. If I was to be rid of him, then it would have to be right here. Tonight.

"Your Majesty," I ventured, making my voice tremble. "Don't be angry with him. I'm sure he has his . . . personal reasons for wanting to usher in another war. That is understandable."

Zixu looked at me with such vehemence I did not have to pretend to flinch. I was half-certain he would forget his position and mine and simply strangle me. "How dare you—I have no personal reasons at all. Everything I say is for the good of the kingdom—"

"Is it really?" Fuchai regarded him coolly.

"Of course," Zixu cried. "Your Majesty knows better than anyone how long I have served you, and your father before you—"

Fuchai's eyes flashed. "Yes, how can I forget? What a loyal servant you were to him."

A dark silence fell over the room.

For a moment I feared Zixu's courage would fail him, that he would cower and crawl outside before the king had the chance to do anything. But Wu Zixu was a stubborn man and a faithful minister. He didn't move.

"We must attack, Your Majesty," he whispered. "If you are to grant any request of mine, let it be this. Your father had devoted his life to building this kingdom for you. Will you really tarnish his legacy by letting the enemy—those who brought about his death—invade our walls? Your father would never have allowed such a thing."

Perhaps another king might have been moved by this speech.

But I understood Fuchai in a way his ministers did not; I had kissed him in the moonlight, had coaxed his worst fears, his insecurities, his weaknesses, out of him night after night. He resented his father as much as he respected him, and any comparisons between the two of them was a sure way to erode what little patience he possessed.

"Enough," Fuchai snapped, standing to his full height and looming over the minister in all his power, his black silk robes spilling around him like a great shadow. It was a scene for the legends: the two figures, one stooped as low as one could go, the other towering above him, the yellow candles flickering in the background, the painted murals of the kingdom's tumultuous, blood-soaked history unrolling on either side of them. I watched Zixu from a distance, knowing how this would play out, and felt a thorn of something almost like pity.

Perhaps history would remember him as a hero. But a hero to many was still a villain to one.

"You are obsessed with the Yue," Fuchai said, taking one forceful step closer, the movement like that of a predator advancing. "You speak of dangers that do not exist. All my other ministers disagree with you."

"You mean Bo Pi?" Wu Zixu lifted his head, his eyes bloodshot. He had never looked so young, so desperate, so human. "Bo Pi cannot be trusted, Your Majesty. He is—"

"So I am not to trust anybody except you, is that right?" Fuchai demanded. "I remember you said the same thing of the Yue minister Fanli." I tried not to react, even as the sound of his name cut my heart open. "And what happened in the end? You wounded him for nothing, and his blood dirtied the palace lanes. It made a bigger mess than it was worth."

"That's what you think now," Zixu said, his voice low and throttled with urgency. "That's what they want you to think. But you never know, in the future—"

"*Silence.*"

Zixu shuffled forward on his knees, then lowered his head so it was pressed to the floor right before Fuchai's boots. My stomach swooped, my shock barely concealed in time. It was the ultimate gesture of submission, like a dog rolling over to display its belly.

"Please," Zixu whispered. His dark eyes shone with—*tears*, I realized, startled. I should have been enjoying this. I should have relished every detail. But it was also discomfiting, seeing a man of such high status be brought so low, down on his knees and begging his king. Knowing that it had everything to do with me. "You're making a terrible mistake. That woman has poisoned your mind." He pointed at me. I stared back with feigned innocence. "You are not thinking clearly. Ever since she came—"

"Speak another bad word about her again," Fuchai said quietly, his voice ringing with danger, "and I will stitch your lips shut myself."

But it was as if Zixu had been possessed by another force, something that propelled him to continue walking the path to his doomed fate. He persisted in a rush, like he already knew he was running out of time. "It's not too late—Your Majesty, if we rally our troops tonight, we can still—"

"Zixu," Fuchai interrupted. His expression was strange, unreadable, his tone almost gentle. He crouched down too, and in a rapid movement, seized Wu Zixu's face. It might have looked intimate, like he was going to close the distance any second now and kiss him, if not for the points where his fingers dug into the flesh of Zixu's cheeks like claws, applying such pressure the surrounding skin went white. "For years, I have let you stay by my side. I have tolerated you, and humored you, and given you much of what you've asked—"

"And I am honored, Your Majesty," Zixu choked out, with an emotion that seemed torn between hatred and raw, wretched devotion. It was the devotion of a believer who would follow his god to the destruction of the very earth. Who would caress the hand that strangled him. "I wish—only to serve you—"

"Yet you defy me?" Fuchai purred. His fingers tightened.

"It is for your own good," Zixu said, panting now. "For the safety of the kingdom—"

"Do you know what some people call you?" Fuchai cut in, still in that silken tone. "They say you're my dog."

For the first time, vivid color crept through Zixu's complexion, making him look alarmingly vulnerable. He swallowed, the sound audible in the closed room.

"But you see, your behavior now is tantamount to treason." Fuchai's hand slid from the minister's cheeks to a spot behind his ear, as if he really were a dog hoping to be scratched. Then his fingers traveled lower to the long column of his throat. It would have been instinct to shy away, but Zixu stayed utterly still, his eyes on the king. "And no owner will keep a dog that tries to bite them, time and time again."

"Your Majesty . . . I beg you . . ."

"It is a pity," Fuchai said, looking genuinely sad as he released Zixu. In the same instant, something heavy clattered to the ground. A sword. I understood the meaning the same time Zixu seemed to.

He showed no surprise, just profound sorrow. Shaking, he reached for the hilt. Drew the blade. It reflected a long slant of silver light onto the crimson walls. Then he paused.

"Will you please do me a final favor?" Zixu asked, hoarse.

Fuchai tilted his head.

"When I am dead," Zixu began, his fingers wavering just a moment over the sword, "cut out my eyes. Hang them on the city gates, so that I may watch when the Yue army invades and captures our capital."

Fuchai's face hardened. Turning away, he commanded without so much as a glance back, "Do not get too much blood on my floor."

But I stayed, staring.

Wu Zixu had always been a decisive man, always determined to follow through with every mission given to him. This was no different. He raised the sword to his own throat as smoothly and steadily as if it were someone else pressed to the blade, and drew it clean across in one swift, sharp line. Blood bloomed instantly. The sword fell. He made a choked sound, then clenched his teeth around it, refusing to surrender even that much of himself. As his heart thudded out its final beats, his eyes fell on me, and my body broke out into a cold shudder. The expression that blazed on his dying face was what transformed humans into hungry ghosts.

He said something right before his body collapsed to the ground, but his voice was already too weak, and thick with blood. In my days since, I have tried to decipher it, circled my way around it, questioned whether I might have heard wrong. Whether I ought to have listened more closely, taken his words to heart. At the time, I dismissed it as a threat, as him cursing me with his dying breath.

All I know is that it sounded like this:

"When the hares have all been caught, the hunting dogs are cooked."

CHAPTER TWENTY

THE NOTE CAME BACK TO ME SIX FULL MOONS LATER, after Zixu's corpse had already been buried deep in the dirt. It was folded into the same white flower, but the inside was different, the complex map and diagram gone, my annotations erased. Now there was only a poem, written in clean, crisp lines. I could still smell the ink on it.

The moon rises white
illuminating your beauty,
your shadow which wounds me
until my heart's devoured

I stroked the words with my fingertips, as if it were some rare creature that would be scared away. Here was proof that Fanli was alive, that he had returned to Yue in one piece. Then I read the poem again and again to myself, silently, my lips parting around the syllables. I'd studied it before in one of the classical texts he'd taught me, but the memory was dim now. He had dismissed it as too sentimental at the time, rushing through to get to the more political pieces, the ones where every couplet contained twenty different meanings.

I remembered teasing him for it: "Are love poems not important too? Perhaps I will memorize this for when I meet the king."

We were both sitting inside his study. He'd cast me an indecipherable look without lifting his head, his face cast in beautiful shadow. "Memorize something else. Not this."

"Why not?"

But either he had not replied, or I'd forgotten it.

I stared down at the flower. Was it a message? A confession? I felt shaken; the pain in my chest was suddenly overwhelming, more violent than a stabbing. I wanted to run to him. I wanted him to answer me himself, not speak in riddles, in inscriptions, in poetry, however lovely. I wanted to wrap my hands around the nape of his neck and feel the warmth of his skin.

But that was foolishness. I read it once more, memorizing it as I would the date of my own death, then fed it to the fire, watching the folded white petals wither in the flames, the ink slowly melting away.

In the following months I tried to forget the poem, the possibility wrapped within those words, the person who'd written it out. To think of him was like pressing my mind up against a knife: the cold, sharp pain of it; the blood running free. But still I did it, again and again.

The ache in my heart deepened.

I woke up in a cold sweat, gasping.

It was late in the night, some dark hour when the sun hadn't even risen yet. My eyes were blurred with sleep, so it looked as if everything was cloaked in white fog. Sweat soaked my inner robes. The air was ice cold. As I took in great, heaving breaths, I caught on to the tail end of my dream right before it could slip away from me.

I had been dreaming of him. Fanli. We were back in Riversong Cottage, but something terrible had happened. A fire, a flood, some great natural disaster—the details escaped me now. All I knew was that he kept telling me to hide, forcing me onto a boat that looked like it would shatter at any second. *It will be safer there*, he'd repeated, gazing down at me with those sad, dark eyes, like he knew something I didn't. I had tried to cling to him. My fingers had twisted into the sleeves of his robes, tears springing from my eyes the way they never did in real life. *Don't leave me.* Even now, my throat felt raw, as if I had actually screamed the words. *Don't make me go. I don't want to—please, I don't want to.* I had known with a burning, knife-sharp conviction that if I got on the boat, if he let me go, I would never see him again.

But then his expression had turned cold, and he'd demanded that I recite the book we'd learned together word for word, in the correct order. *What book?* I'd yelled at him, trying desperately to remember. *Which one is it? Just tell me.* Zhengdan had appeared then too, and the scene changed; we were standing on opposite sides of a river. She was staring at me, her features frozen, her eyes blank as a ghost's. *Do you know? Can you help?* I'd asked her, but when she opened her mouth to reply, she vomited blood. It gushed from her, unceasing. There was so much of it I could see her skin shrink, her complexion turning blue. *Hurry*, she'd croaked out between mouthfuls of red. Even the whites of her eyes were shot through with bloody veins. *Hurry. You promised—*

"Xishi. Xishi, are you all right?" Fuchai was kneeling on the bed next to me, his face open and handsome as ever, yet his eyes were unusually dark. His robes parted at his chest and fell from his shoulders when he moved closer. I could see the tension in his muscles, those hard lines illuminated by moonlight.

"Just a dream," I murmured, rubbing my eyes with my palms. They were nothing new, but they always grew more vivid when I spent the night with Fuchai. Perhaps a product of my own guilt. Still, the dreams had been bothering me more frequently. As if they were leading up to something, something terrible.

My heart, too, had been hurting more than ever. I felt it now, the wrenching pain behind my ribs, so intense that my fingers scrabbled over the front of my robes, feeling for fresh blood, half convinced I had been stabbed in my sleep. There was nothing. Yet still I shivered from the invisible agony, my teeth chattering.

Without another word, Fuchai lifted the blankets and wrapped them around my shoulders. Then he held me. There was no lust in it, no provocation, no ulterior motive—just a simple gesture of comfort. I was so startled I could not speak. Crickets chirped outside the windows, and the blue shadows moved over the walls like souls lost in a ghost city.

"You were crying," he said, lifting a warm finger to my cheek.

To my surprise, I found that my face really was wet. "It's fine."

"No, this is important." In a flash he drew back, his features hardened, the contours of his face sharp and regal. Even in bed, with his ink-black hair rumpled from the pillow, he took on the airs of a king. "Is somebody bothering you? Who? I'll kill them."

I shook my head. He had expressed such sentiments before, and I'd always taken them as proof of his brutality, his ruthless nature. *The Wu monsters*: From kings to convicts, they were all the same. But now it hit me with astounding clarity that it was the most he could do, the most he considered himself capable of. Like how a cook, when something goes wrong, might busy himself making delicious meals; or how a physician, during a disaster, might offer medical advice.

"I'm fine, really," I reassured him. "Only . . ." *Only sad.* But it was the kind of sad that left you hollow, that made every movement feel slow, excruciating, that made all food taste bland. I could not explain it to him, much less tell him why. "It's only my old illness," I said instead. "Some days it hurts more than others."

He made to rise. "Should I call for the physician?"

"No, there's no use." I shook my head, pulling him back down. "If there were a cure, I would have found it by now. And the pain is normally not so bad, when I have other things to distract me."

"It's my fault," he said. He rubbed the small of my spine as he spoke, the warmth of his palm spreading through my robes. "I've been too preoccupied with overseeing the construction of the canal recently; I've neglected you. But don't worry," he went on in a rush. "The canal will be completed very soon, and I'll be yours, every second of every day. What can I do to make you feel better?"

I hesitated.

"Should I behead some servants? Hold a public flogging?"

I didn't know whether to laugh or cry. "No, that's really . . . that won't be necessary."

"Then what?" His hand moved to the back of my head, stroking my hair. His eyes were urgent and completely earnest. "Tell me. I will do anything."

It struck me then, what I had to do. It felt as if a wild swarm of hornets had suddenly dove into my mind. I remembered the poem Fanli sent me:

The moon rises white
illuminating your beauty,
your shadow which wounds me
until my heart's devoured

I had been focusing so hard on the lines of this poem when I should have thought about the poem that came after it, the one Fanli had insisted on analyzing in great depth. It told the story of a king who'd secretly disguised himself as a guest to the enemy kingdom's banquet. After dining and drinking all night, unnoticed, he had not left the kingdom gates, but rather stayed just inside them, preparing to launch a secret attack the next morning.

That was what Fanli meant. I had been wrong; he would never be so sentimental. There was always a hidden message, a mission. A purpose. I swallowed a bitter laugh at myself. What a fool I was to imagine otherwise.

"There is . . . one thing," I began, sitting up.

"What?" Fuchai pressed his lips gently to my exposed collarbone, his eyes meeting mine from under his long lashes. Warmth rushed through my skin at the same time a chill shot through my bones. "I wish only to take your pain away."

I took a deep breath. "What do you say about holding a banquet?"

CHAPTER
TWENTY-ONE

THE PEACH TREES WERE FINALLY STARTING TO BLOOM again. The palace had been cleaned and polished so that you could run a finger over any of its walls or lanes and find not even a single speck of dirt. The winds became gentle, and the grass that had withered in winter grew back again, lush and green as new jade. More lanterns were strung from the curved roofs, their pearl-white light illuminating the ponds and the paths between chambers. Mornings were announced by birdsong, the sun rising earlier and earlier. Spring had come, and the air was fragrant, carrying the heady scent of flowers from Lady Yu's gardens and spices from the royal kitchens.

Inside the great hall, everything had been transformed as well. Gold and silver hangings shimmered from the walls; all the goblets were freshly washed. Two large banquet tables extended from one end to the other, leaving space in between for the dancers and flutists.

"What do you think?" Fuchai asked me with the shy, excited

tones of a student showing his final work to his master. "Is it to your liking?"

I stared around the vast room. The banquet was already in motion, guests beginning to stream in through the doors. We had worked on the guest list together, inviting princes and princesses from distant lands, noblemen and distinguished scholars from the most prestigious families, kings and ministers from neighboring kingdoms. The public purpose of the banquet was to celebrate the completion of the new canal; the private purpose, to lift my spirits. But of course Fuchai did not know the true purpose of what he had helped arrange.

"Everything is wonderful," I said, smiling to hide my nerves.

It was impressive; even I could admit it. The food alone was mouthwatering. Fuchai had demanded the very best cooks be brought in to prepare for this evening, the raw materials gathered from the highest mountains and widest plains, where the soil was tender and the water tasted sweet. There were plates upon plates of dessert: steamed fermented rice cake, the sticky layers rich with the aroma of wine; gaotuan of every shade mixed with red bean paste and salted nuts and sesame, shaped to resemble gold ingots, magnolia leaves, flowers blooming; oil-glazed mooncakes engraved with floral patterns and the characters for peace and prosperity. They were all so beautiful and intricately made it seemed almost a pity to eat them. But the *real* dishes were only just arriving. Servants came bearing clay pots of braised pork, cooked until every slice was golden brown, the lean and fat meat perfectly proportioned, dripping with soy sauce. Eggs had been added to the dish as well, with four clean slices down the sides to let the flavor in.

As the guests took their seats, a bell chimed. The servant stationed at the gates called out, "King Goujian and Minister Fanli of the Yue Kingdom have arrived."

I felt a sudden tightness in my chest, like somebody had gripped my heart. With great effort, I tried to ward off the shaky sensation threatening my body, all rising emotion, hope and panic and fear woven together. I rubbed my arms, faced the gates.

They entered according to their respective roles: Goujian first, dressed in kingly finery for once, and Fanli just behind him. My eyes went only to Fanli. He seemed to have recovered from the sword wound. His movements were fluid, light, his head up. He was dressed in dark navy robes that rippled when he walked, like the surface of a river in a breeze.

He met my eyes, expressionless save for the slight pull of his lips. My pulse throbbed.

"Thank you for the kind invitation, Your Majesty." He and Goujian took their turns greeting Fuchai. Reluctantly, I pulled my attention away from Fanli and focused on the king of Yue instead. He was smiling at Fuchai like they were old friends, but he smiled only with the skin of his face; beneath it, there was a chilling look in his gaze.

"Of course, of course." Fuchai laughed, not noticing. "It has been so long—how good it is to see your face again."

Goujian's smile sharpened. "The sentiment is mutual."

"We had fun, didn't we? Ah, I recall you were quite the helpful stable boy." It was a testament to Fuchai's arrogance—and perhaps his misplaced sense of immortality, believing himself immune to any harm—that he could make such jests without worry of being stabbed in his sleep.

Even I, watching this exchange silently, felt my palms sweating.

"I could never forget," Goujian murmured.

"Well, do sit." Fuchai pulled them over to the seats across his—and mine. I was facing Fanli directly from the opposite end of the table. "We should all have a drink together, for old times' sake." He snapped his fingers, and like magic, a servant appeared with a jug of sloshing wine. Goujian seemed to take note of this. Of everything. His black eyes raked over the halls, every blatant sign of wealth and opulence and comfort.

Then he brought his eyes back to the king standing before him, generously offering a goblet of wine like a gesture of peace. Something flickered in his expression. He took it, downing the liquor in one swig, and flipped his goblet over to show it was empty. "May the king live ten thousand years, and ten thousand years more."

Pleased, Fuchai quickly motioned for the servant to refill the goblet, then clinked his own cup against it. Then he repeated it with Fanli.

"No hard feelings?" Fuchai asked, glancing briefly at Fanli's chest, the place where Zixu's sword had drawn blood.

Fanli smiled, toasting him. "I don't know what you're talking about."

I stood, my eyes darting between them. It felt like some nightmare playing out in real life, everything about it wrong, every world of mine, every side of me—all my greatest wants and fears—colliding. I fought another swell of hysteria, controlled my breathing. This was necessary. And soon it would be over.

When they had each downed at least four full goblets of wine, Fuchai came over, laughing, his face framed by the black of his hair, and laced his fingers through mine. In my peripheral vision, I saw a tightening in Fanli's features. "Come," Fuchai said, tugging me toward the other guests.

As I followed him from table to table, faking smiles and uttering false niceties, I couldn't help snatching glimpses of Fanli. He remained in his seat, composed and polite, the perfect representative from a foreign kingdom. Occasionally he would turn and speak to Goujian in low tones, impossible for a third person to make out. He refilled his wine on his own, drinking goblet after goblet.

I tried not to let my surprise show. I had never seen Fanli drink before; for someone who prided themself on their self-discipline, I'd always assumed it was a vice he avoided.

The banquet was soon in full swing. The dancers moved from sequence to sequence, swishing their long sleeves, the bracelets on their wrists and ankles jangling. The air grew warmer with noise and activity and food, the dishes cleared away and immediately replaced by well-trained maids. There seemed no limit to the wine and lavish food that flowed within the halls.

And everywhere I went, my fingers intertwined with Fuchai's, my crimson sash flowing over my slender arms, the whispers fluttered after us like petals in the wind:

"She is as beautiful as all the rumors say . . ."

"No wonder His Majesty cannot bear to part from her . . ."

"They are a fitting pair, don't you think? The beauty and the king. I'm willing to bet there will be many poems and plays written about them."

But the tones with which they gossiped were not always adoring or admiring. There were darker sentiments too, ones I wished I hadn't heard.

". . . did you hear what the servants said, about that time they walked in on . . ."

"I hear he visits her chambers thrice a day—sometimes early in the morning . . ."

"She looks so innocent. It's hard to imagine . . ."

". . . that night, in the middle of the court, with everyone watching—"

"Your Majesty." The chair creaked as Fanli stood, swaying slightly. There was a misted look to his dark eyes, and streaks of color stained his cheeks. "Please forgive me, but I'll have to retire early . . ."

Fuchai took one long look at him, then burst out laughing. "Drunk already? Do you have such low alcohol tolerance?"

Fanli said nothing, just bowed his head in a subservient gesture. Unfailingly courteous, even with all that alcohol in his blood.

"All right, all right," Fuchai said. Then he swiveled around to me. "Xishi—how about you show him to the guest chambers? He can rest there until the others are ready to depart."

A shock went through me. I could hardly dare to believe it. "Me?" I asked, half wondering if this was some sick joke, another cruel test of his to see whether I felt more for Fanli than I revealed.

But there was no suspicion in Fuchai's gaze. He waved his long sleeve good-naturedly. "Yes, you. I trust that you'll show him how beautiful the palace is."

So that's why he's asking me. He could be so childish sometimes. He wanted to show off, to impress Fanli, rub in the fact that he had the most stunning women and rooms in all the lands.

"Yes, Your Majesty. Of course," I said, standing. I swallowed, tried to suppress the giddy tremor in my hands. The king of Wu had constructed the Palace of Beautiful Women just for me, built a promenade with thousands of earthenware jars that chimed whenever I walked on it, changed the very course of the rivers and commanded that a new waterway be created simply because I'd suggested it to him. He had been nothing but generous, given me his heart and time and affections again and again, spoiled me with the finest silks and sweetest cakes and warmest chambers. But I'd never felt so much gratitude toward him as I did in this very moment. And he didn't even realize what he'd gifted me: time alone with Fanli. Time to speak, to drop our pretenses, to ask how he was. I would not have been so happy even if he'd single-handedly plucked the moon out of the sky for me, if he'd woven me a necklace made of all the stars in the heavens.

I walked over to Fanli, my eyes lowered to the ground. I kept my voice even, mildly polite, the way one would speak to a stranger. "Please follow me."

His voice was equally neutral. "Thank you, Lady Xishi."

Gusts of heat swept over the back of my neck as I led him to the main doors. I could sense his gaze on me, the distance that pushed and tugged between us, the space humming between our bodies. The door swung open under my touch, and the cool night air blew toward me, sweet with the faint perfume of begonias. I breathed in.

We were both outside now. Alone. All the noise from the banquet faded away, muffled by the walls. Crimson lanterns glowed softly down the corridors, illuminating every round, latticed window and carved pillar we passed. Bright-painted murals unrolled on either side of us: immortals dancing in rolling clouds and temples suspended on mountains and lovers sailing together down a river on a bamboo raft.

I scanned the empty, narrow paths around us before speaking. "Are you well?" The sound of my own voice startled me; it was not the sweet tone I used around the king to get what I wanted, nor the commanding tone I adopted to intimidate others into obedience. I had almost forgotten what I really sounded like.

"As well as I could be," he replied. His steps were slower than usual, and his brows were slightly furrowed, as though he was concentrating hard just on walking in a straight line. Surprise coursed through me. I had wondered if perhaps he was faking his drunkenness to get away from the banquet quickly, but now I was certain that it was no act. "No, that's not true," he said suddenly with a soft huff of laughter, as if he could not quite restrain himself. I stared. I'd never seen him like this before. "The truth is . . . and you cannot repeat this to anybody—though of course, of course I know you won't . . ." He paused, leaning against one of the polished pillars, his eyes black as midnight, and made a beckoning motion.

My heartbeat picked up. I stepped toward him, close enough to feel his warm breath grazing my skin as he whispered, "I've missed you, Xishi."

A sharp emotion sliced through me: joy so deep it resembled grief; grief so keen it resembled joy. The two were inseparable. I felt my breathing hitch.

Then, just as abruptly, he was walking ahead again, his head turned back toward me, a half-bitter smile on his lips. "Isn't it ironic?" he asked, his voice barely audible over the wind in the leaves, the silver splashing of water from the garden fountains. "I only have myself to blame. What is that old saying . . . cleverness overreaches itself? Cleverness outwits itself? All these years, I've prided myself on my intelligence, but—"

I held up a hand before he could say anything else, even though all I wanted was for him to continue. My heart was still beating much too fast, my blood rushing through my veins. "Not here," I said quickly, checking around us again. Emptiness, nothing but the shadows of the trees. Still, paranoia clung to me. "Come with me."

My footsteps quickened. We were walking side by side. I kept my eyes straight ahead on the path to the guest chambers, but I felt his cool fingers brush against mine. So quick it might have been an accident. My own imagination. Yet seconds later, his fingertips ran down the line of my palm. Another quick brush, the barest sliver of skin against skin. A small gasp rose to my throat.

I couldn't help sneaking a glance at him. His expression was controlled too, save for the faintest pink brushing the curve of his ears, creeping up the side of his neck, illuminated by the lantern lights. Yet his hand touched mine again; each time it was the barest, subtlest motion, concealed by the darkness and the flowing sleeves of our robes. It felt like a secret, a quiet rebellion. A stealing from fate, or perhaps a reclamation of what had been taken from us. My skin burned with the private knowledge, tingling in every place his long fingers skimmed over my own.

The guest chambers were tucked away in a remote courtyard. The lights were dimmer here, the grass neatly trimmed, but with no flowers growing. No maids positioned outside the gates.

I tugged the doors firmly shut behind us once we entered. The air possessed the stagnant, dusty quality of an unused room, the scent of old incense lingering over the rosewood furniture. I lit all the candles in the room one by one: by the single canopy bed, the drawers, the bronze mirror. Soon, light danced over every corner, suffusing the place in a faint orange glow.

Then I spun around and faced Fanli fully.

It had been so long since I'd seen him, even longer since I'd let myself just look at him this way. His face was as beautiful as ever, fine-boned and sharp-angled; it was what the sculptors modeled their greatest statues after, what poets wrote sonnets about, what artists tried and failed to capture in their paintings. Nothing on earth could replicate it. But all his remaining softness had diminished. Where there'd once been at least a brightness to his eyes, a curve of amusement to his lips, the natural charms of a boy, there was only black ice and cold jade.

And as I stared at him, I was aware of him taking me in too, his eyes trailing slowly from my head all the way down to my feet. It was not that hungry, possessive look I'd come to expect from Fuchai; it was more one of concern, as if assessing me for any signs of hunger or hardship, injury or abuse.

"How . . . have you been?" he asked at last, his eyes moving back up to meet mine. "Tell me everything."

I wanted to. All those days we'd been apart, every time the sun slipped from the sky and the moon rose to take its place, every meal I'd taken alone or with the king while he waited in another kingdom. Everything I'd endured flashed through my mind, but I did not know where to start, how to put it into words. So I just smiled. Shook my head. "I've done everything we agreed on. I received your note. The plan should go smoothly—"

"I'm not asking about the plan."

I looked at him in surprise. The plan was always his primary concern; the kingdom always came first.

"Xishi," he said, his words softly slurred, his voice throttled with some emotion I could not identify. "I'm sorry—"

He was *sorry?*

"You don't have to apologize for anything," I cut in. "Or feel indebted, if that's what you're worried about."

He stilled, then frowned, almost like a chastised child. "You're angry."

"I'm not." At least, I hadn't thought I was. But there was a new tightness in my chest, a tension building in the back of my throat. I thought of the poem again—a confession, or so I'd mistaken it for, only to discover it was another set of instructions. And now we were alone, *finally* alone, and he was apologizing for something we had both agreed to.

"You forget that I was the one who helped hone that mask of yours," he murmured. "I wouldn't blame you if you were angry with me—"

"I'm not angry at all," I said, deliberately sweetening my tone. "What is there to be angry about? I've had a wonderful time in the palace, didn't you know?"

"Xishi—"

"The king is an excellent kisser," I went on. I am not entirely sure what compelled me to say such a thing, but my eyes searched his face, hungry for a reaction. And I was rewarded. His jaw clenched, his whole expression flinching. "Don't imagine that I was *suffering* within these walls—I've never had so much fun. He will do anything to make me happy, and he is every bit as experienced as they say—"

Now his body recoiled too.

"You should see the way he looks at me," I said, every word cutting across the space between us like little blades, designed to hurt, "when we are lying together. Or how he—"

"What is your point?" He spoke like he was in pain, his eyes black-lashed and blazing. It hit me in a rush that he was even drunker than I'd thought. "Are you trying to make me jealous?"

I didn't reply. Couldn't.

"Because I am—a man too, you know," he said slowly, his voice husky and dark as the air around us. "I also feel . . . I have imagined it. I've tormented myself with these thoughts night after night, made myself sick with envy . . ."

I stepped closer. I could feel all the heat in the room rushing through my body. My nerves sang with the thrill of it, the unabashed boldness of my own movements. "So you really were jealous?"

He released a sigh through clenched teeth, his hands curled into fists. Around us, the candles lashed. "Xishi—"

It was as if the air between us had been dowsed with hot oil, lit up in flames. I blew out all the nearby candles in a few quick huffs, and darkness fell over the room like a veil, covering us inside it. I could just make out the soft line of his lips, the lump in his throat as he swallowed. Perhaps I should have stopped there, but it was the first time in forever that I felt so powerful. In control.

"Would you like me to show you, then, how I act around him?" I asked innocently, pressing closer, until I could feel his rapid heartbeat through my own robes. "There is a place, just around the neck—a weakness for him. Or is it that way for you as well?" My fingertips traced the hollow of his collarbone. A shudder ran through him. "I believe it was here." I lifted my hand higher, ran my fingers over the bare nape of his neck. His skin was so hot it burned under my touch.

"Xishi," he repeated again, strained. "Please."

I felt a small jolt of shock. He was begging. And here I'd thought he would never lower himself so as to beg anyone for anything, even if his own life was on the line. Yet my anger was a hard knot inside me; it could not be dissolved so easily. I needed more from him. I needed more for myself. So I continued, my fingers following the fine threads woven into his collar down to the hard planes of his chest. "Or was it here?" I mused. "Or lower, perhaps. Like—"

In the space of a heartbeat, he grabbed my wrist, pinning it to the wall behind me. He had such a scholarly air to him, with his refined beauty and slender fingers, perfect for gripping a brush, that sometimes I forgot how strong he was. How he was as much a soldier as he was an advisor. In another swift, solid movement, he had my whole body pressed against the wall, his other hand firm around my arm.

Then he stopped inches away from me, breathing hard.

Everything felt suspended. Time itself seemed to freeze, to still. But it was the look in his eyes that speared through my lungs. There was longing, but also such deep, incalculable sorrow, as though he understood my rage, my resentment, all that I'd overcome alone. And in response, I let myself deflate. Let my façade fall away from me, my posture slip from its dancer's frame. I gazed back at him without having to smile, to parade my beauty. In the darkness, he seemed to see me more clearly than anybody.

"I know," he whispered. "I know this has been unfair to you. I know you want to go home."

"I want more than that," I said.

He cast me a pained look. "What else, then?"

"You." The crude simplicity of my own words surprised me. In the palace, I had grown accustomed to polishing them into something unrecognizable, alluding to the moon's reflection in the water when I meant the moon itself.

Fanli had gone very quiet, his expression so strained, so close to fearful, that I laughed out loud at him. It was my real laugh, deep and a little hoarse at the edges, rattling free from my lungs. "You act like you're afraid of me," I remarked.

"I *am* afraid of you," he said, the truth tumbling fast from his lips. His body was trembling, even as he held his spine rigid. "I'm afraid of what comes over me when I'm around you. I'm afraid of how tempting it is, to ignore my own rationale, of how many excuses I can invent just to be closer to you. I'm afraid of how much—how much I want. Of what I want. I'm afraid of how easily my self-discipline slips. How quickly my judgment falters. Wherever you're concerned, I have to question myself constantly, evaluate and compartmentalize my own feelings, pick them apart and prod them for weaknesses. Did you know," he said on a broken breath, "that Zixu had sent his men to try to capture me, to bring me to the palace?"

I shook my head, stunned.

"There must have been fifty of them. Multiple attempts on my life. It was quite the nuisance, but I escaped them without much trouble."

"Then . . . how did he—" *How did he bring you here? How did he overpower you in the end?* I had questioned it often in the days after he left, wished we had more time together just so I could ask him, but no matter what scenarios I conjured, I could not produce a viable answer.

"He didn't." The corner of his mouth curled. "He sent a message, saying that you had been gravely wounded, and I came on my own accord. Even though I knew it was a trap. Even though I knew you were most likely fine, that my appearance in this kingdom would only bring trouble to us all. But just the thought—just the possibility, however slim and irrational, that something really had happened to you . . . It threatened to undo my sanity."

"So you came for me." It didn't seem real. I reached out across the tight space, my fingertips grazing the place where the sword had pierced his flesh. Where I had bandaged his wound.

This time, he didn't try to stop me. "Do you understand now?" he asked softly, with a tenderness that felt like death. "My discipline—my intellect—my judgment. Those are all the things I've come to depend on in life. They're what pulled me out of poverty, what lifted me through the ranks, what led me to the king. But now, I cannot trust any of that." His jaw clenched. "I cannot even trust myself."

Distantly, as if from another kingdom, another life, I thought of King Fuchai in that great, cold hall of his, the lantern light cascading over the golden walls, everything shining and bright and false, wine sloshing over goblets and plates heaped with food passing from table to table. I wished to never return.

"You have to go back to him soon," Fanli said, swallowing. How easily he read my mind. How well he knew me. "Go, before I lose the little control I have left."

"Then promise me you will come back," I urged, knowing it was childish, unreasonable, not the request of someone who had already left everything behind, entered the Wu palace as King Fuchai's concubine, a girl forged into a blade.

It was not like Fanli to make such promises either. He was too practical for that. I waited for him to tell me so. At the end of the day our lives were not so dissimilar; we were both weapons to be picked up and put down at King Goujian's will. We didn't have the power to decide these things for ourselves.

But to my surprise, he nodded. "I promise," he said softly, three fingers lifted to the dim air in a vow. "As soon as this ends, I'll come find you, and we'll sail the world together and live somewhere far from here, someplace we can be truly alone. And if my promise breaks . . . then let me suffer for as long as I live."

I stared at him. Then, after a stunned beat, I hit his shoulder.

He made a small noise of protest, though there was amusement laced within it too. "I see you've grown violent in our time apart."

"Why did you . . . I was only asking for a promise—I wasn't asking you to *curse* yourself—"

"I thought it would show sincerity," he said mildly, gazing at me in the dark. "And besides," he added under his breath, as though speaking to himself, "if for some reason I cannot see you again, then I shall suffer either way."

CHAPTER TWENTY-TWO

I CLOSED THE DOORS BEHIND HIM, CAREFUL TO KEEP them unlocked.

Then I stood with my back pressed against the cool wood, gazing up at the sky. The moon was especially clear tonight; scraps of gray clouds blew over it, outlined against its pearlescent glow. You could see every dark impression, every hollow. I remembered the myth Mother used to tell me before bedtime, about the girl who became a goddess, separated from her lover and forced to live on the moon with only her jade rabbit for company. I thought I could make out her silhouette in that play of light and shadow. I thought I could understand her loneliness.

But no point dwelling now. I shook my head, breathed slowly out.

It would be starting soon.

Instead of returning to the banquet, I followed the secret passageway Xiaomin had shown me, taking the shortcut to Lady Yu's chambers. She was in the courtyard this time, sitting alone on the swing, rocking gently back and forth. She lifted her head at the sound of my footsteps; she did not look surprised to see me.

"Remember our agreement?" I asked, not bothering with greetings.

"Unfortunately," she said, her voice weary. She continued swinging, letting the wind do most of the work. "What do you want?"

"Call upon your father first," I told her. "It's time."

Most of the guests had already retired when I finally went back to the king's side. There were men passed out on the table, heads lolling, their goblets bleeding wine. A few giggling noblewomen had snuck off into the shadows with the more charming guards and scholars, the pairs wrapped in a private embrace. Silks and streamers littered the floors; two of the hangings had slid from the walls. The music had died down too. Only a single instrumentalist remained, playing a soft, stirring tune on his guqin. As expected, Goujian was nowhere to be found.

Meanwhile, Fuchai was undoubtedly drunk, lying back on his throne with its raised view of the hall and twirling his crown around his finger like it was a toy.

"Xishi," he slurred as I approached, his eyes focusing on me. "What took you so long?" Before I could even reply, he grabbed my wrist and yanked me onto the throne with him, reaching around my neck, his breath warm against my ear. "Doesn't matter. Just—do not leave my side again."

I wanted to be unmoved. But perhaps it was how he gazed at me, so unassuming and sincere and trusting; perhaps it was because I had just been with Fanli, while Fuchai watched the crowds and waited for me; or perhaps it was because I knew what was coming. A wild guilt tore through my chest, and I pressed my body tighter to his, letting him wrap his arms fully around me. I could hear his thundering heartbeat, that familiar rhythm, always so quick to respond to my presence, my every word.

"What do you want tonight?" I asked him. "Name it, and it is yours."

He pulled back slightly, his mouth parted in surprise. Then he laughed. "What is this? I'm usually the one to grant your wishes."

"I know," I said, feeling that odd, unwelcome pain again. My stomach felt cold. I imagined the scene unfolding outside the hall, beyond the dark city gates. The Yue army would have mobilized already, having taken the route down the just-built canal. I imagined thousands of feet marching, their spearpoints glinting in the moonlight. "I just want to—to repay you. Whatever you ask, I won't say no."

He peered down at me with interest, his eyes intensely dark. "Whatever I ask?"

A flush crept up my neck. I thought I had some idea of what he desired. Part of me was still surprised he had waited so long.

"It cannot be here," he said, rising from the throne. I had to hold his arm to keep him steady. "Come with me."

I went, my skin growing hotter by the second. In his room, surrounded by scarlet lanterns and gilded furniture and forest-green jade carvings, he lay down on the bed and patted the space next to him. I approached slowly, carefully, on tiptoe, shrugging loose the satin sash and my heavy outer robes. My every breath felt fraught.

He waited, patient. But when I took my place beside him, he made no movement to kiss me. Instead he curled his body around mine like a child, his chest pressed to my back. The warmth of his skin engulfed me, not in an unpleasant way; it was like sleeping next to a blazing fire. There was something so . . . peaceful about the gesture.

"What are you doing?" I asked, unable to hide my confusion.

"You asked me what I wanted," he said simply, his voice muffled by my hair. "I . . ." He cleared his throat. When he spoke again, he sounded almost shy. "I want to hold you for a while, like this. Is that all right?"

It felt like someone had jabbed a needle through my heart. I inhaled. "Of—of course, Fuchai."

He sighed, then began to comb my hair back with his fingers. He moved ever so slowly, his fingertips scraping against my scalp, a light brush, there and then gone. "I would give up everything for you, you realize?"

It was not the first time he had said something like this, but in the deceptive quiet after the banquet, in light of everything yet to happen, it suddenly felt ominous. I tried to hide the tension in my body. "Don't say such dire things," I scolded, my tone teasing.

"Fine," he acquiesced. "Then tell me something good. A story. A memory from your childhood."

"My childhood?" If I didn't know better, I'd think he was testing me, searching for information about my background. But his tone was gentle as ever, his touch even more so. A heaviness settled in my bones. "What kind of memory?"

"Anything."

I mulled it over. He wanted something good, but so many of my memories from our village were tinged with some shade of sadness, or fear, or worry. I could not tell him about the days when our grain stores were depleted, when we forced ourselves to go to sleep earlier just to escape the pinch of hunger in our stomachs, the rationing of a single yellow millet bun into thirds, and then fourths, and then fifths. I could not tell him about the plague that had swept through our kingdom, the terrifying and uncertain months where everyone stayed huddled in their houses and covered their faces with scraps of fabric when they went out; how a small scratching sensation in the back of the throat, a faint rash, felt like a death sentence. I could not tell him either about the times the skin on my hands split open, from soaking in the river too long and scrubbing raw silk too hard.

But were there good things? Of course. Even when life was terrible, there was still my mother's comfort, my father's presence, Zhengdan's ringing laughter, the budding peonies and the flowing river.

"We used to play a game," I began. "My parents and I. One would be designated the role of wolf, and the other two were sheep—but you only knew your own role, and not the others. You would close your eyes, and the wolf would choose its victim, and when you opened your eyes again, you had to guess who the wolf was. You only had one chance to get it right."

He nodded at me to go on. He was still playing with my hair. It was surprisingly pleasant, surprisingly soothing—almost too soothing. I could feel my eyelids growing heavier and heavier.

"My mother and I would often team up in secret," I said, ignoring the pang inside me. *It cannot hurt to share this much with him,* I reasoned to myself. Not now. Or perhaps I wanted to give him something honest, something real; perhaps I thought he deserved that much. "It was an ongoing joke between us. No matter who the wolf was, we would always accuse my father. But of course we could tell when it really was him; he was a terrible liar, and he would always ramble when he was nervous, and rap his knuckles on the table. If he suspected that I was the wolf, though, he would try to act like he didn't know. He didn't want to accuse me of anything, even if I was in the wrong—" A lump formed in my throat. I pushed on. "Even if it was only a game."

"They sound lovely," Fuchai murmured.

"What about you?" I asked, eager to shift the focus away from me. "What games did you play as a child?"

"I don't remember much," he said. "Once I was declared the crown prince . . . I stopped playing."

"You weren't allowed to?"

"No." He hesitated. "Well, I wasn't encouraged to—my days were filled with classes on royal etiquette and such. But even when I had the time, the games were never any fun. The other children had been taught to fear me, and so no matter what happened, they let me win very quickly. Sometimes, for the more physical games, they refused to participate at all, for fear they might actually push me or hurt me and be executed for it. Then there were the attendants, who followed me everywhere I went, and always intervened if they thought there was the slightest risk of me getting injured."

I turned around. A mistake. His face was sweet in the dim light, his hair tousled against the sheets.

"Since they would not play with me . . . well, I had to invent other ways to entertain myself. If they were so careful about etiquette, so afraid of offending, then from time to time I would snap at them for the smallest thing and drag them outside to be punished. Just occasionally enough to keep them guessing and on their toes. I suppose *that* was fun, and a game, in a sense. One that only I could play." He spoke in an offhand manner, like it was a joke, but there was a sadness to his gaze. A touch of loneliness.

We were already so close that I could feel the rise and fall of his breathing, but I inched even closer, my body pressed to his, until nothing could possibly stand between us. From the instant I entered the palace over two years ago, I had dreamed of this. I had trained for the moment when Goujian arrived, when all the guards were stationed in their respective positions, when the Yue soldiers—*our* soldiers—marched through the gates. But suddenly I found myself wondering if it wouldn't be quite so terrible to delay it all by another day. Just one day, to give more back to him. To allay my own guilt.

"Is there something wrong?" Fuchai asked, smiling, his long

fingers running through my hair. "I'm not used to you being so . . . open with your affections."

"Do you mind it?"

"Never."

"Really?"

"Of course." A beat. "This is . . . nice," he said softly. "I wish we could stay like this forever."

The heaviness in my limbs grew. I stifled a yawn.

"Xishi," I thought I heard him say. "Xishi."

I was too exhausted to speak. "Mm?"

"No, nothing." I heard the smile in his voice. "Rest, if you need to. I'll look after you."

I don't remember closing my eyes. But even as darkness fell over me, I was aware of the warmth of his body, the evening scent of his skin; all that should have been foreign to me, now as intimate as the back of my hand. As the drums of war sounded in the distance, signaling a new age, a new dawn, there I lay, falling sound asleep in the arms of the enemy.

Somebody was shaking me.

I opened my eyes, squinting. The candles had been lit, their reddish glow casting strange, misshapen shadows over the walls, and Fuchai was standing before me. It was his expression that woke me up completely. He always had a careless look about him, like nothing was quite worth his attention. I had never seen him like this: his hands trembling, his lips pressed tight into a bloodless line. At the same moment, a horn blared in the distance; it was not the first time. Urgent footsteps thundered outside our chambers; cries and the clang of steel. Everything about it was distorting, the peace of the night erupting into violence. The horn blared again, like the shriek of a child.

It's happening, I thought, my blood flashing hot and cold.

Fuchai lifted his hand from my shoulder and rested it deliberately on the hilt of his sword. Then he drew it from its sheath, throwing off a streak of cold, silver light, half blinding me.

I felt the air escape my lungs. He had found out. He knew I was the one who had planned it all, and now he would kill me for my treachery. My thoughts raced with my heartbeat. Perhaps I could beg him for forgiveness, just to buy myself time—perhaps I could weaponize whatever affections he still felt for me, at least until the Yue came—

"Xishi," he said, his tone grave, his eyes black as flint. He lifted his sword.

"I—wait, Fuchai." My voice was still croaky from sleep. I shook my head wildly. "Wait—let me—"

He moved toward me. My entire body froze, dreading the pain, the end of everything. But the blade didn't so much as touch me. Instead he pulled me to him, locking me in a firm embrace, his head bent over the curve of my neck. "Don't be afraid," he murmured. "I'll protect you. Whatever happens—I won't let them touch you."

Relief engulfed me, but it was followed by a wave of guilt. So he didn't know, not yet.

"What's going on?" I asked, letting all my remaining fear seep into my voice. "What's wrong?"

The doors slammed open before he could reply. A guard rushed inside, his cheek smeared with blood and soot. He fell onto his knees halfway across the room and bowed low, the *thud* so loud it echoed. "Your Majesty, the palace has been surrounded—they're coming through the northern gates—"

"What?" Fuchai was still holding me. I could feel the muscles in his shoulders contract. "What happened to General Yu?"

Lady Yu's father. I held my breath.

"There was apparently a—a skirmish near the southern gates." The guard's teeth knocked together. It was a miracle he didn't bite off his own tongue. "He was called down to investigate—we're still unclear what happened. All we know is that half the guards had vacated their usual posts—"

"This doesn't make sense," Fuchai said. Even without seeing him, I imagined the disbelief etched into his features, the slight downward tug of his lips. "How did they get here so fast?"

"They came by—by boat. Through the canal."

Silence. The commotion outside only seemed to grow louder by contrast, screams cutting through the night, orders shouted down the open courtyards and narrow corridors. Torches flashed past the windows, guards sent out one after the other, their armor rattling. The air felt too hot, too sticky, closing in. I could smell something burned.

Without meaning to, my fingers tightened over Fuchai's arm, digging into his robes.

"We have to escape," Fuchai said, as if coming out of a daze. He spoke clearly, with forced calm. "It isn't safe here anymore—"

There's nowhere to hide, I thought in my head, though of course I couldn't say it. *Fanli would have every exit covered. Even if we leave, he'll send his men after you and track you down in days.*

"Your carriage has already been prepared," the guard said in a rush. His eyes kept darting to the doors. The footsteps were getting louder, approaching from both sides. I heard the scrape of sword against sword, frantic yells—then the *thud* of bodies hitting the ground. "Leave now and—"

"Your Majesty!" The doors burst open again, but this time it was a servant that came stumbling in. There was something off about him, not quite in proportion. My stomach gave an awful lurch when I realized what it was. His left hand had been severed.

Reduced to a mangled stump. Blood gushed from it, soaking the floors. When he knelt and bowed, it was only with one arm. He wobbled, fought to maintain his balance, his face bleached white.

Even from here, the sharp scent of rust filled my nose. I thought I might be sick.

"Please—do not forget," he gasped, each word pained, blood gurgling in his throat. I finally recognized him. He was the re-minder Fuchai had appointed. "Do not forget . . . your father's . . . dying wish. Do not forget . . . the Yue—"

And then he crumpled. I watched, a new dread blooming inside me, like a flowering wound. I had caused this. I was the harbinger of death, of everyone's demise within these walls.

Fuchai was tugging at my arm. His voice in my ear. "Leave him. Let's go."

Numbly, I gathered my robes around myself, my cloak pulled up over my hair, and followed him out the side door, flanked by a group of guards. The points of their halberds gleamed around us like gathered stars. I refused to look at their faces; soon they would be gone too. Someone barked out orders, words of warning. *Head straight to . . . Whatever you do, do not stop . . . You'll be safe . . .* I nodded along, my mind buzzing. But at the exit, I faltered. I could still hear the maids screaming from within the palace walls. Would our soldiers spare them? Or kill them all?

It chilled me to realize that I had not given it much thought.

"Wait," I said. "Bring Xiaomin with us."

Fuchai frowned at me, uncomprehending. "Xiaomin?"

"We must go, my lady," one of the guards urged me. The screams grew louder, sharper, whittling into pleas. "There's not enough time—"

"The maid," I insisted. "Please. Make sure she comes too."

"Just do as she says," Fuchai told them, and only when the guards nodded did I let him guide me outside.

The night air stung my skin. It smelled strange, unnatural, like metal and leather and horsehide. Like war. The scene was too dark to be distinct—a relief for my conscience—just black shadows tangled together. It was impossible to tell enemy from ally. But every now and then the torchlight would flash, and the horrors would be thrown into sharp relief: a young face, twisted in pain; a torso with an arrow pierced through it, carrying flesh through to the other side; hair and armor matted with patches of dark blood; a mouth ripped open in a soundless scream. *Suffering*, no matter how or where you looked, no matter who these people fought for.

My stomach churned. And who did they fight for? Goujian. Fuchai. Two kings, born into power, twin sides of a knife. One who was awaiting news of his victory from a safe distance, the other who was fleeing.

The soldiers flowed in from the gates, their bronze plates and helmets gleaming together like a dark, unwinding river, one that extended from the beginning to the end of the world. I saw the banner of Yue fluttering from one soldier's hand, the Wu flag trampled under countless feet. A cold sweat sprang up over my skin.

This is how kingdoms fall, I thought, but I didn't feel as victorious as I'd imagined. My heart was too heavy, a solid stone in my chest.

We were closer to the conflict than ever, and a familiar face burned in my view. General Ma. He was fighting five men at the same time, his sword lashing out. For a few seconds, he appeared to be winning; he thrust the blade into one man's stomach, then sent another crashing down with one blunt kick to the knee.

He was freeing his sword when an arrow shot through his chest.

It was that quick: a blink, a rush of shape and sound. He didn't seem to believe it himself. When he looked down at the shaft protruding from his heart, he wore the same expression of incredulity he'd worn when Zhengdan had beaten him in that duel.

As his body fell silently in the crowd, all I could think was: *Zhengdan should've been here to witness it.*

"Be careful, Lady Xishi," a guard whispered, his shield raised above my head, urging me along as if I had not just watched someone die. He had a kind face, his cheeks full, his eyes round and long-lashed. "Watch your step. We're almost there."

I could barely hear him over all the screaming, the scraping metal. The sounds of splintered bone. It felt like I was moving underwater in a dream sequence, like nothing was real. I had only been trained for the prelude to this, for the catalyst, not the consequences.

Then the guard inhaled sharply. The whites of his eyes shone.

That was all I saw before he collapsed right beside me, a spear twisted into his side. I didn't even have time to react, to grieve. Another guard immediately stepped in to take his place, his back bared to the incoming soldiers.

"Don't be scared." Fuchai had grabbed my hand and didn't let go until we were escorted through the cover of a corridor, and then inside the prepared carriage. The horses were already pawing the ground, their nostrils flaring, uneasiness rippling through their muscles.

I yanked the door shut behind me just as an arrow shot toward us, embedding itself in the carriage wood. The metal tip of it protruded, glinting through the red paintwork. I couldn't stop staring at it with a kind of revulsed fascination, as if it were rising from my own flesh.

"*Go,*" Fuchai commanded the driver, and the carriage jumped into motion, the horses' hooves drumming the ground.

Like this we fled into the night. Mount Guxu awaited us in the southwest; everything had already been arranged. I watched from the window as the palace disappeared behind us, ash-black smoke billowing from all the beautiful chambers and halls, the vermilion walls made redder with blood, soldiers pouring in one wave after another, creating an endless flood of knives and arrows. If you had asked me to describe it, I might have called it beautiful. Beautiful not in the way of a painting or poetry, but a natural disaster: a storm, or a falling comet. The intensity of it drew your eyes in and held you there, the sheer scale of it breathtaking. How many were able to witness history as it unfurled? Already I could imagine the books composed for this very day, the tales told by the fireplace. But I could also hear the dying men's howls and their curses as if they were right beside my ear, addressing me.

I was shaking. I didn't realize it until Fuchai reached over from across the carriage seat and stilled my fingers with his. They were smooth, warm, not a single scar or callus on them. They had likely never touched blood before, not directly. All those men in court, in the training grounds, primed to handle those ugly tasks for him.

"It's going to be okay," he told me, his voice pressed low and soothing.

It wouldn't be, and my knowledge of it strangled me. I couldn't help it. "I'm sorry," I blurted.

"Sorry?" A faint furrow of his brows. He leaned back in that dim, cramped space, surrounded by embroidered cushions. "For what?"

I swallowed. "Because—because the Yue are attacking and . . . and I'm Yue." It was the closest to the truth I could give him.

He studied me for a long time. Long enough to make me nervous. Then he smiled, completely sincere. "You know, if you hadn't said so, I would've forgotten. The truth is," he murmured, "you've long become a Wu person in my eyes. What is home, if not you?"

I smiled back at him, but ducked my head in the shadows, so he could not see my lips trembling.

CHAPTER
TWENTY-THREE

THE SUN WAS JUST STARTING TO PULL ITSELF UP OVER the horizon when we reached the mountain peak. The last time we were here, it had simply been to flee the heat of the summer. A small, isolated room had been carved into the rock, like a temple but without the altars and the sweet incense smoke and red mats for kneeling. But the air here was thick with prayer anyway.

There weren't many of us left. Fuchai and I entered the room first, followed by a dozen or so guards, a few ministers I vaguely recognized, and a handful of maids, Xiaomin among them. She was still in her nightclothes, a flimsy layer of white cloth wrapped around her shivering body. Tears shone on her cheeks.

"Are you all right?" I asked her. A foolish question, but I could not think of anything else.

"My sister," she whispered.

"What?"

"My little sister." She choked out the word, like it might kill her. "She's still somewhere inside that palace—I couldn't find her. I couldn't . . . I couldn't save her. She must have been so scared . . ."

I stepped back, feeling sick. When I'd mounted the horse on the riverbanks, left my home for the palace, I had imagined the world righting itself, the scales tipping back, the balance finally restored in Susu's absence. That was what revenge was. What it promised. But now the ground seemed to sway violently beneath my feet, everything spinning into reverse.

I raised a hand to comfort her, then withdrew it. She would likely wish to scrub her skin raw once she found out what I'd done.

Instead I made myself go back to Fuchai's side. He was staring around the room. The furniture was simple, sparse, designed for practicality rather than aesthetic; there were none of the jeweled vases and intricate tapestries he was used to, the luxuries of a king. All of us seemed to be waiting for—something, I don't know what. Perhaps he would kill someone, or kill himself, or fall to the ground and weep.

Then he shrugged off his traveling cloak and reached for a jug of wine. Popped the seal. Took a swig.

"This really doesn't taste as good," he muttered, but continued drinking all the same.

In my peripheral vision, I saw the looks exchanged, the questions asked by gaze only, with no one to answer. *What comes next?* The maid next to Xiaomin was crying, stifling her sobs with her fist. The guards wore varying expressions of shock, fear, disbelief. These were people who had been taught to obey the king at all costs, to forever place the kingdom before the self. It posed the greatest question of all: Could there be a king without a kingdom?

"Fuchai," I began.

"Come sit with me," he said, lowering himself to the ground until he was sitting cross-legged, like a student in class, then patting the space beside him. I approached slowly.

"Fuchai," I tried again. "Are you . . ."

"I'm fine." He wiped his mouth with his sleeve, resting his head against the faded gray wall, his dark hair falling over his eyes. The future plays about him would all be tragedies, I thought to myself, a small but sharp blade twisting in my heart. "Listen, Xishi . . ." His breathing was oddly staggered. I scanned him in confusion, and spotted the crimson patch staining his left sleeve. It didn't stand out well against the black of his robes, but there was enough blood to reasonably conclude that the cut wasn't fresh.

"You're hurt," I said, frowning.

I waited for him to pout, to lean close, to exaggerate his pain and ask for comfort. But he just shook his head, hiding his sleeve behind him, and drank deeply from the wine jug using his other arm. "Just a scrape," he said, his voice mild.

"But—"

"This is important," he insisted. "Just listen for a moment, okay? This is really—a revelation. I've been thinking about it, and I've decided . . . none of it matters."

"What?"

"The kingdom." He tilted his head farther back, eyes closed. "The land, the lakes, the places of worship. All the gold and the godly statues and the jewels. I'm willing to give them all up," he said, a grin splitting across his face like lightning, "as long as I can be with you always."

I stared. I had not imagined this. It was one thing to know that he desired me, that he enjoyed my presence, admired my dancing, that I occupied a place in his heart few others ever would. But what he spoke of now—it sounded suspiciously like love. "You don't know what you're talking about," I managed.

"I do," he said sincerely.

"You're drunk."

"I'm always drunk."

He was not wrong. "You are a king," I reminded him, gazing around the room at all the somber faces, those who had left their homes and their lives behind just to serve him. "The kingdom is your birthright."

"Is that a no?" He looked more agitated than when the Yue had been on his doorstep. He'd set his jug down, shifting forward to meet my eyes. "Don't you wish to be with me too?"

The words stopped in my throat. I didn't know what to say, how to tell him that none of this mattered anyway. Would it be kinder to feed him another lie now? Or give him the truth?

I was a coward; I shrank from the question, took the easy way out. "We can talk about this another day," I told him gently, knowing there were no days left.

First we heard the hoofbeats. Distant, but growing more distinct by the second, getting higher and higher up the mountain path. Then the swishing of armor.

"Are those reinforcements?" a maid asked hopefully, running to the entrance. "Maybe they're coming to rescue us."

Fuchai had already run through the supply of wine available. He blinked at the noise, as if pulled here from a great distance. Then he rose, supporting himself against the wall with his good arm, and said with sudden, surprising sharpness: "Don't open the door."

Too late.

The maid fell back with a startled cry, and an emissary marched in, surrounded by soldiers. They were all well trained, a perfect line of men in fine-quality uniforms, their hair left long and pinned into sleek black knots atop their heads, the Yue flag flying out behind them. Next to the Wu—the cowering maids, the exhausted guards with their tunics hanging in tatters, the ministers slouched by the far walls—their preeminence was a visible fact, a taunt. The air seemed to solidify around them.

The shriek of a sword. In two strides, Fuchai had stepped in front of me, throwing his injured arm before my body, his sword pointed at the emissary. Someone cried out.

My blood had become ice. Years of preparing for this very moment, and now it was happening too quickly.

"Get back," Fuchai warned.

The emissary was a tall, lean man with a face like a hawk and the build of an archer. He looked like the kind of person Fanli might pick out from a crowd, seeing potential others didn't. He regarded Fuchai with cold disdain, and Fuchai's sword as if it were a stick wielded by a boy. "Do you even know how to fight?" he scoffed.

I could see the color rise up the back of Fuchai's neck. In the palace, everything and everyone was his; nobody ever dared scorn him. Still, when he spoke, he retained the dignity of a king. "Well enough to cut off your head."

The emissary made another scoffing noise, but didn't draw his sword. "No need. You're outnumbered; surely even you can see that?"

Fuchai stared around the room in silence. For every Wu guard and maid left, at least two Yue soldiers stood, armed with polished blades and carved shields. The doors had been blocked, the windows locked tight. Outside lay the sheer drop of the cliff, and a treacherous mountain path that required the best steeds to navigate.

"But don't worry," the emissary said, pacing around the room with leisure. He stopped only to snap a fan open and hold it out over his face so only those coldly gleeful eyes were showing. I wondered if Fanli had specifically asked him to be as infuriating as possible, to better rub the salt in the wound. But no, that was not quite Fanli's style—to be malicious without reason, to stomp over the dead body once it had already cooled. It was more like something Goujian would do. "I'm not here to pick a fight, only to deliver a message from King Goujian."

"Goujian," Fuchai repeated with vehemence. Under the black fury in his voice, I sensed the sting of betrayal too. Perhaps he had genuinely considered the two of them friends. From everything Fuchai had told me, it was not as if he'd had much experience with real friendship.

"He says he can be magnanimous and spare you. If you agree to leave right now, he is willing to arrange for you to travel to Yongdong; you will be allotted three hundred families there to wait upon you for the rest of your days. You will never have to worry about hunger or poverty until your old age; that will all be taken care of."

My heart thudded almost painfully. I knew it was more a calculated jibe than a gesture of goodwill, and yet . . . some weak part of me wished Fuchai would agree to it. His palace lay in ruins; his kingdom, wrestled from his control. Perhaps he need not die too.

I couldn't fully make out Fuchai's features, but when he spoke, there was mockery laced in his tone. "How generous. Is that all?"

"That is all," the emissary said, smiling. Then he caught my eye over Fuchai's shoulder, and recognition flashed over his face. I felt my pulse throb. "Oh, I did also have a message for Xishi."

Everything seemed to go completely still. Then, very slowly, Fuchai turned toward me, confusion written over his features. "What?"

What happened next took even me by surprise. The emissary bowed low, only as one would bow to a king, or a great hero. One by one, the other soldiers joined, a rising tide of motion, their spines bent, their heads dipped toward me.

"King Goujian would like to congratulate you, and thank you for your outstanding service to the Yue," the emissary said, that cold, provocative tone wiped clean. Now he spoke only with respect, his voice earnest. "Without your help, the Yue's resurrection would never have been possible. Your mission is now complete."

All eyes in the room fell on me. But the only ones I could focus on were Fuchai's. I would never be freed from the memory; even beyond the grave, I would see it, that moment of terrible understanding, when everything fell into place. Such hurt blazed in them—as if I had dealt him a physical blow, driven a knife through his flesh. It was the kind of grief that could kill you: grief over the living. His sword arm wavered.

"He's lying," he whispered.

"No," I made myself say. My voice came out remarkably steady, like it was a separate entity from me. "No, Fuchai. I've been lying to you."

He shook his head as he stared at me, just stared and stared. He looked completely speechless, clutching at some wound that no one else could see. No one but me. I watched how every memory we'd ever shared was recast in a different light; every soft word spoken, every tender touch, every quiet promise. He was trembling.

"Since when?"

"Since the very beginning." I let the answer sink in, cutting to the core of him. "It's the only reason I came. To steal your heart, and ruin your kingdom."

The tremors in his hands intensified. "So—Zixu was right."

I could not reply.

The emissary broke the silence. "Lady Xishi, you may take your leave now. We'll handle the rest from here—"

"Don't." The word was breathless, raw. Fuchai was still gazing at me with that wretched, torn expression, his eyes the black of a moonless winter night. "Not—not yet. Tell me something, Xishi. Anything. Isn't there . . ." He steadied his voice before it broke. His hand was reaching for the empty air, grasping at nothing. "Isn't there something you wish to say to me?"

"I hate you," I whispered. I had envisioned this moment ten thousand times over. In my imagination, I spat the words out like a curse. I screamed them at him while I beat at his flesh. I watched with pleasure while he crumpled, recited every crime the Wu had ever committed against the Yue. All our fallen soldiers, all our lost men, all our broken homes. Zhengdan, her hand falling limp on the floor. Fanli, the sword twisting deeper and deeper into his chest. All the vengeance-hungry ghosts rising around me like black smoke, waiting for exactly this. And yet my voice was soft, not a weapon, but a song. I could conjure no flames; I was too hollow, drowning in cold blood, my insurmountable sorrow, my unspeakable grief. How much loss could one soul tolerate?

"What?" Fuchai asked, like he didn't believe it. Refused to.

"I hate you," I said again, repeated it over and over like a chant, like a prayer. As if it were something I was trying to convince myself of. I *needed* to hate him. Everything I had sacrificed led to this. "I hate you, I hate you, I—I *hate you*—" I broke off, breathing hard, unable to continue.

His pupils shrank into two fine points, his face ashen. Then, to my shock, he smiled. It was startlingly beautiful, but it was all wrong. "Good," he said quietly, advancing a step, fingers outstretched as if to brush my face the way he had a hundred times before. There was a rustle of movement; the emissary and the waiting soldiers immediately tensing, weapons at the ready, waiting to intervene. But I gave them a small, silent shake of my head. It was just me and Fuchai: the enemy king, my great tormentor, my heartsick nemesis. "At least you admit you feel something for me."

Then he turned to the emissary, and spoke calmly, clearly, "Tell Goujian that I thank him for his offer, but there'll be no need."

The emissary frowned, not understanding. But I did. My body was frozen to the ground; all I could hear was the violent rushing of blood through my veins, like a hundred rivers churning at once, flowing on to the very depths of the world.

Fuchai was still smiling at me with painful gentleness. Just as gently as one would offer up a bright bloom of flowers, an intricate hairpin, their hand in marriage, he extended his sword to me. "Do it."

"I . . . I can't—"

"If I am to die, I want you to be the one to kill me." His smile widened, like a burst of light in a gray storm, a melting of ice in early spring. And there was the sword between us, the hilt facing me. A choice. An ending. "I want this to be the last of my memories."

"Fuchai—"

"Please," he said. "There can be nobody else but you."

In the back of my mind the images flashed, a roar of noise and color: Susu gasping her final breath, the heavy creases bracketing my mother's lips, the fire blazing in our village, the cracks running through our walls like scars. The cold satisfaction of his gaze as he watched Fanli suffer, the mocking, wolfish curve of his smile.

But also: his face in the dawn light when he was just waking, still drowsy and content, turning to me already. His hands clasped around mine in the winter to warm them. His laughter when I teased him, when he leaned in during a meeting to tell me a private joke. His chopsticks dropping the most tender slice of pork or the sweetest red date into my bowl before his own.

How could I ever forgive him?

Yet how could I ever fully hate him?

I saw my fingers close around the hilt, as if I were a spirit suspended over my own body. I saw my grip tighten—twice. I was shaking so hard I almost dropped it. The sword was so heavy it could have been molded from pure jade or gold. I saw my arms move.

Fuchai closed his eyes, his lashes outlined dark and long against his cheeks, tilting his head back slightly. When the tip of the sword sank in, he flinched, a low sound escaping his throat, but didn't try to retreat. He just stood there, letting me drive the blade through his heart. Ribbons of red spilled over my palms, trickled down my wrists. My skin was too hot, wet and clammy with blood.

And there was blood on his lips, too, a stain of crimson in the low light.

History seemed to be holding its breath, gazing down upon us.

The king of Wu crumpled, and then he was no longer a king at all, but a boy, bleeding against my robes. I held him. His eyes fluttered open, focused on me; it was how he had looked at me in all our time together, across the palace rivers, across the polished floors of his chambers, underneath the moonlight. No matter where we were, he was always the first one to spot me, always the last to look away. As if afraid I would disappear at any moment, like smoke in a breeze. As if he knew that one day, he would run out of time, out of chances.

"Xishi," he said. By now he was already too weak, his breathing shallow, his voice but the faintest whisper. I had driven the sword all the way in. "Let me—see you properly."

I bowed my head, my shoulders shaking. His blood pooled on the floors around us, shining on stone. He stared up at my face for a long time, saying nothing, his black locks spilled over my lap. Something wet splashed onto his cheeks from above. Tears.

Who was I crying for? Perhaps for myself. Perhaps for him.

Perhaps for both of us, the borders of our fate. Now that he was dying, I could finally bring myself to admit it: I did not want to lose him.

We were close enough for me to feel his broken heartbeat. I was used to listening for it, how it quickened and changed in my presence, whenever I smiled at him or touched his hair or simply drew near. Now I listened to it fade, to its faint, final *thud*—

Then everything went quiet.

Those last moments I remember only in flashes.

Someone came to prize Fuchai's body away from me. They told me later that I was weeping, pressing my palms to his chest as if I could stanch the bleeding, as if I could undo the fatal wound. Someone else led me down the mountain, the Yue soldiers following, the glint of their swords and spears like fish scales under water. All of it like a dream. *You can go home*, they kept telling me. But now when I thought of home, my mind was blank. It was a foreign word. I was free, yes. Finished with my mission. Perhaps I could travel across the kingdom, to every place the river water touched the soil, witness all of the four seas. But home? I could no longer even tell you what it meant, much less where it was.

Then—suddenly, it seemed to me—we were offered a sweeping view of the kingdom. The sun shone, bright and piercing, and the winding river threw off silver ripples of light. The sky was a blue so deep it hardly seemed real. Birds glided over the off-white houses and the little bridges and the clustered roads, and the mountains stood layered against each other in darkening shades of indigo. All under Heaven, laid out before me. It was strange. It seemed *wrong* in some vague but fundamental way. In folklore, when the monster was killed, the enemy conquered, there was always some sort of unnatural sign, some rare sighting to mark the birth of a new era. Fuchai was meant to be the problem, his downfall the one solution. But now he was gone, and the world remained the same.

My robes were still stiff with his blood. It coated the hem of my sleeves, stained my hair. I was offered a flimsy cloth to wipe my hands clean, but I refused. I said nothing, except—

"Where's Fanli?" My voice was hoarse, rubbed raw. I had to repeat myself. "Where is he? Is he safe? Is he coming?"

"He's aiding King Goujian with state affairs," came the response from behind me. "But he asked to give you this."

The emissary handed me a scroll. I unrolled it with shaking fingers. It was his writing, his beautiful calligraphy, his familiar, concise tone:

Find me by the river where we first met. And you must watch out for—

I frowned down at the message, my pulse picking up. Watch out for . . . *what?* The side of the scroll had been smeared with blood, stained during the battle. I held it up to the sunlight, but I could only see dark red blots, obscuring the words underneath.

Despite the warmth of the day, a shiver rolled through me. It felt like my scalp was trying to crawl off my head.

Watch out . . .

Instinctively, I turned around to scan the narrow path, but there were only the soldiers murmuring among themselves as they walked.

". . . is dead."

My heart thudded. I slowed my steps and listened harder.

"The Wu minister Bo Pi?" Another voice asked in shock. "You can be certain?"

"It's spread all the way from the palace. He was killed by King Goujian."

It felt like somebody had shoved me without warning. A coldness spread through my bones.

"On what grounds?"

"For disloyalty, apparently. Something about deceiving his king with poor advice and throwing all the realm of Wu into danger."

The other soldier was silent for a moment. "He is a fair man, then; one who weeds out all traitors, even the traitor of his own enemy. He should make a good king."

Those around him nodded in assent, but my blood only grew colder. They did not know what I did. That all of Bo Pi's poor advice, his deception, his lies—they were merely done upon Goujian's instruction. The two of us were Goujian's greatest weapons in the court of Wu, his eyes and ears. To have killed Bo Pi for exactly what he had been bribed to do . . .

Unease prickled over my skin like tiny needles. *You are being paranoid*, I reasoned with myself, forcing my fingers to uncurl. *It has nothing to do with you.* After all, no matter where Bo Pi's loyalties lay, he was still at his core a man from Wu, born and raised in the enemy kingdom. It made sense for Goujian to distrust him. But I was different. I was Yue, just like him, just like the civilians he had sworn to protect. He ought to recognize me as one of his own.

Even so. I had been wondering if Goujian would ever appear and thank me in person, but now I thought it was fine that we didn't meet again at all. Let him have his mountains and lakes, his kingdom and his legacy. I would go to my river in the village, where the water was always cool and sweet, and gaze across the shore for Fanli. My heart reached for him, aching. Not long now. Not long until everything was really over.

CHAPTER
TWENTY-FOUR

IT WAS THE MORNING AFTER WE'D REACHED THE BASE OF the mountain and rested in a nearby inn. I'd gone to sleep thinking of Fuchai's expression as I drove the blade in. I woke up drenched in sweat and shaking. After I changed into a fresh set of robes and stepped down for breakfast, a familiar face rose to greet me by the front doors. It was not the face I most wanted to see, but my heart leaped all the same. Time seemed to bend, and for one sacred moment, I was just the girl in Riversong Cottage again, reliving those warm, bloodless days spent in the haze of the mountain mist, playing the guqin and reciting pretty poetry.

"Luyi," I cried, forgetting all propriety and running forward to throw my arms around him. He smelled like rust and sea salt, and his skin was warm as summer sand under the sun.

He grinned, hardly caring for how the surrounding soldiers and guests eyed us with faint disapproval. He had grown even taller in the days since we'd parted, his shoulders stronger, his skin a little darker. I'd never had a brother before, but as he patted my back and laughed into my hair, I wondered if this was how it felt. "I hear you've been pretty busy. Changing the course of history and all."

I managed to roll my eyes as I pulled back. "How are you?"

"The same as usual. Subject to Fanli's irrational requests. He's been in a dark mood ever since . . ." He trailed off, hastily covered it up with a smile. "Well, you will see for yourself."

My gaze flickered to the open door behind him. I could not help myself—even though I already knew he was with Goujian, that during a critical time like this, with the kingdom changing hands between rulers, he would not simply abandon his duties and come find me. Disappointment pinched my gut.

Luyi noticed. "He wishes he were here; you have no idea how badly he does. And he personally asked me to bring you back to Yue. He trusts your safety with nobody else."

I had been concealing my true feelings for what felt like an eon. I could muster a convincing enough smile in return. "Thank you. Really."

"No, thank you." He looked like he meant it. In fact, the raw emotion in his face was almost too much for me to bear.

I cleared my throat, and tugged my cloak higher over my shoulders. "Well, then. When do we depart?"

I did not know what I was expecting when I finally returned to my village. Perhaps that everything would be unrecognizable. Perhaps that nothing would have changed at all.

But the scene that greeted me was beyond anything I could have imagined. Every single house was lit up with bright colored lanterns, like strings of candies. Streamers fluttered from the trees. The paths had been evened out, redesigned and straightened completely; there were no more loose pebbles and mud, just perfect, flat stone. The architecture as a whole looked better, the windows repaired, the doors perfectly fitted on their hinges, the roof tiles new and gleaming.

All the villagers were gathered at the entrance. Dozens of faces crowded together, eyes bright and smiling. A feast had been conjured—seemingly from thin air—with roasted lamb and glazed duck and sweet congee sprinkled with golden osmanthus flakes and goji berries.

"What's the day? Is there a festival happening?" I wondered aloud to Luyi.

He laughed. "No. It is all for you."

I stared at the spectacle, the lavish meals, the elaborate decorations, the joyous faces. The village bathed in a warm orange glow. It was beautiful and utterly overwhelming. "For—for me? Why?"

"Why? Incredible. You really haven't grown much of an ego in the Wu Kingdom, have you?" Luyi said, amused. Then, in a more serious tone, he went on, "The stories have traveled far and wide. They know what you have done, what you have sacrificed. You stopped a war and saved our kingdom. You're a hero, Xishi."

A hero. The word sounded strange, like it had nothing to do with me. I did not feel heroic at all. I barely even felt human. I remembered again the sticky heat of Fuchai's blood on my palms, the weight of Zhengdan's limp body on my legs, every night passed alone in the dark palace chambers. How long until the memories dimmed? Or would this be another of my sacrifices—that I would carry these ghosts with me for as long as I lived?

Then the crowds surged forward, one by one, reaching out to grab my hand, to seize my arm, just to touch me, as if I had returned transformed into a living legend. I did not so much walk forward as let myself be pushed along by the bodies, passed from one family to the next.

"Thank you . . ."

"You are so beautiful, Lady Xishi . . ."

"A hero . . ."

"You've grown so much—my heavens, you have the air of a noblewoman—"

"A royal—"

"We owe our lives to you . . ."

"I will name my firstborn after you—"

"I will name my seventh-born after you—"

"You've saved us all—"

Their words rang in my ears, the display of colors swimming back and forth in my vision. I tried to thank them back, even though I could not hear my own voice over the commotion. Yet throughout it all, there was a strange prickling sensation in the back of my neck, like I was being followed. I had felt it multiple times on our journey here, but each time I spun around, I couldn't see anyone.

Fanli's message flashed through my head again, a warning chime:

You must watch out for—

Then, abruptly, the chaos died down, the people parting like waves as two figures stepped forward, and my thoughts narrowed to only them.

My throat burned.

They were both older—this should not have come as a surprise. Their skin bore the scars of the sun, the slow erosion of time. My father's hair was almost completely snow white, thinning at the temples. My mother's eyes were set deeper in her face, the creases around them like cracks running through the earth. But they were dressed in luxurious fabrics, their cheeks infused with healthy color.

Mother stopped one foot away from me and just looked. Searched my face like she could fit many moons of memories into this one moment. She was smiling and crying at the same time, and when she spoke, she did not mention anything about heroes, about beautiful legends, about sacrifices. Her hand rested on my shoulder, a restoring of the natural way of things, and she made a soft tutting sound between her teeth.

"You've gotten too skinny," she said, like this were any other day. "Come inside. Let's eat."

And so we ate all through the evening, back in the house where I grew up. I let my mother fuss over my clothes and my weight and my hair; I listened to my father brag about the work he'd done and how pleased our ancestors would be with me. They boiled old tea they'd been saving for my return and showed me around the rooms. Fanli had kept his promise, and more: Everything I'd requested when I left had been repaired even better than I'd imagined it. The villagers kept coming in at regular intervals, bringing a week's worth of food with them, piling them over the tables and craning their necks just to see me. They were hungry for stories: What was the palace like, were the other concubines pretty, was the king kind or cruel to me?

Then the door creaked open again, and the villager standing there did not share any of the radiant joy of the others. She was ashen-faced, with sunken cheekbones and white streaking her hair. Her eyes roved around the room hungrily, desperately. It took me a moment to recognize her, to reconcile this weary old woman with the one who would yell at us to go home before dark, who would at times drop by with baskets of fresh herbs and spices and jars of sweet fermented rice. When I did, my stomach sank to my feet.

Zhengdan's mother had come searching for her.

Her sharp gaze settled on me, and she hobbled over, pushing past the guests like they meant nothing. "Where is she?" she whispered.

You could barely hear her over the cheers and the clinking jugs of wine and the swelling conversation. "Where's my daughter?"

My tongue weighed like a stone. I couldn't bring myself to speak the words, but she seemed to understand just from the look on my face. She staggered back, then righted herself against the nearest chair, her breathing shallow.

"I'm sorry," I said, knowing it was useless.

"No." She shook her head furiously. "No, *she* should be sorry. She is just like her father, that bastard, thankless child. The little fool."

For a moment I thought she would throw her shoe across the room, the way she did whenever Zhengdan forgot to heat the stove or returned from the forest with wild leaves tangled in her hair. But she only stared outside the window.

"She defeated General Ma in a duel," I told her. "She helped us outsmart the Wu military. We would not have succeeded without her."

"What difference does it make?" she murmured, and I was no longer sure if she was still speaking to me. "The kingdom will soon forget about her and move on, but I will not. They have swapped one king for another, but this—*this* is real life." She motioned to the food, the tables, the villagers. "The men will fight for their thrones and their power and their legacies, but to them we are nothing more than crickets and ants, insignificant, expendable. We will continue to worry over the rice and soy sauce and oil, three meals a day, how to escape the cold in the winter and the heat in the high summer, the holes in the roof and the bedding and the taxes. What does it matter who wears the crown, if they will not change any of this for us?"

"But . . ." I was stunned. "But—Zhengdan's father . . . Your husband . . . He was killed by the Wu. Doesn't *that* matter?"

"He was not killed by the Wu," she said harshly. "He was killed by the war. By the will of kings."

I stared at her, shaken. It was like something fixed inside me had all of a sudden come loose. The air seemed suffocating, the bodies packed too tight within the small space. I stuttered another apology, excused myself, and slipped out through the door.

Everything will make sense again, I thought as I hurried down the path. There was a feeling growing inside me, a knowing. Fanli had said that he would meet me by the riverbanks where we met. If I went now, he would be there. I was certain of it. And when we were reunited, he would tell me about Goujian's plans for the future, now that he had secured the throne. I would be reminded again of why it was vital that we conquered the Wu. Why our kings were different. Why life would be better from this point on.

The stars cut through the sky, those silver needle points bright against the darkness. I followed the familiar song of the river, my heart a bird, its wings beating harder. Shadows shifted around me. A twig snapped. Feathers fluttered against the leaves. I had not been in the countryside for a long time. I'd forgotten how the wild filled the trees, how the night could feel like a living thing, breathing and breathing. Watching me.

A chill crept down my back.

I ignored it, continuing down to the banks. The cold, white moonlight fell over the river like fresh snow, the water lapping against the speckled-egg pebbles. The place was empty.

I should have turned around then. But something compelled me to step closer to the very edge of the river. Fanli would come. This was what I kept telling myself. *Now.* Any moment now. My mind was already rushing forward beyond the present to ten days later, a month, a year: He would show up under the moonlight and I would run to him, feel the softness of his lips part against mine. I would tell him about everything I had seen and heard in the palace until my heart was lighter, the pain dulled, and he would listen intently, never losing patience or interrupting. Then we would sail around Lake Tai together, and anywhere beyond that. All wars would cease. All would be at peace. Perhaps when we tired of traveling, we could start a business together, distribute wealth to those in need. I would never have to hide my emotions, never again watch my speech. I would only dance and sing when I wanted, for the pure pleasure of the music—

Something moved behind me.

It happened too fast. I twisted around just as they shoved me with such blunt force my feet gave out. I hit the ground, gasping, my palms splitting open on impact. My head was spinning. *It's not meant to be like this* was all I could conjure. It was the end. It was meant to be over. So why—

I heard a sharp swish through the air. Pain exploded in the back of my skull, stars bursting across my vision. I struggled to turn my head, my eyes blurring. An unrecognizable man loomed over me. His face did not register, but the symbol sewn into his tunic did. It was the mark of King Goujian.

The world seemed to collapse.

Panic clawed up my throat like a frenzied animal. I thrashed, trying desperately to pull myself up, but I couldn't find my balance. There was only the cold air around me, the river, and this stranger. He had some piece of fabric in his hands—a bag—

No.

No, *no, no*—

I opened my mouth to scream, but nothing came out. And then the fabric was yanked over my head, covering everything in black. Rough hands gripped my ankles. I knew what was coming before it happened. Every nerve in me burned, recoiling from the very thought. My breaths came out fast and rapid, strained.

My thoughts were sensation only: pain and panic. I was running out—of oxygen, of time, of strength. I felt the ropes tighten, the rough cords slicing through my skin, weighed down by something hard and heavy like stone. They were going to drown me. They were going to *drown me*. I was going to die. It didn't seem quite real, even as it was happening. Then: the terrible sensation of falling, gravity giving out beneath me.

The water was ice cold.

It poured into my mouth, my lungs. I was sinking, my limbs dead and useless as wood, tied down on either side of me. My chest felt like it would burst at any second. I was stunned—almost too stunned for fear. That came later, when the darkness seeped in fully. There was no way out. No way to live.

Help, I shrieked in my head. Bubbles broke from my mouth. *Somebody help.*

Please.

Help me.

But no hero emerged to save me. The hero was meant to be me—and now I was utterly powerless, a spirit trapped in a frail, mortal body. The cold was unbearable.

Yet already I could feel myself fading, my skin numbing. In those last moments, as the water rose over me, I saw only one image:

It wasn't even a notable memory. Just another morning in Riversong Cottage, one of many. Fanli and I were sitting by the pond together, gazing out at the still waters, the lotus flowers floating over the surface. He had bought a pomegranate from the market and was peeling it for me, picking out the pink, gemlike seeds. We had been talking—about what, I don't remember anymore. Something small, something trivial. But I had laughed and spoken his name, casually, carelessly, and he'd looked over at me with a softness that took my breath away. Again and again, it played over in my mind, until it was the first and last thing I knew. Before the journey down the rivers, before the king's blood stained my hands, before the kingdom fell. When everything still felt like a story, a romantic myth. When we were together and the air was warm and nothing hurt.

CHAPTER TWENTY-FIVE

ACROSS THE RIVER, FANLI GAZES AT THE MOON. HIS hair is windswept, his cheeks still slightly flushed from riding fast all throughout the night.

He doesn't know yet that it's too late. That if he had come only minutes sooner, he would have seen me, and saved me. But perhaps that is asking too much. He has already saved my life once on those shores. Nobody under Heaven is that fortunate to experience the same miracle twice.

He doesn't know either that I'm here, mere feet away, watching him while he watches for me. I cannot be sure what I am now, what I've become. Perhaps I am a ghost. I've heard legends about it: those who die with unfinished business, anger or grief so heavy that it prevents them from floating on to the Yellow Springs of the underworld.

The moon rises higher. A cool wind blows through the trees.

And he waits.

The black veil of the sky has started to lift when he senses that something is wrong.

A twig snaps behind him.

He spins around so fast that all I see is the dark blur of movement, the trees shrinking back from him. His face is half hope, half horror. But it is not me he finds—it's Luyi.

"Where is she?" Fanli demands.

Luyi shakes his head. He cannot speak. He's afraid of the raw look in Fanli's eyes, the sharpness to his tone. Even in battle, Fanli has always been the perfect picture of calm, unfazed in the face of death.

But Fanli steps forward, his gaze pitch-black. "Where is she?" he repeats, louder.

"I—I don't know," Luyi gets out. "They saw her head down to the river but—hours have passed by now and . . ." In a small, frightened voice, he finishes, "I thought she might have gone to you."

Fanli freezes. He is one of the most intelligent people I've met, with a mind that works three times faster than the ordinary man's, weaving together threads invisible to most. I see him understand before anyone else does. His fingers curl into a fist; when his hands flatten forcibly again, his palm has been dented with small, bloody crescents.

"Search the entire village," he says, his voice a low rasp, threatening violence. "Search every single corner, every path, every room."

"It—it might take time," Luyi stammers. "We don't have a lot of people—most of the villagers are too old to walk long distances—"

"Use the soldiers."

Luyi stares at him. After a long beat, he says, "But—I thought they weren't meant for personal use . . . Won't you get into trouble with . . ." He stops himself at the dark expression on Fanli's face. It is how a man looks before walking into flame. "Yes, I'll—I will go do that right now—"

"Wait." There's a knot in Fanli's throat. He breathes in, steadies himself. Swallows. At last he says, so quietly Luyi has to lean in to hear him: "And search the rivers."

At dawn, they finally pull my body out from the water.

A small, somber crowd has formed on the riverbanks. One unsuspecting child catches a glimpse of my corpse and bursts into loud, inconsolable sobs.

Death knows no mercy; it has robbed me of all my beauty. My skin is bloated and starting to slough off, dark veins running under the surface like mountain creeks. Angry red marks are etched into my wrists and ankles from the rope. Strands of wet, black hair cling to my cheeks like seaweed. My lips are colorless and cracked, my eyes closed.

Fanli makes a sound I didn't know a mortal man could make.

Those watching have the sense to move out of the way. And just in time too. He falls to his knees beside me, cradling my corpse. He has never cried before, not even when he was held captive by the Wu, when they tore his back into strips of raw flesh. But he weeps now, his shoulders trembling.

The air is completely silent. Even the birds have stopped singing.

"Fanli, please . . . ," Luyi tries, taking a step forward. He is brave for it; I do not think anybody else would have dared utter a word. "We'll get to the bottom of this. Perhaps she was swept away by the currents— Perhaps it was an accident—"

Fanli hugs me tighter, his hair spilling free from its knot and tumbling over his shoulders, tickling my face. When he speaks, his voice is hoarse, that of a dead man, somebody who has already lost everything there is to lose. His eyes are crimson. "It was no accident." He had tried to warn me. *You must watch out for King*

Goujian. But he had miscalculated; he thought Goujian would wait longer to act. He thought we would have more time.

A chill settles in over the crowd.

Luyi looks at him uncertainly. "What—what do you mean?"

But Fanli doesn't hear him, or doesn't care. He turns back to me, and strokes my hair gently, so gently, brushing it back from my ruined face as if afraid to hurt me. He does not let anybody else approach. He does not speak. He just kneels on the cold, damp dirt, holding me, the river rushing on and on behind him.

A day passes. Two. Three whole cycles of the moon chasing the sun away, of him losing his mind with grief. He doesn't eat or drink or sleep, and refuses any company, any comfort.

"You have to take care of yourself," Luyi tells him tentatively one morning. I can tell he has practiced this many times over, attempting to find the perfect combination of words. But of course, no words could ever be right. "Please, Fanli," he says, his tone low and pleading. Fanli has not responded. Perhaps Luyi mistakes this for encouragement, because he continues, "It cannot go on like this. She wouldn't want—"

It is as if Fanli has been brought to life, jolted by lightning. All of a sudden he moves, swift as a serpent, and in a violent flash, he has Luyi pinned to the ground, one hand fastened around his neck.

Luyi's eyes widen. He struggles uselessly, beating at the dust. Fanli digs his knees deeper into the sides of his stomach, bracketing him with his body. "Fanli— *Stop*— Have you gone—completely insane—"

"Do not speak another word about her," Fanli says with soft vehemence, his pupils dilated. "Do not presume to understand what she wants. You cannot know. None of us will ever know."

He lets Luyi flail a while longer, until the flesh under his fingers has gone stark white, before he finally eases his weight off Luyi's body and lets go. Luyi bolts upright, coughing and gasping.

"Fanli," he chokes out at last. "Just talk to me. Hit me, if it'll make you feel better. I cannot . . ." He makes a helpless gesture with his empty hands. "I hate seeing you this way."

Fanli doesn't even look up. "I regret it now."

Luyi stills. "What?"

"I regret it," Fanli repeats, his voice rusty with disuse. "I should never have trained her. I should never have let her go to the Wu."

"But—she saved the kingdom," Luyi says. "She saved us all. She will go down in history as a hero."

Slowly, Fanli lifts his gaze. His face is hollow, haunted, his eyes black as the darkest night. Luyi flinches. "And who was there to save her?" Fanli rasps.

Luyi cannot seem to find a reply.

He laughs then, a harsh, wild sound. He laughs until tears flow down his cheeks. "Isn't it funny? I used to dream of changing the world. Of working for the greater good. But what good is the world," he asks, "if she is gone?"

That evening, Fanli accepts a shallow bowl of millet porridge. He must be starving at this point, but he drinks it like it's flavorless, like it's just air to him. Sustenance, and nothing more. I watch the relief spread over Luyi's face. He thinks that Fanli is starting to recover. That perhaps he will move on past this, and return to his old self.

But I know him all too well.

Desperate, I visit him in dreams. It is the only place I can go for him to see me.

We're standing in a meadow of some kind, with ten miles of peach blossoms stretching all around us. Vivid pink petals bloom from the slender branches. A pair of white butterflies flutter past in the blue sky, weaving their way around each other.

He's dressed in the same robes as the day we first met. The sun rises behind him, gilding his sharp outline.

"Fanli," I call, stepping forward. "I have to talk to you."

He looks up at me, wild hope and disbelief and grief painted all over his features, and I see his breath catch in his throat. "Xishi?"

I don't even have time to reply when something flashes across his eyes, and he grabs my wrist, tugs me forward. I crash against his chest. Then his lips are on mine, firm and desperate, his fingers tangled in my hair. It feels—real. Wonderfully, impossibly real. The softness of his mouth, the heat radiating from his skin as he deepens the kiss, his hand tightening around the small of my waist, drawing me closer until there's no space left between us at all.

"I should have done this a long time ago," he breathes against my mouth.

"Fanli," I manage, but he kisses me again, even harder than before, like it's all he's ever wanted, like he might go insane otherwise. I can feel his pulse dance under his skin, his erratic breathing, the small shudders running through his body.

I almost cave in. *Let him kiss me until he wakes*, I think dimly. *Let him do whatever he wants.* But then I remember why I wanted to speak to him in the first place, and with all my remaining self-control, I push him away.

It's a gentle push, but he flinches, then stares at me with such open hurt I have to fight the urge to undo everything, to seize him by the collar of his robes and pull him back to me.

"Am I forbidden, even in my own dreams?" he murmurs. "This is all I have left now."

"Focus, Fanli," I tell him, forcing my voice to harden even as my chest twists with a deep, inexpressible ache. "This is important."

"Nothing is more important than you." He sounds like he has never been so certain of anything in his life.

Such sweet words. I would have given up half my soul just to hear them back when I was alive. "I know what you plan to do," I push on. "I know you're going to find Goujian."

He goes very still. "How did you—"

"I'm right, aren't I?"

He makes no point of denying it. "I'll kill him," he says, with a quick, ready violence that is completely unlike him. "I'll make sure he suffers. I'll sever every one of his limbs and feed his heart to the wolves. Everything he has, I will take from him."

"You can't, Fanli," I whisper. "He is the king."

His face is hard as stone, immovable. I imagine him standing alone on some high, jagged cliff, staring down at the tumultuous waters of the ocean, too far away for anybody to reach. "He is the reason you're dead."

"The kingdom will be thrown into unrest," I tell him. I can feel him starting to wake, the dreamscape blurring around us. The petals closest to us have withered and faded to gray. I cannot stay long. More urgently, I continue, "*Both* kingdoms. Everything we've done will be for nothing. Everyone we've lost, every sacrifice—all the civilians whose lives we've preserved. They deserve to know peace."

At this, his eyes focus on me. "You're too good," he says, sounding pained. "They don't deserve you. None of them. Not me either."

"That's not true. I have my own plans for revenge; I just don't want you to get hurt."

"But—"

"If you wish to do something," I tell him, "then work against Goujian in private. Use your intelligence to help the common people, to change the kingdom in ways the king will not. Distribute wealth to the poor, aid them like you aided Wuyuan, create new opportunities for those struggling. That is what matters."

It comes to me now in sharp, stunning clarity, fierce enough to sweep me off my feet. I see the map of the Wu and the Yue and all the fragmented kingdoms, the markers that separate one territory from another, the roads I had memorized until I could draw them out with my eyes closed. I blink, and this time, the perimeters blur like dents in sand, smoothed out by waves. In their place appears the vermilion palace with its gilded roofs and hollow halls, looming high above all the coasts and villages and streets.

The will of kings—that was what Zhengdan's mother had alluded to. The divine order of the heavens, the natural right to rule; those things we were taught as children, trained to accept without question. But King Goujian is not the answer to peace. None of them are. So long as we continue to put mortal men on thrones and hail them as gods, sacrifice our lives to their legacies, history will repeat itself. Just as the ocean tides ebb and flow beneath the moon, empires will rise and collapse, wars will start and cease, and the rest of us will be left to struggle against the currents.

If only I had known earlier.

If only I could go back in time.

Fanli lifts a hand, rests it briefly against my cheek. The sky buckles above us. A wind sweeps through the trees, ripping the petals from their boughs. His image wavers before me, like ink in water, and I can sense my own presence slipping away, as if there is a great wind tugging at me too.

"Promise me," I urge him, my voice already dissolving, too faint. I can only pray he will remember when he wakes.

He wakes with a shudder, a gasp, like someone breaking free from water. He recalls the dream only in fragments, but he knows I was there. Now, in the violet daylight, it is like he has lost me all over again. He buries his face in his hands, crying without sound.

Then he stands, pulls his hair into a high knot, sharpens his sword. It is a new blade to replace the one he had gifted me, with hundreds of thin, parallel marks etched down the side. I would cry too, if I had a physical form, eyes from which to weep. They are the number of days I've been gone. Counting down to the very date of my return, and my death.

Fanli. I reach for him, but it is useless now. I am no more solid than the breeze, passing right through him. *Please. Don't do this.*

He fastens the sword to his belt and leaves for the capital.

When he arrives at the palace, he does not bother greeting the guards or waiting for an invitation to go inside. He just barges right through them, using his sword to knock back their raised halberds and shields like they're nothing but weeds, then marches into the hall where Goujian sits on his new throne of gold.

Once, Zhengdan had said that he did not resemble a king. But he looks every bit like a proper king now, regal and removed, with his crown placed high on his head, his silk cloak shimmering around him. For one eerie moment, I almost confuse him for Fuchai.

Goujian looks up at the commotion and raises his brows. The guards have tried to follow Fanli, some still attempting to hold him back by force, others falling over themselves in apology.

"Never mind," he instructs, waving everyone away. "Leave us. I will speak to my minister in private."

A guard hesitates. "Are you certain, Your Majesty? He looks . . ."

There is no need to complete the sentence. Fanli looks ready to strike the king down in one blow.

But Goujian just smiles indulgently, shakes his head. "No, no. I know him well. He will not harm me."

As soon as the doors fall closed with an echoing *thud*, Fanli crosses the marble floors until he is standing at eye level with the king. I would be nervous, if I were Goujian. There is nothing between them, nothing to block a strike to the heart.

Goujian's brows rise higher. He folds his arms slowly across his chest and regards Fanli like an uncle would his misbehaving nephew, with equal parts amusement and impatience. "You seem rather upset, Fanli. Did something happen?"

When Fanli speaks, his voice is low, barely suppressed, brutally cold. It could freeze a river over in mid-spring. "Why did you kill her?"

I notice the faintest crack of unease in Goujian's expression. No doubt his prized minister has never spoken to anyone this way before, much less him. Still, he manages a low chuckle. "It's just common sense, don't you think? She has served her purpose."

Suddenly I remember Zixu's words, as if from a hundred miles away: *When the hares have all been caught, the hunting dogs are cooked.*

Fanli's knuckles tighten over his sword. I do not know if Goujian notices. I do not think so, or else he would have surely fled in the opposite direction by now. "She gave up her own happiness for the kingdom. She has only ever cared for—" His voice threatens to break. He continues with a terrible air, a killer's resolve. "She has only ever cared for peace. She did everything right. She is the best of every man and woman. She would not be a threat to you."

"Ah, but like it or not, she is." Goujian shrugs. "Apply that sharp mind of yours and think for just a moment: If her beauty is enough to topple the enemy kingdom, who's to say she won't turn around and topple mine? Better to act early, and not make the same mistake that fool Fuchai did."

Fanli is silent, his face turned down, his expression cast in dark shadow. He is trembling all over.

"Are you sad, Fanli?" Goujian steps forward, and pats Fanli's cheek twice. "You know, part of me had suspected that the rumors about you were exaggerated: that you couldn't *really* be devoid of desire. And your investment in her always seemed . . . well, beyond the extent of your duties."

Still, Fanli says nothing.

Stop talking, I scream at Goujian, my voice lost to the air. My nails claw at him, but of course it makes no difference. *Stop tormenting him.*

"It's nothing to cry over," Goujian continues. "I agree that she is beautiful, but I'm the rightful king of both lands now. Since I can be more sure of your tastes, I can give you as many concubines as you wish, from the best brothels in the capital. Enough to fill a whole house with. Just take your pick." He laughs, the sound loud and unrestrained, reverberating through the vast hall. "I bet you will be too well entertained to even remember her—"

Fanli strikes without warning. His hand fastens around Goujian's arm in an eagle grip, and he twists. The sound of snapping bone rings through the deadly silence. Goujian opens his mouth to cry out, his features contorted in pain, but Fanli quickly grabs his face and clenches his jaw shut, preventing any noise from escaping.

Then he hesitates.

His eyes flicker to his sword, then to Goujian's writhing form. He has always been stronger than the king, smarter and faster. It is purely out of loyalty that he never used it to his advantage, but rather to aid the kingdom.

Please, I pray. *Don't.*

One second drags into two. The length of a heartbeat, and

another. A muscle tenses in Fanli's jaw. At last, he loosens his grip slightly and draws his sword, but doesn't raise it.

"I could kill you if I wanted to," Fanli says evenly, over Goujian's labored grunts and gasps. "But I won't. Only because she wouldn't be happy with me if I did."

"You . . . ," Goujian croaks. He's lying on the ground, clutching his arm; it's been twisted at a grotesque angle, broken at least twice over, shards of bone sticking out in the wrong places. "Have you forgotten . . . that I'm your king? I . . . plucked you from obscurity. From that—that dirt-poor village of yours. I recognized your talent when nobody else did. You would be nothing—*nothing* . . . if it weren't for me."

"All I know," Fanli says, his eyes like knifepoints, "is that she is worth more than you could ever dream of becoming. If killing you could bring her back, I would do it without hesitation."

Goujian opens his mouth—perhaps to cry, perhaps to curse him. But Fanli moves forward, stepping deliberately on his injured arm. A terrible whimper, like that of a stabbed animal, escapes Goujian's lips.

"Oh, and in case it wasn't clear," Fanli says on his way out, his robes smeared with royal blood, his eyes set on the doors, "you'll need to find yourself a new minister. I resign."

A sliver of my soul lingers in the palace. Just a sliver—but enough.

I cannot harm Goujian physically in the mortal realm, but that doesn't mean I do not have other ways. That night, Goujian falls into an uneasy, painful sleep, and I let all my anger, all my betrayal and my grief pour into his dreams, filling them with dark shapes, images of my face, my gaze cutting holes into his flesh. His eyes fly open, his pillow soaked through with sweat. There is a terrible, tearing pain in his arm where the bones have been tentatively reset by the palace physician, but that is not what woke him. He had felt like there was river water rising to his throat, the taste of it blooming like blood on his tongue. He stares around the room wildly, his uninjured hand gripping the sheets. For a moment he looks half-crazed.

"Xi-Xishi?" he whispers, like he has seen a ghost.

I do not reply, but wrap my phantom hand around his throat, and it is as if somebody has doused him with cold. He shakes all over and spends the rest of the night tossing and turning, remembering his horribly vivid dream of drowning in a river, of the blackness and the cold and the burning in his lungs.

It is the same dream he will have the next night, and the night after that. Drowning without end. Always as terrifying, always as realistic, until he wakes every morning with bloodshot eyes and an uncontrollable tremor in his hands. He flinches at the slightest sound, sees spirits in the shadows. Whenever he passes by the river, he swears he can hear a girl's weeping. He conceals it well enough in court, but alone, he succumbs to the hysteria, the fear that rattles his very bones.

I am but one of the many who will haunt him for as long as he lives. All those who had died for him, because of him, at his hands.

I will not leave him in peace. I will not let him forget.

Fanli returns to the river.

He carries my corpse in his arms as carefully as someone holding porcelain. It is dusk now, the clouds floating in hazy roseate and violet wisps, the last of the sun's rays slipping beneath the river surface. He has brought a shovel and a jug of wine with him. He tears open the crimson seal, tilts his head back, his throat exposed to the cold air, and drinks alone.

"Xishi," he says, the word soft and half-slurred. He stares down at the broken shadow of my body. Each time, it is like the first: the thunderbolt of agony, the black shock of grief. "You must blame me," he murmurs, crouching next to me, wrapping his smooth, slender fingers around my withered ones. His dark eyes shine, glossy from alcohol and held-back tears. "I blame myself too. I am afraid—even if we were to meet in the next life, you would not want our paths to cross."

Don't be a fool, I wish to tell him. *I will meet you again in every lifetime there is.*

He seems to be waiting for something. A response. But my corpse lies there, still as ice. At last he swallows and grips the shovel with quivering fingers, then begins to dig.

The dirt is hard and unyielding, littered with rough stones. It is not a job for one man, much less somebody of Fanli's rank and dignity. The shovel clips the ground only partly, sending up a spray of loose dirt; he has to throw all his weight into the movement. Soon the sun has disappeared entirely, leaving just the faintest impression of light over the distant mountain slopes, the milky moon rising to take its place.

> *The moon rises white*
> *illuminating your beauty,*
> *your shadow which wounds me*
> *until my heart's devoured*

It is quiet here. The only sounds that can be heard are the repeated *thud* and *hiss* of his shovel against the dirt, and the cicadas chirping from the trees, and his muffled exhalations. Sweat drips from his brow. A streak of dirt is smeared over his cheeks; the sight is disorientating, like mud on the petal of a lotus flower. The skin around his palms and fingers has started to part, breaking open against the hard friction, blisters splitting in angry patches of pink and red. Blood trickles from his hands where they're wrapped around the shovel handle.

When the grave is ready, he stares at the ditch in the earth, his chest heaving.

"I'm sorry," he whispers again and again as he holds my body one final time to lower me into the ground. "I'm sorry, I'm sorry, I'm sorry—" Until they barely sound like words anymore, just noises of inexpressible pain, harsh, rattling sobs in his throat as he fills the grave, then spills the last of his wine into the dirt.

I can feel the Yellow Springs calling to me now, their currents churning from far, far below. It's almost time for me to go.

A few yards away, footsteps crunch over the dry leaves.

Fanli twists around and sees a young boy passing through. The boy immediately blanches, his face bone-white with fear. Perhaps his parents had already warned him about Fanli. *His mind is not stable*, they would whisper at nighttime, in the same breath they tell him about monsters in the trees, murderers roaming the woods. *He is a changed man. There is nothing he won't do because of her.*

The boy tenses as if to run, but Fanli raises one hand to stop him.

"You're not from here, are you?" His voice is rough, like two stones grating together. "The fabric your tunic is made of. It is not yet traded around this region of villages."

"You're right," the boy stammers, stunned.

"Of course I am. Listen, when you leave this place—tell everyone that Xishi lives."

The whites of the boy's eyes gleam, and he darts a quick, terrified look at the uneven mound of dirt that marks my grave, like he is unsure whether to risk his life by pointing out the obvious. "But—but—I'm sorry, it's only—she is—"

"Tell them Xishi is alive, and with me," Fanli continues forcefully, a dark warning flashing over his gaze, a look that says: *Finish that sentence, and I will slit your throat.* "Tell them we are resting together after her mission in the Wu Kingdom. We've decided to set sail around Lake Tai, visiting all the places we never could. Tell them she is brave, and honorable, and happy, and finally free. Do you understand?" Fanli says it with such sharp intensity that the boy freezes in his place, swallows hard.

"Y-yes, I—I think so—"

"Good," he says softly, his eyes no longer on the boy but on the river, as if he can see miles and miles beyond it, to where it reaches its end. "Make sure they all know it. It is the ending she deserves."

The boy nods and scampers off.

When he is gone, Fanli kneels and touches his hand to the dirt of my grave, a lone silhouette in the bleeding darkness. "Xishi," he whispers. "Please, believe in me. I will come find you."

I believe him.

Time in the underworld passes differently than for those in the mortal realm. The years flow by like water, rush past like arrow through light. Above us, the world goes on for the living. The same domestic worries and looming disasters; empty grain stores, separated lovers, cold porridge, brutal murders, warm bedding, permanent scars, missing children, ailing parents, loud festivals. They reunite and part, celebrate and grieve, hate each other and love each other fiercely, irrationally. The moon continues rising and sinking, the sun offering up its new light every morning, wiping away the blood spilled in the previous night.

Those who have died after me have already drifted on, to be reincarnated into the next lifetime and enter the cycle anew. But I stay here, waiting, watching.

Perhaps a century passes. Perhaps only a decade.

All I can be certain of is that for the longest time, there is only darkness, the bone-deep cold of the dead, everything as blurry and insubstantial as white fog—then, one day, on the opposite shore of the Yellow Springs, I see him. His soul is brighter than the rest, a stunning blaze of silver, but this is no surprise. It is what I've always known.

I swim, crossing the water, pushing past the harsh currents until I reach the shore. There is so much between us; the years and the yards of distance. I run through it all until I am standing before him, the darkness devoured by his beauty.

He smiles, and the fog lifts.

ACKNOWLEDGMENTS

I'll always remember the summer I wrote this book. I was twenty-one years old, working my first job out of college, and every morning, when the sun was just starting to rise and I hadn't yet logged in to the real world, I would sit down and let my mind wander to the legends my mother told me when I was a child, and I would type, one word at a time. It is thanks to the efforts of many wonderful people that those words eventually transformed into the book you're reading today.

A huge thank-you to my agent, Kathleen Rushall, who made all of this possible—I honestly don't know what I would do without your unwavering support. I'm so lucky just to know you, let alone to have you in my corner through the many ups and downs of this industry. More thanks to the brilliant team at Andrea Brown Literary Agency.

Thank you to Tiffany Shelton for championing this book in every way possible. Your trust and insight mean more to me than I can ever express, and working with you has been a dream come true. Thank you to the extremely talented Ervin Serrano for the most gorgeous, exquisite cover. Thank you also to my eagle-eyed copy editor, Michelle Li—I am deeply humbled and impressed by every note you've left. All my thanks to Lizz Blaise, Layla Yuro, Lena Shekhter, Lauren Riebs, Devan Norman, Amelia Beckerman, and Dori Weintraub for your talent and expertise.

Thank you so much to Taryn Fagerness at Taryn Fagerness Agency, who has worked tirelessly to help this story reach more readers. I can't tell you how grateful I am for the care and enthusiasm you have shown my books.

Endless thanks to everyone who has worked on the foreign editions and helped bring them into being. Few experiences can compare to the utter privilege and joy of seeing my words translated.

One of the most surreal parts of becoming an author is having your literary idols—the authors whose books you've treasured and devoured and displayed on your bookshelf—read what you've written. Even more surreal is when those authors are so generous and lovely as to take the time out of their incredibly busy schedules to offer the kindest blurbs, so my heartfelt thanks to: Grace D. Li, Sue Lynn Tan, Shelley Parker-Chan, Chloe Gong, June Hur, and June CL Tan.

Thank you to the booksellers and librarians and readers and everyone who's given my books a chance. As someone who's dreamed of being an author since I was twelve, I remain astounded that I get to do this for a living, and it's all because of you.

Thank you to Alyssa for listening to my ramblings and reading my mind and offering such valuable feedback on anything I write. Thank you, and also sorry, for spending your afternoons looking over my books when you should really be studying for your tests. I hope you know that everything is infinitely better when you're around.

And finally, thank you to my parents. I would never have been able to create these fictional worlds if the world you created for me were not so beautiful.

ABOUT THE AUTHOR

Alyssa Liang

Ann Liang is the *New York Times* and Indie bestselling author of the critically acclaimed YA novels *This Time It's Real, If You Could See the Sun,* and *I Hope This Doesn't Find You.* Her books have sold into more than twenty foreign territories. Born in Beijing, she grew up traveling back and forth between China and Australia but somehow ended up with an American accent. She now lives in Melbourne, where she can be found making over-ambitious to-do lists and having profound conversations with her pet labradoodle about who's a good dog.